PRAISE FOR

Maud's Line

"I want to live with Maud in a little farm in a little valley under the shadow of a mountain wall. *Maud's Line* is an absolutely wonderful novel and Margaret Verble can drop you from great heights and still easily pick you up. I will read anything she writes, with enthusiasm."

— Jim Harrison, author of *Dalva* and *Legends of the Fall*

"In clean, spare prose, Margaret Verble describes a people's struggle to maintain a culture and an identity that both sustains and imprisons them. Her observations of the beauty and anguish of this life, and her vivid heroine, make this as good a novel as I've read all year."   — Historical Novel Society

"Margaret Verble gives us a gorgeous window onto the Cherokee world in Oklahoma, 1928. Verble's voice is utterly authentic, tender and funny, vivid and smart, and she creates a living community — the Nail family, Maud herself, her father, Mustard, and brother, Lovely, and the brothers Blue and Early, the quiet, tender-mouthed mare Leaf, and the big landscape of the bottoms — the land given to the Cherokees after the Trail of Tears. Beyond the allotments, it opens up into the wild, which is more or less what Verble does with this narrative. A wonderful debut novel."   — Roxana Robinson, author of *Sparta*

"*Maud's Line* is filled with evocative glimpses of violence, viscera, yearning, and the brusque but communal caring of family ... Verble crafts a story filled with nuance and quiet conflict."

— *Shelf Awareness*

"First novelist Verble, herself an enrolled member of the Cherokee Nation of Oklahoma, does a beautiful job of limning a sometimes hardscrabble Indian life that nevertheless has the comfort that familiarity and extended family bring. Place is especially important to the author's story, and its setting is beautifully realized, as are the characters who populate this gentle novel ... Pair this one with novels by Louise Erdrich."

— *Booklist*

"Maud is refreshingly open and honest about her own sexuality though conscious of her place as a woman in a sexist society ... [Verble] tells a compelling story peopled with flawed yet sympathetic characters, sharing insights into Cherokee society on the parcels of land allotted to them after the Trail of Tears."

— *Kirkus Reviews*

"Writing as though Daniel Woodrell nods over one shoulder and the spirit of Willa Cather over the other, Margaret Verble gives us Maud, a gun-toting, book-loving, dream-chasing young woman whose often agonizing dilemmas can only be countered by sheer strength of heart." — Malcolm Brooks, author of *Painted Horses*

Maud's Line

MAUD'S LINE

Margaret Verble

Mariner Books
Houghton Mifflin Harcourt
Boston   New York

First Mariner Books edition 2016

Copyright © 2015 by Margaret Verble

For information about permission to reproduce selections from this book, write to trade.permissions@hmhco.com or to Permissions, Houghton Mifflin Harcourt Publishing Company, 3 Park Avenue, 19th Floor, New York, New York 10016.

www.hmhco.com

Library of Congress Cataloging-in-Publication Data
Verble, Margaret.
Maud's line / Margaret Verble.
pages cm
ISBN 978-0-544-47019-4 (hardback) — ISBN 978-0-544-47192-4 (ebook)
ISBN 978-0-544-70524-1 (pbk.)
1. Teenage girls — Fiction 2. Allotment of land — Government
policy — Cherokee Nation, Oklahoma — Fiction.
3. Oklahoma — History — 20th century — Fiction.
4. Domestic fiction. I. Title.
PS3622.E733M38 2015
813'.6 — dc23
2014039683

Book design by Greta D. Sibley

Printed in the United States of America
DOH 10 9 8 7 6 5
4500779851

For my mother,
her brothers, and first cousins

Maud's Line

1

Maud was bent over one row suckering tomato plants and Lovely was bent over the next one. They were talking about a girl Lovely had his eyes set on. But a cow's bawling interrupted that. Maud unfolded and looked toward the river. Lovely did the same. The bawling was loud, unnatural, and awful, and it set them to running. They ran first toward the house, not toward the sound, because neither had taken a gun to the garden. Maud stopped at the steps; Lovely rushed in for their rifles. Armed up and not bothering to talk, they both ran straight toward the pump to get to the pasture below the ridge where the howling was coming from. If they hadn't been fearful, they would've run fifty more yards to the gate and gone through it. But they were scared and hurrying, so they climbed the barbed wire just past the pump, and Lovely snagged his sleeve, leaving behind a piece of blue cotton waving like the flag of a small foreign country. Maud did worse than that. She snagged her leg below the knee at the back, opening a tear deep at its top and three inches long. Maud was vain about her legs and Lovely had only three shirts, but still they ran, focused on the bawling, without minding their mishaps.

When they got to the cow, Betty was folded with both her head and her rump sticking up. Between them, smack across the ridge of her spine, were three wide, angry gashes. She was thrashing all over the ground. She'd flattened out a circle of weeds, and, oddly, out of the center wound, a stalk of poke protruded. It was a thick stem of poke and resembled, stuck out as it was, a spear. That's what Maud thought as soon as she saw it.

Lovely yelled, "Her back's axed. We'll haveta shoot her." He moved toward Betty's head and raised his rifle. But then he just stood, cheek on the stock, eye down the sights, finger on the trigger.

Maud yelled, "Pull it."

But the end of Lovely's gun shook like a leaf in a breeze. So Maud raised her rifle, moved a step west to keep from shooting her brother, and waited until she had a good look at an ear.

The blowback of skull and brain splattered onto Lovely's overalls and shirt. He lowered his gun and looked down at his bib. He said, "I'm gonna be sick." Before he completely bent over, he threw up fatback and biscuits over pieces of cow head.

Betty's legs kept flailing. Maud shouldered her rifle again; said, "Move farther back"; looked down her sights; and sent another bullet into the white patch between the cow's eyes. Then she cradled her gun in the crook of her arm, cupped her hand over her mouth, and cried, "Betty, I'm sorry." Her shoulders heaved. She felt the blood trickle down the back of her leg. She looked at the rivulet, laid her gun on the ground, and tore off a Johnson grass blade. She plastered it over the wound and then sat in the weeds and watched the cow twitching to death.

Tears watered Maud's eyes and spilled onto her cheeks. Betty was a tough Hereford with a big heart and strong legs and, the year before, had climbed a fallen tree to escape the worst of the flood. But any dead cow would've been a disaster. They'd lost all but three of their herd to the water. To take her eyes and mind off of Betty's trembling, Maud looked over to Lovely. He was wiping his bib with a leaf. She said, "Don't worry about that. We've got to save this meat."

Maud sent Lovely off to round up their uncles, Blue and Early. The men came back with Blue driving Great-Uncle Ame's 1920 Dodge sedan. He maneuvered it into the pasture as close to Betty as he could get, and the four of them strung her up to the sturdiest tree around. They set to butchering, talking about the meanness it took to ax a cow in the back. They gave Blue the hide to cure and packed Betty's meat in old newspapers and feed sacks. They deposited those on the floor of the backseat and agreed they'd pay Hector Hempel, the dwarf who ran the icehouse, two rump roasts for storing the meat. The men drove off with the car loaded so heavy it didn't rattle.

Maud walked to the house. She first tended her leg and then drew her dress and slip off over her head. At eighteen, she was fit, dark, and tall like the rest of her mother's family and most of her tribe. She was more of a willow than an oak, and her figure and personality had grown pleasing to every male within a twenty-mile radius, to some of the women, too, and to most of the animals. Maud carried that admiration the way eggs are carried in a basket, carefully, with a little tenderness, but without minding too closely the individual. She drew on another slip and dress, tossed her and Lovely's dirty clothes in a tub, and pumped cool water over them until they were completely covered. She left them to soak while she filled one of the front-yard kettles with water and lit a fire under it.

While she stirred their clothes in the kettle, her heart sank further than it'd sunk since the flood, and tears came to her eyes again. Heat rose up to her cheeks, and the fire under the pot made her shins hot. She poked the clothes with the pole and gave in to crying and to some self-pity she didn't much admire. She wanted a washer with a tub and wringers. They were advertised all the time in the papers. So were refrigerators, lamps that turned on with buttons, toilets that flushed in the house. She lifted her dress out of the water with the end of the pole and dipped it again. She wiped her nose with the back of her hand and forced her mind off of the things she wanted. She turned it to the cold kind of cruelty that would kill an innocent cow. She felt Betty's twitching in the wound on the back of her leg, felt her bawling all over again in her heart.

But she was recovered and hanging the clothes on the line when the men got back to the farm. And although they were noticeably tired from the butchering and lugging of meat, and Lovely was still shaken from the whole ordeal, they pitched in and scooped out the wash water, carried it to the garden for the tomato plants, and set wood for a fire in the pit. Maud had saved back enough meat to feed some of their extended family: Blue and Early, of course; and her grandpa, Bert; and her great-uncle Ame and his wife, Viola; and her aunt Lucy and her husband, Cole. She didn't save out any for her father. It was Saturday and late in the afternoon. He wouldn't crawl back until well into the night.

Blue left to clean up and fetch the others. But Early hung around to eat his share of the beef. He was only twenty-six, and his talk was about going to town, gambling, and people of the female persuasion. Maud found Early a lot of fun, and having him to herself raised her spirits some. She teased him about his plans for the evening and fed him the food that was ready, except for the onions. She told him he needed to hold off on those out of respect for the women.

Shortly after Early left, Blue came back in a wagon with his father, Ame and Viola, Lucy and Cole, and their baby boy. He pulled the wagon close to the fire and hitched the mules to the rail. There weren't enough chairs for everybody to sit, so they ate from the wagon bed, some in it, some standing around the tailgate. And it was a feast — beans, onions, biscuits, hominy, the beef, lettuce, asparagus, and two pecan pies Lucy had baked.

While they ate, they talked about who'd murdered the cow. Not that it was much of a mystery. The Mount boys, or men, John and Claude, were the culprits. Everybody agreed on that because of the sneakiness of the crime and because the Mounts had a history of meanness that Grandpa and Great-Uncle Ame swore extended for generations. The Mounts' paternal grandpappy had once set fire to his own dog and blamed it on his neighbor. One of their great-uncles had been the biggest allotment stealer in the Cookson Hills. He'd locked three men in a cabin with a barrel of liquor and wouldn't feed them or let them out until they'd signed their papers over to him. Then when they did, he wouldn't even let them have the rest of the whiskey. And the Mounts' mama, Ame claimed in almost a whisper, had more than a little Comanche in her.

So the talk centered more on what to do. Calling in the law was out. Nobody around the wagon trusted the law nor had any reason to. The law wasn't set up for Indians. But the older folks were against revenge on the practical principle that it multiplied trouble, and the younger ones deferred to their elders by habit and weren't particularly hell-bent in their natures. Blue (according to Bert) had come into the world with an even disposition and a mark on his head, now disappeared, that had determined his name. Lucy was still a young wife who had been tamed by her marriage. Cole was a married-in white; he respected his in-laws' customs and folded to whatever they wanted.

As for the next generation down, Lovely took after his mother, who'd been as calm as the surface of a pond at twilight. Maud was growing more toward their mother's way every day. However, she'd been born with more of their daddy's nature, and his temper was hot. That was how he, as a boy, had come to be called Mustard. His last name was Nail, and as an adult, he was still bad to fight. So even though his daddy had been mostly white, nobody in Maud's mother's family knew of a fullblood in the state of Oklahoma with a more appropriate handle. Mustard Nail would want to kill the Mounts, everybody agreed on that. So after Lovely and Cole had doused the fire with dirt and the stars popped out as the evening wore on, the talk turned to how to break it to Mustard that his cow was gone.

"I think it might be best to lie," Viola said.

"He'll know she's gone. And he spent five bucks breeding her," Lovely replied.

"That's two cows, then," Grandpa offered.

"Hector already knows we put her down 'cause her back was broke," Blue said.

"What did you tell him, exactly?" Lovely asked.

Early had already reported to Maud that Lovely had remained laid out on the backseat of the car at the icehouse, resting from the shock with his arm across his eyes. Maud wasn't surprised in the least. Her brother had always been sensitive. But it wasn't the fault of his name. It was commonly used for boys in their mother's family, and none of the rest of them, five Lovelys in all, had turned out to be anything but tall, unflinching, and good with a gun. At nineteen, Lovely was tall enough, a couple of inches beyond six feet. And he could shoot fairly well when he could force himself into pulling a trigger. But his temperament had caused their mama, while still alive, to coddle him and had put him at odds with their father. Mustard was hard on Lovely and occasionally claimed he had four girls rather than three girls and a boy.

Maud's two older sisters were married and gone, and her mother, Lila, was dead, so it was Maud who stood between Mustard and Lovely. She did it with words and sometimes they worked.

Blue said, "Told Hector you had to shoot her, Lovely. Didn't say much else. He could see yer feet hanging outta the window."

Lovely shooting the cow had been the story Maud and he'd agreed on before he'd gone to fetch Early and Blue. And neither had told their uncles the truth. "You think Hector'll say anything to Daddy?" asked Maud.

"Hard to tell," Blue replied.

"I'll caution him next time I go for ice," Grandpa said. "He knows Mustard like ever'body else."

"I think a broke leg's the best bet. She broke her leg. Had to be shot," Blue said, practicing the lie.

"That sure sounds better than a broke back," Viola said. She picked up her tin, spat into it, and wiped her mouth with a bandana.

With that agreed, the family gazed at the Milky Way, passed Lucy's baby back and forth, and talked about relatives who were on the next farms over, away, or dead. They also talked about Early, who, they figured, was taking money off of some fool drunk he'd lured into cards. The conversation was sprinkled with laughter that kept Maud's mind off of Betty, and the family didn't split up until the moon dimmed the stars and provided them light for traveling.

Maud and Lovely went to bed not long after the others departed, and Lovely was asleep on his back when Maud, half awake and listening to the wolves howl in the wild, heard her father's car stop at their first cattle guard and then at their second one. She was on her side pretending to sleep when Mustard opened the door and tripped on the threshold. He fell loudly on the floor.

After that, he gave out a groan. When Maud determined he wasn't going to stir, she got up, put a pillow under his head, and then settled into deep sleep.

She awoke in early morning light, looked at her father still on the floor, and decided he didn't seem that worse for the wear. He'd managed to get home without visible bruises or swollen eyes, and he wasn't drooling. His left arm seemed a little crooked, but she could tell from her cot that it was just thrown at an odd angle. She glanced at her brother's cot, determined he was still asleep, softly set her feet on a plank, and stood up. She stepped behind a sheet hung on a wire that blocked off a corner for privacy, pulled her housedress off of a peg, and drew it over her head. She checked the rag around her wound and saw a patch of blood dried in the shape of a hammer's head. She decided to leave the bandage in place, slipped out from behind the sheet, and stepped to the kitchen. She plucked her toothbrush from a cup, lifted the dipping pan from the counter, and went out the kitchen door, closing it softly.

When she returned, Mustard was still on the floor, but Lovely was up. Maud had set the kindling the night before, so she fiddled the fire to life and was frying fatback when her brother came in from his morning time alone. She nodded toward the other room. Lovely whispered, "Eggs," and held up three fingers. He sat down in a chair at the table and took up a newspaper that was two days old.

Maud usually waited to eat until her father and brother were fed. But Mustard hadn't shown signs of stirring, so she ate with her brother. The two were finishing off their second biscuits when they heard a faint "Goddamn" from somewhere near the floor beyond the kitchen door. Maud got up with her plate in her hand, set it in the dishpan, and laid another dish on the table.

Mustard made more noise than he did most mornings. The

grunts and groans came first from the front room and then from out in the yard. Maud thought they were for effect rather than an indication of any particular distress. Her father acted badly with the same regularity as the rooster crowed at dawn. But he had a conscience to him, so remorse usually followed soon after the ache of alcohol or the burn of temper had cleared out and gone.

When Mustard finally got into the kitchen, he placed both hands flat on the table and eased into his chair. "You should've seen Charlie Pankins when I left him. Goddamn, he were a mess."

Maud held up the coffee kettle. "You want some before your eggs?"

"I believe I do."

Lovely shoved a saucer toward his father without lifting his eyes from reading.

Mustard scratched the back of his head. "We got our hooch offin a Choctaw who was packing his load in a feed sack."

Maud picked up the saucer, held it about four inches from the table, and poured coffee into it. She set it down slowly next to her father's right fist.

Mustard said, "You might have to pick that up for me. I'm a little shaky."

Maud turned back to the stove, settled the kettle, and picked up the saucer in both hands as carefully as if she were cradling the back of a baby's head. Mustard slurped his coffee, wiped his mouth with the palm of his hand, and said, "Yer the best."

Maud held the saucer until Mustard drained it and poured him another he was able to hold on his own. She knew she was her father's favorite, and this was even with her oldest sister looking more like him than his face in a pond. She said, "Daddy, we've got some bad news for you. Betty broke her leg in the pasture. Lovely had to put her down."

"Say that again," said Mustard.

Lovely looked up from his paper. "Had to shoot Betty in her head, Dad. She was bawling as high as the moon."

"You shot the goddamn cow?" Mustard's face was turning red.

"He had to, Daddy. I saw her myself. She was lying on the ground, unable to get up. It was a pitiful sight. Lovely put her out of her misery."

Mustard wiped his mouth with the back of his hand. He shook his head. He sat there in silence until Maud slid eggs onto his plate and picked out some fatback from a platter under a sugar sack. Mustard ate with a smacking noise until Lovely turned a page of the paper, and then he said, "One shot?"

"Two. She was tough."

"Whatchya do with her?"

Lovely laid his paper down. "Took her to Hector."

Mustard wiped his mouth with the back of his hand again. "I believe I need a cigarette."

Lovely's chair scraped. He went to the main room and slid back into his seat at the table with a cigar box. "Want me to roll and light it?"

Mustard nodded and patted his breast pocket and then his pants pockets. "My Banjo's somewhere. Probably the other room."

Maud said, "There's fire in the stove."

When Lovely finished rolling, he opened the oven door and lit the cigarette on the wood. After Mustard had puffed it to a wet butt, Maud sat down at the table, buttered a biscuit, and spooned some plum jelly onto it. She held it out to her daddy. He said, "Don't mind if I do."

Two mornings later, after Mustard and Lovely had gone off to their jobs, and the dishes were done and the beds made, Maud took a bucket to the pump, primed it, pumped fresh water, and sat down on the platform over the well. She had a clean rag and some Mercurochrome, and she was dabbing the purple medicine onto her wound and wondering if it would leave a scar that would mar the looks of her leg when she heard the sound of a team in the distance. She looked out toward the section line. Coming down it were a pair of horses and a wagon covered with a bright blue canvas. The team was driven by a man she didn't recognize at a distance. Maud forgot about the possibility of permanent disfigurement; she even forgot about the tendency of Mercurochrome to drip off the dipping stick. She sat there on the wood of the well watching the blue canvas jog along until it stopped at her uncle Gourd's house. Maud knew her uncle wasn't at home, but the man called out. He called again. Then he turned the horses toward her and snapped his reins. She hastily put the cap on the Mercurochrome, tore the rag in two, and wrapped her leg with a bandage smaller than the one she'd been using. She stood, threw an arm around the pump, and watched the team, the wagon, and the blue canvas grow bigger and bigger in the bright sun.

The driver was a man she'd never seen before. And with her father at the feed store in Muskogee and her brother in their neighbor's field, and meanness fairly common, Maud wondered if she should, out of precaution, go into the house, where the guns were. But then she recalled Betty's bellowing and felt fairly certain that unless the stranger shot her dead at a distance she could holler loud enough that Lovely would hear her over at Mr. Singer's, jump on his mule, and be to her pretty fast. Then, too, there was something about the blue of the canvas that prevented her from moving. She found it reassuring or, really, more than reassuring, because it was a pretty blue, deeper than the color of the sky and brighter than a heron, a better blue, something new. She couldn't fathom anyone choosing such a blue for any reason other than to please or to draw attention.

The man driving the team was wearing a bowler. That in itself set him apart in Maud's experience. She'd seen bowlers only on undertakers and in magazine pictures of men who were dancing lickety-split with girls who were flappers. Below the hat, he had a clean-shaven face and wore red suspenders and a light-colored shirt. After he closed the second cattle guard, he took off his bowler, waved it in the air over his head, and flashed a smile that glistened like water hit by sunlight. Maud was drawn to the smile like a jay to a piece of foil, but she was a little taken aback by the wave. Was she supposed to wave in return? To a stranger? That would seem forward. But she didn't want to look country and backward, so she raised her right hand and waved her fingers. She kept her left arm slung around the pump.

The man pulled the horses up to the hitching rail about thirty feet away from Maud. By then, his bowler was back on his head, but not so as the brim hid his hair. It was deep brown, thick and wavy. His skin was dark from the sun, but not, Maud thought, Indian. He was definitely a white man; his forearms below his rolled sleeves were hairy. He said in a voice that wasn't a holler, but carried perfectly well, "Looks like you might have some water to spare." Canteens were hanging on the side of the wagon.

Maud nodded. "You can fill up if you care to."

"Just a cup for me, if you don't mind. But Arlene and Evelyn would mightily appreciate a drink."

Maud cocked her head.

"My horses. I named them after my aunts."

Maud laughed. By the time she'd stopped, he'd jumped off the wagon and was walking toward her. He said, "Couldn't call them Sir Barton and Exterminator. They're ladies."

"I can see that."

"And not too fast, either." He took his hat off and scratched his head.

"How did your aunts take to being honored?"

"Haven't told them yet. Aunt Arlene got married and moved all the way to Nashville. Aunt Evelyn is up in Springfield, Missouri. I was going to visit her last year, but then the floods came. I had to stay put and hang on by my fingers."

"Did you lose much? Or were you lucky?"

"Lucky. I live on high ground in Fayetteville. But it sure looked like the end of the world. I bet it was bad around here." He looked away from Maud. "I see the watermarks there on the house."

Maud glanced at the house, too. "If Grandpa hadn't built her on stones, we would've lost her. When the river started overcoming us, we moved the beds and chest into the barn. Hung the beds by hooks from the rafters, put the chest and the drawers on top of the stalls, and slept on the hay in the loft. Lost eleven cows, though. Some of them drowned before we could rustle them up. Ran the others up to the foothills, and they either got lost or somebody stole them. The pigs we ran into the schoolhouse with everybody else's. The chickens roosted with us. Our dog drowned."

The rains had started in the fall of 1926 and continued through the winter. By April of 1927, it was pouring morning and night, sometimes ten inches a day. The water had covered eastern Oklahoma and had run almost all of Maud's family out of their homes. But according to the papers, it had also covered every state from Kansas to Pennsylvania, killed hundreds of people, and swollen the Mississippi to a sixty-mile span at Memphis. The disaster had united the whole country and survivors became friends in minutes. So it was not unusual for Maud and the stranger to settle into a conversation about a mutual experience while he was sipping on a dipper of water and the horses were drinking from the trough.

Maud was gathering bits of information about the stranger like a wind rustles leaves into a pile and was sorting those leaves in her head before she realized she didn't yet have his name or know why he had driven his bright blue covered wagon down their lane. She was thinking about how to ask and not seem like she really cared when he said, "By the way, my name is Booker Wakefield. Please call me Booker." He smiled. There were little creases in the corners of his eyes. The eyes themselves were green, flecked with gold. Maud couldn't tell if those gold flecks were pure color or sparkles of sunshine.

She said, "I'm Maud," but didn't give her last name. It embarrassed her. Her mother's family name, Vann, sounded better to the ear, and she'd always lived among her mother's people. But instead of lying about her last name, she added, "What are you doing around here?"

"I thought you'd never ask," he said. "I'm a peddler. At least in the summertime. Gives me a way to see the world."

"You don't peddle from town to town?"

"The stores in towns have gotten so big and fancy I can't compete. But not everybody can get to a store when they need one. A lot of people still appreciate their goods coming to them. Would you like to see what I'm carrying?" The peddler smiled wide, handed the dipper back to Maud, and walked to his wagon.

He set his hat on the seat and drew the canvas up by pulling on a rope strung across the top of the hull. His wares were secured in place by netting, and he rolled the netting up just as he had the canvas. The goods were stacked on shelves that receded like the steps of a pyramid. On them sat bolts of denim and other cloth in colors pleasing to the eye. There were pots and pans and skillets of every size, suspenders, handkerchiefs, straw hats and fedoras, Woodbury soap, rolls of toilet paper, toothpaste, shaving cream, razors and straps, toothbrushes and pencils, coal-oil lamps, kerosene, and crystal radio sets.

Maud's eyes got wide. And the peddler stretched his arm so that his hand disappeared below the wagon seat. He brought out, between his thumb and forefinger, a spool of red thread. He said, "This is for the water. I think red may be your color."

Maud was wearing a faded green dress, but red was, indeed, the color she pictured herself in. It looked best next to her skin. She ducked her head, but looked up and smiled when he dropped the spool into her hand. He said, "Take your time looking around."

At that moment, Maud didn't have a cent to her name. There was some household money hidden away from Mustard in a baking-powder tin behind the match holder in the cabinet in the kitchen. But that money was family money for flour and sugar and an occasional treat from a store in Ft. Gibson. Maud was too upright to take family money and spend it on herself alone or without talking it over. Her daddy operated that way and it'd caused, over the years, hardship on the rest of the family. She said, "I'll just be looking. I went into town yesterday. Got all my goods there. But thank you for the thread."

He smiled, leaned against the side of the wagon, and said, "Let me know if you see anything you can't live without."

More than anything else displayed, Maud desired the Woodbury soap. She'd gotten a bar for Christmas a couple of years back and was convinced it really did produce skin anyone would love to touch. She also liked the smell, which was, in her mind, as fresh as spring air or an open rose. So she shied away from the Woodbury bars and went to the crystal radio sets. She put her finger on top of a brown cardboard box labeled CRYSTAL EXTRAORDINAIRE, and said, "Do these pick up pretty well?"

"The best in the business. They've got these little earpieces that bring music straight into your head and make you tap your toes a mile a minute." He reached for a box, opened the lid, and held it below Maud's nose.

She peered in. She had a crystal set and so did Lovely. The static they pulled in was more irritating than pleasing, and the earpieces didn't rest comfortably in her ears. She said, "I've got one that doesn't pick up very well."

"You might try one of these. I've got one all put together that I use myself." He closed the lid, replaced the box, and turned to the seat of the wagon. When he did, Maud picked up a bar of Woodbury soap and sniffed it quickly. She'd replaced it by the time he turned back around.

They were far away from any town with a powerful station, but the closeness required for him to hand her the set and give her instructions about how to fit the earpieces in her ears would have overwhelmed a radio signal, even if WLS or WSM had been just one county over. He didn't smell like a white man at all. Or not like the white men Maud was used to smelling. He smelled more like aftershave lotion and leather. The smell made Maud's eyes lose focus.

He said, "Hear anything?"

She regathered her thoughts. "Two or three different stations, all at the same time."

He pointed northeast. "Turn and face that way."

She did, and the sound settled on one station, but she couldn't smell him anymore. She turned back around, took the plugs out of her ears, and said, "I'm really more of a reader, anyway." She handed him the receiver.

His eyelids drooped. He smiled. "In that case, I may be able to tickle your fancy." He put the receiver on the seat of the wagon. "Follow me."

They went to the other side of the pyramid. There, as before, he rolled up the canvas and netting, only this time the steps were filled with books. More books than Maud had ever seen outside of a library. She gasped and took a step back to take them all in. He said, "I'm a reader, too. At night, if I don't have a place inside to sleep, I bunk on my wagon seat, light a lamp, and read longer than I should." He picked out a book and handed it to her. "Ever read this? He may be my favorite."

The book was *A Tale of Two Cities*. Maud had read it, and all of Dickens she could get her hands on. She'd also read Hawthorne, Melville, Cooper, Poe, Irving, Howells, Twain, Hardy, and Austen. She replied, "'It was the best of times, it was the worst of times, it was the age of wisdom . . .' I can't remember beyond that." She opened the book and read out the rest of the sentence.

"You have a mighty fine reading voice. Do you practice it?"

"Not much. I'm the baby of the family. I got read to."

"How many people in your family?"

"I've got two sisters, a brother, and a daddy. My sisters are married and away; my brother's just in the field over there." Maud had forgotten about fearing the stranger, but the reference to Lovely brought that uneasiness back, and she momentarily wondered again if she'd be wise to be afraid. But the lure of the books drew her away from her skittishness, and she set to running her fingers over their covers, pulling out this one and that, and conversing with the peddler in a casual way, as though the books' characters were friends mutually known for the strengths and flaws of their personalities.

Finally, the peddler pulled a book from the lot. "Have you read this? It's a little more modern."

She took it from his hand, opened it, and read the title page. "No. Is it any good?"

"I liked it. I think the author may be a genius. But not everybody agrees with me. His other two books are more famous. I think this is his best."

"What's so great about Gatsby?"

"Well, he dreams who he wants to be and then makes something of himself."

Maud decided right there she needed to read that book. She was thinking about how to get it without spending any money when the peddler said, "Like I say, a lot of people don't take to this book. But I did. Makes you want to go east in the worst way."

It had never occurred to Maud to go farther east than St. Louis or Kansas City, but she could tell the peddler—Booker, as she was beginning to call him in her mind—was thinking about an east that was different from either of those two towns and far out of her reach, even in her wildest imaginings. She felt, at that moment, insignificant under the wide sky, and she was glad they were on the side of the wagon where their backs were to the house. She was suddenly embarrassed by living there. She closed the book and said, "Well, then, maybe I should get it from the library rather than invest in it."

"Tell you what. I'll trade you. If you have a book inside you want to get rid of, I'll exchange it for this one. Even trade."

Maud looked up at him. Those gold flecks in his eyes glittered. Did he know she didn't have any money? Or did he want her to read the book because he liked it? She couldn't tell. "Wait here. I'll see what I have to spare."

Maud had a stack of books under her cot that she'd gathered over time and hoarded. Each one was a favorite she'd read again and again. She pulled from that stack *Moby-Dick*, and she picked it because, it being so thick, she'd read it fewer times than she had the rest and it was less worn. She walked back to the wagon with the big blue book in hand and exchanged it for the slimmer volume and a copy of *Arrowsmith*, which she angled for on the grounds that the Gatsby book was so thin compared to what she was giving up.

The transaction completed, and without much else to say, Maud and Booker fell into an awkward silence that Booker broke by asking for information about who lived around. Maud pointed to the northeast and the west, named aunts and uncles and cousins, and pointed due north and named the Singers. "They have the most folks on that farm and the most money for extras. The man who owns it is Mr. Connell Singer. He likes to read. He has a library and lends me his books."

"Mr. Singer thinks highly of you then."

Maud couldn't tell if that was a statement or a question, but she hoped that either way it indicated the peddler was looking for information about her possible suitors. "He's nice. And generous." She tucked her head and smiled to convey the notion that Mr. Singer was particularly generous to her.

"I see. Those are good qualities in a neighbor."

"Yes, they are. Mr. Singer is the richest person around here. He supplies potatoes to the entire East Coast. Ships them by railroad all the way to New York City and Philadelphia." Maud checked herself after that. She wasn't exactly sure where her neighbor's potatoes went; she just wanted to make it clear that she was familiar with rich people and cities in the East.

"I see. Well, this Mr. Singer, then, probably buys his wares from catalogues and has his books shipped in. Is he a married man?"

"He was. Widowed now."

"I'm sorry to hear that." Booker bit his lower lip. Then he looked to the sky, took a handkerchief out of his back pocket, and wiped his brow. "I guess I better move on before the sun gets higher." He looked to Maud. "It's been nice visiting with you."

"Stop by when you're this way again. Next time, I might not have just been into town."

Their parting was marked by niceties that didn't add to Maud's store of knowledge about the peddler, and by the time his bright blue canvas was rocking away down the ruts of the lane, she was reckoning up all the things about him she wished she'd found out. Was he married (she thought maybe not, he didn't mention any family beyond aunts), what did he do when he wasn't peddling (he'd said he only peddled in the summertime), was he from Fayetteville, Arkansas, or some other Fayetteville (were there other Fayettevilles?), and how did he keep that blue canvas from fading in the sun (that was a complete mystery)? She might have thought about his marital status more than once.

When Lovely came in for his midday meal, Maud had been reading and had forgotten to warm up the beans.

He picked up her book. "Where'd you get this?"

"Peddler came by. Got it off of him."

"Was he driving a wagon with a bright blue canvas?"

"Yes. Did you see him?"

"Didn't see him to talk, but you can't miss that blue."

"Did he go to Mr. Singer's house?"

"Probably. He went back up the line to the highway." Lovely sat down at the table, picked up *Arrowsmith*, and started reading.

Maud hoped that Booker hadn't gone to Mr. Singer's, or if he had, that he hadn't found him at home. Mr. Singer was over seventy, and it would be clear he wasn't a suitor. Maud gave that more worry during her chores, but by the time her father got home in the evening, she'd gotten far enough into her new book that she had taken to disliking most of the characters (except for Nick) and was wondering what Booker, who she now thought of entirely by name, found so wonderful about the novel. She hoped his enthusiasm didn't mean that he was only attracted to rich women and fast cars.

It wasn't until after the meal, when he'd finished reading his paper, that Mustard interrupted Maud's reading and musings. He was sitting in the only chair on the porch, and both she and Lovely had their backs propped against posts, their noses in books, and fans in their hands. He said, "Whatchya reading?"

Lovely spoke first. "*Arrowsmith,* by that Lewis fellow."

"What's it about?"

"A doctor."

"Quack?"

"Don't think so. But maybe."

Mustard looked to Maud. "Mine's about a bunch of rich people," she said. "They don't have much to do. They run up and down the road to parties."

Mustard nodded and fell silent again. But even though he generally was good about letting them read, Maud could tell he wanted to talk. She said, "Anything in the paper?"

"Plans for the new Mississippi levees." Mustard picked his Banjo and a store-bought cigarette package out of his pocket. He tapped the package on his lighter, knocked out a cigarette, and lit up. After a couple of puffs, he started talking about a man who'd come into the feed store trying to sell a litter of beagles.

Maud and Lovely closed their books. Not having a dog was a

problem. They wanted one for the company and to warn them of snakes, and they agreed that any dog that could bark would do. But Mustard wanted a Labrador. He didn't have enough money for a purebred dog, but he liked to talk about shooting ducks down on the sandbar and eating dark duck meat all winter long. He mentioned the pros and cons of various kinds of dogs, described the markings of the beagle pups he'd seen, and told dog stories until dusk closed in and fireflies sprinkled the air with gold.

To Maud's disappointment, they went to bed without any more reading. But she consoled herself with ruminations on Booker until after the moon rose and she could see the front yard lit through the windows. She'd been asleep for several hours and was dreaming about hanging bright blue wallpaper when Lovely shook her by the shoulder. He whispered, "There's a peculiar light in the sky."

She assumed he was talking about the yellow that comes before a tornado. She sat up in bed feeling some dread about having to go to the cellar. Then she saw it was dark outside the windows and the air was tinted only by moonlight. "What color?"

"Like city lights."

"Where?"

"Northeast."

"Above the trees?"

"Yeah. High. Come see."

They tiptoed out to the porch. Maud followed Lovely to the east edge. "Look," he said.

The sky was yellow. But not tornado yellow. Maud said, "Fire."

"Yeah. We better see if it's coming toward us. And if anybody needs help."

"You sure it's not somebody burning off stubble?"

"Could be. But it's got to be late. Maybe two in the morning."

"What were you doing up?"

"Taking a pee."

"Should we wake Daddy?"

"You do it. He'll take it better."

Mustard agreed that fire was in the air, and the three of them threw on clothes and shoes and piled into Mustard's car, a 1919 retractable top Chevrolet that tilted and jiggled so badly that Maud, in the backseat, held on with both hands to the rods supporting the roof. When they turned off the lane onto the section line, she held on with one hand, and peered around her brother's head into the night and the light ahead. Fairly soon, she began to smell the fire in the air, and by the time they climbed the rise beyond a body of water they called a "snake lake," she could see the flames beyond the hood of the car. Passing through the cross of the section lines, she tasted cinders in the air. Mustard yelled, "She's gone!" But neither of his children answered because they, too, could see that the schoolhouse that sat farther up the section line, the one they had both gone to, was completely engulfed in flames.

Mustard stopped the car in the middle of the road. They all jumped out and quickly passed a few other automobiles and trucks until they got to a cluster of people, one of several, watching the fire. Grandpa, Uncle Ame, and Aunt Viola were in that group. Maud touched her great-aunt on the shoulder and was quickly enfolded close to the older woman's hip. Viola said, "Poker woke us up barking like crazy."

"Did anybody get anything out?"

"Don't know."

After that, there wasn't much conversation. At first, Maud worried the fire would get out of control and she watched for that. But, fortunately, the wind was low and the schoolyard mostly barren. Men were shoveling its dirt over the runners. So after her worry about spreading ceased, the fire had a hypnotic effect that drew her into thoughts and images that arose without bidding. She thought of teachers she'd been schooled by in that building, of a day when she'd brought in purple flowers she'd picked on the way, of a boy she had hungered after whose family had come and gone suddenly, of running through hallways with cousins, of a play in which she'd been Maid Marian and worn a curtain on her head, and of her mother, still alive, leading her up the steps. She found she was crying.

She wiped her tears, moved away from Viola, and threaded through the crowd of people. Their faces were lit by the fire almost as well as if the sun had been shining, but their backs were dark, and their shadows mingled with the light in a way that made it seem like the dirt was alive and moving. Most of the people in the river bottoms were there, and about half of them were kin to Maud; for that land, at the time of statehood, had been parceled out to the Cherokees living on it already. Her great-grandfather, Sanders Cordery, had settled in those bottoms at the end of the Trail of Tears. Maud's grandpa, Bert, had married one of Sanders' daughters, Jenny. And Jenny and all of her children, adult and minor, had been given allotments of land. One of Maud's older sisters had been an infant at the time of allotment, and the other a tot; they'd received land of their own. But Maud, Lovely, and Mustard lived on Maud's mother's allotment. Maud's aunts' and uncles' allotments were scattered around them, some with houses, some only farmland or pasture. Her grandpa, her mother's younger siblings, Blue, Early, Lucy, and Lucy's husband and child lived together on Jenny's land. At the moment, Ame and Viola were hunkered with them, too, as Viola's house in the old Creek Nation had been lost to the flooding of the Verdigris River. Most of the people around the fire who were not kin to Maud were white and had moved into the fertile Arkansas River bottoms whenever they could get their hands on Indian land.

Maud talked to her mother's younger sisters, Lucy and Nan; held their babies, one after the other; and watched the fire. But she also craned her neck this way and that, thinking maybe, just maybe, Booker might be there. Her good sense told her that nobody could easily drive a team of horses toward a fire, but she hoped that maybe he'd come on foot. A lot of the people around her had walked to get there. That was dangerous at night because of the snakes, so nearly everybody was armed and had their dogs with them. The lanterns they'd carried were clustered on the ground in groups like the watchers.

After a while, Nan's baby, Andy, got heavy, and Maud handed him off to his older sister and threaded through the patches of people, keeping one eye on the fire and the other on the crowd, still looking (and trying not to seem obvious) for Booker. And that's what she was doing when she looked straight into the eyes and beard of a man who was standing by himself, not staring at the fire, but at her. John Mount. He flicked his tongue out in the air, wiggled it around, and settled it on his upper lip. It and his eyes reminded Maud of a snake. She turned fast and walked facing the blaze to another cluster of people that included several of her former schoolmates. They were talking about what was lost in the fire. They all agreed the building hadn't been the same since the pigs had been run into it during the flood. But still, the loss of a school was a terrible thing, and several of the girls were weeping. Maud shortly got enough of that crying and threaded again through the crowd, this time not so much looking for Booker but trying to avoid John Mount and his kin.

She landed again with her aunts. And in the next group over were some men, including her daddy and her uncle Ryde. It unsettled Maud even more to see them together. She didn't trust either of them to not start a fight, and more often than not, they got into trouble together. Maud noticed that they were facing away from the fire and the other men, and that their heads were close. She didn't take that as a good sign, and she wondered what they were talking about. She couldn't approach them to eavesdrop without drawing attention, but the sight of them together, clearly not watching the fire, disturbed her so much that she set off looking for Lovely.

She found him farther back than the others, leaning against the hood of a truck, talking with Gilda Starr, the girl he had his eyes on. Gilda had gone to school with them in the early grades, but her family had moved into town afterward. Still, Maud and Lovely saw Gilda at dances, fairs, rodeos, and sometimes walking the planks in front of Ft. Gibson's stores. The last time Maud had seen her to talk to at any length was in Taylor's General Store on a day that the rains had been so torrential they'd been trapped there all afternoon. Lovely had been trapped, too, and Maud was of the opinion that it was then when Gilda had grabbed her brother's attention. She was attractive and good-natured, but above them in station. So Maud, as she turned and walked the other way, hoped Lovely wouldn't get his heart broken. She was still pondering that possibility and glancing sideways at the fire every so often when she ran smack into a man's chest.

She sprang back and stumbled before she realized it was Claude Mount's. Then she felt her face take on the heat of the fire. Mount grinned and said, "You needn't look so snakebit."

"I'm not snakebit. You surprised me, that's all."

"You might watch where yer going."

Maud thought Claude Mount had stepped into her path from behind the cab of a truck, but she didn't accuse him of that because she didn't want conversation. She said, "I will," and turned.

But he grabbed her by the arm, and said, "Hey, Maud, don't ya have time to jaw with yer neighbor?"

"Take your hand off my arm."

"No offense meant." Mount held both hands up next to his ears like he was surrendering. He wasn't that much taller than Maud, but he was powerfully built and had a full beard. The hair on the top his head was stringy. He smelled like he'd been wrestling hogs.

Maud said, "No offense taken then." She turned to go again.

"I hear tell yer uncle Ryde is accusing my brother of breaking the back of one of yer cows," Mount said, in a voice loud enough to be heard at a distance over the sound of the fire. Maud looked to see who else was within hearing range. Then she turned to him and said, "I don't know about that. But somebody did."

"Well, it wasn't John. I can tell ya that. He were with me."

"That's a fine recommendation."

"It ain't natural for full brothers to be working together?"

"Depends on what the brothers are working at." Maud looked around. She didn't want to stay in a conversation with Claude Mount, especially that far away from the fire. Most everybody was still turned toward it with the roar in their ears.

"Minding our bizness like ever'body else. You tell yer uncle Ryde the Mounts don't take to false accusations."

Maud saw a gun in a holster below Claude's belt. But she didn't see it as adding to his threat. He was frightening enough without a gun, and the Mount brothers were prone to sneaky violence, not the shoot-you-in-the-chest kind. Besides, to have come without a gun would've been stupid. Cottonmouths were as thick as thistles down where the Mounts lived. She said, "I'll tell him if I see him," a statement she had no intention of fulfilling. Telling her uncle Ryde would make him even more prone to pick a fight and drag her daddy smack into the thick of it. Not that he needed dragging. In fact, Maud knew, it was just as likely that he'd be leading.

She walked off, and as she did, just by habit, shook her hair. It was long and black, and she shook it often for all sorts of reasons. That time she shook it to shake off the smell of Claude Mount. But it provoked a sound from Mount that was animal and unmistakable in intention, and that frightened Maud so much that she felt that she, like her cow, had been assaulted in the back. Her muscles contracted around her spine, and her legs extended to their fullest stride without running. She walked straight to her aunt Nan, took Andy again, and stood there watching the blaze until she was carried away into its depths.

By the light before the dawn, the fire had lost its height and most of the building had fallen. Volunteer firemen from Ft. Gibson had arrived in a fire truck with hoses they didn't bother distending. Whenever it looked like any arm of the fire was going to run away, somebody shoveled dust over it, threw on it a bucket of water they'd drawn from the truck, or took a wet feed sack and slapped it out. People were beginning to tire, and Maud was starting to find Andy heavy again. She passed him to his sister and walked toward a spot where she could see if Lovely was still talking to Gilda without having to go past where Claude Mount had been. It was during that walk that she overheard some man she barely knew say the word *peddler*.

She stopped, folded her arms under her breasts, and turned toward the fire. Three men were in a conversation with one woman. They were all white and the woman was doing most of the talking. She was answering the men's questions, relating the details of a visit Booker had made to her place. Maud wasn't exactly sure where that was, but she thought it was a little house between the highway and Ft. Gibson. The men wanted to know if the woman found him strange in any way. Where was he from? Did his manner seem shifty? It was clear to Maud the woman was enjoying the attention, and she talked at length about his visit. As for shifty, he'd cheated her on some cloth and she'd noticed he was carrying a lot of kerosene on that wagon.

At the mention of kerosene, Maud turned and stopped her pretense. She said, "I visited with the peddler. He seemed like a good Christian to me."

One of the men spoke. "How do you know that?"

"He tried to peddle me a Bible, but I already had one. So he read some scripture to me. He had a fine reading voice. One whole side of his wagon is taken up with books."

"Most of those were novels," the woman said.

"Some of them were. Some were schoolbooks, some were Bibles. He had all sorts of books. He's an educated man, as far as I could see."

One of the men smiled at Maud. "That helps clear up some of the suspicions about him, I guess. Thank you for your remarks." He touched the brim of his hat.

The woman said, "I wouldn't be too quick. He's here this morning and then tonight this." She gestured toward the fire. "It's not like many strangers come through."

"What makes you think somebody set the fire?" Maud asked.

"We were just speculating," another man said. "Most fires start in winter."

Maud couldn't deny that. "Well, I can tell you, I spent a good deal of time going through his wares and buying books from him, and he's a fine man with a good family. Named his . . ." She

realized she had gone too far. Anybody would find naming your
team after your aunts funny, even people who obviously had no
senses of humor. She finished the sentence by mumbling.

One of the men said, "I didn't quite get that."

Maud said, "Named all the books of the Bible in the old part.
Just rattled them off. It was impressive."

She left after that and resumed her search for Lovely. She saw
him still standing with Gilda, decided she'd waited long enough,
and marched over to them. The three of them were still talking
when the sun hit the rim of the earth and, at the same time, a
Packard rolled down the section line at a creep. Maud, Lovely,
and Gilda all recognized the car, as did everybody else, and when
it rolled to a stop, one of the men standing close to it walked over,
spoke to the driver, and then opened the door and held it. A slim
man with a white goatee and moustache and hair to match appeared from inside the car and walked with a cane toward the fire.
Gilda said, "I was wondering where he was."

"Did he just now show up or is he coming back, do you think?"
Maud said.

"It takes him a while to get organized," replied Lovely. "He
hasn't been feeling well."

The old man, Connell Singer, took several steps toward the
fire, spread his stance, and planted his cane. The man who had
opened his door had been treading behind him and stopped behind his shoulder. That man made a motion with his hand that
was clearly for the purpose of calling other men over, and they
came, a single man at first, and then several others. They stood in
a half arc around Mr. Singer, leaving an opening so that his view
of the fire, what was left of it, was unobstructed. Maud couldn't
hear a word of what was said. But she witnessed arms extending
into the air and enough general gesturing to be able to tell that the

men were giving Mr. Singer a full description of how high the fire had climbed, where the walls had fallen, and how the runners had been stopped in their paths.

Maud shortly got bored with watching a conversation she couldn't hear and that she felt confident was passing on information she already had, and she turned again to the fire. In daylight and dying, it looked less magical and more like a big mess that would take a lot of work to clear. Little patches of flames were still dancing, but they were separated from one another and resembled fires that might be used for roasting or camping on the river. Smoke rose from most of the wood, and some of it, Maud thought, would burn for days unless rain came. She was looking at the sky for any sign of that and recalling when rain clouds were the last things she wanted to see when Gilda said, "Mama's waving to me. I better get going."

Maud said, "We better go, too. I'll round up Daddy. Good to see you." She left quickly so that Lovely and Gilda could privately say whatever they wanted in parting, and as soon as she got out of earshot, she stopped and searched the clusters of people still standing around. Her aunts were gone, and with them, her cousins. Neither did she see any of her uncles or her grandpa. She turned and took a few steps, looked toward the cars and trucks, and didn't see her daddy's. She thought maybe she wasn't looking in the right place, had disremembered in the excitement where they'd parked, so she looked this way and that until she'd focused on every car there and realized that her father's really was gone. Then she turned back toward Lovely and saw him walking Gilda toward her family. She decided that might be interesting to watch and, suddenly feeling weary, looked around for a place to sit down. There wasn't any sitting place except in the dirt, so she stood.

The parting took longer than Maud expected. Evidently, Lovely and Mrs. Starr had found something to talk about, and Maud was thinking about ribbing her brother about that on the way home when her eyes again drifted over to the cluster of men around Mr. Singer. Three of those men were the same ones who had been talking about Booker, and the woman they'd been talking to was also with them. Maud knew there was only one thing that would draw that woman into a conversation with Mr. Singer and a whole group of men, and she suddenly felt the same way she felt whenever she found a snake in a hen's nest. She backed up from where she was standing and frantically looked around for any kin. She spied Early far across the fire, standing with his cowboy hat shoved forward on his head and scratching his back with his elbow in the air. Beyond him, she saw no other kin except Lovely. He was still talking to Mrs. Starr. Maud couldn't imagine what he could think to say that would take that long, and she suddenly felt a grinding irritation with him. She looked back to the group standing around Mr. Singer. The woman was nodding.

Maud was transfixed by that conversation. She couldn't join it, but she also couldn't leave while it was going on. She stood there and fumed, smelled the burnt wood in her nose, and tried to will Lovely to get out of his idiotic conversation and walk toward Mr. Singer. She glanced repeatedly his way and then again back at the group around her elderly neighbor. Eventually, she saw the back-sides of the Starrs as they walked away; but Lovely, the idiot he was, walked over to Early and started talking with him. Neither of them looked in her direction, and instead of crossing to the other side of the fire to join them and maybe picking up a little of the conversation still going on around Mr. Singer, Maud stayed where she was until Mr. Singer turned back toward his car. Then she turned away from it all and started walking home.

Maud had only gotten as far as the Beechers' place on the near side of where the section lines crossed when she heard Lovely's voice calling her name. She kept walking without turning. She heard him running. Finally, he shouted, "Hold up, will you?" so loudly that she couldn't pretend she hadn't heard him. She slowed her walk and threw a look over her shoulder that she hoped telegraphed displeasure. When Lovely caught up to her, he panted, and said, "What've you got a bee in your drawers for?"

"You took too long. We've been up all night. Can't you think of anybody but yourself?"

Lovely drew his chin in and pulled to his full height. But he didn't snap back. He fell into a pace that matched Maud's and walked in silence at her side until she couldn't stand it any longer. She said, "Where the heck do you think Daddy went off to?"

"Work?"

"I doubt it. He left too early for that."

"Maybe he's home, trying to get some sleep?"

"Could be, I guess. It'd be nice if he'd thought to take us with him."

"Nice? Dad?"

The reminder of their alliance against their father put Maud in a little better mood, but it wasn't better enough to confide in Lovely her fears about Booker; if she did, he'd recognize that her interest extended beyond the realm of justice. She didn't want to have that discussion, so she said, "Are you courting Mrs. Starr or her daughter?"

Lovely didn't rise to that bait. He replied, "I wonder where the schooling will take place come fall?"

"Mrs. Benge's, probably." Maud named the closest school on that side of the highway, the one on the bayou.

"Ft. Gibson's would be nearer."

"Maybe there then. I don't really know."

"I know you don't know. I was just making conversation."

"Well, make it about something interesting. Did you get Mrs. Starr's blessing?"

"Wasn't looking for it. Was just listening to her tell how they'd been awakened in the night by the sound of cars starting. Evidently, they're light sleepers."

Maud didn't care what kind of sleepers the Starrs were, but she did recognize that her brother's mention of the sleeping habits of Gilda's family was more connected to thoughts of beds than to a concern for their health. She said, "Did you make any progress on the daughter?"

"Taking her to the dance Saturday night."

"What dance?"

"The one in town. Down on the corner. Gonna be fiddling."

"How are you getting in?"

"Early's gonna take me on the back of his horse."

Envy wasn't a large part of Maud's nature. But it'd been a long night, and worry over Booker hadn't left her. As she looked down the long dirt road that led straight to more dirt then to a wild of cane and tangled scrub and eventually to the sandbar and the river, she felt the same desolation she felt the day Betty was killed. The thought of a dance with fiddling and lanterns and people dressed up in clean clothes without her being there was almost too much to bear. A tear formed in her left eye, the one closest to the sun, and she wiped it away with a flick of her wrist, hoping that Lovely hadn't seen it.

If he had, he didn't mention it. Maud took a deep breath, set her jaw, and distracted her mind by thinking about the chickens she needed to let out and feed and then about whether or not her father was at home in bed. That thought sent her eyes searching the dirt for tracks that might have been laid that morning. But there had been more traffic than usual on the road, and she couldn't distinguish new tracks from old. She walked on in silence before Lovely finally said, "Gilda thinks a lot of you."

Maud knew Lovely had just made that up to get her into a conversation about his girl, and by that time, she'd reined herself in enough that she didn't begrudge his romantic interest. She kept the conversation going in the direction he wanted all the way down the line until their house came into sight and she could see that their father's car wasn't there. She said, "Where do you think he's off to?"

"Work, I hope."

"What do you think the chances are?"

"Maybe pretty good. He'll want to tell everybody about the fire."

Maud hoped Lovely was right. But her father wasn't an eager employee. He avoided taking orders like a calf avoids a rope, and his skittishness didn't endear him to his superiors. Over the years, he'd had a number of jobs — construction work, road building, even a little grave digging — but he'd always wound up in a fight with somebody, often his boss, and either stormed off after a brawl or, more often, wound up on the ground knocked out and dirty. Mustard usually got the first lick in, but not always the last one.

Maud let out the chickens and fed them while Lovely milked the cow. Then they both sat to breakfast, ate quickly, and Lovely left to clear timber. Maud tended to her other chores, changed the bandage on her leg to a smaller one just to keep dirt out of her wound, and then walked down the lane and back up the section line to her aunt Nan's. She found Nan on her back stoop churning butter in the shade of a tree, and Maud took over the churning to give her a rest.

Nan was about the same age Maud's mother had been when she'd died, so Maud was partial to her, and Nan gave Maud what mothering she could. They talked at length about the fire, recounted how they'd become aware of its burning, what they'd done to get there, who'd said what to whom, and what they thought of the flames, the smell in the air, and the charred remains of the school. They wanted to return to the ruins, but Nan didn't have the energy to round up her children and Maud was too tired to walk the road in the sun alone. So they took turns churning and talked about their imaginings of the fire's site in broad daylight and their hopes for a new school. In the midst of that talk, Nan mentioned that Ryde hadn't come home.

The butter was setting up. Nan took over the churning to finish it off. Maud flexed her fingers to get her hand back into pliable shape and said, "Daddy didn't come home, either. At least not as far as Lovely and I could tell."

Nan pursed her lips.

Maud said, "I saw both the Mounts at the fire last night."

"They're bad'uns. You stay away from 'em."

"I'm trying. You heard about our cow?"

"Yeah. You can bet it was the Mounts. They been acting like that since the river was laid in its bed."

"We hadn't really wanted Daddy to know it."

"Something like that's hard to keep. As soon as Ryde heared it, he was ready to take off after 'em."

"I think he told Daddy. I hope they didn't take the law into their own hands."

Nan kept churning. Maud looked off into the distance at the hills on the horizon. Eventually, Nan spoke. "Nothing would surprise me."

Maud looked down at the dirt between her feet. A thing like

an axed cow could get a lot of people killed. She recalled Betty writhing in the weeds. A shudder ran down between her shoulders and through her body to her breasts. She wiped a bead of sweat from between them. She wanted away from the violence as much as she wanted indoor plumbing and brighter light to read by at night. She applied her moist thumb to the dust on the toe of her left shoe. Worrying wouldn't fix what was out of her control, and she hadn't yet spoken a word about what else was on her mind. She said, "Did that peddler with the blue covered wagon stop here?"

"Sure did. I bought some cloth with my egg money."

Maud didn't want to talk about cloth, but she knew how the conversation was supposed to progress. She prompted Nan to tell her the color and what she was going to make the material into. Only after she'd heard that, did she say, "Some white woman at the fire was accusing the peddler of starting it and cheating her, too."

Nan cleared her throat. After a while she said, "That's Miz Pratt yer talking about. I heared her, too. She ain't never in her life got the good end of a deal."

Maud felt relieved. That Booker could be a cheat hadn't set too well with her. She said, "What did you think of him?"

Nan let up on the churning. "He's a good-looking feller. Did ya buy from him?"

Maud told her the titles of the books she'd gotten in trade and then added, "Do you think he'll stay around long?"

"Well, Maudy-Baby, he's a peddler." Nan started churning again.

Maudy-Baby had been her mother's name for her, and a lump came up in Maud's throat. In the dust at her feet, she imagined her mama dying in the yard, twisting on the ground. To get that image out of her head, she nudged her aunt with her shoulder. "I know. But he sure is pleasing to the eye."

Maud played with the baby while Nan patted the butter into molds, took the noon meal with her aunt and cousins, and walked home, having secured a ride to the dance. She was lost in thinking about the fun of Saturday night when she walked through their first cattle guard and realized that the gate was open and lying on the ground. She felt certain she'd closed the guard behind her when she'd left. And, that morning, Lovely had taken a sack meal to the field because he was late getting started. There wasn't a car, wagon, or horse ahead at the house. She looked to the front pasture for the cows and saw Carrie, the milk cow, and her yearling lying in the shade of a pecan tree. She pulled the gate up off the ruts into place and looked to the second cattle guard. That gate was down, too. Her heart suddenly thumped fast. She felt stupid for leaving home without her gun. She looked hard at the house.

It was two rooms of unpainted boards resting on stacks of sandstones. When it had gotten so crowded that her grandpa and the rest of the family moved to another house, they'd left her close family in that one, and her uncle Blue and her daddy had built a porch across the front and the west side. Its tin roof was supported by five posts, four of which were visible from the lane. The house seemed empty, its two front windows like blind eyes, its two doors like cave mouths. She looked to the yard. It was a few patches of grass, a lot of dirt that she kept swept with a broom, and a line of sandstones winding from the porch steps to the pump. Some chickens were scratching around. But what Maud's eyes rested on was a tall and broad live oak tree. Its foliage was lush and many of its branches dipped to the ground. During the hottest days of summer, she retreated to its shade, and when she looked out from its cover, the rest of the farm appeared as separate as another country. Maud, as accustomed as she was to hiding beneath the branches and leaves of the oak, recognized the possibility that it could be concealing somebody as well as the house. At the distance she was from both, only a marksman could hit her. And although she didn't really believe she was likely to get shot in her own lane, stranger things had happened, and she did think it was within the realm of possibility that somebody who she couldn't see or sense was watching her. She looked in the dirt of the ruts for footprints, saw her own, and recognized Lovely's. But Lovely, even if he'd come back, wouldn't leave the guards down any more than she would. She looked for tire tracks and for those of wagon wheels. There were several sets, but she had stepped on many of those and none had rolled over her prints. She turned and reopened the first cattle guard and looked for prints beyond it. The same confused pattern speckled that dirt. She pulled that gate closed again. Then she walked back up the section line, watching the house and the live oak on her left as long as she could.

She went back to Nan's. Two of her cousins were playing in the yard. She spoke to the girl. "Renee, did a wagon or car come by while I was in the back with your mama?"

"None that I noticed." The child was flat faced and brown headed.

"But you'd see one, right? You were in the front yard most of the time?"

Renee held a stick in her right hand. Words she'd drawn in the dirt to teach her little brother to read were between her and Maud. "I guess so. That'd be hard to miss."

The house sat so close on the line that dust was always a problem. There wasn't any noise in the bottoms beyond the buzz of insects, chicken arguments, cow complaints, and the sound of

Mr. Singer's tractors. Lately, those hadn't been in any of the fields close around. Probably, a car or a wagon would've been heard by all. Maud said, "How 'bout a horse?"

Renee squinted. "Looking for company?"

"No. Just wondering. Go back to your words."

"You wanta play with us?"

"I'd love to. But I gotta . . ." She didn't know what she was going to say until she added, "Catch up with Lovely."

Maud didn't have to walk far before she saw Lovely in the distance between a stand of trees and a potato field, using a mule to move limbs into a pile. Mr. Singer had hired him to clear the trees for planting because the woods bordered both on their mother's allotment and their grandmother's.

Lovely looked up while Maud was still walking the road. He started unhitching the mule from the limbs before she got to him. When she was within talking distance, he said, "You want to ride her back with me?"

Lovely threw his tools in a pine box sitting on two stumps under the trees. He threw the ropes over the animal's back and led her to another stump. He mounted first and pulled Maud up. They were on the section line before she said, "We may have a problem at the house."

"What kinda?"

"I went to visit Aunt Nan, and when I got back, the guards were down on the ground."

"Both of 'em?"

"Yep."

"You think I need to stop at Aunt Nan's?" Lovely said, over his shoulder.

"Might oughta."

Lovely kicked the mule in the side. He often brought the animal home rather than return her to Mr. Singer's for the night, and so there was no worry about being considered mule thieves, and as they clip-clopped along, Maud described her fear of going up to the house with the gates on the ground. Lovely had a handgun in the saddlebag he carried to the field, and when they got to Nan's, Maud slid off of the mule and borrowed a rifle.

They rode as far as the intersection of the section line and their lane, and stopped at their uncle Gourd's house. Gourd was laying out with a woman, and when he got one of those, he could be gone a whole season or until the woman, whoever she was, threw him out. So they tied the mule to Gourd's porch post and went inside. When they came back out, Lovely untied the animal and mounted her from the porch, and Maud slipped off the planks, went behind the house, and scooted down the ridge, carrying the rifle in her left hand. She used her right hand to grab on to weeds to manage the incline. On flatter land, she took the cow path below the ridge west toward the house.

Maud had climbed through the fence and was leaning against a large tree just under the ridge with her rifle pointed when Lovely came out on the porch and shouted her name. She recognized the shout as urgent, but not terrified, and she laid her gun on higher ground and used roots as steps. She stepped high until she got out of the weeds. Lovely was still on the porch when he said, "We've got a problem in the kitchen."

"What kind?"

"A dead dog."

"In the kitchen?"

"On the table."

"That's just meanness," Maud said.

"You betcha. Shot in the head and slit in the throat. It's a mess in there. One of us will have to clean it up."

Maud figured who that was likely to be. "I guess I better take a look."

"It's pretty bad. I've already seen it."

Maud felt like she might, on the strength of that remark, get out of having to bury the dog. And she wasn't above using her gender to her advantage. She said, in a voice that was a little less assertive than she usually used with her brother, "How bad?"

"There's blood everywhere."

"What kind of dog was it?"

"Dog, dog."

"It's the Mounts' doings." Maud leaped to that conclusion without even drawing a breath, and for a few minutes, she and Lovely distracted themselves from the carcass in the kitchen by discussing their neighbors. They took into account that they'd found Betty in the Mounts' pasture, or what the Mounts called their pasture, which was really just scrub in the wild between real pasture and the river. And they took into account a fistfight Mustard had had with Claude Mount during the last election. They also counted in the real possibility that Mustard and Ryde had done something in the early morning light to settle the score with the Mounts over axing Betty's back. But then they figured it might be just as likely that the Mounts would've gone after Ryde, and they knew no meanness had taken place at their aunt's. So they left it at that, and Maud asked, "Do you think they actually killed it in the kitchen?"

"Don't know. I can't see them bringing it into the house to shoot it. But there's a lot of blood for them to have kilt it somewhere else. I got some on me." Lovely held up his hand and spat on it.

"Why are you spitting on yourself?"

"I got a thistle poke." He massaged his palm with his thumb and then swiped his hand on his overalls.

"I've told you to wear gloves a thousand times."

"I was wearing gloves. It poked me through one."

Lovely looked toward the river. The sun was past four o'clock. "If Dad doesn't stop off somewhere, he could be home in an hour."

"We better get to digging, then."

"Let's dig in the garden. We can make fertilizer."

"Do you want to drag it out, or do you want me to?"

"Well, I've already seen it," he said. "And it didn't get to me like Betty did. I'll drag it out. You get the shovels."

They dug a hole three feet deep and a foot longer than the dog. While they threw dirt, they talked about whether the dog belonged to somebody or was one of the feral ones that lived in the wild of the river, roamed the sandbar, and sometimes took up with the wolves. It was a dog they'd never seen. But dogs and cats turned up around the house on a regular basis, and if their father hadn't been so particular about the kind he wanted, they could've had their pick of a half dozen or so. This dog was mostly black and a little long-haired, but not speckled with burrs. Lovely had dragged it to the garden wrapped in the only tablecloth they had, and with a good bit of regret, Maud agreed to bury it in that cloth. Lovely shoved the carcass into the hole with his boot. It raised a little dust when it hit the bottom. He said, "Should we say something over it?"

"Like what?"

"Don't know. It might've been somebody's pet."

Maud looked around. Sunflower stalks were growing at the north end of the garden. They weren't yet blooming, but they had the makings of buds. She walked over to them and broke a stalk off. She walked back to the hole, knelt, and laid the stalk on the tablecloth.

By the time Mustard got home, Maud had Lovely's overalls soaking in cold water in the kettle in the yard and the kitchen looked as usual except for the bare wood of the table. Mustard came in weary but carrying news of various conversations about the fire. He reported on arguments about its origin and was halfway through his meal before he rubbed his thumb along the grain of the wood, and said, "Cloth on the line?"

Maud was at the stove picking a biscuit out of the oven. Lovely was at the table with his father. He cleared his throat. Maud straightened up, dipped some beans onto her plate, and said, "We've got a little problem, Daddy."

Mustard grunted.

Maud sat her plate down and slid into her chair. "Do you want a cigarette?"

"Not through eating. What's the problem?"

"Well, I went visiting Aunt Nan, and when I got back, the cattle guards were down."

Mustard had hominy on his knife. He threw his head back and dropped several kernels into his mouth. Then he waved the knife in front of Maud's face. "That reminds me." He pointed the knife at Lovely. "You kids lied to me about Betty. Her back was axed. If you wasn't so big, I'd whip the tar out of you both. As it is, as soon as I finish this meal, I'm gonna kick yer butts."

Maud and Lovely glanced at each other in a communication they'd used since before their mother's death. It was barely noticeable to anyone else, but it said between them, *Don't run. He's just bellowing.*

"We're sorry about that. We didn't know how to break it to you, and she had to be put down, no matter." Maud rubbed her thumb over the headdress of the Indian on the Calumet baking-powder tin they used as a pencil holder. She was glad the tin had been on the floor and unsplattered with blood after the dog had been left on the table.

Mustard pinched the end of his nose. "I can't for the life of me figure out why anybody would want to protect the Mounts."

"We were protecting you, Dad." Lovely spoke. "If you stormed off and shot one of 'em, then where would you be? In jail, we reckoned."

"Somebody would have to catch me first. Haven't you got any faith in me?"

"We do, Daddy. But you've been known to fly off the handle," Maud said.

"Somebody bring me an ashtray."

Lovely got up, went to the front room, came back, and settled a clear glass ashtray on the table. Mustard took his Banjo, a pouch of tobacco, and papers from his shirt pocket. After he'd rolled his cigarette and taken a couple of puffs, he said, "Ryde figured three hogs to a cow. But then I told him she was carrying, so we upped it to four."

"When did you do it?"

"While everybody was watching the fire. Any attention grabber can be an opportunity. Remember that."

Maud and Lovely were used to Mustard's parental advice. It included "Cut up, not crossways," "Hit 'em before they know yer mad," and "Stomp 'em if you can; yer a lot less likely to break a hand." They saw his recommendations as signs of affection but tried not to dwell on them. Maud was imagining the dead hogs when Mustard added, "Shot 'em in the head and then cut their throats for good measure. Little hogs, though. Not big-hog season." He said that with a tone of regret.

"Well, they got even," Lovely said.

"How's that?"

"Killed a dog and threw it on the kitchen table."

Mustard pursed his lips and trimmed the ash off the end of his cigarette. "Is that it?"

"It was pretty bad, Dad. Shot it in the head and slit its throat. Blood was everywhere. Ruined the tablecloth and Maud had to soak steel wool in vinegar and use it on a spot on the table where the blood leaked through."

Maud moved a plate. "Didn't get it all. I think it's gonna have to be sanded."

Mustard extended his hand and fingered the spot. "I can take care of that."

Lovely reached for the honey pot, dipped a spoon into it, and let the honey drip onto a biscuit. Watching the honey's slow move, Maud recognized that she'd been expecting storming and threatening. Maybe her father figured one dog against four hogs and thought he'd gotten the better of the Mounts? She didn't want to encourage more retaliation, so she said, "Thanks, Daddy. It wasn't really all that bad. Was it, Lovely?"

Lovely was as practiced as Maud at settling Mustard's temper, and he hopped back into the conversation with "Naw. We used the tablecloth to lug him to the garden and buried him there. He'll grow fat onions next season."

Mustard lowered his eyebrows and winced. Then he took a long drag and stumped his butt out in the tray. "The Mounts generally go up in their meanness, not down. Keep yer eyes wide fer something sneaky. One dog fer four hogs ain't exactly enough."

2

Maud often found her uncle Ryde as difficult as a cow with a twitchy hind foot. But she conceded that he was the best square-dance caller around. Her job on the way to the dance was to protect his fiddle from his children. She rode in the back of his buckboard on a quilt with her cousins, Morgan, Renee, Sanders, and Andy, holding the instrument in her arms as if it were a baby. The sun was still shining on the potato plants and Maud's back was against the west planks of the wagon bed where she was trying to stay squeezed into a little patch of shade. When they arrived at the schoolhouse rubble, Ryde stopped his horses in the middle of the line. He said fire was still burning under the ash and the only thing salvaged from the building was a book that had been locked in the safe because it was dirty.

"What was its name?" Maud asked.

"Don't know. It's about a bunch of people walking to church, telling each other tales. Some of 'em stories will scald you bald."

When the wagon started rolling again, Maud's mind stayed on the dirty book. It tickled her to think about people telling naughty tales on the way to church, and she decided that if she saw Booker, which was her primary wish, she'd ask him if he was familiar with the book. As the wagon rolled along, the combination of naughtiness, literature, and Booker focused Maud's attention like pollen focuses bees. She clutched the fiddle so tightly that it made creases on her arms.

When Ryde pulled up at the dance corner, Maud was relieved to turn the instrument over and eager to walk the streets with Nan and her children. The town's two drugstores, two cafés, and the Golden Rule Grocery excited her, but her favorite place of all was Taylor's General Store. And that was where she, Nan, and her brood headed to first. Once they got there, Morgan ran off to play with other boys, and Renee was charged with minding Andy and Sanders out on the front porch. Maud and Nan went inside and marveled, fingered, and yearned so much that Maud temporarily forgot about looking for Booker. It wasn't until they reemerged into long afternoon shadows that her mind once again veered to her main mission. By that time, the streets were filled with wagons, horses, mules, automobiles, and people. Maud parted ways with Nan, walked in and out of stores on Lee Street, spoke with people she hadn't seen in a while, and let a boy she knew from school buy her a Coca-Cola. After finishing the soft drink, she extracted herself with the promise of a dance and with the excuse of needing to give Lovely a message from her father.

Maud didn't really think Lovely and Early had yet made it into town; Lovely hadn't started washing up when she'd left, and Early would want to make a late appearance so he could make the women wait. As for Mustard, Maud didn't think he'd take the occasion to slip down to the Mounts' to extend the feud because, for the moment, he had the upper hand. She figured he'd spend the early part of his evening near his bootlegger's and come to the dance shouting drunk but before he was falling down.

She did keep her eye out for the Mount brothers so she

wouldn't be taken by surprise again. But with the town filling up, it was hard to scan the crowd well enough to be certain someone wasn't coming up on her from behind or at her from a catty-cornered direction. She stayed mostly on the planks in front of the stores, looked in windows for items that struck her fancy, and talked to girls she knew, and to more boys, too. She'd promised several dances and had gossiped about a friend's upcoming marriage when, from down the street, she heard the fiddlers tuning up. She loitered some more, went into and out of Berd's Drugstore without buying anything, and wound toward the dance corner looking for the bright blue canvas that was to her mind the prettiest thing ever set against the sky.

Near the corner, she walked the length of the Pierce building, hesitated for a moment, and then peered through its two arches to the fiddlers' stage. Above it, men were hanging lanterns and behind them were two rolls of blue sitting atop the hull of a wagon. The rolls sucked Maud's breath into her chest. Her heart began to flutter like a bird that wants out of a cage. She spun around and put her hand on one of the stone columns that supported the second story of the building. Her other hand she drew to her breast. She needed a plan to get over to the wagon. She couldn't think of one; her wits had suddenly scattered. So instead of walking toward the bright blue, she crossed the intersection, brought a buckboard to a halt without noticing it, and walked entirely in the opposite direction. She passed clumps of blanket Indians sitting on the curb wearing black hats with feathers, passed their wives and children parked in groups not far away, passed a small house, and walked even farther up the road until it bordered a long, deep lawn in front of the Nash Taylor mansion.

Mr. Taylor had been dead since Maud was a little girl. But his grandson (who was also Mr. Singer's son) lived in his grandfather's house and ran the general store that still bore the Taylor name. The home was the grandest Maud had ever seen, even bigger and better than her Mr. Singer's, and although she'd never been inside, she'd toyed in her imagination with the home being her own from the first time she'd laid her eyes on its two-story center section and double front porches. She didn't actually hope to live in that house, but she hoped to live in one just like it. And whenever she glimpsed the home, she used it as a guide, much like a sailor uses the brightest stars in the sky. She sat down on one of the sandstone slabs in the front lawn and positioned herself at an angle so that she could see the house without appearing to watch it, see the road, and also, in the far distance, see a corner of one of the blue rolls over Booker's wagon. The house and the blue canvas anchored Maud while she tried to plan.

She was still cogitating when she heard the first tune, "When the Red, Red Robin Comes Bob, Bob, Bobbin' Along." After only a few bars, she bolted up with the notion that she needed to retrace her steps quickly and get to Booker before other girls started swishing their skirts around him. The very thought of him clasping some girl's forearm and twirling her around made her feel as frantic as if she'd found a thief in the house. She passed the clumps of blanket Indians so quickly that she didn't smell the smoke from their pipes and cigarettes, nor did she realize that she'd stepped right into the middle of a penny-pitching contest that stopped to let her go by.

When she got to the dance corner and saw all the men, women, and children standing at the edge of the square just tapping their toes and not yet dancing, she felt foolish. She knew as well as anyone that nobody danced the first dance and that all parties had to get started by some brave couple who took the floor (or the watered-down dust) and showed off enough to erase everybody else's embarrassment. Her uncle Ryde yelled out, "Who's gonna claim this ground?" and Maud craned her neck to see one of the Benge boys and his new wife step into the patch. The Benges were kin to nearly everybody standing around the dirt square and the new couple was, Maud agreed, the most attractive in town. So by the time the fiddlers started "Red Robin" again, four squares of couples had moved into position. Booker wasn't in any of the squares, and the crowd in front of Maud had thinned out enough that she could see the onlookers on the two other sides of the patch as well as she could see the stage where Ryde and the other fiddlers were. She scanned the crowd. Booker wasn't in it.

About that time, she felt a tap on the shoulder. Jimmy Foreman, a good-looking, skinny boy she'd known most of her life, led her into the dirt. They joined a new square and danced two more dances before Jimmy was cut in on by Henry Swimmer and Henry was cut in on by John Leeds. Maud decided that she looked better on the floor than she would've looked standing around it and that dancing was the best place to be appreciated by Booker. She figured he must be looking on, even if, as her eyes searched the rims of the dance patch, she couldn't locate him. The light was now entirely cast by lanterns. Maud couldn't make out the blue except in her imagination. But she could see a canvas roll. Booker's wagon was still there.

And it continued to be when the fiddlers broke and the dancers went off in clumps to drink lemonade or stronger brew sold out of the trunks of cars. But Maud, instead of availing herself of any refreshment, took the break as an opportunity to do what she'd been wanting to do for at least five dances. That was to go to Booker since he wasn't coming to her. But as soon as she reached an angle where she could see the wagon and its owner well enough, she realized that Booker was there to sell, not to dance. She felt foolish for having spent so much time thinking anything else. He was beside his wagon, holding a pot out to a woman she couldn't place. But she could tell from a distance that Booker was reciting the advantages of that particular pot over all others on this Earth or any other planet.

Maud felt a jab of jealousy. She fought an urge to stride over to the wagon, grab that pot, and buy it herself. To contain that feeling, she looked around at the people who had wandered in back of the stage, and she saw, at a distance, Billy Walkingstick. He was talking to two other boys she knew, but she also knew she could lure Billy into anything, even a briar patch. So she walked in a direction that would both avoid the wagon and catch Billy's eye, and sure enough, like a bass following a lure, Billy disengaged himself from his friends, and shouted, "Hey, Maud, don't be highfaluting."

Maud replied, "Oh, Billy, you surprised me. I didn't know you'd taken up square dancing."

Billy said, "Haven't. Didn't have anything better to do. You been dancing?" He fell in next to Maud.

"A bit," she said, and kept walking. But then she suddenly stopped. "That peddler over there has something I want to look at."

"What is it?"

"Several things. Women like to look. You know that." She took off toward Booker's wagon.

Billy dropped his cigarette, crushed it with his boot, and caught up with Maud in a couple of long strides. She was pleased he did. His puppy eagerness and Indian good looks made him the perfect escort to be seen with.

She went straight to the Woodbury soap. She picked up a bar, read its wrapper, and held it close to her nose for a sniff. Booker was making change with his back to her. She was afraid he wouldn't turn her way until she sniffed the bar silly, so as soon as that transaction was completed, she said, "How much did you say this was?"

Booker turned around slowly. He looked at Maud's face and then at the item she held in her hand. He stretched his hand out to hers, brushed it slightly, and said, "Let me see." He turned the bar over and found 5 c marked on the back. He said, "A nickel, normally, but for you, two cents." He touched the rim of his bowler and smiled. Then he turned to Billy. "Howdy. Are you Maud's brother?"

Maud spoke quickly. "No, a friend. This is William Watie Walkingstick. He goes by Billy."

Billy brought the fingers of his left hand to the rim of his cowboy hat and inserted his right hand into his front pocket. "I'll pay full price for that." He drew out a nickel.

Booker took the coin with one hand and delivered the bar to Billy with the other. "Glad to do business with you, Mr. Walkingstick. Fancy anything else for your girl?"

Maud made a noise that was more of a catfish growl than a word. Both men jerked a little and looked to the source. Maud knew she was turning red. She hoped the dark of the night and the dark of her skin were combining to protect her. "Thank you, Billy." She held her hand out for the bar. To Booker, she said, "He's one of my oldest friends. Fishes with my brother."

Booker said, "I see." Maud hoped that he both did see and didn't. And she was trying to sort out some kind of response that would straighten things out but not give her away when Billy said, "You sell soft drinks?"

"No, they're not in my line." Booker shook his head.

Maud said, "He mostly trucks in books. Booker, would you show Billy your books?"

Booker held out his arm toward the side of the wagon facing the back of the stage. "What kinds of books do you like to read?"

"Whatchya got?"

Booker, in a singsong cadence that spoke of practice, recited a litany of books, and Billy's eyes took on a glassy gaze. But shortly into that, to insert herself back into Booker's attention and also to get Billy off the hook, Maud said, "My uncle was telling me about a book that escaped the fire. Did you hear about that?"

"Heard about the fire. Hard not to." Booker had a smile on his face.

"I meant did you hear about the book?"

"No. I assumed all the books were burnt. I went by there the day afterwards. It was a mess if I ever saw one. You can even see the pile from the bridge."

"You've been over the bridge?"

"Went to Muskogee. Had to pick up more goods at the railway station."

"I'm surprised you didn't stay over there."

"I did for a couple of days. But I wasn't having much luck competing against the stores."

Billy said, "How much will ya take fer this book here?"

Maud had forgotten about Billy. And she'd never known him to read a lick. She said, "What is it?"

"Lasso tricks. See here?" He held out a page illustrated with several pair of hands and ropes in different positions. "It shows all the angles."

Maud pretended interest in the pictures, and Booker named a price. Billy pulled more coins out to pay and then stuffed the book into his right hip pocket. Maud couldn't see a graceful way back to the original conversation. Worse, she didn't see any way to dump Billy without looking heartless, and she knew males sometimes sided with each other in their sympathies even if they were rivals. She didn't want to look cruel, but she didn't want to leave. So

she was stuck. And she was fishing around for something to remark on when a commotion arose on the other side of the wagon.
Booker said, "Excuse me," and stepped away.

Maud was still on the book side of the rig, her view blocked by
the pyramid, when she heard an official-sounding voice: "Are you
Mr. Booker Wakefield?"

Both she and Billy moved toward the voice, and Booker said,
"Yes, sir. What can I do for you?"

"You can come with me."

Maud knew the sheriff. And she was about to say, "That's just
stupid gossip," when Booker said, "What for?"

"It's about the school burning."

Booker rubbed the back of his neck. Then he laid his hand on
the edge of his wagon and gripped it, his elbow stiff. "Do you have
probable cause?"

The sheriff said, "Do ya want to come peacefully, or should I
persuade you?" He put his hand on the butt of his gun.

The crowd had grown thicker. The faces were lit by lanterns.
Most were women of childbearing age with little ones at their
skirts. Husbands were sprinkled around in groups behind their
wives. The deputy was at the sheriff's right shoulder. Booker said,
"I need to close up. I can't leave my wares."

Maud felt heat rising up beneath her dress and her slip, and
with it, the urge to blurt out, "That silly woman just wants attention." But she realized that accusation would only complicate the
situation and that she didn't have any proof except her intuition.
Besides, she knew it made matters worse that she was there, that
men hated to be humiliated in front of women. She felt embarrassed for Booker and wanted to back away, to disappear, and then
to reappear again, maybe at the jail, to save the day. But she also
recognized that was a foolish desire. Heroic moments happened

only in the pages of books. She touched Billy on the arm and jerked her head as a signal to step away.

They moved outside of the ring of light, and Maud watched without speaking as Booker, in silence, rolled down the netting over his goods, rolled down the bright blue canvas, killed his lanterns' lights, and hung the lanterns on hooks on the side of his wagon. By the time that was done, most of the crowd had dispersed and one child's voice was yelling in the distance, "They've arrested the drummer!" Only the glow of the dim yellow lights of the dancing patch remained in the air. But that was light enough for Maud to see Booker look in her direction. As though they were alone in the world, he shook his head. She nodded and mouthed the words *I know*. Then he climbed into the seat of his wagon, picked up the reins, and after the sheriff climbed in on the other side, flapped them, and clucked at his horses.

Maud said to Billy, "There's no justice in that. Some ignorant woman accused him and the sheriff needs someone to pin the fire on."

"What makes you so sure he's innocent?"

"I don't have to be sure. They have to be. That's how the law works."

"Really?" Billy looked at Maud sideways.

"Well, no. But that's the way they tell it."

"They tell a lot of things, Maud. None true as far as I've ever seen."

There was no denying he was right. So she and Billy walked in silence around the back of the stage, up the side of the dance patch, and into the light again. Billy didn't ask Maud to dance, but a couple of other boys did. She turned them down, watched Lovely dancing with Gilda through two songs, and then she and Billy walked down Lee Street into the dark. They made a stop at the back end of a car. Then they sat on the front steps of a lawyer's office, drank choc beer, and smoked cigarettes. Eventually, they fell to necking as, even to Maud, that seemed to be the only thing left to do.

She awoke the next morning thinking about Booker in jail. Her father had spent many a night with the sheriff and was, in her estimation, safer behind bars than out. So while still on her cot, she convinced herself that a night on a feather mattress probably hadn't produced any hardship on Booker beyond humiliation and that the danger to him would pass for lack of evidence. Booker's being guilty didn't even cross Maud's mind.

When she finally got up and let the chickens out, they scattered like shot from a barrel. She pumped water, went back in, lit the fire, and started making biscuits. Her father was still snoring. Lovely came in the kitchen door from his time outside. He slid between the wall and the table and said, "How'd you get home?"

"With Aunt Nan and Uncle Ryde."

"Where'd you go?"

"What do you mean?"

"Well, you disappeared. You were dancing and never came back."

Maud turned from the cabinet, flour on her hands. "I did come back. I watched you and Gilda for quite a while. Make any progress?"

Lovely looked to the other room and then back to Maud. "I think I did."

She turned back to the counter and took up her rolling pin, thinking Lovely would keep talking. But he didn't. So, finally, while cutting biscuits, Maud's curiosity overtook her, and she said, "What makes you think you made progress?"

"She danced with me all night. Even when Charles Howell headed to cut in, she waved him off."

"I thought she dated Charles in school?"

"She did."

"What else?"

"What do you mean, 'What else?'"

Maud was cutting the dough quite deliberately. She twisted with added pressure. "This is like pulling teeth. What else makes you think you made progress?"

Blood came up into Lovely's ears. "Not what you think."

"How do you know what I think?"

Lovely looked to the other room again. Then he said, "Are you gonna take forever with the biscuits?"

"You may not get any biscuits unless I get some details."

"A decent man doesn't tell."

Maud looked around at Lovely, widening her eyes for effect. She slipped the biscuit pan into the oven and then sat down at the table. She looked to the main room, confirmed that her daddy was still asleep, and said in a whisper, "You didn't . . . ?"

"I did not." Lovely acted indignant.

"Don't pretend."

"I'm not pretending. We didn't."

"I didn't think you did. But don't pretend you didn't want to."

"I'm not pretending anything." Lovely spread his hands.

"Then what was 'A decent man doesn't tell' all about?"

"I was just piquing your interest. I know how you like to run your imagination."

"I do not!"

"Then why are you asking?"

"That's half the fun of a dance. Talking about it later."

Lovely shook his head and swatted the air like he was going

after a fly. He looked once again toward his father's bed and then leaned into the table. "The thing is, Gilda's a Christian. She won't do anything but kiss."

Maud straightened her back and looked at Lovely with a wrinkle between her eyes. "There's nothing wrong with not being fast." She bit her lower lip. While still on her cot, she'd begun feeling guilty about necking with Billy. Not about the necking itself, which they'd done before, but about necking when Booker had been carted off to jail, and about necking after meeting Booker at all. She told herself that had she not known Billy expected it, had she not been light-headed from the cigarettes and beer, if it hadn't been dark, and if she hadn't been feeling like she was ready to burst, she never would've done it. She was hoping that none of that showed on her face when Lovely added, "She gave me her Bible to read."

"Her Bible? She brought it to the dance?"

Lovely put his head in his hands. "No. We walked over to her house to get it. All the Starrs are Christians."

Maud smiled. "Not all of them. Some are outlaws. The rest have to look respectable just to live down their bank robbers and killers. Don't worry about it." She got up, opened their little icebox, took out some fatback, and started slicing it. After she'd slapped several pieces into a skillet, Lovely added, "I think I'm gonna read it."

"You should. It's got interesting stories." Maud's mind swam to Jonah and the whale. She'd learned the tale in school, and it had captured her imagination the same way *Moby-Dick* had. Maud didn't feel any particular animosity against individual Christians as much as she was inclined to see the hypocrisy in their religion. Beyond that, she was too mixed blooded to have any truck with the Keetowahs, and there weren't any other faiths around. So she hadn't given religion much thought beyond recognizing that powers in the universe, like the river and the sun, were mightier than humans and had to be reckoned with. She did hope there was a force that would propel her into a better life, but she felt like that could only be a combination of pleasing looks, some education, and her wits.

About that time, a grunt came from the next room, and the conversation about the Bible died. But as soon as Mustard slid in at the table, he was eager to swap news. He'd arrived in town with some of his running buddies as the band was closing up and a fight was being organized on the dance square. He'd laid a bet on who'd win, and he reached into his pants pocket and drew out several large bills. "By damn, don't ever bet against an Indian if he's fighting a white man. If the Indian's sober, you'll lose ever'thing ya got. I'm gonna get my dog with these winnings. Lovely, after breakfast, we're gonna build us a dog house and pen. We'll use them boards and wire we salvaged from the roosters' coops."

Maud did her chores while they hauled from the barn wire and boards that had, before the flood, been fighting cocks' pens. The posts were still standing, and as they strung the wire, she sat in her daddy's chair holding *Arrowsmith* and thinking about Booker in jail. When Mustard left to ask Blue who he knew with a ready litter, Maud was so busting to talk about Booker that she blurted out even before Lovely's butt reached the stoop, "The sheriff arrested the peddler for setting fire to the school."

Lovely had heard that. "Does he have any evidence?"

"Only vicious gossip. And him selling kerosene."

"He's a stranger," Lovely added.

That was, of course, the root cause, at least in Maud's estimation. She knew there were strangers in No Man's Land where, for all of her life, they'd come from every corner of the continent to make money in wheat. She also knew there were strangers in the central part of the state where oil was gushing, and in the Osage oil fields in the Outlet. But around the bottoms and Ft. Gibson, strangers came only to dig potatoes. And it was too early in the season for them to start dribbling in.

Maud and Lovely chewed on the possibilities facing Booker, and as they did, the urge grew in Maud to walk into town, go into the sheriff's office, and testify that she . . . well, that was just it. She couldn't provide an alibi; she couldn't even be a character witness for someone she'd talked to only twice. But Maud knew, in the way women do, that the stranger in the bowler carrying the books on his wagon was the most interesting man she'd ever met. She had a pulling on her heart that was taking it out of her body into a space she didn't have a name for yet. Maud was so in tow to that tug that Lovely's attempts to bring the conversation around to Gilda felt like the irritating tap, tap, tapping of a woodpecker. But at the same time, she didn't have anything to say about Booker that she hadn't said ten minutes in the past, and she didn't want to share with Lovely feelings that she couldn't even describe to herself and that were also private beyond any she'd ever had. So not on Lovely's first attempt, but on one soon after, she gave in, pulled her mind back to the porch, and talked over with him everything they knew about the Starrs. They were trying to work out exactly how Gilda was related to one of the Starr outlaws, Henry, when they heard the sound of a car. They turned toward the section line to see who was coming and were disappointed when they saw it was only their father.

But Mustard was in a fine mood, and he brought more news. Blue knew of someone who had a litter of three-week-old Labs and he thought there were four not spoken for. Mustard had a name and a number he was planning to call the next morning from the feed store. The three of them fell into talking about the dog and how Mustard was going to train it, and into anticipating ducks, geese, and all sorts of good birds to eat. It wasn't until they'd finished that talking, had eaten supper, and were back on the porch that Mustard, between puffs of a cigarette, said, "Blue saw John and Claude Mount in town last night. They was selling whiskey and drinking at the fort."

Maud said, "I didn't know Uncle Blue still drank."

"He don't. He was over there sparking some woman. But when he seen the Mounts and their gang, he came in and sparked closer to town." Mustard took a long, last draw, crushed his cigarette beneath his boot, and added, "John Mount had already been fighting. Blue said his right hand were bandaged."

The next morning, after Maud had done her usual chores and both of the men had left the house, she filled a tub with water, shed her clothes, and bathed with the Woodbury soap behind a corner of wood erected for privacy out next to the pump. Midmorning wasn't her usual time for a bath, but Maud had determined she was going to put on her hat and walk into town and see what she could learn about Booker. Shortly afterward, she passed Nan's without stopping, passed the lane that led to where her grandpa and his brood were living, and didn't even yell to Lovely, whom she saw in the distance struggling with the mule and a tree stump. But as soon as the ruins of the school came into sight, she focused on them, and when she got up to them, she circled the mountain of rubble, found a little piece of wood that was burnt only on one end, picked it up, and carried it away in her hand. She was almost to the highway when she looked northwest toward Mr. Singer's potato barn and house. There, as clear as smoke signals on the plains, was a bright patch of blue. She clutched her little piece of wood tighter, brought her fist to her heart, and headed toward the blue like a hard rain falls to earth.

As outbuildings go, the potato barn was the most substantial structure in the bottoms. Its two long stories of brown brick had small windows close to the roof and two tall, wide doors on either side in the center. There was a potato stand several paces in front of the building, and Maud had, on occasion, bought potatoes at that stand. But she'd never been inside the barn. It was for the storing and sacking of huge amounts of potatoes all year round, and Maud found the odor of potato multitudes overwhelming. However, potato stink was the last thing on Maud's mind. Even the building shrank. The only thing she saw was the blue — that is, until Booker walked out of the barn with a sack thrown over his shoulder and followed a woman to her car. The woman opened the back door and Booker laid the sack in. Then he shut the door and stood next to the car, clearly in conversation. Seeing him talk like that both relieved Maud and infuriated her. How dare he be out and around and talking to some woman when she'd been worried sick about him.

She hadn't set out to buy potatoes, and although she had money for food back at home, she hadn't tucked any into the little pouch pinned inside her slip where she carried her valuables. She didn't have a cent on her. And besides, they had planted their own potatoes. Booker had surely noticed their garden when he'd driven down their lane. So Maud marched through a potato field, heading straight toward Booker without the strength to turn around, but also without any money or any excuse to be out there, without anything except a piece of partially burnt wood in her hand, a hat on her head, and a will to get to Booker as fast as she could without looking eager.

While she was walking, another car pulled up to the stand.

Booker went over to it and talked to somebody sitting inside. Then he walked back to the potato barn and came out with a sack on his shoulder again. It was when he turned toward the car that he saw Maud. He raised his free hand. His smile made Maud forget the predicament she was in. She slowed her walk so that she'd arrive after the car left.

By the time they were face-to-face, Maud didn't make any pretenses. She said, as honestly as she had ever said anything in her life, "I've been worried sick about you."

"I've been worried about myself. Mr. Singer sprang me. But the sheriff says if I leave these parts, he'll come after me with a warrant."

"What've they got on you?"

Booker rubbed the back of his neck. "Not much that I know of. Some woman says I was acting suspicious, and she thinks I gave her a raw deal on some cloth she bought. Evidently, it had a flaw down in the bolt. If we'd unrolled it to the end I would've caught it, but she wanted to make curtains out of it, and I was trying to give her a deal and not be left with just a remnant, so . . ." He shrugged his shoulders. "Lesson learned, I guess."

"I saw that woman. I don't know her. But she was talking to some men at the fire." Maud wanted to tell Booker that she'd taken up for him, but she knew full well that most men didn't like being defended by a woman. So she held that back. She said instead, "Mr. Singer's given you a job?"

"Fortunately, I made a better impression on him than I did on that woman. He doesn't much like her, and he figures I can sell, and I can. So he has me selling potatoes and is letting me sell my own wares to anybody who stops. You were right. He's a nice man."

That remark caused Maud to recall that she'd tried to make Booker think that Mr. Singer was a suitor. She felt heat rise up her neck. She placed her hand on the top of her hat and shifted it so that it covered her face a little more than it had. Before she could think of what to say next, Booker added, "I guess I'll be around these parts for a while. That might not be all bad." He took a deep breath.

Maud looked past Booker at the potato barn and then down at her shoes. "No, it might not. You could get to liking it."

"I already like it. But I have a real job back in Arkansas."

Maud looked up. "What might that be?"

"I'm a schoolteacher."

"A schoolteacher? What do you teach?"

"All sorts of things. English, geography, math."

Maud felt like she was being pulled along by a strong river current. "A schoolteacher," she said, like she might have said *a pharaoh* or *a president.*

Booker smiled. The smile went all the way up to the gold flecks in his eyes. He said, "Do you mind if I come calling?"

Maud ducked her head. "No, I don't mind at all. I can try to make up for the sheriff's lack of hospitality."

"I'd sure appreciate that. A little kindness goes a long way."

At that moment, a horn honked. A car neither one of them had noticed had pulled in off the highway. The man behind the wheel was someone Maud had never seen. He yelled, "Do you know how to get to Tahlequah?"

Maud pointed and said, "Take the highway in that direction. It's twenty miles."

The man said, "What's in that rig over there?"

Booker said, "Wares. I can show them to you."

The man said, "Don't mind if I do. I need to stretch my legs." He opened the door and unfolded out of the car.

Booker turned to Maud. "When and where?"

Maud wasn't ready to have Booker meet her father. She didn't really want to share him with anybody at all. And there wasn't anything in the bottoms except farms and a couple of snaky lakes, the burnt school building, and two cemeteries. One of those was so close to the snake lakes they couldn't visit it without guns. But the other one was farther away from the cottonmouths. She said, "Tonight. See that stand of trees over there. That's our family's old cemetery. I'll meet you there."

"You're not superstitious?"

"I am that. But I'm not afraid of my family. Not of the dead ones, at least. After eating but before the sun sets. It's snaky on down closer to the river after that."

The man said, "How much for these suspenders?" and Booker turned around. Then he turned back. "About six," he said.

Maud left her father and her brother whittling and reading on the front porch, and walked, with a newspaper in one hand and a snake stick in the other, down the lane and up the section line. She left the paper with Nan according to a plan she'd made with her aunt after seeing Booker that morning. Beyond Nan's house, where the section lines crossed, she headed through the potato fields on a path that gave her a good view of where she was walking because, although the cottonmouths weren't as thick beyond the snake lakes as they were below them, the largest lake wasn't far from her. She watched the dirt in front of her and to her sides, and couldn't help but think about her mother's death. That particular snake had been hiding from the sun under a rosebush. Her uncle Gourd, newly home from the Great War, had been sitting on his front porch when he heard her scream. He saw her run in a circle and fall. When he got to her, he cut her ankle, sucked the blood, and spit it out again and again. But her mother went rigid and died before Gourd got her into the house. Maud hadn't seen the death herself. She'd been in school. Her aunt Lucy had come to her classroom door along with her principal. She had gotten up from her desk and slowly walked toward the door frame, knowing from Lucy's face, and mostly from her presence at all, that something terrible had happened, something that was going to change everything forever. And so it had. Once her mother was buried, her father chopped down the bush with a hatchet and went on a bender with Gourd that lasted so long it seemed like it was going to be permanent. Only when he eventually sobered up and stayed that way for three weeks did her aunt Lucy and her grandfather move back to their house on the other side of the swale.

That was nearly half of Maud's lifetime in the past, but she still carried that sadness and didn't want it on her date with Booker. She regretted suggesting the cemetery even though it wasn't the one her mother was buried in. So she tried to shake all of that out of her head and simply watch the ground for snakes. When she did finally raise her eyes, she saw Booker riding to her on the back of one of his horses. She veered out of the potatoes to the section line and stopped to let him come to her. He pulled up about fifteen feet away, took his bowler off in a flourish, and said, "Would madam like a ride?"

"Madam would. Where'd you get the saddle?"

"Brought it with me. Keep it between my shelves. I sleep in there, too, when the weather's bad." He dismounted.

"You're teasing me."

"No, I'm not. There's a little house in there. Right between the shelves."

"I don't believe you."

"Well, I'm telling the truth. Do you know how to get up on a horse or do you need some help?"

"I'm mostly Indian. What do you think? Look the other way."

Maud handed Booker her snake stick, grabbed the horn, and put a foot in the stirrup.

When she was astride, he said, "Do you want to keep this stick?"

"I sure do. It's my snake stick."

"You carry a stick around to beat snakes to death?"

"No, silly. I carry a stick around to rustle snakes up and scare them away. Are you going to get up here with me or are you just going to walk around not even knowing how to protect yourself?"

"I need protection from two-footed creatures." He smiled. "We better find a stump. I don't want to pull you off." He put a hand on the harness and began to walk.

And while Maud swayed on the horse's back and looked down at Booker holding his bowler and her snake stick in his other hand; while they were out there surrounded by potatoes and a little corn; while the sun was still above the tree line in the west and the air cooler than it'd been all day; while the sky filled up with wisps of clouds and bobwhites called to each other and the smell in the air was of horse, dirt, and just a little moisture; right then, Maud made up her mind about what she intended to do with the rest of her life.

She didn't get back toward home until nearly dark. Booker stopped the horse beneath trees hanging over the section line, slid off its rear, and held out his arms. When Maud's feet touched the ground, he embraced her, and without asking, kissed her long on the lips. He stepped back and looked at her with a gaze that took in her face, her whole head, her hair, and her shoulders. He said, "Tomorrow?"

She nodded.

"I'll come down here."

"Not to the house. Let me prepare Daddy."

"Where?"

"Come this far. I'll figure it out. He's not against courting. But he's combustible."

"Combustible?"

"High tempered."

"Should I be afraid?"

She shook her head. "I'm just cautious. You're already on the bad side of the sheriff."

He kissed her again.

That went on for as long as Maud thought proper or, really, longer, because, in spite of what she'd just said, she'd given in back there on the horse. Now she was hoping she was what Booker wanted and that she could keep him wanting. That was her plan. It didn't have details. It existed more as a primal urge, a force that was like a river sweeping everything downstream.

As Maud walked the lane, she saw Lovely in the porch rocker reading in the last of the light. When she got nearer, he closed the book and looked in her direction. His face was in a shadow, but it seemed to Maud that the tilt of his head was odd, and she wondered if he was thinking about where she'd been. She next looked to the lean-to. Her father's car was there. She wondered why he wasn't on the porch. She moved from one possibility to another until she got to the steps. She whispered, "Where's Daddy?"

"In bed," Lovely whispered back.

"It's early for that."

"He was whipped."

"What're you reading?"

"Gilda's Bible."

"How is it?"

"Sorta snaky. Not too bad, though."

Neither of them was totally ignorant of Christianity. They'd been taught to say they were Christians when asked, to bow their heads during prayers at school, and to imitate whatever Christians took in their minds to do. They hadn't been old enough to question their mother about that before she died, but Maud had since figured out on her own that the safest route was to go along. However, some of her friends were tormented by questions like "If God is good and loves us, why did He send all this rain to drown our crops and stock and ruin our houses?" Maud thought those kinds of questions were worth asking, but she never came to the same conclusions her friends did. She thought God, if there was one, didn't give a shiny penny for what they were doing or what happened to them. And he seemed particularly unpartial toward Indians.

Lovely said, "Where've you been?"

"Aunt Nan's."

"You changed your dress to visit Aunt Nan?"

"*Shuuu*. Did Daddy ask where I was?"

Lovely leaned toward Maud and lowered his voice again. "Naw. He's too interested in getting a puppy to think of much else. Says he's going up toward Wagoner to look at a litter on Wednesday. They aren't ready to leave their mama, but he wants to pick his out and make a down payment."

Their daddy burnt through money like fire through wheat stubble. They had a car only because he'd sold some of his Seminole allotment. Maud knew that the offer of a down payment was his way of trying to make sure he didn't blow all his dough before he got his dog. There really wasn't much to say about that and she wasn't ready to talk about Booker, so she left Lovely out on the porch and went to bed.

She was too excited to sleep, and she lay on her cot reliving every look, word, and feeling until she realized that her brother still hadn't come in. She figured she'd been lying there for a while, and her father was breathing a deep rhythm, so she quietly got up, opened the screen, and went out on the porch. She was expecting to find Lovely asleep in the chair or laid out on the planks with his head on the Bible. But he wasn't there. She looked to the yard. She saw him by the pump, facing the river, his back to her. He was standing straight and still. As far as Maud could tell, he was fully clothed and his legs weren't spread, so he wasn't taking a leak. She watched him for more than a minute. He didn't turn, didn't move. She quietly slipped back inside, and this time, soon after she laid her head on her pillow, she drifted to sleep.

The next morning, Mustard left out as usual. But Lovely was quiet even after he went, and he didn't seem in a rush to get to the field before the sun rose higher and made his work hotter. When Maud went out to dump her dishwater, she found Lovely in Mustard's chair on the porch, one boot on, his other foot covered by a sock, its boot in his lap. He was staring down at that boot like it was an object he didn't entirely trust.

She said, "Lovely, you okay?"

He looked up. "Yeah. Thinking."

"You going to work?"

"Yeah." He shook his head like he felt a shiver and looked again at the boot in his lap. "I'm putting on my boots."

"I can see that."

Lovely moved the boot off his lap, brought his knee up, and put his foot in. Shortly afterward, he rode the mule down the lane.

Maud worked like a dust devil all that day. That was the fastest way to make time pass, and by midafternoon she'd done everything she usually did on Tuesdays and had done the wash, too. By the time Lovely got in from the field and Mustard from work, a pot of Tom Fuller had brewed. The three of them ate it, accompanied by cornbread and dog talk.

After that, Maud again left her menfolk on the porch and walked down the lane with a day-old paper in her hand. Her daddy hadn't seemed suspicious and her brother had his nose so deeply in the Bible that he hadn't bothered to tease her. As soon as she got out to the section line, she saw Booker on his horse ahead under the shade. She looked toward her house and saw her father still facing in the other direction. She waved to Booker with the paper.

They couldn't go toward the river without being seen from the house. They rode back up the section line, and this time, as Maud knew would happen sooner rather than later, her uncle Ryde was on his porch and her cousins were in the front yard around a tree with a tire swing on it. Ryde grinned in her direction. The children yelled and waved.

"That's my family. We have to stop."

"I sold the woman there some cloth."

"I hope it didn't have a flaw. Uncle Ryde is bad with his fists."

The whole bunch of them got introduced. Maud handed Ryde the paper, and Booker and Ryde discussed how bad the flood had been up in Booker's direction. Maud talked to Nan and played with the kids. After what she considered a respectable time, she said, "We were after fresh air."

As soon as they got away from the house, Maud, who this time was seated in the back, turned her head and looked over her shoulder. Nan was at the edge of the porch with a pan and a rag washing Sanders' face. Ryde was holding the paper but looking in their direction. Maud waved and turned back around. "I guess the cat's out of the bag."

"Am I not presentable?"

"Well, you are under suspicion."

"Your uncle doesn't care. He said the sheriff's an idiot."

"Being on the sheriff's bad side will automatically put you on Uncle Ryde's good side. That's the way it works around here. It's probably the best thing that could've happened."

"Will he tell your dad I've got you out for a ride?"

Maud thought Ryde would and said so, but she also thought that Ryde and Booker had gotten along fine, and felt that bode well for her intentions. Her family, as a whole, was liberal in the area of romance. They all saw mating as a natural action — and a good source of entertainment and amusement. She was painfully aware she lacked the means to go to the teachers' college in Tahlequah and knew she was of a marriageable age. She thought everybody would expect her to do exactly what she was doing. So as the two passed through the cross of the section lines, waved at the Beechers, and veered off onto the path to the cemetery they'd gone to the day before, Maud left her worries along the road, enjoyed the smell of Booker and the horse, watched the wind ripple the tops of the potato plants, and felt that life was glorious in general and that her life in particular was turning out better than she could've hoped. After they dismounted at the edge of the thicket protecting the graves and had taken a respectable amount of time looking at one stone and then another, they fell rather quickly into a pattern of necking, saying silly things, and necking some more.

Later, Booker dropped Maud off in the shade where he'd dropped her the night before, and standing beside his horse, they necked again. Afterward, they agreed that they would meet there the following day and Maud would take him up to the house to meet her brother. Maud figured that Mustard would be in Wagoner and that way she could let Lovely tell her father about Booker when Mustard got home and ease him into the idea.

She saw Lovely alone on the front porch, and she figured Mustard was inside asleep. This time, however, Lovely was propped against a post reading by the light of a lamp, and as Maud walked the lane looking at the lamp's glow, she recognized that as contrary to his habits, and she thought it meant he was deeply hooked into the Bible. She said so when she got to the porch, and Lovely said the book had a lot of rules in it, but it had a lot of action, too. He had gotten as far as the flood and was enjoying it. They settled away from the windows on the steps so they wouldn't wake their father, and they spent the rest of the evening whispering about the likelihood that somebody could build a boat big enough to get two of each animal into it, and if somebody had, what it was like living with all that livestock. They agreed that two days in the barn with the chickens had been bad enough, and Maud said that she thought Noah's ark was a story handed down through generations and had lost some of its realistic details.

The next morning, Mustard left, eager to pick out his dog, and took biscuits with him to stave off his hunger on his drive home. Maud thought Lovely had left with her father, but when she went to the front porch, she found him there, staring toward the river with neither of his boots on his feet. "Lovely, you're getting lazy," she said.

He turned toward her with a puzzled looked on his face. "Why do you say that?"

"You haven't even put on your boots."

"I'm not wearing them today."

"You have to wear your boots. Put 'em on."

Lovely picked up his right boot and slipped it over his sock and then slipped on the other one. He seemed so far away that Maud was tempted to blame the Bible reading. But she put that down to prejudice on her part, and she went to the garden without giving Lovely another thought.

That night, she walked the lane as she had the two before, but this time she waved Booker to her and held the first cattle guard open as he rode through it. He dismounted, led his horse, and they walked holding hands. After they'd secured the wire of the second guard, they stopped in the lane and faced the river. The water couldn't be seen from where they stood, but the tangled brush, cane, and reeds that rolled out in front of them didn't seem to meet up with the hill on the horizon. Maud told Booker that broken joint was where the river ran.

Shortly, they turned and walked to the house. Lovely, by agreement, and after a little kidding, had stayed inside until Maud called, "We're here," and then he came out to the porch for a proper introduction. Lovely was taller than Booker by a few inches, but Booker was the thicker of the two, and Maud, as she stood between them, looked from face to face as closely as though she were reading coffee grounds to divine their futures.

Booker and Lovely talked at some length about the flood they'd all lived through, but after that, Lovely said he needed to tend to something in the barn and left Maud and Booker alone on the porch. Maud wasn't given to shame. But she was well aware there was a whole other way to live that included heat in winter, light inside, indoor plumbing, and enough chairs for everybody to have one. So she wasn't ready to let Booker see the inside of the house. Cardboard was nailed to the walls in there. A sheet was hung on a wire; behind it, their clothing was in crates. The only furniture in the main room was a chest of drawers, Mustard's iron bed and feather mattress, two cots, and two rocking chairs. In the kitchen was a table and straight chairs, a bench, a counter and sink, a little icebox, a dipping pan, and a wood stove.

To keep Booker from seeing any of that, Maud said, "I have a surprise. Wait here." She disappeared into the house and came out with a dish filled with cookies. She handed the dish to Booker, went back in, and came out with a pitcher of milk and two glasses. And she and Booker were sitting on the top step, enjoying the cookies and milk, and also enjoying watching each other chew, when they were startled by a howl from the barn. They jumped up and ran.

Lovely was on his back in the dirt in front of the shelf against the far wall. He was holding his head in both hands. His fingers were bloody. A scythe was on the ground beside him. Maud said, "Goodness, what's happened?" She knelt and moved Lovely's hands away from his forehead. She found a large gash. Lovely said, "He attacked me."

Maud immediately thought of the Mounts. She leaped to her feet and wildly turned her head. To Booker, she said, "Check the loft. No, wait." She pulled a hammer off the wall. "Hold this. I'll get a gun."

Booker took the hammer. And Maud didn't see his startled look because she was already running to the house. When she came back with her mother's pistol, Booker was still holding the hammer, but Lovely had risen to a seated position. He was still holding his head in his hands.

Booker said, "Who are we planning to kill?"

Maud knew better than to name anybody in particular. She didn't want Booker hearing about the feud with the Mounts. She looked to Lovely to warn him to keep quiet. But he seemed not to have heard. She said, "Just protecting us against whoever's attacked Lovely."

"I see," Booker replied. "Do you want me to go up into the loft?" He held out his hand for the pistol.

Maud licked her lower lip. She didn't want to get Booker shot or banged in the head. But she couldn't say, "I'll do it," and unman him. She addressed Lovely. "Do you think he's still here?"

Blood was draining through his fingers and dropping into the dirt. "Don't know. Couldn't see him. He was yelling."

Maud looked to Booker. She hadn't heard any yell except the lone howl. Booker shrugged his shoulders. She said, "Did he hit you with the scythe?"

Lovely shook his head. Maud glanced to Booker again. "He must have escaped. Did you hear anybody in the loft while I was away?"

Booker shook his head.

Maud decided then that there wasn't anybody in the loft and that it would be safe to send Booker up there. She held out the pistol. "Would you check, just to be sure?" To Lovely she said, "We need to clean your cut. Take your shirt off."

Booker took the gun and headed toward the ladder to the loft. Lovely lowered his hands from his head one at a time. They struggled getting his arms out of his sleeves. When the shirt was finally clear of his body, Maud pressed it to Lovely's forehead and held it. Booker came back, reported that nobody was above them, and then sat down on a barrel, still holding the gun. The dust motes danced in the fading rays of sun. A horse fly buzzed. Lovely's chest rose and fell with the sound of breathing. Nobody spoke until Lovely finally said, "I was swinging the scythe. I couldn't see him, but he was here, yelling. I must've swung too hard. I think I hit my head on the shelf."

Maud looked up. On the edge of the shelf was a dark spot she recognized as blood. She wished she'd seen that before she went for the gun. The whole story sounded strange, and she was still afraid Lovely would say something about the Mounts in front of

Booker. "Whatever happened, we need to get this cut cleaned out." She tapped Lovely's shoulder.

Booker leaned the scythe against a stall and gave Lovely a hand to get up. His face was streaked with blood and dirt that looked like war paint drawn on by a child. His chest, which was bare except for a small tree of hair, was spotted with red. Booker said, "It probably looks worse than it is. The forehead is filled with vessels. Any head cut will stream blood."

Maud said, "Let's get to the pump and survey the damage."

Lovely put his head under the pump and Booker worked the handle. Maud went to the house and came back with a flour sack, a pair of scissors, and the bottle of Mercurochrome. She laid the cloth on the platform, cut it into strips, and dabbed Lovely's wound with one of them. She made him hold his face to the sky as she applied the medicine. Then she tied two others strips together, and she wrapped them around Lovely's head in a band. When she finished, she stepped back and said, "You look just like a wild Indian." She smiled.

They left Lovely's shirt soaking in a tub and went back to the porch. The cookies had attracted flies, but Maud went back inside and brought out more, and when Mustard's car lights shone on the lane, the three of them were enjoying the lingering sweet of sugar cookies and watching fireflies. Lovely went inside before his daddy got to the porch, but Maud and Booker stayed where they were.

Mustard turned his head toward the horse at the hitching rail on his way from the car. When he got to the porch, he said, "Ryde said we probably had company." Booker stood up, walked down the steps, and offered his hand. Mustard ignored the hand and scraped his boot on the bottom step. Booker dropped his hand and turned to Maud with a startled look on his face. Maud couldn't tell him right then that Indians didn't shake hands unless they were trying to act white. She smiled instead. "Daddy, this is Booker Wakefield. He's a schoolteacher."

Mustard scraped the sole of his other boot. "Whatchya teach?"

Booker stuck both hands in his back pockets. "Oh, just a little of everything."

Mustard looked off toward the barn. "I see. Well, we need teachers. I've had a long day. Nice to meetchya." He didn't move.

Booker glanced at Maud and took his hands out of his pockets. He rubbed his palms over his suspenders. "Nice to meet you, too, sir. I'd better go." He made a slight nod toward his horse.

Maud said, "I'll walk you to the rail," and on the way there, Booker whispered, "He didn't take to me, did he?"

Maud couldn't explain her father's Indian ways within earshot. She was trying to come up with an answer when Mustard called out, "Watch fer the snakes!" Maud smiled. "I believe he did take to you."

"Maybe he just doesn't want me to die in his front yard."

Maud poked him with an elbow. "You'd be good for the garden. Don't worry. That's just his way."

She and Booker said a hasty good-bye. Then Maud walked back to the porch where Mustard had settled in his rocker. "I sorta had you figured for Billy Walkingstick," he said.

Maud felt a blush rise to her cheeks. She was glad for the dark. And she didn't want to talk about Billy or even think about him. She sat down against a post facing away from her daddy. To distract him, she said, "Tell me about your dog."

"I picked out a bitch. The only girl left in the litter. She's got the prettiest eyes I've ever seen on a dog." Mustard straightened a leg, reached into his front pocket, and pulled out his money. "I want ya to do something fer me, Maud." He licked his thumb and separated three bills from the rest. "I want ya to take this, and no matter how bad I beg, I want ya to hide it from me 'til I go after that dog." He held the bills out.

Maud felt embarrassed for her father. But she felt a surge of love, too. Not only did he not make a fuss over Booker, he was trying to control himself. She reached inside the collar of her dress, unpinned a cloth purse from her slip, and held her hand out. Mustard handed her the bills and said, "You better not put it in such a public place."

Maud yelled, "Daddy!" got up from the porch, and let the door rattle shut behind her. As she drew her dress over her head behind the sheet, she heard Mustard chuckling.

Mustard saw Lovely's forehead at breakfast the next morning. He started questioning, and when he got vague answers, his tongue sharpened. To blunt it, Maud asked again about the dog. And she led her father so far with dog questions that the subject of Lovely's wound was completely forgotten. But when Mustard's car was safely stopped at the first cattle guard, Maud said, "Now, tell me the truth. What happened?"

Lovely touched his headband. "Don't know. Do you ever hear people around here?"

"People other than us?"

"Yeah."

"No."

Lovely bit his lip. "It must be my imagination. I thought I heard someone yelling at me. So I grabbed the scythe. Then I got to swinging 'cause he wouldn't show his self."

"Was it one of the Mounts, do you think?"

Lovely shook his head. "Maybe I read too much."

Maud didn't know what to say. So she said, "Let's see how that cut is. We better do it at the pump."

They were at the pump, and Maud was enjoying the relative cool of the morning and wrapping Lovely's head with the rest of the strips, when he said, "I'm gonna lay 'round here today. I feel a little light-headed."

Maud stood back from her work. He did look hollow eyed. "I'm not surprised. That was a blow."

"Will you put the mule to pasture?"

"Sure. You think you're getting sick?"

"Might be."

She felt his earlobe for fever. "You may be a little hot. It's hard to tell this early in the day. Should we bring out your cot?"

They set the cot and its pillow on the west porch, the coolest place in the mornings. Lovely settled in with the Bible and Maud went about her chores with her mind turned to Booker and herself. She was sweeping the front yard, thinking about how her mother would take to her pick, how she would be proud of her and like Booker, and how he would like her, when she heard Lovely call. She went to the west side of the yard to find that he had pitched up his breakfast over the side of the porch. Chickens were pecking in it.

Maud's first thought was to protect her own health. She didn't want to get sick so early into courting. Rather than bring the dipping pan and dipper out, she drew water in a bucket and brought Lovely a cup. She put the bucket and cup down beside him, and, as she backed away, told him that she would bring him more food. Lovely washed his mouth out, spat at the chickens, and lay back down on his cot. He turned his face toward the wall of the house.

When the sun hit the cot midday, they moved it beneath the branches of the live oak tree. In the late afternoon, Blue brought in a mess of fish, and Maud cleaned them by the pump. She, Blue, and Mustard ate fish, and gave Lovely the only food he wanted, a hushpuppy. By the time Booker rode up, Maud was convinced Lovely had the influenza, and she used his illness as a reason for them not to linger. She left her father and Blue discussing politics on the front porch and Lovely still on his cot under the tree and rode off behind Booker on his horse.

They went again to the cemetery. They took the horse into the shade with them to scare away any snakes, tied her to a branch, and settled on a stone that marked the grave of a great-great-uncle. They moved from necking to petting and, in between bouts, began telling each other every significant event that had happened in their lives and many of the insignificant ones, too. Booker was thirty years old. He'd been married. His wife had died in childbirth, and so had the daughter she'd carried. After that, he took to peddling to remove himself from daily reminders of loss and distract himself with new horizons. He was not interested in any woman back home and hadn't found, until now, anybody who interested him. He'd often thought he'd never find anybody again. The reawakening of feeling wasn't as frightening to him as he had imagined, but it was surprising. He'd thought romantic life would pass him by, that he would be a witness to it, but only a sad one.

Booker's tragedy made him all the more attractive to Maud and also made him seem more reliable. Maud wanted someone as stable as her daddy was shaky. Someone who would talk to her about books and ideas, who would take her to exciting places, who thought indoor plumbing and electricity were basics of life. Booker seemed to fill that ticket, and it didn't hurt that he was also handsome, sexy, and sweet smelling. She rode home holding on to his waist with her face against the back of his shirt, listening to the slow clip-clop of his horse and thinking that she'd never dreamed this kind of happiness would find her. Her contentment lasted until Saturday night.

3

Maud was standing at the stove on Saturday morning when she heard a groan from the other room. Mustard was outside doing his business. It had to be Lovely. Through the door frame, she saw him holding a hand to his head. Between his other forefinger and thumb was the band of cloth he'd worn to bed. It dropped to the floor. Maud went to the main room. Lovely's scab had come off with the band. She returned to the kitchen and moved the skillet off the burner. She took Lovely to the porch, settled him in the chair, and went back in to get from the chest a patch of cloth she'd set aside for a quilt. She wet it in the dipping pan and gave it to Lovely to hold to his wound. He didn't want anything to eat. So after she finished cooking for Mustard, she took Lovely to the pump, doctored his head with Mercurochrome, and bandaged it again.

She ate and went about her chores. Mustard went about his. Lovely stayed on his cot. When the sun reached its peak, Maud helped Lovely move his cot back outside under the live oak tree and fed her father and herself. In midafternoon, Mustard was in the barn and Lovely still under the tree. Maud bathed behind the privacy fence at the pump and went back to the house to finish dressing. The window curtains were closed against the sun and the room was dim when she opened her drawer in the chest. But she instantly saw that her good clothes had shifted since she'd picked up her Woodbury soap. Not much, but into some disorder. She opened the little box that held her mother's cameo. It was there. She counted her handkerchiefs. All three were present. So were her two good scarves, her good gloves, her good handbag, and her visiting hat. She checked under her cot. The edges of her books were uneven. That confirmed her suspicion: Her father had looked for his money while she was behind the fence. He wanted it for Saturday night. She chuckled. He could look all he wanted. She'd hidden it in a jar behind a row of canned beans in the cellar. He wouldn't go to the cellar unless a tornado was climbing his tail.

Maud made cornbread and left it along with onions, beans, fatback, and gravy for her men to eat. Then she walked to Nan's. She found Sanders crying out on the porch and heard Ryde shouting before she went in the door. Renee and Morgan had been frightened into silence. Andy was on the floor happily playing with naked thread spools. Ryde went out the back door cussing. Nan handed Maud a hot iron.

Ryde had entered Andy in the Prettiest Baby in Ft. Gibson Contest. He was agitated about winning. Maud understood he needed the prize money. And she understood the usefulness of contests for cattle, horses, hogs, pies, and quilts. But a prettiest baby contest seemed mean-spirited to her. She figured all women probably believed their babies were beautiful, and she felt it was cold-hearted to spoil that illusion. But she also thought that Andy was dark enough that he had a good chance of winning. Babies with Indian blood seemed to win more often than pale little things. While Maud ironed, her mind went to the children she might have with Booker. She hoped they'd be dark. But, standing next to the stove, she felt as hot as a firecracker, and with her cousins more lively with their father out of the house and Nan tired before they'd even left, she also hoped that whatever children she and Booker had were far off in the future and few. She turned her mind to perspiration. She wanted away from the irons and the stove, and hoped, on the way to town, she could maneuver into some shade in the wagon.

She assigned her cousins seats in the buckboard based on where the sun was most likely to hit, and she slid down into a little patch of shade. But when they came to a point on the section line where she knew she'd be able to see Booker, she sat up high. He was talking to a man next to a car. She waved twice but couldn't catch his eye. She leaned again into the shadow of the tailgate and tried to avoid both the sun and the dust. She wished for rain and asked Nan how long it'd been since the last good one. Nan told her to the day, and for the rest of the journey, Ryde cussed the heat, worried aloud about his corn and onions, and talked about his crops wilting.

When they arrived at the circle of trees where the contest was, the photographer sponsoring the event had already set up his backdrop and camera. However, not many contestants had shown up, and Maud, having been to other photographic contests, knew that the Indian mothers weren't very particular about time. She knew the photographer, too. He was white and clock finicky. Maud spent much of her time watching him crane his neck, take his watch out of his pocket, and wipe his brow with his handkerchief. The rest of her time she spent trying to ensure that Andy stayed in a better disposition than the photographer did. From where their quilt lay, Maud also watched the wagons, cars, and horses on the main artery into and out of town. With so much to look at and Andy so wiggly, she gave little thought to

Lovely sick at home or to her father searching for his money while she was gone.

Booker joined her in time to see Andy win, Nan get a free set of pictures, and Ryde get the ten-dollar cash prize. Shortly afterward, she and Booker escaped on his horse over to the remains of the fort, where the food was spread. They were eating fried chicken and wilted lettuce on a log near the fort's well, and she was telling Booker what she knew about the efforts to rebuild the stockade when she saw her cousin Renee running their way.

Renee stopped, heaving for breath. Maud said, "Just take your time, take your time," wishing the child would gulp in enough air to say whatever she'd come to tell.

Finally, Renee spit out, "Daddy said to tell you, John Mount was bit."

Maud laughed, relieved. "Well, that's too bad. Did your daddy bite him? Or was it somebody else?"

Renee's eyes grew wide. "Not Daddy. A dog. A rabid dog."

Maud felt like a fist grabbed her heart. "When, Renee? When did this happen?" She stood. Booker laid his plate on the log and stood, too.

"I don't know. A few days past."

"Last week?"

The child nodded.

Maud turned to Booker. She hadn't told him about the dead dog. And that smacked her almost as hard as Renee's news had. He would realize she was holding back. While she was trying to decide how to justify that, Booker asked Renee, "Is John Mount a friend or a family member?"

"Neither," Renee said. "We hate the Mounts. Last week, they left a dead dog on Uncle Mustard's kitchen table."

Booker turned to Maud. His eyes were wide. "I see," he said. Then he added, "No, I don't really."

Maud put her hand on his arm. "I was going to tell you. I was just looking for the right time. Then it slipped my mind."

"That happens. Dead dogs in the kitchen are as common as biscuits."

"It just . . . It's part of a feud. It goes way back."

Maud was remembering her daddy telling Lovely and her to keep their eyes wide for something sneaky when Renee added, "The Mounts axed one of their cows in the back."

Booker's chin pulled in. "When was that?"

"Last week. Sometime before the dead dog," the child added.

Booker frowned and cleared his throat.

Maud's mind was caught like a shoat in a fence between trying to read Booker's mind and the possibility of the dead dog being rabid when Renee turned to her and said, "You told Mama that Lovely's sick."

"With more than the knock on the head?" Booker asked Maud.

She was trying to recall the symptoms of rabies. They weren't coming, except for the fear of water. She'd left a cup and a bucket freshly drawn under the tree. She was focused on the image of that bucket when she answered. "He has the influenza or something. He's running a fever."

"Is he turning away from water?"

"I was just trying to think. I can't say for sure."

"Did the dog bite him before it died?"

"No, it was dead when we found it. But Lovely touched it."

"I don't think you can get rabies from a dead dog. I think it has to bite you."

"What if you get some of its spit on you?"

Booker ran his hand over his mouth. "I don't know about that. Maybe."

"We better get home."

"We better get a doctor," he replied.

They sent Renee back to her parents, left their food on their plates, and rode to Dr. Ragsdale's office in the middle of town. A sign on his door said his hours were during the week. They walked to Berd's Drugstore. John Berd didn't think rabies could be carried without a bite. He thought the skin had to be broken for the virus to get in. It was then that Maud remembered Lovely's thistle poke. Her mind's eye saw him massaging his palm with his thumb. She felt sick to her stomach. She leaned against Booker.

They left Berd's and stopped everybody Maud knew. No one had seen Dr. Ragsdale. But one woman said she'd seen his car in front of Taylor's General Store. They went there. Booker knew his employer's son and Hugh Singer knew Booker's position with the law. He went with them to ask the sheriff to run the doctor to ground. But the sheriff and neither of his deputies were in, so the three of them walked back to the store, and the merchant placed a telephone call to the doctor's home. His wife said he was on the bayou fishing, that she didn't expect him home until after dark. Singer asked that the doctor call him at his home and he took down from Maud a list of Lovely's symptoms.

By that time, Maud was racked with worry. She was too anxious to meet up with her family or attend the speeches at the fort. But she was afraid to go home to see what was happening with Lovely. All she wanted to do was stay with Booker and cling to him like silk to an ear of corn.

They rode toward the bottoms, Maud clutching his waist. They stopped at Mr. Singer's. Booker had hidden his wagon in a clump of trees between the potato barn and the main house. He parted the blue canvas. They crawled into the nook between the shelves and onto his pallet. Alone and in relative private, they did what came naturally — up to a point.

Maud told Booker she was too worried about Lovely to go any further than they'd already gone. And although she felt some guilt over using Lovely that way and more over not going home to tend to him, she didn't feel guilty for enjoying herself as much as she could. Sex felt as natural as sunshine and weeds. But she wanted out of the bottoms and into a stable life with Booker, and she didn't want to be in a family way until she had what she wanted.

Eventually, Maud asked Booker to take her home. They left the shadows of his bunk in the moonlight and rode south down the section line. The piles of the school's remains looked like giant watermelons looming up from their vines. The Beechers' house, under the trees, was dark. Lamplight in Nan and Ryde's front room spilled out onto their porch. At the end of the line, Gourd's house looked like it'd been abandoned for years. Booker said, "I think the guard's down."

Maud was on the back of the horse. She leaned so she could see. "Maybe Doc Ragsdale came and didn't put it back up."

She slipped off the horse and walked not far in front of it because she didn't have a snake stick. She closed that guard and the next one. Mustard's car wasn't in the lean-to or anywhere in the yard. Neither was any other. Booker dismounted at the hitching rail.

Lovely was in the chair on the east end of the porch. He didn't move. Maud called his name. He turned and looked at them. The moon lit his features.

Maud said, "How're you doing?"

"Had the shakes. They're better now."

"Maybe your fever's lifting."

"Maybe."

"Did the doctor come by to see you?"

"I don't think so."

"You don't know?"

"I've been sleeping off and on."

Maud was close enough to Lovely to see him well. He didn't look completely himself. But she thought maybe her guilt and worry made him seem odd. She put her hand on a post. "Are you gonna sleep outside?"

"My cot's under the tree."

"Is there anything I can get you? Some water, maybe?"

"No. I'm fine. Howdy, Booker."

Booker returned the greeting. Then he asked Maud to walk him to his horse. He asked if she was planning to tell Lovely what they'd learned in town. She didn't have a ready answer, and with moonlight on their shoulders, they whispered about the wisest course of action. Maud enjoyed their sharing something, even a problem, and neither of them stuck to a firm position, and not just because they were trying to please each other. They both thought Lovely had a right to know, but they also agreed that telling him could cause unnecessary fear. In the end, they decided to let the subject rest until the doctor could explain it with some authority and reassurance.

After that, they talked about whether Booker would stay the night. He said he'd sleep on the porch using his saddle for a pillow. And in making his case, he used kisses to be persuasive. Maud didn't want to send Booker away; his body turned hers like the sun turns the face of a sunflower. And she was also afraid of being alone with Lovely's strangeness. But she didn't entirely trust Booker not to slip inside to her bed or trust herself if he did. And she didn't want him there, or anywhere near, if her daddy showed up drunk. She knew full well how drunkenness looked to most white people. So in the end, she sent Booker off down the lane.

The next morning, Maud looked first to Mustard's bed. It was empty and untouched. Then she looked to the pile of books that Lovely's cot usually hid. The piles were coated with a sheen of dust. She rolled onto her back and looked to the ceiling. There was a crack in the cardboard up there that she sometimes imagined as a river, sometimes as a fissure in the earth, sometimes as a scar on a face. But she felt too worried for the crack to suck her in. She hoped Dr. Ragsdale would show up as soon as the sun got higher. She thought again about the possibility of rabies. The more she thought about that, the tighter her stomach grew. She began to feel like she was going to throw up. She decided that would be a good thing. Lovely had a bug. She caught it. She swung her feet over the side of her cot. She didn't hear Lovely outside on the porch, and the sun was too high for him to be sleeping unless he was even more poorly. She got up and peeked out the door. Lovely wasn't on the porch. She stepped outside. He wasn't anywhere to be seen. She walked to the outhouse and called his name. She went to the live oak tree, parted its leaves, and found his empty cot in the shade. She went back in, dressed behind the sheet, and began to feel hungry.

Lovely didn't turn up for breakfast. He didn't return while Maud was feeding the chickens, milking the cow, or sweeping the dirt in front of the house. He didn't come back to help her hoe. And neither did Mustard or the doctor show. She didn't expect Booker; Mr. Singer was taking him to church to sit in his pew to be seen. So she was left to her own cogitations. And, slowly, as she chopped weeds and grass that seemed more attracted to garden dirt than to the yard, she decided that if she wanted something done she was going to have to do it. She'd visit the Mounts and see if John Mount had gone mad or was just his usual mean self. She didn't intend to get right up on them or have an actual conversation. She didn't even intend to get within running distance. She knew a place down in the wild where she could climb a little rise, peek over, and see their house. At that time of day, they both should be outside. It was too hot to stay in.

So Maud changed into a shirt and a pair of overalls that she'd inherited from Lovely, slipped her mother's pistol into her pocket, and picked out her Winchester from the cluster in the corner. She walked the lane, turned at her uncle Gourd's house, and took the ruts to the river. Not far under the ridge, she veered off east onto a cow path. The vegetation on either side was tall. It rustled with the breeze, buzzed with insects, and was full of nettles. She knew the cottonmouths were thick, and she kept her eyes on her boots and repeatedly used the barrel of her rifle as a snake stick. She wondered how on the face of the Earth the Mounts, or anybody, could stand to live in such a forsaken place. The sun was high in the sky. Beads of sweat broke out on her forehead, her crown, and the back of her neck. Patches appeared under her arms.

At some distance into the wild, Maud found the spot she'd come looking for. It was a hill of sandy soil, not high, but higher than anything else around except the other little rise that the Mounts' house sat on. While climbing the mound, Maud realized that she didn't really know if the Mounts' house was still there. It was so close to the river that it could've easily been swept away in the flood. The thought made her heart sink. She'd come out far into a place she'd always avoided, a place so wild with poisonous creatures and wolves and occasionally even bears and wildcats that her mother had used it to scare her into good behavior. Maud shifted her rifle to her left hand and freed her right one to grasp a root to lift herself to the rim of the rise.

In the distance, she saw what remained of the Mounts' house. The porch was gone. The single front window and the door were so high above the ground that they looked like they were part of a second floor. Wooden steps to the door were of a different color than the wood of the house. Maud figured they'd been laid after the flood had taken the porch. Next to the house stood a willow. The movement of its limbs was the only movement around. Maud had been worried about the Mounts' dogs smelling her and barking, but she didn't hear a sound beyond the low rush of the river. She looked south and saw a ribbon of water. She turned back to the house. She looked for dogs. She decided the Mounts had put theirs down, fearing the spread of rabies.

She was squatting below the crest of the hill, watching the house for movement and listening to insects, when the ripple of a shadow glided across the tangles in front of her. She looked to the sky. A buzzard had flown over. It circled out toward the river and circled back in. Another buzzard came in from the southeast. It was higher and circled in a clockwise direction. The first buzzard landed next to the Mounts' stovepipe. The second buzzard disappeared behind treetops. The buzzard near the stovepipe dropped off the house out of sight. The other buzzard flew back in and landed on the roof. It flapped its wings. Then it, too, slipped below Maud's line of vision. A third buzzard flew in.

When the third buzzard landed on the roof, Maud's fear of the Mounts disappeared and was replaced by a fear so great it propelled her to stand. She made her way quickly down the hill and then ran the cow path toward the Mounts', past their cow lot to their front yard. She heard whooshing noises, flaps, and hisses.

She climbed the steps to the door, entered the house, held her breath against its filth, and walked to the only window in the back wall. That window was open. Beyond it, on the ground below, were twenty to thirty black buzzards and turkey buzzards. They were in two groups, stabbing, tearing, raising their heads to swallow, flapping their wings, and jabbing at each other.

Maud's breathing grew more and more shallow until she felt faint. She steadied herself with the butt of her rifle against the floor and a hand on the window frame. She turned toward the room. There was a cast-iron stove in the corner, two chairs and a table in the middle, a dipping pan on a table, and two beds against opposite walls. Maud used her gun to steady herself, walked to the table, and sat down. In front of her was a bowl crawling with green flies, a saltshaker, a tin cup, and a box of matches. The birds made a loud racket.

Maud pushed the bowl to the far side of the table. The flies hardly stirred. She studied the saltshaker. It was glass, smudged with dirt, and half full. The salt in it rose higher on one side than on the other. Her eyes were still clamped to the shaker when she heard the flapping of wings nearby. She looked to the window. A turkey buzzard was sitting on the sill, its red, wrinkly head cocked at her. Her hand went to the bowl. She threw it and hit the bird. The buzzard rocked backward, hissed, and disappeared. The bowl fell out of the window. The swarm of flies filled the air. Their buzz was shrill.

Maud's mind focused. She walked to the window, swatting flies. The birds were still tearing away. She took her mother's pistol out of her pocket and fired at the ground. Wings flapped in every direction. Some birds landed in trees close by, some on other spots on the ground. They looked at Maud like she looked at them. She steadied herself in the frame but then recalled that the buzzard had stood in that place. She stepped back, stumbled over to the dipping pan, cupped up a handful of water, and wiped it over the back of her neck. She sat down at the table again and tried to think.

The Mounts were dead. Past dead. Being eaten. She didn't know how they'd died. She wouldn't put it past them to have shot each other. Or maybe John Mount had gone mad with rabies and killed Claude and himself, too. She was sure it was them, not because she had seen the remains well enough to tell, but because they weren't around. They ran a still. One of them stayed near it most of the time. Her mind went from the bodies to the birds. She didn't know if buzzards could carry rabies. But if they did, they could infect all of the wildlife and then the domesticated animals all over the area.

Maud racked her head for everything she'd ever heard about the disease. She eventually recognized that her thoughts were jumping like fleas. She felt certain of only two things: aside from dogs and cats, skunks and bats carried rabies. She didn't think skunks ate carrion, but she thought bats might, and she knew they ate insects. By night, the remains would be crawling with those. She needed to alert somebody so the bodies could be removed before dusk when the bats were flying. It was well past noon already.

Maud eased up from the table with her rifle. There were four birds outside, still pecking the heads. Maud raised her gun to her shoulder and fired. One bird hissed and toppled over. The other three flapped their wings and flew. Maud lowered her gun. She turned from the window and scanned the room. She stepped over to the nearest bed, took a quilt from the foot, and threw it over her shoulder. She picked up another quilt from the foot of the other bed. The thought of lice crossed her mind. She shook that away, went over the threshold, and carefully descended the new steps.

At the back of the house, she found the buzzard she'd shot clawing the ground with a wing and making a grunting noise. The sound was so peculiar for a bird that Maud looked around. There was no other movement except the wind stirring the branches of trees. The buzzard's body made a thumping noise against the ground. Maud threw the quilts off her shoulders and shot the bird again. Then she picked up the quilts, and as she moved closer, she tilted her head so that she saw the human bodies only out of the sides of her eyes. About ten feet away from them, she threw the top quilt to the ground, laid her rifle beside it, and took the second quilt in both hands. She flapped it open, and with her head turned, spread it over the remains of one of the bodies. Then she picked up the other quilt and flapped it open. She held it in front of her so that it hid the sight of the second body until she saw the sole of a boot. Next to the heel was her father's lighter. Maud dropped the quilt and ran.

She sped down the cow path and around the hill and was almost to the ruts of the road when she lost all breath, bent over, and placed her hands on her thighs. She stayed bent over with a pain in her side until she dropped to her knees. She panted. The sun was in front of her, its heat on her forehead. She swiped away the sweat rolling into her eyes. She wiped her mouth. She began hearing insects. Her breath came back in an even rhythm. She squatted, sat on her rear in the dirt, and embraced her knees. She needed to go back to retrieve her father's Banjo and her rifle. She had to do that right away. She got up, turned, and walked long strides. When she got to the house, she stopped before rounding the back corner and listened. She heard movement; she thought it was buzzards again. She was right. She put her hand in her pocket and felt her mother's pistol. But instead of shooting, she yelled, "Go away," and the birds did. She grabbed the lighter and tucked it into a pocket of her bib and spread the second quilt over the carcass. She picked up her rifle and quickly walked away.

On the path out of the wild, Maud murmured, "Lovely, please be back. Please, please." But after a while, she felt calm enough to realize that Lovely might not be able to help her. He'd helped move the dog, but he couldn't shoot Betty. And he was already sick. Could he stomach human bodies picked to pieces? Could he move them to the river? Or roll them into graves? Graves would arouse less suspicion. Bodies in the river, even weighted with rocks, had been known to wash ashore. The only people who visited the Mounts were looking for rotgut. They would take what they found and not look around. The Mounts' family in town didn't associate with them. If they came sniffing and found graves, they'd figure somebody had been kind enough to bury them.

But John Mount was probably seeing the doctor for shots. And Doc Ragsdale would be concerned about him getting one every day. If John didn't show up, the doctor could go looking for him. A new grave, certainly two, would raise the doctor's suspicions. She needed to find out for sure if Dr. Ragsdale was giving John Mount shots before she could decide how to get rid of the bodies.

Her thoughts turned to her daddy killing the Mounts. She knew why. But how? Shooting, probably. Shots in the wild of the river were so common she might've even heard the exact ones. Was his rifle in the corner with the others? Or gone? She tried to visualize the cluster. She couldn't recall which guns were leaning there. She gripped her rifle even harder and touched her mother's pistol. Her daddy hadn't taken it, but he probably wouldn't have used it to kill someone, even if no other gun had been available.

The thought of her mother made Maud feel ashamed. She'd disapproved of her father's fighting roosters and wouldn't even drown kittens unless the puss was so poorly she couldn't nurse them. Maud's mind saw her mother turn her face away from the remains on the ground. But then her mother's face turned back around. She would, in the end, do whatever had to be done. She'd often said that none of them would be alive if their old folks had given up on the Trail. People had to rise to difficult conditions and keep going. Her mother had been thankful just to have land that was hers. For a plot to grow crops. For vegetables to eat. For plum jelly. For side meat.

Maud regretted not feeling the same. But she couldn't help herself; she wanted away from meanness, away from death, away from buzzards and rabies. That wasn't too much to ask. People in the East were living in heated houses, dancing fast, and cutting their hair. In No Man's Land, ignorant city slickers were raking in money in wheat. Even the Osage were driving Cadillacs and wearing fancy rings. The whole world was booming. And she was scaring buzzards away from human meat.

Maud's yearnings had distracted her, but as she climbed toward the crest of the ridge, she shook them off like a dog shakes off water after a swim. She had dirty work to do and she needed to be about her business. By Gourd's house, she looked ahead to hers. Dr. Ragsdale's car sat smack in front of it and startled her. She couldn't be caught coming up from the Mounts', particularly with an extra gun. She skirted behind Gourd's shack, slid from the far side onto the porch, and, hidden by the bedroom wall, reached out and turned the knob, thankful Gourd had so little to steal that he didn't have a lock. She slipped inside and opened his little icebox. It was empty. She stashed her mother's pistol in it, came back out, slipped off the east side of the porch, circled behind the house, and slid back down the ridge. From there, she walked the cow path west. She rose up again close to the pump.

Dr. Ragsdale was in her father's chair. Mercifully, he was looking into a black bag on his lap. She wondered if he'd found Lovely and put him to bed. She decided that the doctor being there was the best possible thing that could've happened, and she was feeling relieved by her good luck when Booker came out the front door. He'd been inside. He'd seen what it looked like. And lying to him would be harder than lying to Dr. Ragsdale. Her lucky feelings scattered like dandelion blowballs spread by wind. She inhaled, gripped her rifle tighter, and took bold steps. She wished she'd worn a dress.

Booker waved and smiled. By the time Maud reached the porch, Dr. Ragsdale was standing up with him. Lovely was inside and so was his cot. He had a headache and fever, and had taken water. The doctor didn't think he had rabies, but he'd given him a shot and thought it wise to give him the entire round of twenty-one.

Maud felt relieved to have the subject drawn to Lovely. She asked the doctor, "Could he have influenza?"

Ragsdale was a short, wiry man. He had a moustache, a cleft in his chin, and a shock of brown hair that hung in his eyes. He brushed his hair back with the heel of his hand. "I don't think so. It's not that season. His headache could be a result of the knock he got. The wound's not infected, but he could've suffered a concussion. More likely, he needs glasses. He's squinting a lot and says he's a big reader. More concerning to me . . ." The doctor paused and looked toward the door. He jerked his head.

Maud and Booker followed Ragsdale to the yard and his car before he continued. "More concerning to me is that he seems to have lost traction." He tapped his temple with his middle finger. "Up here."

Maud looked down at her feet. She'd worn brogans and she was standing in dust. She swiped a little dirt with the side of her boot. "He's always been sensitive. But lately, he's been staring off a bit."

"Did that start before he knocked his head?"

Maud looked up, bit her lip. "I think. But I can't say for positive. He gets to thinking about things and goes off somewhere. We both do, if the truth be known." She looked at Booker. "Sometimes, you just wish you were somewhere other than here."

The doctor said, "When I went off to St. Louis to school, I thought I'd died and gone to heaven. My folks didn't have electricity 'til I got back." He lowered his voice. "Still, you might keep an eye on him."

Booker said, "There's nothing wrong with being dreamy. Everybody wants something better. But it could be the fever, couldn't it?"

Dr. Ragsdale looked out over the wild of the river. He squinted. "It could be. Hard to say." He tucked his lower lip under his top teeth.

Maud hoped the doctor would tell them what he was thinking. She watched baby toads hopping in the shadow of the trough and waited. But Ragsdale said, "I better get going. Can you or Mustard get him in every day?"

Maud was startled to hear her father's name. And it brought the buzzards back. She sucked in air. Booker looked at her and squinted. She coughed to cover her reaction. Then she said, "I don't really know. Daddy's gone up to Wagoner, I think. He's been talking to a man up there about a retriever. I don't know exactly when he's coming back." She looked over again at the toads.

Booker said, "I've got an extra horse. I'll bring one down for Lovely. Unless the shots will make him too sick to ride?"

"They probably won't a grown man. But some tolerate them

better than others. I'll come down here tomorrow. Give him his shot and see how he is. If he's better, your horse would be the ticket." Dr. Ragsdale turned to Maud. "These shots are a precaution. I don't really think Lovely's got rabies. But I do understand from Mr. Wakefield here, that . . . I don't know how to put this delicately . . . there's been some meanness here lately. Something about a dog. Do you have any reason to believe you need shots, too? I'm expecting John Mount to come in for his this afternoon."

The mention of John Mount rattled Maud to the point that she hoped she wasn't visibly shaking. But she quickly realized she had the answer to one of her questions. "I'm fine. I didn't touch the dog. I scrubbed some blood off the table, but that's all."

Booker said, "Is it carried in blood?"

"As far as we know, only in saliva. There're myths, of course. People get frightened and think wild things. But Mount is worried, and he has a right to be. If you're bitten by any dog, you should get the shots. Almost none of the dogs around here have had theirs. But then again"— Ragsdale pulled on his moustache —"we haven't had any rabies in a while. It could be that dog turned on Mount for some other reason."

Maud wanted to say, *Because he was an animal killer*. But she checked her tongue by biting her lower lip. She had to guard against giving away that she knew Mount was dead. And she suddenly realized she was about to be left alone with Booker and would have to lie to him both outright and by holding back. That would be hard. To keep the doctor a little longer, she said, "How much will we owe you for this? We'll need to save up."

Dr. Ragsdale winced. "Let me jaw with your dad over that. I know him fairly well."

Maud didn't want Dr. Ragsdale to say anything about her father in front of Booker. He often doctored him after his fights. Her fear spun to that as Booker said, "I appreciate your coming out here with me."

"Glad to. Do you want a lift back to Mr. Singer's?"

Booker looked at Maud.

She could tell he wanted to stay. She felt like she had her leg in a trap. She blinked hard, ran her tongue around her lips. "I've been checking on Grandpa's cow. I have to report to him. They'll expect me to stay and visit."

Booker frowned. He opened his mouth like he was going to say something to Maud, but he closed it and then said instead, "Thank you, Doc. I'll get my jacket and hat." He turned and walked toward the porch with a slight slump in his shoulders.

Maud wanted to call him back. But she had to get him out of there. She extended her hand to the hood of the doctor's car to keep from running after him. The hood was warm; the heat on her palm focused her attention. She said to the doctor, "Thank you for everything."

"Glad to help. Don't want you to worry too much." He, too, looked toward Booker's receding back. "I saw the sheriff in church. Evidently, children were seen around the school the evening it burnt."

At first, Maud didn't know what the doctor was talking about. Her thoughts were on the bodies, her heart racing. "Children?"

"Yes." The doctor nodded toward Booker coming out the door. "Ever'body knows your friend here got tangled up in that. That's gonna get cleared up. It was probably children."

Maud's mind skipped off the bodies, over Booker, and onto Nan's kids. They lived closest to the school. If they burnt it down, her uncle Ryde would beat them to death. "What children?" Her eyes grew wider.

Dr. Ragsdale peered at Maud. He squinted. "A group of boys, I think. No doubt smoking. Kids shouldn't be allowed to smoke 'til they're fifteen."

Morgan, Nan's oldest, might be in that group, but the rest wouldn't be. Maud moved her palm off of the car and rubbed it with her thumb. Booker was almost to them. She said, "Is there something particular I should do for Lovely?"

Dr. Ragsdale looked up at Booker and then back to Maud. "I'm a little worried about him being out of his head. I don't think he'll try to fight you, but watch him."

Maud didn't understand what the doctor was saying. But Booker was there with his hat in his hand, his coat thrown over his shoulder, and obviously displeased. She needed to push him away before she apologized and begged him to stay. "I sure thank you for your help, Doctor. Booker, I'll be seeing you around."

Booker turned pink in the face. "Certainly." He put his bowler on his head and let out a breath that sounded like a huff. Then he turned and walked to the passenger side of the doctor's car.

Maud stood in the yard until the car reached the first cattle guard. When Booker got out to take that gate down, she hoped he would turn and look at her. He didn't. She moved to the porch and watched again, with the same result at the second guard. When the car turned onto the section line, she went in, feeling Booker's displeasure like a feed sack slung over her shoulders.

Lovely was on his cot, his knees in the air, an arm over his eyes. The room was hot and shadowy. The only light was slanting in through the windows. Maud pulled a rocker to the side of his bed. She sat down, glad to have a moment of quiet. She felt exhausted. "How're you doing?"

"Not too good." Lovely dropped his arm and slid his feet to the bottom of his cot. "Does Mama ever come visit you?"

Maud shook her head. "I wish she did."

"She came to visit me. I saw her clear as that woman there on the wall." He pointed to a calendar blonde holding a soft drink and smiling.

"That's nice, Lovely. I hope she looked as happy."

"You don't understand, Maud. I really saw her. She was as real as you are."

Maud didn't know what to say. She patted his shoulder.

"Honest, Maud."

"Mama loved you, Lovely. If she knew you were sick, she'd be concerned."

"I think they're here, Maud."

"Who?"

"All of them."

"All of who?"

"You know. Mama, Grandma. That baby Mama lost."

"Grandma died when we were little. I can barely remember her."

"I hear her talking. There're other people around. Some of them aren't friendly."

Maud's mind shot back to the bodies. She couldn't believe she'd forgotten them, and she felt frightened all over again. "Lovely, I need to go see Grandpa. Do you know when Daddy's coming back, or if he is?"

"He was here last evening."

"When?" Maud looked to the corner that held the rifles. Her father's was gone. He really had been there.

"Sometime. I don't know. It was nearly dark. Ever'body was visiting."

"Ever'body?"

"Mama and Grandma. The other folks. The mean ones."

"I see. And Daddy took his rifle?"

"I guess so. I don't know."

"Did he take anything else?"

"Just his dog money, I think."

"How did he know where it was?"

"I told him your hiding places."

"Creepers, Lovely. Why'd you do that?"

"He wanted to buy his dog."

"Not at night, Lovely."

Lovely rubbed his brow above his scab. "Well, that's what he said."

Maud sighed. She leaned back in the rocker, drummed her nails on its arms. "Where did you go off to in the middle of the night?"

"Did I go somewhere?"

"You weren't here when I got up."

"I can't remember. It seems like I've been everywhere lately."

"Did you go with Daddy?"

Lovely rested his arm above his scab. "Maud, I can't remember. There's been a lot of coming and going. I'm telling you Mama was here. And people I don't know."

Maud hoped that if her mother had been there it was to keep Lovely from going with their father. She thought about asking if he knew the Mounts were dead. She hesitated. Lovely wasn't in his right mind. If he didn't know, and she told him, he could tell somebody else. He'd spilled her hiding places. In the state he was in, he couldn't be trusted. And surely her daddy wouldn't have taken him to kill the Mounts. But he might have taken Ryde. The light had been burning at Nan's in the night. "Lovely, I'm going over to Grandpa's. Aunt Lucy and Viola will've cooked Sunday dinner. I'll bring you some back. You can tide yourself over with biscuits. I'll get you a cup of water. I want you to drink it."

"I can't right now."

Maud's heart jumped. "You're afraid of water?"

"My belly still hurts from the shot." He rubbed his stomach. "Don't worry. Doc watched me drink."

Maud left the house and went straight to the cellar. It was a log dugout covered with a sod roof. She pulled back the door and looked at the steps and dirt floor. The sun hit them both. She held her breath and listened for snakes that occasionally retreated to the hole in the heat of the day. She heard nothing but silence interrupted by insect and chicken sounds. She stepped down, palming the dirt of the wall. The first thing she checked was the shelf where she'd hidden her daddy's money. The jar was gone. She muttered a curse on her brother, moved the bean jars back into place, and reached for a jar of plum jelly from the shelf below. She slipped that jar into the pocket of her overalls. When she did, she recalled Booker seeing her dressed in them. She felt ugly.

But Maud knew she couldn't waste time thinking about her looks. She had a pressing job to do. She climbed out of the hole, shut the door, and secured it. Then she got her rifle from the porch and set out through the back fields, avoiding Nan's house because she didn't want to see her uncle Ryde until she had a notion of what to say to him. She directed her mind toward her grandfather's place. Early would probably be there. He was prone to telling tales in town, embellishing even the plainest plank on the porch to make it sound like the yellow brick road. But if anybody listened close enough, they usually heard kernels of truth. She didn't want any of those spilling out.

Who else would be there? Uncle Ame and Aunt Viola, for sure.

She needed to talk to Viola about Lovely, and her grandpa and Ame worked as a team. But Lucy, Cole, and Blue would be there, too. And it was Sunday; other family might've drifted in. Maud turned off onto another cow path, hoping to see as few kin as she could.

When she got to the horse pasture, she was relieved to see that Early's and Blue's horses weren't there. She looked ahead to the house. At that time of day, folks would be in the side-yard shade. She wouldn't be able to tell who until she was close. But to her relief, it turned out to be only the older generation. They were sitting on the ground, leaning against a tree trunk and stumps. She took a deep breath and waved to them.

Maud wanted to blurt out her trouble. But she needed to be certain somebody hadn't just gone into the house. She sat down on the ground and quickly found that Early and Blue had gone into town. Lucy, Cole, and their baby were at Nan's. She heard, too, rapid fire, that Lucy's feet were swelling and Blue was courting a white woman who had a bit in his mouth. After that gossipy spray, Maud wanted to run a straight line. She announced without warning, "The Mounts are dead. Killed, as far as I can tell."

Her grandfather's eyebrows ran up to the wrinkles of his forehead. He cocked his head like he'd heard a near owl during the middle of the day.

"They're down at their house, out in the back. Buzzards have been at them. I covered them with quilts to keep them away. Daddy's Banjo was by one of their boots." She reached into her bib and pulled it out.

Maud's grandfather and uncle Ame both cussed. Then they put their hands on the ground and stood. Ame was small and bowlegged. He looked like a fullblood, wasn't a talker, and wouldn't look anyone straight in the eye. Her grandpa was over a head taller; one of his shoulders was higher than the other, but his legs were straight. He was also dark, but lighter than his brother. He ran his hands down the sides of his overalls, looked up to the sky, and said, "Did the Mounts have any hogs left?"

Maud tried to remember hogs. "I was in such a state I can't recall."

His next remark was to Viola. "What'd you and Lucy do with them brooms?"

"They's against the back stoop."

"Get 'em fer us."

Viola got up. Maud said, "What're we gonna do, Grandpa?"

"Ame and me'll take care it, Maudy-Baby."

Maud felt such relief that she was suddenly glad the Mounts were dead. She wanted to throw her arms around her grandpa's neck, press against his bib, and cry. But he wouldn't take to that.

He said, "Anything else we need to know?"

Maud couldn't bear to put words to what she'd seen. "Daddy's rifle's gone. I'm thinking he thought the Mounts gave Lovely the rabies. But Doc Ragsdale was down. He doesn't think Lovely's infected. Giving him shots just as a precaution."

Maud's grandfather nodded toward her hand, the one that held the lighter. "Did he drop it or leave it on purpose?"

"Don't know."

"Did he kill 'em alone, or did Ryde help?"

"Don't know that, either."

Ame said, "I wouldn't put it past Ryde."

Grandpa said, "Me. neither. And then get scared and leave the bodies. Neither one of 'em can think through a damn thing." He looked toward the sun and squinted. "Did Ragsdale go on down to the Mounts?"

"No. He went back to town. He was depending on John Mount to get to him. I guess he's afraid to go into the wild."

Ame said, "That's a good thing."

Viola had returned with the brooms in time to hear her brother-in-law's last question. She said, "Bert, if Mount don't show for his shot, that doctor'll go looking fer him. That's what Pappy would do."

Bert said, "We better get going."

"What are you gonna do?" Maud said.

Her grandpa looked over her head. "What I want you to do is poke around Nan's. See if you can find out if Ryde had any part. If he gets to talking, we could have a real problem on our hands."

"I'd say two bodies is a problem." Viola picked up her spit can and turned her head.

Maud sighed. Murder was awful. The thought filled her with shivers. But in a deep crevice inside, she felt pleased that her father had defended Lovely. It was the first time in her memory he'd done that, and she thought that if she saw her daddy again she'd thank him for it.

Her grandpa continued, "Be cagey with Ryde. Ifin he didn't have a hand, we don't want him finding out. Jist visit pleasant like."

He and Ame walked off toward the horse lot, each carrying a broom. Maud and Viola turned to the house. There were two front rooms, a kitchen in the back, and, attached to the main structure by a porch, another room where Blue and Early bunked. Viola went into the south room in the main part of the house. Maud sat on the side of a bed in the other front room and gripped its iron footboard. From the south room, Viola said, "Pappy told me when yer grandpa and Ame waz boys, there waz a neighborly killing 'round here. Yer great-grandpa drove it. But yer grandpa played a part, and yer great-uncle Coop pulled the trigger. Mr. Singer's mother waz in on it, and his brother took the rap. It were a long time ago. I never heared the full story. Ame's never said a word about it, though we've been married since '99. My pappy warn't no killing man, but he were in the thick of it, trying, as best I recall, to heal yer grandma's wounds. She waz a little girl and the wolves had been at her."

Maud had never caught a whisper of that story. And hearing it told from another room made it feel as spooky as a critter creeping out of the mist covering a field. Maud recalled her mama saying that time moved in a circle, not like an arrow. She felt dizzied by that circle and clutched the iron rod to hold herself to the mattress. She was still holding on when Viola came into the room.

They set out to Nan's carrying with them Maud's plum jelly and a slingshot Bert had whittled for his grandkids. They agreed on a story about Bert and Ame going fishing. But then it occurred to them that nobody put much effort into fishing on Sunday after dinner was eaten. They settled on a story about leaving the men at home with their heads under the hood of Ame's car.

Maud didn't know Viola as well as she knew the rest of her family. Her uncle Ame had married her and moved with her to the Creek Nation after his first wife had died. Except for long visits, Maud hadn't seen either one of them since. However, Viola was somehow also blood kin to her through her mother. Maud didn't know enough to untangle that web, but she felt that if her own grandmother had lived she'd be much like Viola. She kept her gait slow to match the older woman's walk and watched her out of the sides of her eyes.

Viola was dark to the bone, her skin wrinkled by weather, her eyes deep set. Her hair was braided down her back and a wad bulged her lower lip. She drew a bandana from her dress and wiped sweat off her brow. "Give me the lowdown on Lovely."

The question led Maud to where she wanted to go. "He's not right in his head. And, like I said, the doc doesn't really think it's rabies." She described Lovely's accident in the barn. Then she added, "He's seeing things. Thinks Mama's come to visit him. Thinks other people are talking to him. I haven't told him what I found at the Mounts."

"How high's his fever?"

"Not so high he should be seeing or hearing things."

Viola peered out toward a field of potatoes and moved her wad to the other side of her jaw. They'd walked another fifty feet when she finally remarked, "The men'll come up from the wild by Gourd's. We'll look in on Lovely after we finish this visit."

At Nan's, they found Maud's aunt Sarah and four of her kids had come over from Muskogee in Sarah's oldest boy's car. They admired his new Chevrolet and caught up with Sarah's family gossip. Ryde and Cole had taken the buckboard to Ft. Gibson before Sarah had arrived. With Ryde gone, Nan seeming normal, and with other kin around, Maud's mind let go its grip on the events of the morning. Food revived her energy. By the time she and Viola said their good-byes and walked the section line toward her house, Maud was almost feeling like she'd imagined the bodies the same way Lovely had imagined their mother dropping by.

She was drawn back to reality when Viola said, "I don't know if we'll get much out of them men when they come in. Ame and Bert try to protect you younguns. They think book learning is the way to go. Couldn't read much themselves 'til they waz grown."

Maud recalled nestling in her grandfather's lap, reading out loud from whatever book was in the house, and him drawing out pennies for her from a little black purse in his bib when she finished. Now she wondered if he was encouraging her, or was learning with her. "Can they read Cherokee?"

"No, yer grandma could read it real good. But Ame and yer grandpa waz raised over in Arkansas, away from the rest. I think their daddy may've been mostly white."

"Don't they know?"

"Not total sure. They waz orphaned in the Hard Times. Come here as kids 'cause their mama had told 'em this waz where her people lived. Her name waz Margaret. She waz a great-niece to my grandpappy and to yer great-grandfather. They waz brothers."

Maud understood that her great-aunt was trying to educate her and that she ought to remember what she said. But she didn't think she could. That type of information was important in times past when roles were compiled and allotments handed out. But she had too many other things to think about. She said, "I need to mark all that down," just to be polite.

"When ya get the chance. Now people can't keep up."

They were in the shade of the swale trees before either one of them spoke again.

"Was your pa a real medicine man?" Maud asked.

"Sure waz. Prutty good one, too."

"Did he give shots?"

Viola cackled. "He didn't have those. He gathered medicine the Breath Master gives us and doctored with it."

Maud knew something about the Creeks' Breath Master. He wasn't much different in his creating ways from the Genesis God. Maud started to say that Lovely's girl had him reading the Bible. But she checked her tongue because Lovely had been too sick to spark. She hoped he didn't lose Gilda because of that.

When they passed the trees, they saw that Bert's wagon wasn't at the house and that Lovely was in Mustard's chair on the porch. There was, it seemed, a whiff of moisture in the air, and they talked about the possibility of rain until they got to Gourd's, where Maud went inside to retrieve her mother's pistol.

They found Lovely with the Bible on the planks next to his chair. He looked perkier than Maud had expected. She gave him some food from Nan's, and they talked about Sarah's kids until the wind came up. Then Maud left to milk the cow and close up the chicken house. When she got back, drops of rain had speckled the dust. They moved the rocker against the wall. Lovely and Viola slid to the planks and sat. Maud took the chair.

Thunder rumbled. The tree branches swished with the wind, dark clouds rolled in, and lightning zigzagged in the sky over the river. When the rain came, it played on the far side of the porch like the shake of a rattle. The three of them were lost in the show and saying very little when Bert's wagon appeared on the crest of the ridge by Gourd's house. The mules stopped. Bert and Ame sat still in the downpour. Then they got off the far side of the wagon and went into the house. Maud told Lovely they'd been down at the river to see if anything worth salvaging had been thrown up on the sandbar. The lightning and thunder died, but the rain continued. As dark descended, Maud, Lovely, and Viola went inside one at a time and lay down to sleep.

But Maud couldn't fall off. She felt fairly certain that the Mounts had been taken care of, but Booker arose in her mind like a ghost at the foot of her cot. She was worried about him being mad and unhappy that he hadn't returned on his own. But she was also thankful for not having to lie to him, and she thought that she wouldn't have come back had she been him. Her feelings were running at crosscurrents. She rolled from shoulder to shoulder. She was awake when Lovely got up from his cot and went out the front door. She assumed he was taking a leak. And she lay there in the dark, listening to the rain on the tin roof, waiting for him to return, and determined to turn her face to the wall and go to sleep when he did. But the time grew longer. She listened for sounds over the rain, but it had grown harder and its beating was all she could hear. She sat up on the side of her cot. There was more light outside than in. She used the light from the windows to steer by and went to the porch. Lovely wasn't standing at the east edge, as she'd pictured. The chair was empty. He was nowhere to be seen.

She went back in. Viola was on Mustard's bed rolled in a ball that made her look smaller than she seemed when she was awake. Maud sat down next to her. She thought about touching her foot, but she had a dread of waking old people too quickly, so she was sitting there, not moving, when Viola said, "Is he gone?"

"Yes."

"Not on the porch?"

"No."

Maud shifted sideways. Viola swung her feet to the floor, grabbed the iron of the headboard, and stood. She pressed her hands down the front of her slip and then rubbed her mouth. She sat back down next to Maud. "He's tetched," she said.

"Bad tetched?"

"He walked out in a gully washer."

They listened to the rain hit the roof until Viola said, "Well, we can't go out looking in this. We better go back to sleep. It's the loony time of night. Even when it ain't raining sheets."

Maud got up. "I'll try. Not having much luck."

Viola rose and walked to the window. She took a pouch on a

leather strap off over her head. Lightning struck; she dug her fingers in. She held up her thumb and forefinger and said loudly, "Come here." Maud did. "Open." Viola stuck her fingers in Maud's mouth, drew them out, and said, "Swallow."

Maud felt a hard little kernel between her tongue and gums. She swallowed it. "What was that?"

"Sompthing to put you to sleep. But jist as a matter of practice, if anybody else asks you to do that, ask what it is first." Viola turned and crept back to Mustard's bed.

When Maud woke, the sun was slanting through the windows but the room was cool. The smell and sizzle of fatback floated in the air. Her grandfather and Viola were talking in the kitchen. She ducked behind the sheet, dressed, and slipped out the door to the outhouse. When she came back in, she found they'd eaten, but more food was warming in the oven.

Maud said, "How'd it go?"

Grandpa said, "They had five pigs they hadn't fed at all. Found their still."

"I still got a little buzzing in my ears," Ame added.

"Coffee's jist about done," Viola said.

Even if she could have pried them out, Maud didn't want more details. She used a feed sack as a potholder and opened the oven door. Nobody spoke until she slid onto the bench against the wall with her plate. Then Viola said, "Lovely ain't showed. We waz talking 'bout tracking him down."

"The rain'll make that hard," Maud said.

"How far off in his mind is he?" Grandpa looked at Maud.

She looked at Viola.

Viola lifted the pot from the stove and poured coffee into Bert's and Ame's saucers. She turned to the cabinet, got a cup, poured coffee into it, and handed it to Maud. She poured coffee into another saucer on the table, deposited the pot on the stove, sat down, and drew the saucer to her. She took a long sip and wiped her mouth. "Sometimes tetched is a good thing. Pappy saw things other people couldn't see. Helped him all his life. Could be that Lovely's gonna turn out like Pappy. Do a lot of good fer folks."

There was a pause for more sipping. Then Maud said, "What if he doesn't turn out like your father?"

Viola pursed her lips and wiped them with an old flour sack. "Well, he might have the rabies. Or he might start living in a different world. It's too early to tell. Watch him, though. Ifin you can find him. He needs more shots, don't he?"

Maud recalled then that Dr. Ragsdale would be coming. Booker was also due with a horse for Lovely. She looked up from her plate and shook her hair. "Yes. What time of day is it?"

Her grandfather looked out the screen. "'Bout eight o'clock."

"I slept late." Maud looked to Viola.

Ame said, "I gotta see a man 'bout a dog."

After he came back in, the old folks left in the buckboard.

Maud went about her chores, eyeing the section line every few minutes. Midday, she turned her father's chair east so she could watch the road but not be glued to it while she ate and read. She was having a hard time retaining what she was reading when she heard the beat of hooves in the distance. She got up quickly and went inside. She checked her looks in the mirror and brushed her hair and bit her lips to make them fuller until the sound of the hooves was close to the house. She went out on the porch.

Booker was wearing a cowboy hat. He pushed it back on his head and put both hands on his saddle horn. He didn't say anything. Maud said, "Look who turned up."

"I keep my word." He swung his leg over his horse. He tied the reins of both horses to the hitching rail and then stood facing Maud with his fists on his hips.

Maud figured he was waiting for an apology. She felt he deserved one, but she also felt justified in doing what she had to do. "Was the rain a problem for you last night?" she said.

He walked toward her. "No. I pulled my wagon into the potato barn." He licked his lips.

Maud didn't know what to say or do. "I'm almost done with *Arrowsmith*." She pointed to the book beside the chair.

"Maud." Booker took another step toward her. He licked his lips again.

"I'm worried sick. Lovely's gone."

Booker took his hat off. "Where to?"

"I don't know. He's taken to laying out. That's not all that strange for the men around here, but he's still not right." She tapped her temple.

Booker ran the edge of his hand down the crease in his hat. Maud shook her hair. She sucked the insides of both cheeks. Booker said, "We could go looking for him." He nodded toward the horses.

Maud smiled. "Let's sit a while. Doc Ragsdale is due. I need to be here when he comes. I like your hat."

Booker climbed the steps and looked Maud so deeply in the eyes that a blush came to her cheeks. She felt like a covey of quail had fluttered up in her heart. He brushed a strand of hair away from her face. "Is anybody else here?" She shook her head. He said, "It's cool enough today to go inside." He kissed her.

They were on Mustard's bed when they heard a motorcar. Their clothes were partly on, partly unbuttoned, partly off. Booker jumped up. Maud said, "Did you leave the guards down?"

"No." His fingers worked his bottom shirt button.

"It takes a while to get through them." Maud straightened her slip, got up, and went to the mirror.

Booker said, "I got a problem that needs to get resolved before the doc gets here." He flipped up his shirttail and smiled.

Maud turned from the mirror and took a good look. She raised both eyebrows and smiled. "Keep your shirttail out, then."

"He'll know what we were doing."

"He's gonna know anyway. He's not a fool."

"Maybe I could go out the kitchen door and walk around the side of the house?"

"Don't be taking care of yourself in the pots and pans."

Booker turned red. "I can't believe you said that."

"I've been around men all my life. I don't see how you all live with those things. They take more time and energy than a woman puts into her hair."

Booker looked down at the front of his pants. Maud looked there, too. She said, "Looks like your friend is dwindling away."

"I'll get you."

"You'll have to catch me first."

Maud went out the door. She was at the edge of the porch smiling when Dr. Ragsdale stepped out of his car. But her lips tightened when she saw the doctor's face. His eyes were wild. His cheeks were pale. He was breathing hard. He stopped at the steps as Booker came out of the house. The doctor looked away toward the river and back up at Maud and Booker. "I've been to the Mounts'. They're dead. Or somebody is. There're pieces of bone in the mud in the hog lot."

Booker said, "Human bones?"

The doctor nodded. "I need a drink of water." He gripped the edge of the porch with both hands and lowered his head.

Maud went to the kitchen. She took the dipper off its hook and lowered it into the pan. She took it out carefully. Her hand was trembling. It would give her away. She set the dipper down in the pan and grasped its edges with both hands. Water splashed out of the pan onto her dress as she stepped to the door. She put a shoulder to the screen without splashing any more. "I thought you might need a lot." Maud looked to Booker. He took the pan and lowered it to the floor of the porch, close to the doctor. Dr. Ragsdale looked up at him, tried to speak, but couldn't.

Booker winced and bit his lower lip. He held up a dipper of water. "Take some."

Maud sat down in the chair. The doctor was as pale as his shirt. His sleeves were shaking. He said, "I haven't seen anything like it since the war. In Belgium, we came on a mass killing. The wild boars, or wolves, or something, had been at the bodies. Their bones were gnawed to splinters. But they'd been that way for some time. These bones are still wet."

Maud said, "It rained."

The doctor nodded. "Maybe that's it. But John Mount couldn't be dead long. I saw him day before yesterday."

"How do you know it's him?" Maud said.

The doctor wiped his mouth with the back of his hand. "I don't. There's nothing but parts of skulls. I'm not even certain how many bodies."

"They ran a still, you know," Maud said. "We hear shots from down there nearly every day. There's no telling what kind of meanness goes on."

Booker said, "Have you heard shots lately?"

Maud furrowed her brow and stuck out her tongue at the corner of her lips. "Hard to say. They're as common as wolf howls. We don't pay them much mind."

Booker blinked several times and then turned to the doctor. "What do we need to do?"

"Get the sheriff," Ragsdale replied.

Booker looked off toward the river. "Let me do that. I need to look law-abiding. You stay here."

"Take my car," Ragsdale said. "If you know how to drive."

"I do. Traded my car for horses when I started peddling."

Maud told the doctor to take the rocker. She went inside, pulled the last biscuits from the oven, buttered and jellied them, and returned to the porch with a plate. She held it over the doctor's arm. He took it and set it on his lap. She sat down, her feet on a step, and watched the doctor out of the sides of her eyes. She was afraid she'd say something that would give her away. Ragsdale didn't say anything, either. He finished both biscuits and dipped up some water. He wiped his mouth with the back of his hand. "I need to give Lovely his shot."

"He's not here. He's taken to wandering."

"Is this a recent development?"

"Yes. Daddy lays out all the time, but Lovely's a homebody."

The doctor took another sip from the dipper. "Do you happen to have a light?"

Maud went inside. She'd deposited her father's lighter in a gourd bowl on the chest where he emptied his pockets. She picked it up. Anybody who knew him well would know he wouldn't go anywhere without his Banjo. She tucked the lighter in his drawer, went to the kitchen, and retrieved a box of wooden matches. She gave the box to the doctor.

He went through two cigarettes, one lit from the other, and had smoked down to the butt of the second one when he said, "Do you think your brother went visiting family?"

"Could be," Maud replied. "But he left in the middle of the night. Aunt Viola was visiting. We watched for him for a while, but he didn't return." Maud spoke while looking toward the river.

"That'd be Viola Vann?"

"Yes."

"I'd heard she was around. Her daddy, Fox, was a famous medicine man. Was he kin to you?"

"Her mama was, I think. But they're mostly Creek."

The doctor lit a third cigarette and drew long. "Her father had a concoction that everybody swore would heal an abscessed tooth without extracting it. Burnt the dickens out of the mouth but drained the puss and cleared the infection." He shook his head. "I wish I'd paid more attention when I was a little boy. Mr. Singer's mother was sort of a doctor, too. You don't pay any mind to old folks. When they're gone, you realize how much they took with them."

Maud fell into a conversation with the doctor about old-time remedies that worked or didn't. She didn't often talk to anyone with a college education, so talking was a treat, and she noticed, too, that the doctor spoke to her like he would to a man and without appearing to have ulterior motives. Once again, she let her fears go and almost forgot the situation she was in. That reprieve lasted until she heard a rumble on the section line. They both looked toward the road. The doctor's car appeared first. The sheriff's car was following close.

The sheriff and the doctor had a short conversation. They went off in the sheriff's car and left Maud and Booker on the porch. They sat down on the steps and swapped information. Maud was concentrating on not giving herself away and was facing the pump, so Booker noticed Lovely first. He came from the direction of the chicken house. Maud and Booker stopped talking. Lovely was smiling and had a glassy look to his eyes.

Before he got to the steps, Maud said, "Where have you been?"

"Visiting Aunt Nan, then over to Blue's allotment."

"Why did you leave out in the rain?"

Lovely stepped up to the porch. "Any biscuits left?"

"They're all eaten. You didn't answer my question."

"Sorry. My stomach got me. My days and nights are mixed up. I couldn't sleep. The rain seemed inviting."

"Are you an idiot? You didn't even take your rifle. You could get killed stepping on a snake."

"I took a stick. And this." He pulled his pistol from the back of his belt. "Could I have some biscuits or are you Judge Parker?"

Maud went in the door without saying another word, pulled out the biscuit bowl, and starting mixing flour and lard into dough. But she kept her ear cocked, and she heard Booker tell Lovely that the doctor and the sheriff were at the Mounts' and that somebody down there was dead. She crept closer to the door of the main room and listened harder. Lovely didn't seemed surprised. She hoped that was only because he had every right to hate the Mounts. She turned back to the kitchen; stirred the ashes from the morning fire; stuck some paper and two more sticks of wood into the stove; and as the fire got going, tiptoed to the door again. They were talking about how Lovely felt. He thought his fever was gone, and he didn't want to take any more shots. The first one still hurt.

Lovely had finished eating, and they all were back out on the porch again when the sheriff and the doctor returned. They sat in the car for a long time. When their doors finally opened, the doctor walked toward his car and the sheriff wiped his boots on his runner. He walked toward the porch, stopped, and rested his hand on the butt of his gun. "Mr. Wakefield, we were in such a hurry I didn't tell you that you're no longer under suspicion. The fire was accidently set by boys smoking. You're free to go, or stay, if you wish. As for the business down there in the wild, that's another bucket of fish. The doctor and I suspect it's murder. He says it's two individuals. Not much doubt it's the Mounts. But I'll check with their town kin before I draw a line under that. Do any of you know anything about any of this?"

Maud said, "We're not close neighbors."

The sheriff rubbed his hand over his mouth and then put it back on his gun. "I understand there's been some meanness."

Maud said, "The Mounts could have easily killed each other."

"Normally, I'd agree with you there, miss. But they didn't kill each other and leave a quilt burnt in their still."

Maud felt the color in her face rise all the way to her hair. She gripped the post she was standing near. Booker looked to her and back to the sheriff. Lovely said, "What are you saying?"

"I'm saying we found a couple of burnt pieces of quilt in the still's pot. I'm guessing whoever killed the Mounts tried to burn a quilt for some reason. Then the fire got dampened by the rain somehow." The sheriff scratched his head.

The doctor walked by the sheriff, carrying his bag. "I need to give Lovely his shot." He stopped on the bottom step.

The sheriff said to the others, "Where's Mustard?"

Maud said, "At work, I guess."

"Did you see him this morning?"

Maud gripped the post until she felt her hand cramp. She let go of the wood, bit her lip, and ducked her head, trying to look a little embarrassed. "He laid out last night. I think he's sparking."

"Who's he sparking?"

"I haven't asked."

"I see. So you have no idea?"

"You know Daddy, sheriff. He doesn't take to his kids meddling in his business."

"But you feel sure he was sparking last night?"

"I didn't say that. I said I thought he probably was. I was here. I can't see into the distance."

The sheriff drew a pad out of his shirt pocket and a pencil from behind his ear. He scribbled and then looked at the tip of his pencil. He looked at Booker. "Mr. Wakefield, you still working for Connell Singer?"

"Yes. I came down here to help Dr. Ragsdale by dropping off a horse. But I better be getting back." He looked to Maud. But she turned her eyes to the sheriff. In a defiant tone, she said, "Sheriff, there're plenty of people who would kill the Mounts. Whiskey and killing go together like ice cream and cake."

Booker's brow furrowed.

The sheriff said, "Mr. Wakefield, you can go on."

"Maybe I should stay."

"Look, you just got on my good side. Let's leave it that way. Doc, you go on and give this boy his shot. Then I want to sit down with these folks and get some answers." He turned and walked toward his car.

Booker looked at Maud. But she looked at Lovely. "Mind yourself," she said softly.

Booker's eyes cut to each of their faces. "What do you mean by that?"

The doctor moved to the porch. "Lovely, let's go inside and let you lie down on the bed."

Maud said to Booker, "Lovely hasn't been in his right head. I don't want him saying anything that could get someone hung."

"Do they still hang people around here?" Booker's right eyebrow went high.

"It's a saying. Lovely, do you hear me?" He was going through the door the doctor held open.

Booker looked two or three different ways. Then he said, "Maud, do you want me to stay?" His mouth was close to her face. His hand on her arm.

Maud looked up at him. "You'd better go."

He dropped his hand and took a step back. He squinted. "Okay, if you want to be that way, I will. But I have to say, Maud, this feels a little fishy. Your menfolk keep disappearing, and then these Mount people are dead. And now you're telling Lovely to keep his mouth shut."

"What are you suggesting?" She looked toward the sheriff to be sure he couldn't hear her.

Booker rubbed the back of his neck. "I don't know, Maud. But I'm a Methodist. I'm not real big on killing."

"I'm not big on killing, either, Booker. But we don't even know for sure who's dead. And if it is the Mounts, they're moonshiners. Moonshiners get killed all the time. Surely that's not any different over in Arkansas."

"No, it's not." Booker ran his hand over his mouth. "But what about your daddy and Lovely disappearing?"

The sheriff had just shut his car door. Maud lowered her voice even more. "Look, Booker, you just heard me explain that to the sheriff. I don't know what else to say." She widened her eyes to emphasize her innocence.

"Okay, I guess. You're sure you don't need me to stay?"

Maud was sure she didn't want Booker hearing any questions or answers. But she also didn't want him to go, and he was so close that she felt the tug of his smell. "I'll come to you."

"You promise?"

"Of course I will."

By that time, the sheriff was coming back with a couple of pencils in his hand. Booker said, "Let me know if there's anything I can do," to nobody in particular.

The sheriff stopped at the steps and let Booker pass. He put one pencil behind his ear and held the other one over his pad. "Miss Nail, is it still?"

"Yes."

"Do you care to come down here?"

"I don't care one way or the other."

"Then why don't you come out here in the yard with me. Let's go over to the pump." He turned and walked away.

Maud looked toward Booker. He was headed toward his horse. She hesitated momentarily and then stepped down. Booker turned when he got to the hitching rail. "Tell Lovely he can have Arlene as long as he needs her."

"Thank you."

Booker cocked his head and stood still. Then he put his hat on and mounted.

Maud turned her eyes from him. She walked to the pump, stopping short of it by a couple of feet. She said to the sheriff, "What do you want to know?"

"I want to know who killed the Mounts."

"I understand that. But I have no idea. There's no crime in being somebody's neighbor."

"No. But I also understand John Mount left a dog on your table. That's why your brother's in there taking a shot in his stomach. It may be why he's gone off in his head."

"He's gone off in his head because he's been poorly. He's been drinking water."

"Have you seen him drink water?"

Maud paused. "No, not really. But he walked out in the rain last night. Nobody with rabies would do that."

The sheriff made a note. "Where'd he go?"

Maud felt like she'd made a misstep. The sheriff didn't know when the Mounts had died. He might think it had been in the middle of the night. But she couldn't take her words back. "Told me he went to Aunt Nan's. I stayed here."

"What time did he go?"

"Sheriff, you know people don't tell time in the middle of the night. It was raining. We'd been in bed a while."

"And he walked right out into the rain?" The sheriff had a blank look on his face.

"I wouldn't say that. I thought he'd gone to take a leak. He could've been on the porch until the rain slacked for all I know."

"You didn't get up to check where he was?"

Maud wanted to cover for Lovely, but she didn't want to give away how long the Mounts had been dead. She was trying to figure out what her brother and Aunt Viola would say when they were questioned. She said slowly, "I did. Eventually. By that time, he'd gone. But I couldn't say when it was. Wouldn't want to. I might be wrong."

"So you went back to bed?"

"Yes."

"Who else was here?"

"My aunt Viola."

"She's living with your grandpa, I believe."

"For now."

"They're right up the road?"

"Yes, north of this house beyond the swale."

"Was her husband with her?"

"No."

"Did they have a fight?"

"No fight. She came to doctor Lovely."

"And how did that go?"

"What do you mean?"

"I mean, what was her diagnosis?"

"She didn't diagnose him. She just sat and talked."

"I thought she came to doctor?"

"She did."

"Well?" The sheriff looked up from his scribbling.

"Look, Sheriff, you surely don't believe my elderly aunt has anything to do with the Mounts and what may have, or may not have, happened to them. What's the point you're trying to make?"

"Miss Nail, I'm just trying to figure out where everybody was between the time the doctor last saw John Mount in town on Saturday afternoon and the time he and I found the . . . what we found."

Maud had decided it'd be best to hear what he'd found to cover anything she might reveal without having a source to attribute it to. "And what was that?"

"It's not fit for a woman to hear."

"That may be. But I'd like to know what my menfolk are being accused of."

"I haven't accused anybody yet."

Maud didn't know what to say next. She looked over at a toad by the trough. The sheriff looked off toward the river. "Do you happen to know where your grandpa and uncle were last night?"

"Not with me. Aunt Viola and I went visiting our other kin. And then we came down here. She would've walked back, except the rain came up."

"She would have walked in the dark?"

"She's a fullblood."

"I see." The sheriff paused. He put his pencil point to his pad and stuck his tongue out between his teeth. He eventually spoke. "So, you and your aunt were here asleep, sort of. Your brother was out walking around in the night. Your pa is . . . we don't know where. And your grandpa and . . . his brother . . . were at your grandpa's house?"

"I can't really speak for them. You'll have to ask them," Maud said quickly.

"And did your brother take a gun when he went for his midnight walk?"

"He took a pistol."

"So he left out knowing he was going somewhere he'd need a pistol?"

"You need a pistol to go to the outhouse around here."

"And that would be why?"

"Because of the cottonmouths."

"They're that thick?"

"They crawl back and forth between the river and the lakes all the time. Is there anything else you want to know? The Mounts weren't snakebit to death, were they?"

"Hard to say. But if I had to guess, I'd say they were shot."

"You couldn't tell if they were shot or not?"

"No. There wasn't anything much left. Except pieces of head."

"So how do you know it was them?"

"Bones are in their hog lot. They're not around."

"I see." Maud put her arm around the pump.

The sheriff questioned Lovely, too. When that was finished, he and Dr. Ragsdale left. Lovely came out on the porch and reported to Maud how he'd answered: He'd thought he'd heard a woman calling him. He went out to find her, but nobody was on the porch. He came back in and got his pistol because he was scared. Then he heard the woman again. He thought maybe it was somebody he knew. Maud interrupted. "Who?"

"Grandma, actually. But I didn't tell the sheriff that. He probably knows she's dead."

"Whatchya do after that?"

"Walked farther up the line. Took shelter with Nan and Ryde, just like I told you. Ate breakfast there. Then walked over to Blue's allotment and home."

"Did you tell him that?"

"Yep. And I told him I slept all night here the night before."

"That's not true."

"Sure it is."

"You were gone when I got up."

"That doesn't mean I wasn't asleep in the night."

Maud was disturbed by Lovely's story and she didn't know what the sheriff would make of it. But she didn't really think her father took Lovely with him to kill the Mounts. Lovely wouldn't have been much help. If he'd taken anybody, it would've been Ryde. She still didn't know about that. She looked to the sun. It was a crimson ball of fire in the west.

4

Maud wasn't ready to see Booker. She was afraid of lying to him and being found out. For two days, she tended the animals, swept the yard, chopped weeds, canned until she ran out of lids, and scrubbed clothes on a board until her knuckles looked like strawberries. When she finally let up, she bathed standing in the tub by the pump, looking out over the wild toward the river. Her mind spun away from her labors and the killings, and tilted toward Booker. A tingle arose. Then a physical sensation gripped her so hard, she ran a hand down to the patch beneath her stomach before she recognized what she was doing. At the first shudder of relief, her mind came to her. She realized she was butt naked in broad daylight and her own brother was on the far side of the wood fence reading a book on the porch. He could see her head if he looked. She flushed, felt the sky and the wild watching like parents, and quickly stepped out of the tub onto a board. She drew her slip from the fence and pulled it over her head and shoulders. She waited until she felt like her face wouldn't give her away, then tilted the water out of the tub. By the time it had made the dirt look like rolled dough, she'd made up her mind to ride Booker's horse to the potato barn the next morning.

• • •

At the schoolhouse ruins, she saw Booker in the distance talking to a man. A sack of potatoes sat on the ground between them.
Close by, a woman sat in a buckboard and a child was standing
in its bed behind her. Maud used the family of strangers to settle
the feeling in the part of her body that sat in the saddle, and by
the time she reached the buckboard, she thought her face was no
more flushed than it normally would be from riding. She talked
with the woman until the man picked up his sack and turned
toward them.

She and Booker didn't speak until the buckboard pulled out.
Then he said, "I want to show you something." He took Maud's
hand and led her to the side of the barn facing the fields. In its
shade, he kissed her full on the mouth, pulling her hips to his.
When they finally let up, he said, "I have to be with you." He kissed
her again.

Maud had imagined the women in East and West Egg taking
pleasure in men like men took pleasure in them. Those images
confirmed her inborn inclinations. Only ambition hemmed her
in. But against Booker, giving into the pull of love was as easy as
limbs swaying in the breeze, as fish swimming downstream, as
puppies tumbling in play. She pulled her dress up and he slipped
in, their only witness a cow that, before they'd finished, had
turned away.

Once that dam broke, Maud and Booker embarked on easy ways
in the heat of summer days. At every opportunity, they took pleasure in each other's curves and angles, smells and juices. Maud
wanted Booker before sex, during, and also after, when he was
soft and tender, and she was melted into a puddle of love. She
wanted him when they were together and apart, for those days
and for days far away. And Booker, too, seemed as aroused by

love as by sex. He talked with eagerness about how she had awakened him from a life half lived and about a future together that included books, indoor plumbing, electricity, and children. He also confessed how he'd felt hemmed in — not by his wife — but by his job, the community's expectations for a teacher, and by his parents, who had turned to Bible-thumping and teetotaling as they'd aged. He liked having an Indian maiden. Inside, he had an untamed streak himself.

Maud thought Booker hadn't yet figured out that Indian maidens weren't exactly the lovely wildflowers they were made out to be in books. But she didn't mind pretending. She felt that was best. She told Booker her father had gone to look for work in the Seminole oil fields. And she avoided the subject of the Mounts. And so did Booker, except for one conversation when he admitted he'd been shocked by the sheriff's suspicions until he'd realized that he had more reason than anyone to know that the sheriff jumped to conclusions. He apologized to Maud, and she accepted his apology, remarking, "Uncle Ryde's right. Sheriff Talley's not bright."

They used Mustard's bed whenever Lovely was off sparking Gilda, even sometimes when he was around and out in the barn. Once, they didn't hear his footsteps until he hit the planks of the porch, and they had to jump up and hide behind the sheet. After Lovely found them there, whenever Booker was visiting, he started whistling whenever he came back to the house from the barn.

Several days into their bliss, Maud, Booker, and Lovely were sitting on the porch, all three in rockers, because, by then, the heat of the summer even in early evening made chairs useless inside. They each had a feed-store fan in hand. Lovely had Gilda's Bible on his lap. As Booker was telling a story about the Fayetteville superintendent of schools personally holding the Bible for every teacher to make an abstinence vow, they heard a rumble on the road. They turned their heads to see who was coming.

Both cattle guards were closed. The sheriff got out and fumbled with the gates. While he did that, the three on the porch agreed to let Booker do most of the talking. Lovely had grown quieter in the past week, didn't always make sense, and wasn't talking to anybody he didn't have to. Maud was on guard about what she'd seen at the Mounts' and didn't want any of it slipping out under questioning. She'd discussed it with Lovely only enough to be convinced that he hadn't had any part in it and to caution him again about keeping his mouth shut.

Booker was standing by the time the sheriff unfolded from his car and put on his hat. "Sheriff Talley, come on up. Take my chair."

Maud offered the sheriff a dipper of water. He drained it and handed it back. She hung the dipper on a nail on a post and took her seat. The sheriff looked to Maud and Lovely. "I'm a little short of time, so I'll cut to the chase. I've come out here to ask if you've seen yer dad. Laswell, over at the feed store, says he hasn't showed to work in a while."

Booker said, "He's gone to look for work in the Seminole oil fields."

The sheriff looked to Maud. "Which ones?"

"Near Bowlegs."

"Bowlegs. Now that would be . . . ?"

"Close to Wewoka. He's from there."

"Have ya heard from him since he went?"

"He's not high on writing," Maud said.

"Do ya know when he's coming back?"

"If he got work, he'll be staying."

"Do ya know where he's living?"

"He's got a sister over there. He was gonna park himself with her."

"Her name would be?" Talley took a pencil and pad out of his shirt pocket.

"Aunt Matilda."

"Aunt Matilda what?"

"I don't know what she goes by. Her maiden name was Nail. But she's been married a couple of times and may be married again, for all I know. We aren't close to Daddy's people. They're Seminoles."

Booker interjected, "Is there a particular reason you're looking for Mr. Nail?"

The sheriff tilted back in his rocker and rubbed his eyebrow with his eraser. "He ain't been seen since the business down at the Mounts. First, he's in Wagoner trying to buy a dog. Or that's the story. Then he's sparking. And now he's over in Bowlegs working in the oil fields and visiting his sister."

Maud said, "It's normal for Daddy to lay out and around."

The sheriff looked out toward the wild of the river. "That so? He's visited my jail so many times that I've often wished Mustard would go off somewhere else."

Maud's temper rose. She wanted to kick the sheriff for running his mouth in front of Booker. She tapped her foot but held her tongue.

The sheriff turned to Lovely. "How're yer shots going?"

"Got my last one today. I'm sore in the belly but don't have the sickness."

The sheriff took in a deep breath. "Is yer daddy sending home any money?"

"Not yet," Maud said.

"When he does, I'd like to know. Particularly if there's a return address. I told Western Union to call me if Mustard wires anything. I want to talk to him."

"That would be about the Mounts?" Booker said.

"Yes, it would."

"Have you come to any conclusion on that?"

"I've narrowed some things down. We're positive it's them. Neither has showed his face anywhere since. Can't figure out the quilt, though. Don't make sense that somebody would kill them and then burn a quilt."

Maud looked at her hand resting on the arm of her rocker. She made an effort to keep her fingers stretched out. "You think Daddy had something to do with it?"

"He has the motive. And yer uncle Ryde seems particularly jumpy. But I don't want to leap to conclusions." He looked at Booker. "I'm capable of learning."

They watched the sheriff leave through the cattle guards. Then Booker said, "Maybe he's smarter than we thought." Lovely said, "I'd like to find Dad myself. We need to pay Doc for my shots."

Money from Blue's renting their fields wouldn't come in until the crops did. The only money they had was Lovely's wages, and he hadn't been able to work full days. They were more broke than usual. But Maud hadn't mentioned that to Booker. And she didn't want Lovely dwelling on it in front of him. She said, "Show Booker your belly."

Lovely lifted his shirt. His stomach was bruised and covered in welts. "If I had known how bad these shots were, I would've killed the Mounts myself."

Booker said, "I don't know your father well. Do you think it's possible he could have . . . ?"

Maud answered before Lovely could say anything. "Daddy's

more of a fighter than a killer. I think probably somebody unknown got mad over liquor and killed them. They mostly sold poison."

"What about the quilt?" Booker said.

Maud regretted the quilts. And she should've realized that the hogs would finish off the bodies — if she'd just taken the time to locate the pen. She felt dumb over that. "For all we know, they could have burnt the quilt themselves. There wasn't a woman in their house that I know of. And it's not winter. Maybe one of them got sick all over it, and rather than try to wash it, they burnt it. Stranger things have happened. Why don't you come help me close up the chickens?"

Booker wasn't staying at the house overnight. After he took his leave, Maud drew water from the pump and went to the kitchen to wash up the dishes. While she waited for the water to warm, she mulled her predicament. She didn't want Booker knowing any more about the Mounts than he already did. She sure didn't want him knowing she'd found their bodies and thrown the quilts over them. She kicked herself for the quilts once again and felt a tenderness rise in her throat for her grandfather and great-uncle. Neither had spoken a word to her about the situation. They'd done their duty, but she felt certain they'd taken no pleasure in it. Her mind turned to her father. He had, in his own manner, been protecting Lovely by killing the Mounts. It was like him to mess up whatever he did, but it was exceptional for him to take up for Lovely. She could hug him for doing that, but she was glad he was gone and hoped he would stay away. She moved the pan from the burner to the sink, slid the dishes in it, and turned her mind to the future.

She and Booker had a heap of hope. People in Oklahoma were growing rich in ways not possible in Arkansas or most other places in the country. Booker's mouth watered for something bigger than teaching school and peddling, something more exciting than high school ballgames, showing up to church, and Sunday afternoon drives. They agreed they would marry and return to Fayetteville only until the school could get a replacement and they could lay firm plans. Maud was more pleased with that vision than she'd been with anything in her life, and she resolved to write each of her sisters the next morning and tell them about her wedding plans. She'd like her sisters to see her get married, but she also thought there was an outside chance that her father was with Peggy, her sister in Sapulpa. In her mind, she worded Peggy's letter to warn him to stay away.

Her thoughts turned to selling eggs to bring in money. Booker could display them on his wagon and see her as a wife who'd help make a living. But when she glanced over to her egg basket, she recalled she'd collected only eight that evening and twelve the evening before. The heat was affecting the laying, and it would until it broke. As she dried her last dish, she tried to think of another way to get a few dollars. The thought of river rocks popped into her head. Nan had some pretty ones sitting on a windowsill; so did Lucy, in a pot next to her bed. The Arkansas polished stones to all shapes and colors; many were beautiful; some even had holes through them and could be strung. They were there for the picking up. Maud had settled on that course by the time she threw the dish water onto a clump of grass she was trying to nourish in the yard.

The breeze had come up from the river and cooled the evening down. Lovely was hunched over the Bible in the fading light. Maud sat down next to him. He closed the book and said, "I wish I was making the progress with Gilda you're making with Booker."

"She must like your reading."

"She does. But she's all eat up with holding out for marriage."

Maud felt a little stab of guilt at that remark. She would've done the same if . . . well, if she'd been able to, and if Booker hadn't already been married before. Men who were used to having a woman didn't play cat and mouse very long. After the first time, she'd used that to justify her actions. She said, "Have y'all talked about marrying?"

"Not directly. I gotta provide. I need a better job than I have. I've lost time to the shots, but I'll have that field cleared by the end of summer."

"Has Mr. Singer got more work?"

"He'll always hire for the potato fields. But it doesn't pay much."

"How 'bout a job in town? You can figure and read better than most."

Other than meeting Booker's parents, who she was certain wouldn't like her skin, Maud's only concern about marrying was leaving Lovely behind. She worried about him fending alone. But she told herself he was surrounded by family and had two bachelor uncles, three counting Gourd. Blue or Early could move in with him and lighten the load for Lucy after her baby came. But if he married Gilda, even better; he could move in with her family. Most men she knew did that. Maud and Lovely talked more and rocked as darkness grew and the stars came out. The farm was peaceful with their father gone. With the crickets and tree frogs singing, Maud's plans seemed to be unfolding as easily as a rose opens from a bud. She had a feeling of deep contentment when she went inside to bed. Lovely soon followed.

In the middle of the night, Maud awoke with a start. Lovely was yelling. She looked to his cot. His head was on his pillow, but his arms were swinging. She shouted, "Lovely, wake up." She swung her feet to the side of the bed. She'd been sleeping in her father's since he'd gone, and she held on to a post at its foot and shouted at Lovely again. The second shout brought him to a seated position. He shut up. Maud crossed the floor but stopped short of being close enough to be hit if he started swinging again. "You were fighting in your dreams."

Lovely gasped for breath. He swung his feet to the side of his cot and grasped its frame with both hands. "I was drowning, Maud."

"In the river?"

"In the snake lake. Cottonmouths were swimming all over me."

Maud stepped closer. Everybody in the bottoms was afraid of the snakes. But since their mother had died, Lovely and she had been haunted by them. His nightmare was similar to others that plagued them both from time to time. She said, "I'll get you a dipper of water and we'll go back to bed."

"It was the drowning that was so bad."

"Worse than the snakes?"

Lovely rubbed his face with his hands. "The snakes were bad, too, I guess." He shook his shoulders. "But I swear, Maud, I think sometimes I'm losing my mind. Just drowning."

Maud thought he was losing his mind, too. But she didn't know what was causing it or if it would stay lost or come back. She didn't want to frighten him more. She touched his shoulder. "It was only a bad dream, Lovely." She walked to the kitchen and came back with a dipper of water. She held it out to him and sat down on his cot. She described a reoccurring dream she had about them drowning in the flood. When she got back in bed, to get all the drowning out of her head, she focused her mind on the material in Taylor's General Store that she'd picked for her wedding dress.

• • •

The next day, she wrote letters to her sisters and then walked the ruts by Gourd's into the wild. She searched the dirt for new prints, the weeds for signs of passing. But when she got to the Mounts' cow path, she looked the other way and listened to insects and the far-off hum of the river. When the brush along the ruts eventually came to an end, pure sand took over and, at the river's edge, turned in spots to pebbles and rocks. The water was rapid and wild, the sandbar deserted except for an occasional bird. The tracks were those of animals that came in the night. Apparently, a pack of wolves had been there recently, a lone deer and a fawn, a cat larger than a barn one. Maud walked several hours near the river under hot sun. Her skin turned browner and redder.

Within a week, she looked like a fullblood. But she'd picked up stones that would sell. All were rounded by water into ovals or balls; many were multicolored red, brown, and gold; and a few had holes in them. The holey stones would bring the most money, and to make them even more appealing, Maud threaded strips of leather through them. Booker displayed them as necklaces. The project brought in a little money for payments on the shots and necessities, and Maud enjoyed the scavenging. She always took her gun against the snakes and the wolves, but, with the Mounts gone and the allotments closest to the banks belonging to her relatives, there were never any strangers on the sandbar or, really, any people at all. The river was deadly; and the sand, in spots, could suck; but she'd been taught to respect their ways. She often took a fishing pole and returned to the house loaded with dinner as well as with rocks. Booker came every evening, sometimes bringing a paper, and Lovely seemed more like himself. After supper, he cleared out to spark Gilda or visit kin and gave Maud and Booker some space.

Then one evening when she and Booker were lying on Mustard's bed talking about asking Mr. Singer if they could marry on his front porch, they heard a car rumbling down the section line. Booker rolled out of bed and fetched his pants from the floor. Maud rolled out on the other side. Her clothes were at the foot of the bed. She pulled on her drawers and threw her slip and dress over her head. They heard the car idling. Booker walked to the window. "It's Talley again."

Maud slipped behind the sheet, picked up her hairbrush, and looked in the little mirror hanging by a wire on the wall. "Maybe he's found Daddy." She'd heard back from her sister in Sapulpa. If he was there, Peggy hadn't mentioned it.

"Would that be a good thing?" Booker was putting on his shoes.

Maud laid her hairbrush on the top of a crate holding clothes. They hadn't returned to the question of who killed the Mounts since the sheriff's last visit. And she'd convinced herself Booker knew the answer and didn't care. She opened a bottle of lotion he'd given her, poured a dab into her palm, and rubbed her hands together. She said, "We're getting ready to find out."

They were on the porch by the time the sheriff closed the second cattle guard. They offered him a seat and a dipper of water. They talked about the weather, about Amelia Earhart's speaking tour, and about Will Rogers' mock campaign for president. Rogers was a distant cousin of Maud's, and she puffed up a little during that conversation. While she was in that afterglow, Talley slipped in, "I took a little run over to Wewoka and Bowlegs."

Maud looked to Booker to see if he would speak. He looked to her. She blushed. "Did you find Daddy?"

"Nope. Found your aunt. She said she hadn't seen Mustard since '24." He leaned back in his rocker and ran his thumb and fingers over his moustache. He rested his boot on his knee.

Maud was used to silences in conversation and knew she

could wait out any white person. She looked out toward the river. A couple of straggling chickens that hadn't gone to roost were scratching in the dirt close to the front bumper of the sheriff's car. They squabbled over something too far away to be seen from the porch.

Booker said, "He hasn't been back here, has he, Maud?"

She looked at the sheriff. "No. I thought he found work."

"You haven't seen him at all?"

"Nope."

"He's not in the house?"

"No. You can look if you want to."

"He's not in the cellar?"

"He only goes to the cellar if a tornado's on him."

"How about the barn or smokehouse?"

"Look, Talley," Booker interrupted. "Make yourself at home. Check the hen house if you want. You can see for yourself there're no recent tracks around here. Yours is the only car that's pulled in since the last rain. That was a week ago. We wish we knew where Mr. Nail is. He's left Maud and Lovely without much money coming in."

Talley looked down at his boot. "Ryde Foxworth says that if Mustard did kill the Mounts, it wouldn't be any of the law's business. That the Mounts needed killing by someone. I'm betting that with the help of some liquor yer uncle might get to flapping his tongue."

Maud's brow wrinkled. "Does the law usually warn the family that they're arresting someone?"

"Oh, I can have Ryde arrested before you can get up the road to tell it. I'm just trying not to waste good liquor on him. It's hard to come by."

"It's illegal, for one thing," Booker said.

"I've heard that," the sheriff replied. "I'm totally against it my-self. But I recognize its medicinal properties. I was hoping to get some information down here that would make things a little eas-ier for yer girl's aunt and cousins."

Maud's breathing got shallow with dread. She'd not asked her uncle Ryde about the business at the Mounts' and he hadn't vol-unteered any information. She said, "Well, that's mighty nice. But we can't help you. I haven't seen Daddy in some time. Lovely hasn't seen him, either. We thought he went to Wewoka because he'd been talking about it and because his sister's allotment's near there. If he's not there, I don't know where he is. And I'd be sur-prised if Uncle Ryde does."

The sheriff leaned over and picked his hat up off the boards of the porch. He stood and put it on. "Well, that remains to be seen. Nice talking with you all. If Mustard shows, ask him to come see me."

Maud and Booker stayed seated and silent until the sheriff closed the first guard. Then Booker looked at his hands. "Maud, is there anything you'd like to tell me?"

Maud had thought she'd dodged that question. But she had a ready answer. "I don't know if Daddy killed the Mounts. Maybe he did, maybe he didn't. It's not the sort of thing he'd tell me about. I know this, though: If Talley puts Uncle Ryde in jail, Aunt Nan and my cousins will starve to death. Morgan's only twelve. He can't earn a decent wage."

"Do we need to go up there?"

"I'll go alone in the morning. Aunt Nan's too Indian to talk in front of you."

Booker raised his eyebrows. Maud added, "She likes you. She just doesn't talk to white people."

"She talked to me when she bought that bolt of cloth."

"Did she? Or did she use one of the kids?"

Booker looked off toward the river and scratched his cheek. After a moment, he said, "Come to think of it, your female relatives don't have much to say. Why won't they talk?"

"I can't explain Indian ways. Just be glad I'm some white. You'd have a hard time if I wasn't."

"Oh, I would, would I?"

"Yes, Cherokee women have high standards. We only marry into whites to keep y'all from killing us off."

"Well, as it so happens, I was just now thinking about doing terrible things to you."

"Really? Don't forget I carry a gun."

"I'm not afraid." He got up and leaned over Maud with his hands on her rocker's arms. "I'm thinking I need to do some more to take your mind off your worries." He kissed her long and tenderly, and she kissed him back.

The next morning, she awoke to find Lovely hadn't returned in the middle of the night. He'd been so regular for several days that it concerned her. She hoped he'd stayed at the Starrs' and then gone on to work. She could see if he was in the field after she walked to Nan's. She hurried through her morning chores, figuring out how to get far enough away from her cousins for the conversation she planned, and, deciding Renee would be more of a problem than the boys, she carried with her a copy of *The Wonderful Wizard of Oz*.

Renee said her mother was burning trash. And Maud walked around the house to find Nan standing in a field beside a metal barrel with the smoke curling from it like a snake raising its head. She could tell from a distance that her aunt was pensive, and rather than call out as she normally would, she walked through the grass and weeds, listening to them rustle. Maud thought Nan heard her, but she didn't turn. She got right up on the barrel before Nan said, "Did the idjit tell ya he was arresting Ryde?"

"Yeah. How long's he holding him?"

"I hope he lets him go today. We've gotta start picking corn." Nan threw a rag into the fire.

Maud looked at the corn. The stalks were loaded with ears. "What do you think Uncle Ryde's telling Talley?"

"Ryde makes things up as he goes."

"You think they both killed the Mounts?"

Nan picked up a long stick and stirred the fire. "I think Ryde might've been with Mustard. I doubt he pulled a trigger. Ryde can't shoot worth a damn. I have to shoot ever' damn thing 'round here."

"You don't think Uncle Ryde'll tell the sheriff that?"

"He wouldn't turn the bucket over on Mustard. Too partial to him and that would get hisself in trouble." Nan bent down and picked up a pail of dirt. She reached into it, drew out a handful of soil, and threw it on the fire. She threw a second one.

"Have you talked to Grandpa?"

"Ever'day."

"He told you about going down there, I guess."

"He feels bad 'bout them quilts. Feels like he didn't plow that field deep enough."

"He couldn't predict the rain."

"Can most of the time. Smells it."

"Well, I created that problem. Not him."

"We ain't raising you kids fer killing. We're raising ya fer book learning. How's that feller of yers?"

Maud felt relieved by the turn in the conversation. She told Nan that Booker and she were planning on marrying on August

18. And they chewed on the wedding by the fire barrel until Sanders interrupted them, complaining about the way Morgan was treating him.

Maud ate the noon meal with Nan, and while they cleaned up, they talked about Lovely. After that, Maud walked on up the line. Lovely and his mule weren't in the trees by the swale. She went on, and by the time she neared the potato barn, her dress was patched with sweat and she was feeling foolish for walking in the heat of the day.

Booker was sitting on a crate reading a book in the shade of his wagon. When he looked up, she said, "Whatchya reading?"

He looked at the cover like he was discovering the title. "*Leaves of Grass.*"

"You've got good taste in poetry, even if you don't have any manners. Are you gonna offer your lady a seat or are you just gonna sit there?"

"I was thinking maybe a crate wasn't worthy of a certain person's bottom."

Maud looked around. "Don't say *bottom* out loud. Somebody might hear you."

Booker stood up. "And who might that be? That oriole up in the tree?" He pointed to branches not far away.

"Could be. I've got an uncle who thinks birds are his enemies come to spy on him."

"And which uncle might that be?"

"Uncle Gourd."

"Oh, yes, the mysterious one nobody ever sees."

"People see him. He's just laying out with Mrs. Adams. She's got a nicer house. And speaking of laying out, is Lovely's mule in the barn?"

"Didn't he show last night?"

Maud shook her head.

"I should've stayed. I don't like him leaving you down there by yourself." Booker's brow furrowed.

Maud poked her forefinger into his stomach. "I'm not usually by myself. Besides, nothing's going to happen to me now that the Mounts are dead. Worry about something else. Like where Lovely is."

"If I worried about every disappeared man in your family, I wouldn't have any space left in my head," Booker said. But he rolled the canvas down over his wares. They walked to the livestock barn. The mule wasn't there. But she was in the lot beyond it, standing under a tree, flicking her tail. "He's on foot. We know that at least," Booker said.

"Maybe he's visiting the Starrs. He's getting on with Gilda."

"Do we need to go over there?"

Maud would normally go back to the farm and hope Lovely showed for supper. But her conversation with Nan worried her. "Aunt Nan thinks he's still a little off in the head."

"I thought you thought he'd been some better in the last few days."

They were standing in the shade of the livestock barn, looking toward the lot. The day was burning hot; flies and other insects were buzzing. In the distance, Mr. Singer's house sat under trees that shaded it from the sun. It looked peaceful and solid. Maud said, "I do think that. Don't you?"

"Sort of. I haven't known him a long time, though. Your aunt has."

"He's always been a little peculiar. But I don't necessarily see that as a sign of anything. We've both always gone off into other lands in books. Maybe he just wants to be to someplace better than here."

"Ambition's natural in a man. I'd blow my head off if I had to teach school all my life."

"Lovely doesn't have ambition in the usual sense. He dreams more than he calculates about how to get ahead."

Booker brushed the dust with the toe of his shoe. "I don't understand that. I've got to get ahead. I want us to have everything we want. There's no reason we shouldn't. I can make money. I know I can."

Maud placed a palm on Booker's arm. "I don't doubt you for a minute. But today I need to locate Lovely. I'm going to Gilda's."

"I'll take you."

"Can you leave your wagon in the middle of the day?"

"I'll park it behind the potato barn."

They rode into town on separate horses and found Gilda shelling peas in the swing on her parents' front porch. She invited them to sit, went into the house, and brought out lemonade. The three of them fell to talking about the weather and wound slowly enough to the real point of the conversation to be polite in their indirection. Maud said, "We've come into town looking for Lovely."

"Is he in town, do you think?" was Gilda's reply.

"He didn't come home last night. He may've stayed with some of our folks. But he didn't pick up Mr. Singer's mule this morning and he's not at the swale. I'm sort of worried about him."

Gilda's tongue ran over her bottom lip. Her eyebrows closed into a V. "I haven't seen him since Saturday night. He came to supper, and we walked over to the fort. There was a banjo-picking contest over there."

Maud knew Lovely had hitched a ride to town with Early on Saturday. But he'd come home in the middle of the night and had been there Sunday morning. "You didn't see him last night?"

Gilda touched her hair. "No. And I thought he was coming to church on Sunday. He said he would. Daddy held off going until the last minute. But Lovely never showed. Daddy's an usher, so we couldn't wait any longer."

Maud hadn't heard anything about Lovely going to church. And although it might have cost him a little ribbing, it wouldn't have been enough for him to withhold that he was intending to go. But Maud couldn't feature Lovely saying he'd go to church with Gilda and then not showing. She felt a little spike of fear. "That doesn't sound like Lovely. Has he seemed odd to you lately?"

Gilda wore her hair up. Wisps of it had escaped her barrettes. She undid a clasp and swept up a strand. She rotated her head, undid another, and did the same. "Well, to be honest, Saturday night he was agitated and talking about how the Mounts were going to come back and kill ever' last one of you, down to your uncles and aunts. He was fretting something awful about that. We left the fort and walked into town for a soda, but he couldn't sit in the drugstore. Said there were too many people in there. So we walked the planks, looking in windows. But he was so jumpy that it started getting on my nerves. We were out on a date, you know. It was Saturday night."

"Do you think he didn't come back on Sunday because he thought you were mad?" Booker asked.

Gilda bit her lower lip. "I don't think so. We had a long talk. And I felt more sympathetic when I saw how bad off he was. It's embarrassing to say, but he started crying. Does he do that very often?" She looked to Maud.

Maud's thoughts scattered like thrown corn. She figured Lovely must have told Gilda that their father was suspected of killing the Mounts. He would know murder wasn't exactly un- usual news to the Starrs. But Gilda's parents had pretenses. So maybe not. She hoped Gilda wouldn't say any more about the

Mounts. Surely she had enough sense not to do that in front of Booker. Maud was parsing that out when Gilda said, "He does me this way, too. Is that a family trait y'all have?"

"Does you what way?"

"Goes off in his head."

"I'm sorry. I was just thinking. But, no, you're right. Lovely thinks a lot, too. About the crying, I don't know. We lost our mother when we were little. That marked him, I think."

"Daddy's a little afraid for me to be going out with him."

Maud stiffened.

"It's not a big objection, and Daddy's not mean. But it irritated him when Lovely didn't show up for church. And he thinks Lovely's peculiar."

Maud felt relieved Mr. Starr's objection didn't have anything to do with murder. "Peculiar?"

"I shouldn't have said that. I'm sorry, Maud. I can handle Daddy. Or at least Mama can. And she likes Lovely a lot. She's been encouraging him to get a better job. He's book smart. He just doesn't seem to want to get ahead. But I think he would if he had a family."

Maud raised her eyebrows.

"We haven't talked about that much, really. Do you think he's seeing anybody else?"

Maud was relieved by the turn of conversation. "You're the only girl he's ever been stuck on to my recollection. And I would know. He's had little crushes, like all men do." She looked to Booker to see if color was rising in his cheek. It wasn't, and she turned back to Gilda. "But he's stuck hard on you. And, no, I don't think he's seeing anybody else. He hasn't given any hint of that."

"Why would he think the Mounts would come back and kill the whole family?" Booker asked Gilda.

Maud raised her hand before she could stop herself. But Gilda only said, "He didn't say." Maud patted her hair with that hand. She felt thankful Lovely had picked out a Starr. If Gilda knew, she wouldn't say anything. But Maud wanted the subject changed fast. "We think maybe the shots have made Lovely a little touched in the head. But he's seemed better to me lately." She turned to Booker. "We ought get on with hunting for him." She turned back to Gilda. "If you see him, could you send him home? And tell him to wait there if we're not back?"

Booker and Maud rode as far as the center of town and stopped at the hitching rail in front of Berd's Drugstore. Booker told Maud to stay on her horse, but he dismounted and tied up his reins. He said, "Maud, it seems you haven't given me the full story on the Mounts. I'm going to go inside and buy us a couple of Coca-Colas. When I get back, I want you to spill the beans."

"You don't want me to come, too?"

"You'll get distracted and distract me. I want you to think hard on what you want to say. I'm tired of being left in the dark."

"I can't tell you here." She looked around. There were people out and about. She knew some of them.

"I'll get the soft drinks, anyway. I'm thirsty again. I'm sweating everything out." He turned and walked away.

They rode to a tree in a vacant lot next to the First National Bank. The shade was on the side away from the street, and the roots were large and worn with sitting. Booker and Maud settled on them, their backs to the town. She took a long sip through a straw. Then she took another. Booker said, "You planning on draining the bottle before you say anything?"

"I'm hot."

"Well, then, take your time." Booker laid his hat on another root and leaned against the tree.

Maud could tell that he was determined and that she was going to have to tip the bucket somewhat. But she hoped she wouldn't have to turn it all the way over. "I didn't see Daddy after we found out John Mount had been bit by a dog. I can't totally testify to his thinking. But it was pretty clear to everyone that the Mounts tried to give us rabies. I'm guessing he killed them because of that. They deserved it."

"You know for sure he did it?"

Maud sipped again. She sighed. The day was so warm and the air so still even the shade felt hot. Or maybe the hot was inside her, she didn't know. "Well, he's suddenly disappeared."

"Anything else?"

It was clear Booker was going to dig until he turned something up. Maud put her palm under her bottle, gathered the moisture there, and wiped it onto her forehead. She took a deep breath. "I found his lighter down at the Mounts."

Booker leaned away from Maud. His eyebrows met in a V. "You were down there?" His voice was louder than before.

"I went down there. That's where I'd been the day you brought the doctor out to see Lovely."

"Why on earth did you do that?"

"I was worried Lovely had the rabies. I wanted to see how John Mount was doing."

Booker brought his bottle to his forehead. He rolled it a little. When he brought it back down, he shook his head and said, "Crap, Maud. You could've been killed."

"I know how to keep from getting killed, Booker. I'm not a fool. I didn't walk up and knock on the door."

"What did you do?"

"I laid out on a sand hill and watched the house."

"How'd you find the lighter?"

Maud didn't want to tell Booker about the buzzards. He was upset enough. She was thinking about how to justify finding the bodies without explaining the birds or looking too daring when he interrupted her thoughts with "Tell me the truth now, Maud. Don't cogitate something up."

"I'm not cogitating, Booker," she said, louder than she'd intended. "I'm trying to remember. When you run up on bodies, it's distressing. You get excited and it's hard to recall anything right."

"You actually saw the bodies then?"

Maud hadn't meant to say that. Booker was pulling more things out than she wanted revealed. She wished he could leave well enough alone. She said, "I think something just bit me." She stood up and scratched the back of her leg.

Booker turned his face up to her. He had a hard look she'd never seen. And he didn't say anything. She thought she could wait him out, but then he tucked his lower lip between his teeth and squinted one eye. It was clear he wasn't going to speak.

"I didn't kill them, Booker. I just saw them dead."

"I wasn't implying you killed them. I'm just trying to get the story straight in my mind. It's a lot different from what you've been telling. What happened next?"

"I came on back to the house. You know the rest."

Booker was sitting with his legs spread, his forearms on his knees, his Coca-Cola bottle in both hands. He lifted the bottle and finished it off. "I have to say, Maud, this doesn't sit well with me. What about the mystery quilt? Do you know anything about that?" He threw the bottle into a patch of weeds.

"The quilt in the still pot?" Maud asked, buying time.

Booker put a hand on the ground and stood up. He looked Maud full in the face. "Yes, that quilt."

Maud could feel herself blush. She hoped her skin was so dark it didn't show, but to get away from the stare, she turned, walked over to Booker's bottle, and picked it up. "John Berd gives money for these."

"Fine. Save it. Are you going to answer my question? Or are you going to scour the lot for more bottles?"

Maud wanted to say, *I'm going to do what I please.* But she caught herself by holding her tongue between her teeth. She swallowed hard. "The Mounts lived like pigs, Booker. There was no woman in the house. That they burnt things instead of washing them isn't surprising to me."

"You're sure?"

"No, I'm not sure. I wasn't there. And I'm getting tired of the third degree. Can't you just let this be?"

Booker picked up his hat and put it on his head. "I'll need to think on this, Maud."

"We need to find Lovely. That's what's in front of us now."

"I agree. What do you want to do with your bottles?"

They dropped the bottles by Berd's, but they didn't find Lovely or anybody who'd seen him. They returned to the potato barn, left one of the horses there, and rode on to the bottoms. They put the chickens up, milked the cow, and ate supper, but they didn't make love. They'd settled on the front porch when they saw a wagon filled with Maud's old people and Blue headed their way. Booker took Maud inside the house and kissed her. But when everybody was seated, he said he'd better be going. He turned at the last cattle guard and waved his hat in the air. Maud, sitting on a step, returned his wave. Then Booker galloped away.

The porch conversation quickly turned to Ryde being arrested and Lovely's whereabouts, but the stream of talk meandered. Maud's grandfather told stories of Sanders Cordery's disappearances that Maud had never heard. She thought they were a little outlandish. But they confirmed that the men of the family had laid out for generations. It was in their blood. And after that, the talk moved to Gourd enjoying Mrs. Adams' hospitality in town. The conversation continued as the breeze cooled the air and the stars came out. Visiting broke up later than usual, and Viola stayed behind to give Maud company during the night.

When Maud awoke the next morning, her great-aunt was stirring the fire in the stove and cleaning her teeth with a twig. They made breakfast and ate together. While they were drinking coffee, Viola said, "Them men think Lovely's jist off learning the ways of nature. They might be right about that or they might not. Nan knows him a lot better than me. She thinks he may be funny turned, and not in a good way."

Maud thought Nan had probably said more to Viola than she'd said to her. What she didn't know made her uneasy. She was trying to calm herself into a response when Viola added, "Let's turn the cup. I can read the future better that way."

Maud tried not to let any expression show. But she was as startled as if a bird had flown up in her face. She'd heard about cup turning all of her life, but she'd only done it as a child in play. She was curious, but she also considered the practice an old-fogy superstition or maybe some mysterious Creek Indian way. Still, Viola's father was a legend. Maud figured he'd passed down some of his secrets. And she wanted to find Lovely and didn't want to insult her great-aunt. She drained her cup and handed it to Viola.

Viola reached for Maud's saucer, held Maud's cup over it, and gave it a quick shake. The grounds plopped out. Viola gently shoved the saucer out of the way and peered into the cup. She bit her lower lip. A humming sound arose from deep in her chest. She clicked her teeth together and hummed some more. Finally, she sat back, looked to the ceiling, and frowned. "I'm not getting anything about Lovely."

"What are you getting?" Maud felt stupid as soon as she'd said that. But it was out of her mouth; she couldn't take it back.

"Jist diddly-squat." The old woman looked around the room. "I better be getting on. Lucy will've cooked the breakfast, but people'll want dinner later on. She's getting so full in the stomach, she can't be tending to men all day." Viola pushed up from the table. "If Lovely don't show this evening, you come on our way. No need for ya to stay down here alone. Even with the Mounts gone, it's not the best situation."

Maud told Viola she might take her up on the invitation, but she had no intention of doing so. Booker would be back at the end of the day, and with Lovely gone, he'd spend the night. She didn't anticipate being lonely or afraid. She figured her great-aunt knew that and was just being polite.

Maud spent her day doing chores and reading. And she was in the hen house gathering eggs in the late afternoon when a shadow fell through the door onto the dirt floor. She froze. She hadn't noticed any change in the level of chicken noise, hadn't heard a car, a wagon, or hooves. She picked one more egg out of a nest, held it in her hand, and turned. Lovely was in the door frame. "You scared the dickens out of me! I've a good mind to throw this egg at your head. Where have you been?"

He took a long breath. "Maud, something's happening to me."

Maud was in a narrow space between two walls of nests and the wire in front of the roost. Lovely was blocking the door. She suddenly felt trapped. "Step back. Let me out of here."

Lovely stood still. Maud said the same thing again before he turned from the door. In front of the chicken house, she said again, "Where've you been?"

"Away." Lovely rubbed the back of his neck, rotated his head. "Are you hurt?"

He seemed to think about that. "Don't think so. Not in the usual way. But I think those shots did something to me."

"They were hurtful. No doubt about that. Let's go to the house. Let me take a look at you."

Maud set the egg basket on the kitchen table and came back out to the porch where Lovely was sitting on the edge. She looked down at him. His neck and hands were dirty. So were his clothes. His overalls had a new hole in the knee. "Have you been in the wild? You didn't even take a gun."

He looked out into the dirt. "I was down on Blue's allotment. Remember that place he took us when Mama died? The trees in the circle? I always liked it there. It's cool under those trees."

Maud stepped off the porch onto the ground close to Lovely's knees. He seemed hollowed out in the cheeks. His face was as dirty as his neck and hands. She said, "It's cool under the live oak tree. And not nearly as far. You need to get in the tub."

"I don't want a bath."

"You're as dirty as a dog in a dust hole."

"I want some food."

"I'll get you some. But you need to bathe. Go out there by the pump and clean yourself up. I'm not letting you in the house the way you are. Mama'd have a fit."

"Is Mama here?"

"You know what I mean."

"Maud . . ."

"Go on now. Go to the pump. I'll get you a bar of soap." Maud stepped back to the porch and went in the kitchen door. She came back out with soap and Lovely's second pair of overalls. He was still seated. She nudged him with her shoe. "Here, take these.

And don't go off anywhere. I'll be inside cooking. Come in when you're clean."

Lovely washed up, but he didn't come in. Maud brought plates of food to the porch. She watched the road for Booker as they ate, let the subject of where Lovely had been alone, and told him what had gone on while he'd been away. She left out visiting Gilda and her conversation with Booker under the tree. But she left in looking for him and Viola spending the night and turning the cup.

Lovely didn't ask questions. After he'd eaten two plates of food, he got up from his chair and walked to the edge of the porch. He looked down at the ground. His silence made Maud uneasy. And she was becoming irritated with Booker for being late. She, too, got up from her chair. She piled Lovely's plate on top of hers, went to the kitchen, and poured water from a bucket into the washing pan. She placed the pan on top of the stove and stoked the fire to heat the water. Then she scraped their scraps into the slop bucket. She thought she knew the time, or thereabouts, but she wished she had a clock to confirm her sense of the sun. But she mostly wished she knew what was holding Booker up. She hoped he didn't turn out to be one of those men who was never around when they were needed, and to distract herself, she was counting in her head which of the men in her family fell into that category when Lovely came into the main room and started making noises. She turned to the door.

Lovely had thrown his sheet onto their father's bed. He was breaking his cot down. "What're you doing?" Maud said.

"Moving my bed."

"To the tree?"

"I'm gonna sleep in the chicken house."

"You're not sleeping in the chicken house. That's a fool thing to do."

"It's safer in there."

"Safer than what?"

Lovely looked around the room. "Safer than here."

"There's nothing here to fear. Daddy's gone."

"Where'd he go?"

"I wish I knew. You're not going to the chicken house."

Lovely continued folding his cot. Maud grabbed his shoulder. He jerked loose from her grip and backed away. "It's not your bed."

"Of course it's not." Maud ran a hand through her hair. "But why on earth sleep in the chicken house?"

"Are you not listening to me? It's safer in there."

"What do you think's going to happen to you in your own home?"

Lovely ran his hand over his mouth. "I'm not sure."

Maud stepped toward him. "Look, you've been poorly. You're not yourself. But you're with me now. I'm not gonna let anything happen to you. Remember how I took care of you when you had the throw-ups? I'll take care of you again. Nothing's going to hurt either one of us. If you don't want to sleep inside, you can take your cot to the porch and sleep out there. Or you can sleep under the tree. But you can't sleep in the chicken house. It's dirty. And you'll upset the chickens."

"They won't care."

"They will, too. They'll stop laying. They've almost stopped because of the heat as it is. We need eggs. You can't be irritating the hens."

Lovely seemed to consider that. Then he unfolded his bed and Maud handed him his sheet. "Why don't you go on out to the porch? There's still some light to read. Get your Bible or one of the books Booker brought. He's coming soon. He'll be glad to see you."

Lovely turned and walked out the door. As soon as Maud felt he'd stay in his rocker and not wander off, she turned back to the kitchen. The water in the washing pan was moving with the heat. She tested it with her finger and set to washing dishes.

Booker hadn't come by sunset. And Maud sat in a rocker long after Lovely had brought his cot out to the porch and fallen asleep. The moon was dark. She finally went inside and lay on her father's bed. She lay there all night, fighting to sleep, winning toward morning, but waking to the first crow of the cock. In the gray of dawn, the chest stood against the wall like a hunkered bear. The sheet hung like a ghost. Maud felt queasy. She rolled over and closed her eyes. That didn't help. She got up feeling sluggish, wished she'd had more sleep, and checked on Lovely. He was still knocked out on his cot when she went to do her business.

She came back in, fed kindling into the stove, stoked up a fire, and poured flour into a bowl for biscuits. She was cutting lard into the flour when she suddenly felt like she was going to throw up. She made it to the side of the porch. Then she went to the pump and washed her mouth out. Lovely was up by then. She told him he needed to make the biscuits and fry the eggs and side meat if he wanted to eat. Then she sat on the porch and rested her head on the back of her rocker until he called her. She slid into a chair at the kitchen table and ate half a biscuit. That made her feel better. She went to the main room and lay on the bed. She quickly fell to sleep.

She woke sweating with the heat. Her first thought went to Booker, her second to Lovely. She went outside. Lovely was nowhere to be seen. She came back in. Next to the Calumet tin on the kitchen table was a note in Lovely's hand. He'd milked the cow and gone to work. She felt relieved. She pulled the pan of biscuits from the oven and ate two with some honey and a piece of side meat. She dressed and let the chickens out. She took her rifle from the corner and walked the lane to the road.

She went right past Nan's without going in and without, apparently, being seen. She saw Lovely and the mule pulling a log toward a pile. At the cross of the section lines, she checked their mailbox. It was as empty as usual, except for a flyer addressed to the Beechers and misplaced in their box. She took the flyer to the Beechers' door and talked to Mrs. Beecher about the weather and the crops, but she turned down an offer of buttermilk. Then she walked on. When she got to the ruins of the school, she barely noticed them because her eyes were focused ahead, searching for the rolls of blue. She didn't see them or the wagon. The potato barn grew bigger and bigger.

She was close enough to the barn to smell the potato stink when a man she'd never seen came out. He looked at her rifle. She said, "It's for the snakes."

"Sometimes they lay in the spuds," he said.

"Do you work in the barn?"

"Not usually. I work the fields. But the feller who was selling the spuds has up and gone."

Maud felt like she was going to sink to the ground. She steadied herself with her rifle. "Where to?"

The man scratched his head. "Don't rightly know."

"Is Mr. Singer in?"

"I reckon. I ain't seen his Packard go out. You want some spuds?"

Maud shook her head. She held her breath through the potato barn and walked out the other side. The Singer house was painted white. It was double storied, sat facing south, and had a large back porch. A summer kitchen sat not far behind the house; a wisp of smoke curled from a chimney. Maud climbed the back steps and knocked on the door. Inside the screen, she saw a long hall and the back of a staircase. She heard footsteps descending the stairs. The outline of a woman was coming her way. At the door, the woman said, "Can I help ya?"

Maud had seen the woman before when she'd borrowed books and returned them, but she didn't know her by name. "I'm Maud Nail. I'd like to see Mr. Singer if he's in."

The woman bit her lower lip. She was a Negro. She was wearing a white apron that went down past her knees and her hair was done up in a red kerchief. She held a broom in her right hand. "I'll see ifin he's around. But ifin he is, leave yer gun on the porch."

Maud propped her rifle against a window frame, turned toward the summer kitchen, and clasped her hands behind her back. She stood there, straining to hear what was going on inside the house. But the sound of a tractor prevented that. She was caught by surprise when a voice behind her said, "Maud, I suppose you're looking for Mr. Wakefield."

Maud turned as quickly as if she'd been tapped on the shoulder by a finger from the grave. Mr. Singer was standing inside the screen. He was slighter than she last recalled, and through the screen, he looked pale. He opened the door and stepped out. Maud wanted to step back, but she was at the edge of the porch as it was and she didn't want to step down. She put her hand on a post.

Mr. Singer had on a white shirt, its cuffs rolled up to midforearm. He took an envelope out of his pocket. "He left this for you."

Maud reached for the envelope. "Thank you."

Mr. Singer pursed his lips. He looked off over Maud's head but didn't move. She felt her hand trembling. She didn't have a pocket to put the letter in, and she didn't want to open it in front of Mr. Singer. She said, "Is he going to be gone for long?"

Mr. Singer seemed to consider that question. Then he said, "You'll probably know more than I do when you read the letter." He paused, said, "Good to see you," and turned back into the house.

Maud grabbed her gun and left the porch quickly. She veered away from the potato barn to avoid its odor and another conversation with the man she'd talked to earlier. She chose a path that went up a rise and ended at the highway near the Arkansas River bridge. She'd crossed the road all of her life, but she was rarely afoot that far west, and she heard the roar of the water and the sounds of traffic on the planks. When she got near the road, she stopped in the shade of a tree and stared at the envelope. Her future was in it. Booker's hand had written her name across the front; his tongue had licked the flap. Maud started to open the letter right there but hesitated. She was a long way from home on foot. What if it said something she couldn't bear? She leaned against the tree, then sunk to a root at its trunk. She heard a car rattling the planks on the bridge. She watched it pass. She looked at the letter in her hand, studied the writing for any sign it could give.

After a while, she reached inside her dress, undid a safety pin, and fastened the envelope to her slip over her heart. She sat under the tree until a wagon and three more cars passed, all from the direction of Muskogee. Booker had gone over there to pick up more wares on more than one occasion, and Maud began telling herself that was where he'd gone again. She got up from the root, walked the road to the edge of the bridge, and looked at the planks stretching to the far side. She stayed there until another car came onto the bridge, and then she crossed the road quickly before it went by. She walked a path down to where an old ferry had been.

Maud had ridden the ferry as a child and knew that Mr. Singer had hired her grandfather to steer it when he'd first arrived in Indian Territory. She envisaged those days as she walked deeper into the bottoms, forcing her thoughts away from the letter by using her imagination as she always had to carry her away from her father's drinking, her mother's death, and the dust and hard work.

She hadn't walked the path from the river to her mother's allotment very often but she knew the way. When she finally came through the field behind the chicken house, she was weary and her feet hurt to her shins. Lovely was sitting on the edge of the porch. When she got to him, he said, "Where the dickens have you been?"

"You lay out. Can't I do the same?"

"You can, if you are of a mind. I was just thinking about supper. You weren't here when I came in for dinner."

"I wish men would learn to cook."

"I had some biscuits and side meat. That's all I was getting anyway."

"Did you take the mule back to Mr. Singer's?"

"She's in the pasture over there." Lovely pointed with his thumb.

"Was Booker's wagon at the potato barn when you got her this morning?"

Lovely's brow furrowed. "I don't reckon it was. Has he gone off somewhere?"

Maud sat down on a step close to Lovely's leg. "Seems that he has."

"Well, he'll be back. What's for supper?"

"Have you picked anything from the garden?"

"Not yet."

"Do that, and I'll cook it up. You're lucky I'm hungry myself."

Maud watched Lovely's back as he walked away from the porch. When he got to the garden gate, she unpinned the envelope from her slip and held it in her hand. Her name was written in ink; her sweat had smeared it some. She placed her thumb over the smear. If she opened the letter, she would know her fate. She felt as certain of that as she was of the cock crowing at dawn. She turned the envelope over, moved her thumb to the fold. Both the thumb and the hand holding the envelope trembled. She bit her lip. A cow mooed in the distance. A small toad hopped out from under the house. Maud got up, opened the screen, and went inside. The curtains were drawn, the room dark. She went to the chest and opened her drawer. Her little handbag was in there. She undid its clasp and tucked the letter inside.

Maud was limp from her walk and from lack of sleep. She followed the sun to bed, slept soundly through the night, and awoke at the first crow in gray morning light. She was again cutting lard into flour when nausea hit her. She got as far as the yard and threw up there. She washed out her mouth at the pump and cupped her breasts in her palms. They felt tender. Her visitor should be on her.

She walked back to the house. She kept track of her cycle, the dates of plantings, and the numbers of eggs with notes on the calendar on the front room wall. She took the calendar off its nail, flipped to the previous month, and counted. Forty-one days. She was late, but she wasn't that regular; and Booker always pulled out, had never not. She bit her lower lip.

The door banged. Lovely sank to a chair at the table. Maud went back to making biscuits. They talked a little and eventually ate. Then Lovely took off to the pasture to get the mule. Maud let out the chickens, milked the cow, and did her inside chores. By that time, the heat was too high to work in the garden, and thoughts of Booker were filling her head until she felt like it was busting. She was afraid of the letter he'd left her and wanted out of the house and away from it. She picked her rifle out of the corner and decided to see if her uncle Ryde had escaped the sheriff.

She found Nan in her side yard at her kettles, washing clothes. Ryde was back at home in the cornfield with Morgan and Renee. She pitched in to help Nan, and by the time the clothes were flapping in the wind with a noise that sounded like they were being paddled, she felt better than she had in a couple of days. They went to the porch to rest. Andy was asleep in a wagon in the shade. Sanders was building a stick fort on the side of the house away from the wind. They positioned their chairs so they wouldn't be covered by blown-up dust, shelled beans, and talked. Eventually, like Maud had hoped, Nan asked about Booker. She told her the full story, holding back only the counting of her days.

Nan told stories about various men in the family laying out, and she told them with such good humor that Maud felt reassured. But after that, Nan said, "Do you remember yer first cousin, Able?"

"Sort of. He's not around much anymore."

"He ain't around at all. He's up in Vinita."

Able was, Maud believed, her aunt Sarah's next to oldest child. Sarah had married at thirteen and started having children a year later. Some of her ten kids were a good bit older than Maud, and Sarah had lived in Muskogee since before she and Lovely were born. Maud didn't know those cousins as well as she did her others. But she did know that the ones she'd seen recently had cars and went to college, facts that gave her hope. She said, "Is there a college up there?"

"Don't know about that. There's a hospital fer people who are tetched in the head."

Maud sucked her breath in and looked toward the side of the porch. She could see the top of Sanders' head. She looked back down to her hands. "Why are you telling me this?"

"Figured you didn't know it. Happened 'bout the time Lila died. You was little and grieving. And nobody talks about it much now. But it nearly broke yer aunt Sarah's heart. She can't get over it."

"Why'd she do it then?"

"His daddy did it. Sarah fought it. But I believe Carter waz right. Hadn't been right about much in my book, but right about that. Able got to acting wild. Not jist the usual wild. But talking to people who weren't there and seeing things. He got hard to handle. He was already big. Eighteen or nineteen and well over six foot. And he got one of his little sisters by the head. I can't remember now which one. But he wouldn't let go, and he nearly broke her neck before the rest of them boys got him off her. That did it for Carter. You know, he's a successful man. He always ran around on Sarah, and then up and left her for good. But he's taken care of his kids. Is sending little Early and Buddy to college. Gonna send them to law school. But he sent Able to Vinita. I 'spect he had to."

"Does it run in families?"

"Don't know. Don't know what it is, neither. But it's peculiar."

After that, Nan moved to talking about a bull her uncle Coop had had that wouldn't mount any cow. Maud wasn't sure what the bull had to do with Lovely or Able, and she was trying to figure out if anything more than peculiarity linked the stories together when Lovely and his mule came toward them on the line. Ryde and his older kids came in shortly after that. They all ate together, and when the meal was over, the wind died down, and Ryde and Lovely went to the porch and the children to the yard while Nan and Maud cleaned up. After that, the two women settled with their legs dangling over the edge of the porch. That was when Ryde said, "Heard anything from Mustard?"

Maud looked to Lovely to answer. But Lovely looked to her. She said to her uncle, "No. Have you?"

Ryde was cleaning his fingernails with his knife. He scraped under the nail on his thumb. "He might need to stay away. The sheriff's looking fer something on him. So far, his only clue is the burnt quilt." Ryde arched his eyebrow at Maud.

"That was stupid. I wasn't thinking."

"You happen to mention it to anyone?"

"Not outside the family." She recalled her conversation with Booker. Her mind had gone to his letter when her uncle said, "We didn't kill John. Claude did."

Lovely said, "Why would he kill his own brother?"

"Accident. Trying to kill yer daddy. Missed. Shot John instead."

Maud licked her lips. She wanted to hear the story, but she was also pulled in the opposite direction. Renee was sitting in a wheelbarrow, reading a book. Morgan was pitching rocks toward a mark in the dirt. Sanders was picking the rocks up and bringing them back to Morgan. Any of them might be listening. It was Lovely who asked, "How'd Claude get killed?"

Ryde pulled a hand-rolled cigarette from his pocket. He pinched one end and put the cigarette in his mouth. He picked his lighter up from the porch, lit up, took a deep draw, and leaned forward in his chair. He spoke softly. "I'm not saying we didn't go down there to kill 'em both. We did. They both did the deed with the dog. We got that from a reliable source. But Mustard wanted 'em to know who waz killing 'em and why.

"We laid out at a distance and saw John going into his outhouse. When he come out, yer daddy showed hisself. He told John he waz gonna kill him fer giving Lovely the rabies, and held his gun up. When he did, a shot rang out, and John jist stood there wide eyed. A red patch appeared on his shirt, jist like somebody had throwed a ripe tomato at him. He waz completely stunned. So waz we. We jumped back in the trees. I stayed there shouting insults to distract the shooter, and yer daddy took off 'round about. John waz still standing, and he started walking. To tell ya the truth, I thought about shooting him again. But I got all these kids, and, anyway, he waz leaning and sorta crisscrossing. I could tell he waz gonna sink to his knees. Meanwhile, Mustard cut up the rise, went back down again, and took Claude by surprise. Mustard said he waz jist standing at the corner of the house looking toward John, still as a tree, strickenlike.

"After they both waz down, Mustard put another bullet in each one of 'em so they wouldn't suffer, and we moved 'em together, tried to cover our tracks, and got out of there. If we'd been smart, we would've let the hogs out on 'em ourselves. But by the time we got to thinking straight, we couldn't risk going back."

Maud was a little stunned by the story, but it wasn't far off from what she'd imagined, and she felt thankful it wasn't any worse. She didn't want her cousins going hungry because their daddy was in jail, and she was glad to hear that her uncle had some thought for his family. As for her father, well, maybe he was off in the oil fields or in No Man's Land getting rich. She hoped so. She was only worried that she'd said too much to the sheriff. She should have sent him in another direction. "Do you know where Daddy is now?"

"Said he waz headed toward his sister's. But the sheriff didn't find him, so I told him he went to the Osage Hills." Ryde chuckled and coughed at the same time. "Talley don't know how much Mustard hates them particular Indians."

5

By the time Maud and Lovely rode home, stars
blanketed the sky. Maud, swaying on the mule, felt dozy. When
they stopped at the cattle guard, she jerked full awake and
grabbed Lovely's arm to slide off. She opened and closed the gate
and walked in front of the mule to the next one. But even had she
been alert, her thoughts were too tumbled to sort. When she got
to the house, she fell straight to bed.

She woke the next morning feeling sick. And three days in a
row were too unusual not to arouse her suspicion. She told Lovely
to cook and went to the garden to avoid the smells of breakfast.
She felt both happy and panicked while plucking weeds. She filled
almost half of a bushel basket. Then she moved to picking cherry
tomatoes. She was tempted to eat one but was afraid it would
make her sick. She picked a passel of them and set them on top of
the weeds.

After Lovely rode off, Maud quit working and looked toward
the house. It hadn't felt empty to her with her father gone, and
staring at its gray boards and tin roof, she realized that was because Booker had taken his place. She placed a hand on the front
of her dress. Under it and her slip could be a little seed that held

her and Booker together. The breeze whipped her skirt against her legs. She wished the wind would lift her off her feet and carry her high enough to see the entire bottoms and the Arkansas River, to see the water cut beneath the foothills, coil to the Mississippi, and flow to the sea. Maud stood, her hand on her stomach, held by her vision. She walked toward the house, her basket on her hip, feeling eternity inside her.

In the kitchen, she discovered that Lovely hadn't washed the dishes. Every bowl they had was dirty. She smelled coffee. It nauseated her. She went back out to the porch, plucked the tomatoes out of the basket, and set them in rows against the wall. Then she walked to the chicken house and dumped the weeds behind it. She came back, went in the main room door, and set the basket on the floor. She opened her drawer in the chest, pulled out her little handbag, unsnapped the clasp, and drew out Booker's letter. Before she closed the drawer, she took out a handkerchief, too.

She chose the rocker that always stayed on the porch. But as soon as she sat, she felt the wind getting gustier. It hadn't rained in a while, and the gusts picked up the dust into brown swivels that danced like dirty little ghosts in the yard. Grit hit her face; dust hit her eye. She squinted and realized the wind was rolling the little tomatoes across the porch like they were being pushed from behind. She set her handkerchief and envelope down by her chair and put her handbag on top of them. She went inside for the basket.

She came back out and began scooping up the tomatoes. They'd scattered in such a disorganized fashion that she recalled the baby toads that lived under the house and around the troughs. One tomato rolled over the side of the porch, bounced on the ground, and burst open. A chicken ran and made a grab at it. Maud said, "Take it." She picked up a tomato with a little brown spot and tossed it to the hen. The wind lifted her dress. Her skirt hit her in the face. She batted it down and sniffed. The wind was carrying more than dust. She looked to the sky. Dark clouds were rolling over. She felt thankful for them and scooped up more tomatoes that were rolling toward the edge of the porch. She turned to pick up her letter, but her handbag had fallen over. The handkerchief was lodged against a rocker. The letter wasn't there.

Little red tomatoes rolled in all directions. Maud paid no attention to them. Her eyes searched the yard and the air. The wind was blowing toward the garden. She looked to it. A white rectangle was caught against the fence. She scrambled down the steps. She tripped. She flew over the bottom step, hit the dirt with the heels of her palms. She sprung up and ran.

She was within ten paces of the fence when a strong gust of wind shot the envelope straight up. It whirled and dipped over her head. She reached for it, even though it was twice as high as her open hand. It glided like it had wings. It soared straight up again and turned high in a twist. It rode on a current of air toward the lane and dipped again. It hit a bramble and stuck. Maud felt grateful for thorns. She said, "Stay right there," and ran toward the bush. But as she did, she was pelted with drops of rain the size of quarters. They stung in their falling, but she didn't care. Her eyes were glued to the letter. It stayed stuck on the bush. She jumped the hump of the lane. She grabbed the envelope.

The first thing she saw was her name, written in bold blue ink, streaking into rivulets that looked like blue icicles hanging off a roof on a bitter day. Maud tore open the envelope at its end. She drew a single page out. It was thin paper. Rain drops pelted it. She started reading at the top, "Dear Maud." In the first line, "I want to" was clear; after that, a circle of melted ink. Another clear word stood out here and there. One was "later," another "maybe." A word that could be "would" or "should" melted down the page into another word that she took for "horse," but could've been "house." She clutched the letter and envelope to her breast, sunk down on her knees in the dirt, and fumbled to get her safety pin unfastened. Her fingers crumpled the paper as they worked. The pin drew blood. She stuck it through the paper. It tore. She snapped the pin closed. She put her hand over her breast to protect the letter and raised her face to the sky. She yelled, "Damn it, damn it, damn it!" A clap of thunder shook her so hard that it seemed like the ground was quaking in dance.

By the time she got to the house, she was soaked. She tore the letter again trying to get it unpinned. Her fingers trembled as she smoothed it out on the table. Her palm was wet. It smeared the writing even more. Drops fell from her hair and her dress. Every sentence was smeared. She tried to read what she could. But the more she hovered over the letter, the wetter it got. Her tears mixed with the raindrops. She crumbled the envelope in her fist.

Maud was in the barn sitting under the scythe when Lovely came in on the mule. Her knees were drawn up, her head cradled in her arms, her face hidden. She didn't look up. He led the mule into a stall, came out, and said, "It's rained so hard the swale's crossing the road." Maud didn't answer. "Did you hear me?"

Maud had heard Lovely come into the barn and had heard him speaking. But his voice sounded like it was coming from a long, long way away, maybe as far as the other side of the river. And his words didn't sound connected to one another. She couldn't raise her head. Lovely laid his hand on her arm. It felt cold and rough.

She woke up in the big bed. The coal-oil lamp on top of the chest was lit. It cast a yellow light and long shadows. Lovely was sitting on the edge of his cot. A form was huddled in a rocker by the door. At first Maud thought the form was Booker. She called his name. But when the form stood up, it didn't stand tall, and it had on a dress and an apron. Viola said, "Snakes swimming the section line. No good out there tonight." She put her hand on Maud's forehead.

Maud turned her face to her pillow. Viola said, "Lovely, go out on the porch. I'm gonna undress her now."

Maud woke again in daylight. Sounds were coming from the kitchen, but so were smells, and when the smell of coffee hit her stomach, she bolted up in bed like she'd been sharing it with a rattler. She hit the door with the palm of her hand. She didn't have anything to throw up, but she retched anyway, and when she finished, she headed to the pump. Her feet were muddy when she got there, but she didn't care. She took a bucket off the pump, drew water without having to prime it, and took the pail behind the fence. She washed her mouth out and stripped off her slip. She threw the slip over the railing, picked up a sponge and a bar of lye soap, and dipped them into the pail. She scrubbed herself so hard that the tops of her thighs turned red. Then she scrubbed under her arms and in the crevice between her legs. When she finished, she threw the water past a sandstone that sat between the pump and the one she was standing on, took her slip off the fence, and drew it down over her head. She pumped more water and walked back to the house, carrying the bucket and avoiding the slickest sandstones by veering off onto clumps of muddy weeds. She washed her feet again on the steps of the porch.

She got a whiff of fried pork. She sniffed some more. She thought maybe she could tolerate the smell. She went in the kitchen door, slid into a chair, folded her arms on the table, and rested her forehead on them. Viola sat a plate with two eggs and a biscuit in front of her and turned back to the stove. Lovely said, "We can't both go crazy, Maud."

Maud raised her head. "I had a letter. Do you know what happened to it?"

Lovely blinked hard. "Don't know about a letter. There was a wad of paper on the floor. And a piece on the table this morning. Nothing you could read."

"Where are they?"

Lovely nodded toward the stove. "Used them to get the kindling going."

Maud was stunned. Tears welled up in her eyes.

"Were they important? I couldn't make out any words."

Maud put her arms on the table again and rested her forehead on them. She couldn't look at anybody and didn't have the strength to run. She bit her lip to keep from sobbing. She stayed that way for a long time. Eventually, Lovely said, "Can I have another biscuit?"

Viola started talking. She said something about their grandmother. Something about making biscuits. Something about Mr. Singer's mother. None of it made sense to Maud. She wished Viola would stop talking. She lifted her head to tell her to shut up.

Lovely said, "I guess I did the wrong thing. But I swear there wasn't anything to read."

Maud bit her bottom lip so hard she drew blood. She knew the letter was unreadable. She'd tried and tried to make the words out. She ran a hand through her hair and pulled it forward over the side of her face. She rested her forehead on the heel of her palm.

Viola set a cup down next to her elbow and poured coffee into it. Maud shoved it away. Viola handed the cup to Lovely and poured herself one. She sat down next to Maud and tilted her coffee into her saucer. She said, "Check Singer never did cook much on her own. Always had help. But Pappy said she could cook if she wanted to. I 'spect that was true. A woman who can't cook is like a bull without balls."

Maud felt as hot as if somebody had dumped grease over her. Viola's talking didn't make any more sense than chicken squawking. She picked up a biscuit and bit into it to keep from screaming. Lovely said something about a skunk under the floor of the Singers' summer kitchen, about Mr. Singer's last wife tossing mothballs under there.

Mention of Mr. Singer focused Maud's mind. He probably knew what Booker was up to. What was the best way to get it out of him? Just ask outright. He'd always been nice. And he surely knew she and Booker were courting. He couldn't help not. He'd given her the letter. She just needed to work up the courage and the words. That's what she'd do.

She grew restless for Viola to go. She decided the best way to hurry that was to eat something. But she didn't know if she could. She nibbled more on her biscuit. It wasn't bad. But the thought of coffee seemed like poison, and she didn't think fried meat would do her any good. She said they needed to make the meat last. They weren't raising pigs and she didn't know when they could afford to again. Viola and Lovely took over the talk from there. Maud nibbled the biscuit down to crumbs and worked up enough appetite to put butter and plum jelly on the next one. She needed to pump up her blood to walk to Mr. Singer's.

After Lovely left for the field, Maud said she needed to go into town to make another payment to the doctor. She offered to walk Viola home, and she set out, twitchy on their walk. They talked about the damage the storm had done to the trees, avoided the puddles in their path, and complained about how heavy the air was. Maud felt thankful Viola was a fullblood and wouldn't ask questions other people might. Still, as they got closer to Viola's turnoff, Maud felt she needed to thank her for coming. Lovely had gotten her sometime in the night. And getting there probably hadn't been easy. But a "thank you" might tilt over a bucket of minnows she didn't want swimming out. So in a way that she knew didn't sound natural, she chattered about the barn cat having a litter of kittens, about her irritation with three hens she thought weren't laying at all, about a book she was reading that was set down in Texas. Maud avoided asking Viola anything. What she wanted to know — did she have any secrets for the morning sickness and how was Lucy feeling with only weeks to go — were subjects she didn't want mentioned.

After she parted ways with Viola, Maud walked straight toward Mr. Singer's. She felt guilty to be thankful to be rid of her great-aunt, and she resolved to be nicer the next time she saw her. Then she turned her mind to practicing what she'd say to her neighbor. When she got to the highway, she kept walking west toward the bridge. She was avoiding the potato barn and the bare patch of dirt in front of it, where Booker's wagon had been.

Under the tree where she'd pinned the letter to her slip, she stood on a large root, took her shoes off, and used a leaf to wipe them clean of mud. She cursed the rain and wind as she wiped. That cursing felt bold and boosted her confidence. She put her shoes back on, set her shoulders straight, and walked in long strides on the least muddy path toward Mr. Singer's yard. When she got there, she almost kept walking to the back of the house. But she didn't want to do anything that might dampen her courage, so she strode right up the front steps to the porch and used the knocker. She banged it three times and took a step back.

The same Negro woman who'd answered the door before answered it again. Maud asked for Mr. Singer. The woman disappeared down the hall without closing the door or inviting her to take a rocker. So Maud stood, looking out over the yard at the trees around the house and at the incline of dirt that had been piled when the bridge was built. She recalled her mother leading her and Lovely by the hand to watch the construction, and a lump came up in her throat. It was threatening to overtake her when she heard steps. The screen door opened. Mr. Singer came out on the porch, and said, "Hello, Maud."

"I hate to bother you again."

"No bother."

Maud had decided to dump the small talk. "That letter you gave to me the other day, it got destroyed in the storm before I could read what it said."

Mr. Singer's eyebrows rose over the rim of his glasses. His goatee and moustache twitched. He looked out toward the trees. Finally, he said, "You seem to have an unusual amount of patience. I know it's not a lack of curiosity."

"Lovely's been sick, as you know. I got behind in my chores. I try to put business before pleasure."

"Is that so?" Mr. Singer smiled with his eyes.

Maud felt she was blushing all the way down to her toes. She cleared her throat. Her voice came out higher than usual. "The truth is, Booker and I've been courting. I hurt his feelings and now he's gone. I don't know where he is. I need to find out."

Mr. Singer winced. "So that's what happened. I figured it was something along that line." He scratched his cheek.

"I reckon he told me where he was going in that letter, but I foolishly didn't read it immediately. I don't know why. Afraid of what was in it, I suppose. You know how up and down sparking is." She regretted that as soon as she said it. Mr. Singer's sparking had probably always gone his way. She mumbled, "Your mind sort of leaves you sometimes. At least a woman's does."

"So I hear." Mr. Singer clasped his hands behind his back. He was quiet.

Maud felt comfortable with people taking their time to respond. And she knew that for all his light skin Mr. Singer was a Cherokee, too. She looked at a tree that had a wide split in it.

Mr. Singer finally said, "I don't know that I can be much help. He was agitated. Said he had to leave. I asked him if he was going home; I didn't think it was time for him to go back to school. But he said he didn't know where exactly he was going. He needed time to think."

"Did he say if he was coming back?"

"I'm afraid he didn't say anything about that." Mr. Singer looked down at the planks of the porch and winced again. Then he added, "But he didn't say he wouldn't."

Maud couldn't help the tears that came up in her eyes and rolled down her cheeks. But they prevented her from speaking.

Mr. Singer looked off into the distance and ran his hand over what was left of his hair. "Why don't you come inside and pick out some books? You still like to read, I bet."

Maud wanted to run. But she'd told Mr. Singer the truth when she couldn't tell her own great-aunt, and she suddenly saw him as the only real friend she had. He was certainly her only link to Booker. And the only way she could get messages. Booker probably wouldn't have noted her route number, even if he'd ever seen it. She couldn't damage her connection. "I'd like that. Thank you."

They went into the room on the right behind the front parlor. Maud had been in the room before. A desk and three chairs were at the far end, and all four walls were lined with bookshelves. Mr.

Singer stopped in front of the north wall of books. "Have you ever read any history?"

Maud wiped the tears from her cheeks. Mr. Singer drew a handkerchief out of his back pocket and handed it to her. "I recall you like novels best. You're welcome to borrow some of those. But I find history sort of gives me the long view."

Maud turned and blew her nose. She clutched the handkerchief tightly as she turned back. "Sorry. I'll wash it and return it." She took a deep breath. "No, I haven't read much history except in school."

"Now, this one"—he pulled a thick book from the shelf—"is about Henry VIII of England. Lots of stories about beheadings. Mighty fine reading to take your mind off to another world." He held the book out toward Maud.

She was about the same height as Mr. Singer. She thought he must have shrunk with age, and she felt bad looking him square in the eye. She dropped her eyes to the book and took it in her hand. "That will be fine."

Mr. Singer took a step to his side. He reached for another book. "Now, you could be more interested in Cherokee history." He held out a bright green volume.

"Cherokee history is written down?"

"Some of it is. This fellow Mooney went and lived among the ones left behind. Their elders talked to him. He wrote down what they said."

Maud took the book. She opened it to a page headed "Formula for Love Charms." She quickly closed the volume. "This looks interesting. Thank you."

Mr. Singer smiled. "Be particularly careful with it, if you don't mind. My grandfather is mentioned in there. My great-great-grandfather, too. And a couple of my uncles."

"Were they named Singer?"

"No. My father was a white man. They were named Morgan, Sevier, and Lowrey."

"No Rattlinggourds or Tenkillers?"

"Well, there's a Ghi-go-ne-li and an Oo-loo-tsa, I believe. But we got white as fast as possible." He smiled.

Maud smiled, too. And when she did, she thought for the first time in a day that she might live. Perked by that idea, she asked, "Do you think I could take a fiction book, too?"

"Yes, of course. If I have one you haven't read. They're over there, you know." He nodded toward the west wall.

Maud added *The Complete Sherlock Holmes* to her collection and felt lifted by Mr. Singer's kindness. She told herself that he wouldn't have been friendly if Booker had said anything terrible about her. She clutched at that notion even though she didn't think Booker was the kind of man to gossip with his employer. Or the kind of man to gossip much at all. White men held their business closer than Cherokee men did. Maud felt thankful for that.

By the time she got to Nan's, she felt well enough to go in and visit. And by the time she got home, she felt well enough to do her chores, even going out to the barn and incurring the wrath of the cat to take a peek at the kittens. By evening, she'd settled into the belief that Booker was just laying out and would return when his feathers were slicked. She didn't think he was suited to oil-field work, knew he wasn't suited to farming. He was probably up in the Outlet, selling soap and pots to riggers' wives, raking in coins and bills.

She started reading the books that Mr. Singer had lent her. She only wished she hadn't borrowed all three so she could return them quicker and see their lender sooner. Within a week, other than her morning sickness, her major concern was lack of money.

She returned to the sandbar to fish as a way of conserving their salted meat for cooler weather. And it was during one of those walks that she remembered the meat Hector Hempel was holding for them. She decided she would organize Lovely and Mr. Singer's mule to visit the icehouse on Saturday.

On Friday morning, she told Lovely to bring the mule home, and the next morning, after she was sick again, they rode her together up the line, over the highway, and on toward Ft. Gibson. They found the usual combination of automobiles, wagons, and horses in front of the icehouse, and while they were waiting their turn, she caught up with folks she hadn't seen. She was talking to Sissy Sisson, who she'd gone to school with, when she glanced up and saw Billy Walkingstick. He was on the icehouse platform, talking to a cousin of his. They both were wearing fancy shirts and cowboy hats. Maud turned quickly to face the other way. She got still and kept her head down. She was barely listening to what Sissy was saying for plotting an escape when she heard Billy call out to Lovely. She didn't look up. She asked Sissy a question to keep her talking.

While Sissy chattered away, Maud whirled in thought. It was no mystery why Billy called to Lovely; they'd been friends since they were kids. She didn't mind, in theory, them talking; but she was worried about what Lovely might say. A lot of days, his sense was scattered in the wind. A few days before, he had proposed moving out to the cellar. Another day, she'd had to convince him to take his boots off to go to bed. But he was back sparking Gilda, going to see her that evening, and he'd been in his right mind riding in. Maud asked Sissy another question. She hoped Lovely wouldn't bring Billy over to see her. Surely he had more sense than that.

She was still listening to Sissy when Hector Hempel called "Nail." Maud turned. He was holding the ends of a burlap sack in both fists. The sack was almost as big as he was, and its bottom was dark with melting ice. Lovely took the sack from Hector, then turned toward Billy. Maud hugged Sissy and mumbled about needing to get the meat home before their ice disappeared. She headed toward the mule, went to the far side of it, away from the platform, and looked off into a field. She was swatting at a horse fly and wondering if Lovely was ever going to get his butt over there when she heard him say, "Look who I lassoed!"

Billy put his fingers to the brim of his hat. He smiled real big. "Lovely's asked me to take yer meat to the farm. You, too, if yer of a mind. He wants to stay in town." He pointed. "I've got a buckboard over there." He rolled his tongue around the inside of his lower lip. He smiled again. His teeth were even and white.

Maud pulled her leg back to kick Lovely's shin. But she stopped. Billy would see that. She said between her clenched teeth, "Gilda's not expecting you until this evening."

"How do you know? Did she tell you?"

"No, you told me coming in."

"Well, I'm here now. No use going back to the bottoms, turning around, and coming back."

Maud was so irritated with Lovely that she was barely civil to Billy. She told him that once they deposited the meat and ice in their chest at home, she had to go to her grandpa's to invite her folks to Sunday dinner. She said she'd need to stay and visit, as old people expected that. But Billy got to talking about his own old people in such an endearing way that Maud forgot she'd just made the invitation up, and she began to look forward to cooking for her family the next day. She and Billy were coming upon the ruins of the school when she recognized in the road ahead her uncle Ame's car full of people. The car slowed to a creep. When they stopped to talk, she spit her invitation out with real pleasure.

But that left her with no excuse to escape Billy. And she was figuring out how to stretch the meat enough to invite Nan and Ryde and their whole brood and use the need to visit them as a new excuse when she saw her uncle Ryde's wagon. Billy said, "Looks like yer whole family's on the road today."

Maud said, "Seems so," and felt irritated with the entire bunch.

After that invitation, she settled back against the wagon seat, asked Billy a question about rope tricks, and got him to talking so that she could think. Her thoughts went to feeding all those people. She would need to cut the meat into chunks for stew. She had potatoes, okra, tomatoes, corn, onions, carrots, and asparagus. Lucy and Viola would bring pies. So would Nan. She would have to use the cooking kettle in the yard to hold all that food, and dishes would be a problem. She could raid Gourd's for extra bowls. She hoped he had more than two and thought surely he did because a woman had lived with him in the past. She hoped that the woman hadn't taken her dishes with her. She was thinking about having enough spoons when Billy said, "Word is you've taken up with the peddler who burnt the school."

Maud flushed so suddenly that she felt like a fever had overtaken her. "He didn't burn the school. That's ridiculous!"

Billy leaned sideways away from Maud. "Don't get yer back up. I'm jist trying to get the lay of the land."

"Well, spreading vicious gossip isn't the way to do it!"

"Seems like it's worked pretty well." He pulled on the brim of his hat.

After that, they rode past the swale in silence. And Maud's mind was still working on what to say about Booker when Billy hopped off the wagon to open the guard. When he got back in, she said, "I was seeing him. But he's off right now."

"Where's he gone?"

"Peddling. He has to make a living like everybody else."

Billy got off the wagon to close the guard, and Maud said, "I'll do the next one."

She walked the rest of the way to the house, and Billy threw the sack of meat and ice over his shoulder and took it in for her. He set it on the kitchen table and squatted to open the ice chest. He looked inside, stood back up, picked the dipper out of the pan, and took a long drink. He offered the dipper to Maud, and she did the same. He said, "I'm not sure it'll all fit in there."

"We have another one down in the cellar. I better cut the meat into hunks and divide it up."

"Want me to help?"

"You do kitchen work?"

"I cut meat. Do you have a sharp knife?"

Maud turned to the counter and opened a drawer. She pulled out a butcher knife and tested it with her thumb. She pulled a whetstone out of the same drawer. "It could use some sharpening." She held them out.

Billy stroked the knife against the stone so quickly it sounded like fiddle tuning. He pressed his thumb to the blade. "You got an ice pick?"

Maud drew one of those out and held it up.

They set to cutting meat and chipping ice, and because they were working against the heat, they got the meat packed in ice and stored in both of the chests fairly quickly. After that, they rewarded themselves with biscuits, butter, and honey.

During the course of all of that activity, Maud began to enjoy Billy's company. He could be charming. He was easygoing and lived for the minute he was in. In those particular minutes, he entertained her more than she'd been entertained since Booker had left. They talked about people they knew, talked about Billy's new job driving a tractor for Marty Benge, talked about the oil fields, and about everybody getting rich but them. They laughed and carried on in such a way that Maud forgot her predicament.

When the sun finally dipped so that it caught the tops of the trees, Billy helped her do her chores, and then she opened up some canned beans, seasoned them with grease, tomatoes, and onions, and made some more biscuits. They ate out on the porch. After they finished, Billy said, "I might have a little wine under my wagon seat."

"Wine?"

"Yep. Want some?"

Maud wanted any new experience. "I'll take just a tad. I may not be able to stand the taste."

"I'm betting you'll like it." Billy got up from his rocker and went to his wagon. He returned with a bottle of purple liquid.

Maud brought out a couple of glasses. Billy stood on the ground at the edge of the porch and filled the glasses up. Maud sat down on the planks. "Who'd think there'd ever be wine in the bottoms? I don't know anybody who drinks it."

"Nobody around here is high-toned enough. They drink it all the time over in Tulsa."

"How do you know?" Maud took a sip. It didn't taste like anything she'd ever tasted.

"I went to Tulsa with Marty to pick the new tractor up. There're eating places there, Maud, that sell wine by the bottle, just like it's legal."

"Maybe it is there. I can't keep all the liquor laws straight."

"I don't think it is. We had to keep the bottles under the table."

She took another sip. The liquid didn't taste like she'd thought it would. It was warm and smooth and a little like juice. And drinking it made her feel like she was somewhere nice, maybe a place in a book.

They didn't have enough wine between them to make them anything but tipsy. But the wine made Maud feel like she was connected to the larger world. She wanted to go to a dance in a skirt at her knees, wear long strings of beads, bob her hair. As she listened to Billy describe the glories of Tulsa, it sounded like East Egg to her. Maud sat on the edge of the porch with her legs dangling off, thinking about riding in fast cars, drinking gin from a slipper, dancing on tables, and singing snappy tunes.

While her head spun with dreams, Billy's eyes scanned her lips, her hair, her eyes, her hips. He got in a way that would be hard to hide if anyone looked below his belt. He got up from sitting beside her, adjusted himself with a hand on his pants, and then walked down the steps. He turned to face Maud, looked down, and said, "I think I may need to do something about this."

Maud saw what Billy meant. The bulge beneath the buttons on his pants was rather attractive and so was Billy's smile. In a move that was more natural than intentional, Maud spread her legs just a little.

Billy put a hand to his lump. He rubbed it. Maud licked her lower lip. Billy said, "Maud, if you could just . . ." He put his other hand on her waist. "I want you so bad I'm busting."

"Billy . . ."

But then he moved his hand to her neck and brought her face down to his. He kissed her with his tongue in her mouth and she, after going stiff, went weak and returned his kiss. He pulled her off of the porch, moved his chest against hers, and wiggled his body between her legs. "Open my pants, please, Maud. I'm in pain, I want you so bad." He started panting and moved her hand to his buttons.

Their fingers fought. But then Billy unbuttoned his pants himself and brought his penis out. He put Maud's hand on it, and she felt a shudder go all through her body down to her toes and up to the crown of her head. His skin was warm, his member hard, and she felt wet between her legs. She was panting, too. And her mind sort of left her. Her back was against a porch post, and Billy was against her and inside her, grunting and moving up and down, and she was being carried far, far away into a land that was beautiful and peaceful and totally removed from her present existence. Maud had, with Booker, grown to like sex. She felt comfortable with her body taking its pleasure and giving it back. And she discovered right there next to the porch that her pleasure was in her own control and not entirely linked to a man who had up and left her with no warning.

The two of them, locked together, rocked back and forth and up and down for quite a while. When Billy's relief came, Maud's did, too. And they were so breathless they gasped together and heaved for air until Billy inhaled, turned away from Maud, and let out a whoop that was so loud it lingered. "Damnation, Maud, I love you more than all the stars in the sky."

It was then that Maud came to her senses. She pressed the front of her dress down, ran a hand through her hair, and pulled up her underwear. "We shouldn't have done that, Billy."

"Why not?" Billy tucked himself in and started on his buttons. "I sure wish I had a cigarette."

Maud wanted a cigarette, too. "Don't you have any?"

"No, I'm completely out."

"I don't think there're any here. Daddy's gone. I'm sure he took his with him."

"Can you check?"

Maud wanted to do more than check for cigarettes. She wanted to clean herself up. "I'll look in his drawer. Hold on." She climbed the steps, went in, and in a few minutes came back with a hand-rolled cigarette and a wooden match. She sat down in a rocker and Billy sat down in the one next to her. "I can't believe he missed this one," Maud said.

"Where's he gone?"

"To the oil fields, I guess."

After that, they talked until the moon came up, round and bright, but they didn't talk about what they'd done. Maud's mind was too jumbled to say anything definite; she didn't know what her feelings were, let alone how to explain them to Billy. And Billy talked mostly about world events — Amelia Earhart crossing the Atlantic, the Hoover-Smith race, reports of polio. Billy said visiting Tulsa had made him want to see other places. He confided to Maud that he wanted to change his name to Walker, go someplace where people had never seen an Indian, and make something of himself. He liked airplanes more than tractors, and he wanted to fly in one. They talked about flying off into the sky and seeing the bottoms and the river from the air. That talk lasted until they heard the sound of a horse coming their way.

Maud's first thought was that the horse carried Booker. She jumped up from her chair and stepped to the edge of the porch, feeling panicked. But she could see by the light of the moon that the horse carried two people, and she realized with a mixture of relief and disappointment that Early and Lovely were the most likely combination. When the rider on the back of the horse fell off trying to dismount at the guard and then crumpled to the ground, her guess was confirmed. She and Billy walked to them. Lovely was so drunk he was either playing possum or really couldn't get up. Early wasn't completely sober himself. But he and Billy each took an arm and lugged Lovely to the porch. They brought out his cot and settled him on it. Then they brought out Maud's for Early to sleep on. Maud told Billy he better get home; she had cooking to do come morning. When he left, she was suddenly tired to the bone. She went inside to her father's bed and slept without turning.

When she awoke, she expected to feel ailing. She lay on her back looking up at the ceiling, waiting for the nausea to hit. She tracked the crack, pretending it was a road on a map that led to Tulsa and on to Oklahoma City. She did that for several minutes, her mind wandering to the previous evening until she determined she might not get sick. She got up slowly, went to the door, and looked out on the porch. Lovely's face was covered with his arm. Early was asleep with his hat over his eyes. She decided that if she was going to throw up, she best to do it before they woke up. So after her morning business, she pulled some side meat out of the ice chest and sniffed it. The sniff didn't turn her stomach or even make it uneasy. She wondered if she wasn't really pregnant, or if wine was the ticket to feeling good. She slapped the meat into a skillet and started making biscuits, figuring on how to get a private word with Lucy later in the day.

Maud didn't know much about pregnancy beyond what she'd observed watching animals and a little she'd heard from her aunts. Her mama had lost a baby. But she hadn't realized her mother was pregnant until she had going-down pains, and when that happened, her grandfather had taken her, Lovely, and her sisters out of the house all the way to Ft. Gibson. He'd bought them ice cream. Maud got to thinking about how good that ice cream had tasted, and she was half finished preparing breakfast before she realized she still didn't feel sick at all. She went out on the porch and shook the men awake.

While they were taking their time getting up and going about their business, Maud ate her breakfast without any queasiness. But she found she'd lost her taste for coffee. She finished quickly and made trips to the garden and cellar to get the fixings for the dinner. After she fed the men, she asked Early to build a fire under the kettle outside, and she sat Lovely down on a little stool next to it and made him stir the pot with a long-handled wooden spoon. Early squatted with Lovely to remind him to stir. Maud walked to Gourd's to raid his dishes.

The first person to arrive was Blue, and he sat out by the pot with Early and Lovely. Maud could see them talking and hoped they were gossiping about Saturday night in town. She feared they might be gossiping about Billy and her or Booker and her. But she didn't have time to do anything about that, and she sure didn't want to get into a conversation with them or get any ribbing. She shied away from the pot until the entire family arrived and naturally split into groups of men, women, and children. The women commanded the kitchen and porch, the men the pot of stew, and the children the yard and the live oak tree.

The men ate first, the children next, and then, after washing two rounds of dishes, the women ate. While they did, the men set cigarette butts on the tops of the fence posts against the wild and took turns shooting them off. The sound of gunshots and children laughing felt so reassuring to Maud that she, for most of the afternoon, forgot about wanting to go anywhere else and was perfectly content with her family around her, as country and as dark as they were. She only wished that her mother was sitting at the table with them, that her father was taking his turn with the gun, that her sisters, Rebecca and Peggy, lived closer by. Her mind didn't return to her troubles until Lucy said, "I wish this baby would hurry itself up."

Nan snorted. "It'll be a pile more trouble when it comes."

"I'm tired of peeing ever' fifteen minutes," Lucy replied.

Maud thought about her own peeing. It seemed normal. "Remind me when it's due?"

"Gonna be a Virgo."

"You'll have an easy time. Mark my words. Easy delivery, easy tempered," Viola said.

"Renee's a Virgo," Nan said. "She's gitting as high tempered as Ryde." She rolled her eyes.

"Well, the daddy figures into it, that's fer shore," Viola said.

Nan put a golly rag to her lips. She cut her eyes at Maud. They twinkled.

Maud knew Nan was hiding a grin. She felt a blush down to her toes. There wasn't such a thing as privacy in the bottoms. As gossipy as her family was, the likelihood that Viola hadn't spread that she'd had the morning sickness was as remote as a breakfast without biscuits. They might not say they knew it, but that was just so they could giggle and make fun behind her back. Maud felt her temper rise. "Can't anybody have anything to themselves around here?"

Nan drew her chin into her neck. Viola looked down at the table. But Lucy, bolder than either of the other two when her husband wasn't around, cackled and said, "Well, if ya parade up and down the section line, ya could be seen."

"I can't get to my house without going down the line!"

"Yeah, that's unfortunate," Lucy replied. "I'm shore glad Daddy moved us up closer to the highway."

Nan said, "I sorta like Booker." She looked out the door.

Maud felt her heart pounding. She hadn't begun to sort her feelings, and they were being laid out on the kitchen table and fingered like knives and forks. "I like him, too, but he's taken a powder."

"He'll be back, I 'spect," Lucy said. "Men do that all the time."

"Uncle Cole doesn't," Maud replied.

"No, Cole, he stays as close as a tick on a dog. But he's an exception."

Nan said, "Where you think Booker went to?"

Once Maud gave into the conversation, she did so with relief. "I don't know. He left me a letter, but it melted in the rain." She told them the full story of the letter and what Mr. Singer had said. When she was finished, Lucy shook her head. "I don't know how you put off reading it. I couldn't've stood the suspense."

"I won't again," said Maud.

Outside, one of the children yelled. That drew only the slightest turn of heads, as it was a scream of playing wild, not of distress. But the yell focused Maud's attention on the rest of her circumstance, and she blurted out, "How do you tell for sure if you're in a family way?"

All three women pulled their eyes away onto spots somewhere in the distance. Maud waited them out, letting them pretend they didn't already know. Lucy finally answered, "Different fer different babies. This one, I got to feeling like a stuffed hen the next morning. The first one, I didn't even know he was in me until I noticed I wasn't on the rag."

Maud's thoughts went to her calendar. She could go in the main room, get it, and figure the days again with her aunts. But that would be a public reckoning she wasn't quite ready to make. She looked out the screen door. Three of Nan's children were playing tag in the dirt. Lucy's baby was waddling after a chicken. It suddenly occurred to Maud that she didn't really care for children. That realization hit her in the face so hard, she gulped. As she did, Lucy said, "When'd yer visitor last call?"

Maud brought her mind back to the table. "I'm not sure." She looked at each of her aunts in turn. Viola had a dip in her lip; so did Lucy. Nan was picking a bit of pie crust out of a pan. None of them seemed anything but calm. While Maud was struggling for a way out of the conversation without having to get the calendar, Viola said, "A lot can happen to a baby this early on."

After that, Nan and Viola got up from the table and started in on the dishes again, and Lucy told Maud about a snake she'd recently found in a hen's nest. Maud felt thankful for that particular snake, and the talk dribbled away from what was on her mind to the daily hazards of living, the hope for a break in the heat, and the antics of people they all knew and mostly were related to. After the dishes were done, the women went to the front porch, and the men left off shooting and got to looking under the hood of Ame's car. The older children climbed in the tree. The younger ones napped on a cot on the porch. The day melted into evening before they all went home.

Maud was tired and went to bed early. But she was as far from sleep as she was from the Mississippi River. She lay on her back, listening to Lovely's chair creak on the porch. Her mind rushed ahead like water rolling to the sea. If Booker didn't return, a baby would tie her to the bottoms, the heat, the dirt, and the hardship, for the rest of her life. Even if she told Billy it was his and married him, it would tie them both down. And the baby, if there was one, could turn out to be light rather than dark. Billy would be able to see every day that it wasn't his.

Maud woke to the cock's crow and looked at the crack in the ceiling. The curl at the closest end seemed to be a snake dipping its head, trying to hold her with its eye. Maud ran her hand down her belly. It was flat. She was circling her stomach with her palm when she realized she didn't hear any sign of Lovely. She glanced to his cot. He hadn't been on it. She swung her feet to the floor and rose. He wasn't on the cot on the porch. She went to the outhouse and to the pump. There were no signs anyone had washed up. While she was brushing her teeth, she realized for the second day in a row that the only pang in her stomach was hunger.

Maud studied the calendar through her meal. By her calculations, she'd missed one visitor entirely and was due for another one. She felt her breasts. They were tender and a little larger than usual. She went about her chores wondering where Lovely had gone off to and trying to settle into the idea of being a mother. While she was doing that, she visited a red hen she had setting in a little brooder house next to the chicken coop. Trying to hold the hen's attention by clucking, she stuck her hand under her feathers. The hen flashed a peck at her arm. It drew blood. Maud said, "Hussy!" But she knew she didn't have any business bothering the hen; she'd done it on an impulse to see how the chicken would react. And the hen's temper wasn't too far off from what she had expected. Or from what she felt herself. She didn't want to be sitting on an egg if Booker had up and left her for good. The irritation she might have otherwise felt at being pecked she directed toward the whole male race.

Lovely didn't come in for dinner. Maud thought about walking up to the swale to see if he was working, but decided he couldn't be without either breakfast or a noon meal. So she spent her afternoon reading, perched on a little stool in the shade under the limbs of the live oak tree. She'd read the Sherlock Holmes and the Henry VIII, and her attention was on the second section of Mooney's book, *The Sacred Formulas of the Cherokees*. Formulas existed for all sorts of things, many for curing, some for hunting, a few for love. Maud was studying the love formulas when she caught the beat of hooves in the distance. She looked out from the cave of branches. She saw Billy riding her way.

She hadn't thought of him all day. She looked to the trunk of the tree. Boards were nailed there. They'd held Morgan and Renee only yesterday. Maud laid her book on the ground and grabbed a board. She pulled herself up, squirmed onto the largest low branch of the tree, and stuffed her skirt under her legs. She made her breathing shallow and looked out from between the leaves.

Billy went up to the porch and peered in the screen door. He went inside. He came back out and sat in a rocker. There he stayed. Maud settled into the limb. She thanked her elders for teaching her stillness with hunting and fishing. She didn't even feel particularly unsettled. Eventually, Billy walked to the pump, splashed some water out, drank, and rubbed some on the back of his neck. After that, he walked his horse to the first guard, which he'd left open in the lane, secured it again, and did the same with the far one. Maud waited on the limb until the sound of hooves died away.

She spent the rest of the evening reading and fanning herself. Occasionally, she lifted her eyes and wondered where Lovely had disappeared to, wondered if she really was carrying, wondered what she could do if she was. In all that mulling, she decided her top tick-off was to find where Booker was and get to him. She thought that if she could make her way to Fayetteville, she might find him there, or find people who would know where he was. She went to bed with that plan planted in her mind.

The next day, she copied out on a little lined pad the formulas Mooney had recorded in both Cherokee and English for making children jump down and for destroying life. The formulas for destroying life relied on the wild parsnip, a plant she'd never seen. But she routinely substituted ingredients while cooking and she thought a parsnip was a cousin to a carrot. She had some of those left in the garden. She spent most of her spare time during the day pulling from the book other secrets she thought might come in handy. Then she ate an early supper and walked to her uncle Gourd's, carrying his bowls, Mooney's book, and her notepad.

The house was hot from being closed up, but there was enough light inside to read. She sat at Gourd's table, poured over the book, and made notes until she heard the beat of hooves. She slipped to the floor below the window. She kept reading until the light was too dim and the hooves beat away up the line.

Maud was too busy with her worries about Booker and the little bean that might be lodged in her belly to give much mind to Billy. She appreciated his attentions when she wanted them, and she'd always found him handsome, even exciting. He could be worked like dough, which had both its good points and bad. But her mind and her heart were given over to Booker. And with that in mind, the next day, she walked the line toward Mr. Singer's with his books and handkerchief in a flour sack. She looked toward the swale and didn't see Lovely there. At the section lines' cross, she opened her mailbox flap, hoping her sister Rebecca had finally answered her letter. A dirt dobber flew out into her face. Maud ducked and said, "Dammit, get out of here!" Then she took a step back and peered into the hole. There were three mud nests in there, but no more dobbers and no letters. She looked under the box for a hole the wasps could be using to get in. She didn't find one and decided she'd left the flap a little open the last time she'd checked the mail. She pushed it closed and then pushed it harder with the butt of her gun. She walked on, feeling irritated with Rebecca until she recalled that her sister had three children under the age of five.

On up the line, two big machines for moving dirt were across from the burnt school. As she got closer, she saw several men.

She decided to avoid the men even though she had her rifle. She cut west across the potato fields on paths that had been laid before she was born and then took the river path. When she got to Mr. Singer's, she went to the front door. It was open except for the screen. The same Negro woman came to it. She said, "Mr. Singer ain't in."

Maud felt irritated with herself for not checking to see if the Packard was in the garage before she knocked on the door. If she'd come by her usual route, she would've seen that. "Is he expected back soon?"

"Can't say." The woman had on glasses. She lowered her chin and looked at Maud over the top of them.

Maud didn't like that look. But she didn't want to get on the wrong side of the woman guarding the door. So she smiled and said, "I don't believe I know your name."

"Miz Lizzie."

"Well, Miz Lizzie, Mr. Singer loaned me these books." Maud held up the sack. "He generally likes to quiz me on what I've read. So if you'll tell me when I can catch him, I'll come back."

"Gone into town. Don't tell me his intentions."

"Well, then." Maud pulled the sack to her breast. "Tell him Maud Nail dropped by and will come again."

"I'll tell him. Youse Jenny's granddaughter?"

Maud stepped back. She hadn't heard her grandmother's given name in a long time. "Yes, I am. You knew her?"

"Knew her well."

Maud took a deep look at the woman on the other side of the screen. She was short and wide. She was well fed, which wasn't usually true of Negros, and she had on those glasses, which was unusual in the same way. Maud couldn't tell how old she was by looking at her. If she'd known her grandmother well, it would've been as children. Adult Negroes and other people didn't mingle. Maud was trying to calculate how old her grandmother would've been had she been living when Lizzie said, "Sit there in that chair. I'll bring ya some lemonade." She turned from the door.

Maud was surprised by the hospitality and thankful to sit a spell. She was hot, and the books and gun had weighed her down. She didn't feel the energy she usually had, and her tired blood confirmed her suspicions. She was brooding on those when the screen door opened and Lizzie brought lemonade out on a little tray. Maud gulped it without stopping, put the glass back on the tray, and wiped her mouth with her fingers. "That was delicious."

"I 'spect yer looking fer yer man."

Maud leaned sideways, her eyes up at Lizzie, wide as saucers. "Yes, yes, I am. Do you know where he is?"

Lizzie looked toward the incline that held the road. "Can't say. But he went thaterway." She pointed to the bridge.

Maud was astonished. She'd gotten more information out of this stranger than she'd gotten from anyone. She asked if she knew any more. Lizzie didn't, but she asked Maud about Lovely. She said he'd done her a favor a few weeks back and she knew he'd been poorly. Maud said he hadn't entirely recovered from his shots, and both to change the subject and to satisfy her curiosity, she blurted out, "What kind of favor?" As soon as she said it, she realized she shouldn't have, and she feared she'd given offense to someone whose help she needed. But Lizzie seemed unfazed. "Moved a rock fer me. From the swale where he's working up here to the house. I'd taken a shine to that rock as a girl. It waz gonna get lost in the plowing."

Maud left shortly after that, taking the flour sack of books with her as an excuse to come back. But she walked away feeling like she'd made an unexpected ally. She climbed the rise and sat for a while beneath the same tree by the highway close to the bridge that she'd sat under before. Then she walked the old path by the river to avoid the men and machines, and because she could just as easily go that way to get to her grandpa's.

Of the adults living at her grandpa's, she found only Viola and Lucy. Lucy's little boy was napping on a pallet in a little red wagon under the trees, and the three women went to the kitchen to keep from waking him. That kitchen was bigger than Maud's and there was a round table in the middle. They strung beans while they talked. Maud, both to avoid the subject niggling at her mind and because she was worried, told her aunts Lovely was gone again. The talk centered on him. Everybody in the family was worried. Nobody thought he'd acted himself on Sunday. Lucy had talked to Sarah about his behavior a couple of weeks in the past. It was much like Able's, only milder. But then Lovely had a mild disposition. The three agreed that his disappearances were beyond the usual laying out, and Viola said she'd send the men looking for him if he didn't return by Saturday.

The subject of laying out brought up Mustard's whereabouts. The women speculated on where he could be and if he'd slip back after a spell. Lucy thought that was likely; the sheriff didn't have any evidence to pin him to the crime and the Mounts needed getting rid of. Viola thought Mustard's returning was less sure. People were getting rich in the oil fields. Mustard liked money as well as anybody else. Then Viola said, "That's probably where yer fella is, too."

By then, Maud was glad to have the subject turned to Booker. She told her aunts what she'd learned from Lizzie, that he'd headed west. They both thought Booker was most likely working in the oil fields outside of Oklahoma City. But Maud felt certain oil work wouldn't be an attraction for him. It was too rough;

her father would fit right in; but Booker was a little on the dandy side. Maud couldn't picture him working on a rig or even peddling to men with black hands, sweat-stained shirts, and headbands. Maybe to their wives, but not to the men.

However, she really didn't know. And the speculation about Booker eventually deflated her. She turned the conversation to Lizzie, who she was, and how she'd known her grandmother. Lucy, who was one of Maud's grandmother's younger children, had never heard anything about Lizzie beyond her being Mr. Singer's cook and housekeeper. But Viola said, "Pappy told that tale. If I rightly remember, she waz with yer grandma the day she waz lost to the wolves."

Maud didn't think her grandmother had really been lost to wolves. Nobody would survive that. Viola was using some old-fogy phrase, and Maud didn't want to know any more about those ways. She said, "So she knew her well?"

"Don't know 'bout that. I was about Lee's age." Viola nodded toward the side of the house where Lucy's baby was asleep under the trees.

"She's a good bit older than you are?"

"I guess. Hard to tell with them folks."

"Hard to tell age on anyone," Lucy contributed. "White people look like they's a hundred and one when they's only about forty-six."

After that, the talk dribbled into observations on the weather and the habits of their animals. Maud began to feel the comfort that familiarity and family bring, a comfort she sorely needed. She took supper at her grandpa's and waited to walk home when the moon was up and it was too late for visitors.

6

The next morning, Maud ate breakfast with the calendar by her plate. August 18, the date she and Booker had set for their wedding, was sixteen days away. If Booker came back, it'd be before then. The eighteenth grew larger in Maud's eyes than the other dates, and scribbles about the numbers of eggs gathered and checkmarks she'd made figuring her monthly cycle disappeared off the page. When the one and the eight began looking like a skinny man with a shapely wife, Maud realized she'd lost track of her day.

She hurried through her chores. By midday, the heat was too high for walking the section line or the ruts to the sandbar, and the air too thick for any activity except sitting under the live oak tree and reading. Through the screen of low-hanging branches, the house and the yard seemed like they belonged to somebody else, to folks she didn't know or want to know. The sounds of insects and birds sawed on her nerves. Her whole existence seemed hopeless. The thought that other people in other places were doing things that she'd never do made her angry. She wanted off that pitiful patch of Indian land. She stood up, determined to do something other than wait for the next two weeks. She brushed the limbs aside and stepped into the heat of the afternoon sun. A cow mooed. The rooster scratched in the dirt close to the front steps. A hawk drifted toward the river on currents that didn't touch the tops of the trees. She felt completely alone.

Maud wished Lovely would get his butt home. She'd intended to walk into town and talk to Gilda the day before, but the conversation with Lizzie had distracted her. It was too hot and too late in the day to start that walk now. And she was at the far end of ruts at the end of a section line in the middle of nowhere. She walked to the pump, disturbed a cluster of toads, and jacked the handle up and down. Cool water running over her hand and arm made her feel better. She sat down on the wooden platform and looked out over the wild. She missed Booker. She missed Lovely. She missed her daddy. Evening would come and the only company she'd have would be cows and chickens, and if she went to the barn, the mean cat and her kittens. She thought about taming one of the kittens for company. But if she and Booker went to Fayetteville, that wouldn't be fair. Maud picked up a pebble and threw it. She looked down toward her feet for another. That was when she began to wish Billy would show.

And he did. He didn't ask any questions about where she'd been. But he came in a clean shirt, and with a half a pack of cigarettes in his pocket. They ate and smoked on the porch, and then Billy stood up and leaned over Maud's rocker. He placed his hands on each arm, pushed down, and tilted her forward. He kissed her tenderly, little pecks around her lips and then square on them. He kissed her neck. He was kissing her collarbone when Maud said, "We'll be more comfortable on the bed."

They fumbled at first, then hurried like a couple of animals. After a while, they made love a second time in a way that was gentler but more satisfying to Maud. She let out a moan that could've been heard on the river, and then she gasped until she got her breath. She kissed Billy all over his head. He kissed her all over her breasts. And then they both curled up and slept.

When the cock crowed, Maud woke with a start. The crack on the ceiling seemed to have grown in the middle of the night. She looked over at Billy. He was asleep on his stomach. She put her hand on her belly. It seemed almost as flat as usual, but when she touched her breasts, they were a handful. If she wasn't pregnant already, she soon would be. Maud sighed. Billy shifted his leg. She breathed more shallowly. She didn't want to wake him and face whatever he was going to say.

Maud slowly shifted her weight and slipped out of the bed. She was completely naked. She pulled back the sheet on the wire, stepped behind it, cleaned herself with a rag, and drew one of Lovely's shirts over her shoulders. It hung down to the middle of her thighs. After that, she put on clean drawers, went outside, did her business, came back in, and started a fire. She had biscuits in the oven, coffee on the stove, and fatback frying when she heard the front door. She peeked out. Billy was relieving himself off the side of the porch. Her mother had trained her father and brother not to do that during daylight.

Later that morning, Billy gave her a lift to the highway. Then he rode east to work and she walked toward Ft. Gibson. A milk truck picked her up. She rode with the milkman as far as the Pierce building. She'd come into town to see Gilda, but at first she window-shopped; she rarely got to do that and she was starved for a taste of life beyond dirt and chickens. Then she thought about going to Taylor's and looking at her wedding dress material. She headed quickly in that direction. But once she got to the store, she was afraid to go in. She might cry if she saw the bolt. Instead, to keep her heart from aching, she lingered at the window and read a newspaper clipping about a loaf of bread that came presliced in a package. The sliced bread settled her some, and she was wondering about the usefulness of it and if sliced bread tasted better than unsliced when she heard her name. She turned to see Gilda crossing the street.

They went to Berd's soda fountain. It being early in the day, they had their pick of booths and they took the one in the corner. Gilda bought herself a chocolate milkshake and bought Maud a vanilla one. They didn't say anything of significance until the shakes and straws were at their table and John Berd had finally worn out his talkative welcome. They'd sipped a quarter of their drinks by then, and Maud was determined to make hers last, but she had Gilda in front of her so she asked straight-out if she knew where Lovely might be.

"He's not at home?"

"No, he left Sunday night after a big family get-together."

Gilda rubbed her straw with the tips of her thumb and forefinger. Then she put both palms on the table. "Maud, we broke up Saturday night. I really care about Lovely. But he's gotten so strange he gives me the jitters. And Daddy's been throwing a fit." She slumped against the back of the booth but kept her hands on the wood. "He took it hard. I couldn't stand myself if anything happened."

Maud felt a surge of friendship for the girl across from her even though she'd dumped her brother. She understood why she would. "Do you mind telling me what he's doing that's so strange? He's strange at home, too. But it seems to me that if there was a pattern to it, it might be easier to cure."

Gilda bit her lower lip. "It's not so much what he does. He's not mean, or violent, or anything like that. It's more like he's deep. We've got a rosebush next to the front porch. And Saturday night, he cut off a rose with his knife and got to talking about bugs crawling in it and ruining it and everything going to dust and rot. Not what you usually talk about on a date. And he didn't want to go to the dance. He didn't want to see anybody except me. And sometimes he looks at me like he sees straight through me. I don't mean like I have something to hide. More like he's looking through my face to a wall behind me. Does that make any sense?"

It did. In some respects, Lovely had always been like that. But there was no doubt he'd been worse in the past few months, and Maud understood Gilda's jitters. More to buy thinking time than to disagree, she said, "Our mother was killed by a snake hiding under a rosebush. Roses don't bring the best out in Lovely."

"I'm sorry. I'd forgotten that. Maybe that explains the rose conversation. But really, Maud, he's that way about other things, too."

Maud told Gilda she understood. She was just thinking it through. And the two spent the rest of their shakes trying to figure out where Lovely could be. Maud didn't think he was in the bottoms. Somebody would've sent him home or sent her word. He could be camping on the sandbar. She hadn't been down there since he'd disappeared. She asked Gilda if Lovely had been on his mule Saturday night. She said he hadn't. And Maud knew Lovely had come back to the bottoms on Early's horse. Drunk, too, which was unusual for him. She started to ask Gilda if he'd been drunk with her, but she decided to let that dog lie. She went back to thinking about the mule. Lovely wouldn't want Gilda to see him riding a mule and had probably left it at Mr. Singer's on Saturday afternoon. The milk truck had picked her up too far away from the mule's usual pasture to have seen if it was there. Still, Mr. Singer might've seen Lovely. And the mule was another reason to talk to him. Maud wished she'd brought his books. She didn't want him to think she wasn't planning to return them. She could explain she'd come to town without them. She was sorting out how to put it all to Mr. Singer and not look like a pest about missing men when Gilda said, "He still has my Bible."

That brought Maud's mind back to Lovely and made her feel that Gilda could tell she was thinking about books. But that had to be a coincidence. Without being able to recall where the Bible was, Maud replied, "I'll get it to you. Don't worry about that."

"You could read it yourself, if you want."

"I've read parts when Lovely wasn't around. It's good."

"You could come to church with us anytime you want. I've been praying for Lovely morning and night."

Maud knew how conversations with Christians went. And she had a strategy for closing them. "I sure appreciate that. I have my own devotional every morning. Would go to church if I had reliable transportation. Can't be troubling others. I'm a Baptist. What are you?"

"We're Methodists. Lovely didn't say anything about you being Baptist."

Maud knew all the churchgoing Starrs were Methodists. But she felt stupid for not figuring in Lovely's and Gilda's conversations. She took a long suck on her straw that made a slurping noise she apologized for. "Lovely was never baptized. We have to be a certain age before we're dipped. I got dipped, but he was afraid of the water, so my parents held off on him. Then Mama died and things got out of whack." Maud said that with a straight face and silent thanks for the conversations at school between girls who thought dipping was the only way to heaven and ones who thought baby sprinkling was foolproof.

Maud and Gilda agreed to get each other word when Lovely turned up. And as soon as they parted, Maud headed toward Mr. Singer's. She was picked up by a couple she knew and given a ride as far as the highway. As soon as she got close to the potato barn, she checked the mule's pasture and saw her standing under a tree with a couple of horses. Neither of the horses was Booker's.

When Maud walked through the barn, she saw Mr. Singer sitting at a table on his back porch. She was already brought to tears by the familiar smell, and she'd hoped to have a few moments to pull herself together before talking. But Mr. Singer looked up and smiled. Maud felt touched by the smile, and it brought out more tears. She wiped them away with a knuckle.

She explained she'd gone into town on another errand and didn't bring his books with her. She said Lovely hadn't been feeling well and apologized for his absence from work.

Mr. Singer had a ledger and four yellow pencils laid out on the table. A fifth pencil nestled in the ledger's crease. He reached into his front pocket, drew out his knife, and pinched out a small blade. He picked up a pencil and carefully whittled a sharp point. He said, "I've been worried about Lovely for some time. Even before we thought he had rabies. He's down at the house, is he?" Mr. Singer held the pencil up, eyed it, and laid it down.

Maud had hoped to get information without having to confess Lovely had up and gone. But now that would require an outright lie rather than just a little skirting around. "No, to tell you the truth, he's not. I've been in town talking to the girl he's been sparking. She hasn't seen him, either."

Mr. Singer picked up another pencil and whittled again. Before he got that one done, he asked, "How long's he been gone?"

"Left out Sunday night after a big family meal."

"Any of them know where he is?"

"They've all been worried about him, too. If he was at one of their houses, they would've sent word."

Mr. Singer laid the pencil down next to the other sharpened one. He leaned back in his rocker and called, "Lizzie!"

Lizzie appeared at the screen door of the summer kitchen. She said, "Lemonade, tea, or buttermilk?"

Mr. Singer looked to Maud. She said, "Any's perfect for me," and he said to Lizzie, "Whatever's easiest. Thank you."

Mr. Singer talked about varieties of potatoes, the effect of the flood on his crop, and the competition from northern states until Lizzie brought out a pitcher and two glasses on a tray. Maud tried to catch the cook's eye with a smile, but Lizzie had a blank look on her face that Maud read as *no trespassing*.

Halfway into their buttermilk, Mr. Singer was still talking potatoes. The men in Maud's family did the same about cattle, horses, dogs, corn, wheat, and every blame thing in the bottoms. She was tired of male talk and was thinking about how to turn the conversation to Booker when Mr. Singer said, "Have you heard from our friend?"

Maud was startled that Mr. Singer had read her mind. "No, I was hoping you had."

Mr. Singer twirled an end of his moustache. Then he bit his lower lip. "You know, I have four daughters. Love them ever' one. Never could stand to see one of them hurt. Maybe you should forget Mr. Wakefield. You're a lovely young woman. There are as many men walking the Earth as fish swimming the river. You'll find another easy enough."

Maud's first thought was that Mr. Singer had heard about Billy. She flushed. But then a worse notion crept over her; Mr. Singer was saying Booker wasn't coming back. Her tears reappeared.

They dropped onto her cheeks, and, when she ducked her head, onto her lap. Mr. Singer pulled out a handkerchief and handed it to her. She cried, her shoulders shaking; and he twirled his moustache. He said, "Now, now," and put his hand back to the knife and started cleaning under his fingernails.

Maud pulled herself together enough to say, "I don't mean to be silly."

"No, no."

"We were talking about getting married."

"He said something about the front porch." Mr. Singer tilted his head in that direction.

Maud was surprised. Booker had asked for that favor without telling her. The tears came out again. "We didn't mean to impose."

"No imposition. I was happy to agree to it."

"When did he ask you?" She gulped some air.

"I can't rightly say. It was before he left, of course."

"Right before?"

Mr. Singer clicked his teeth together. "I was just trying to recall. I don't think it was the same day."

She looked at the handkerchief. Mr. Singer was going to run out of handkerchiefs if she didn't stop crying. "If it happens to come to you, it would help me know his intentions."

"How so?"

She wasn't sure. "Maybe if it was right when he was leaving, it would mean he was planning on coming back?"

Mr. Singer winced. She read from that wince that Booker had asked him for the use of his porch at an earlier time. She was sucking air for another sob when he said, "Well, I reckon if he's coming, it'll be in time for the wedding. When was that planned for? I can't recall."

"The eighteenth. Two weeks tomorrow."

Maud left Mr. Singer's company wanting to talk to Lizzie again. But the cook was in the summer kitchen and it was directly across from the porch. Her only excuse to go in there was to return the buttermilk glasses. She'd offered to do that, but Mr. Singer had told her not to bother. So she headed back toward the bottoms by the river way again, both to avoid the men on the machines and to take a long look down the planks of the bridge that headed toward Muskogee. She wondered if Booker was just over there. It was too far to walk to and get back from in a day. But it was easy on a horse; and she began plotting how to get a ride over there. She wasn't very far into that plot when she realized that Billy would be back that evening. She wasn't ready to see him with Booker spinning in her head. She detoured to her grandpa's and took supper there.

She was washing dishes and Viola was drying when Lucy stood up from the table and said, "I think this baby's coming early."

Maud handed Viola a plate and smiled. Being with family had raised her spirits and she'd convinced herself there was a good chance Booker was just over in Muskogee. She said, "What makes you think that?" and turned and looked at her pregnant aunt. There was a puddle at Lucy's feet. Maud's eyebrows went almost into her hair. "You mean right now?"

Lucy nodded.

Maud's instinct was to flee out the back door, go to Nan's and get her, go home, milk the cow and put the chickens up, then go to Gourd's house and hide under his bed. "I'll get Aunt Nan," she said, wiping her hands on her apron.

Viola said, "We need to get them men outta here." She left the room, speaking loudly enough to be heard in the kitchen: "Baby's on its way. Y'all get on over to Nan's. Blue, Maud's cow and chickens need tending. Bert, send Nan this way. Cole, you

go, too, and take Lee. Early, scat." Viola came back to the kitchen
and said, "Maud, pump a lot of water and set it to boiling. Lucy,
come with me."

Maud opened her mouth to protest. But by the time a sentence had formed on her tongue, Viola was leading Lucy by the
hand through the door. Maud was left standing by the sink, dishwater dripping off her rag. Early came in and grabbed what was
left of a pie. He said, "I hear tell it's worse than calving." He escaped out the back door.

Maud had cleaned up the puddle on the floor but was still in
the kitchen when Nan arrived. She was scrubbing the counters
like they hadn't been cleaned in years when Viola barked from the
next room, "Got the water hot?"

Maud's mental time had been spent plotting and discarding
escapes. She'd forgotten about the water. She knocked the dipper
to the floor in her hurry out the door to the pump. But by the time
Viola came back in, she had three pots of water roiling and was
soaked with the heat of the fire.

Viola said, "This is gonna be quick. You come help Nan hold
Lucy in position."

Maud didn't budge. "I'll just get in the way."

"No, you won't. Come on."

"No, really. I'll tend the water."

"You need to see this. It'll be practice fer you'un." Viola used
her elbow to point to Maud's stomach.

Maud had once seen her daddy stick his hand up a cow's rear
to get a calf out. But she'd never seen a human being in the misery her aunt Lucy was in, and she knew Lucy was no complainer.
There was nothing about childbirth that looked appealing to
Maud, and a lot that seemed downright appalling. The blood was
as bad as hog killing, and she thought that if Lucy screamed one

more time she was going to have to slap her. Even when the baby
was held up, tapped on the rear, and started wailing, Maud didn't
feel the miracle of birth. She thought the little girl looked as slimy
as a catfish. And she had a black head of straight hair that, upside
down, looked like a boot brush.

Viola cackled. "We got us a little Indian."

Maud sat down on a windowsill. She clutched the edges. Lucy
looked like a dying horse. The baby looked like a critter that
needed drowning. And it wouldn't stop screaming. Maud thought
she was going to be sick. She jumped up from the sill, ran through
the kitchen and out the back door. She threw up her dinner beside
the steps. She was sitting on the back stoop with her head in her
hands when Poker started licking her throw up.

The baby, Nancy they called it, upset everybody's living arrangements. That was the only good thing Maud saw about it. Her
grandpa, Uncle Ame, and Uncle Blue moved into her house. Early
and Cole moved into Gourd's. Lee came home to his mother, and
Maud was put in charge of him. Viola took charge of Lucy and the
baby. Things stayed that way for more than a week, and then the
men started straggling in.

Cole came back first. The next day, Ame and Blue returned.
On the next, her grandfather took dinner with them rather than
at Nan's. After dinner, Maud found him alone in the side yard at
his usual seat on the ground against a stump. He was shining a
dried gourd with a flour sack, making a rattle for the baby. She sat
down on a block of wood. "While you were down at the house,
did Billy Walkingstick happen by?"

"Shore did."

"Did he ask about me?"

"He mentioned you."

"Say anything in particular?"

Her grandfather had several sticks and a little bowl of dried seeds and beans at his side. He picked up some seeds and dropped them one by one into the gourd. After several were in, he shook the rattle close to his ear. "I told him where you was. I don't think he wanted to dip into the baby business."

Maud had been banking on that. "Anything else?"

"Well, he come down ever' night. That was saying enough."

Maud was glad for the information, but she felt like her whole family knew her business. And that irritated her. She was out of sorts with the whole lot and out of sorts with herself, Booker, and Billy, too. She had been, every day, walking the path around the river bend and into the potato fields far enough to see if Booker's wagon had returned. It hadn't. Each day brought her closer to the eighteenth and put her in a blacker mood. And being in a family way didn't help. She'd started trying to decide if she was going to marry Billy and pass the baby off as his or try to abort it. Every day she awoke with those thoughts. As the days went on, she see-sawed from one choice to the other. Billy loved her. And she was attracted to him. But he was no wild Indian with movement in his veins; he was a Cherokee, and a fairly full-blooded one. As forward thinking as he seemed, he would eventually, she thought, want to squat on a piece of land, hug it like a blanket, and not give it up. She would spend a life with him out in the country. Buying a new tractor would be big news. There wouldn't be pretty clothes, parties to speak of, shiny cars, or dancing on tables in nightclubs. There wouldn't even be indoor plumbing or electricity. And, Maud knew, there wouldn't be many books or any discussion of ideas beyond current events that took place so far away that they seemed in a dream.

But Booker wasn't coming back. He would've already returned

if he was. And he had been run off by the very type of thing she wanted away from. Or maybe he'd been run off by her not confiding in him sooner. She occasionally admitted that into her calculations. But telling the man you love that you helped cover up murder wasn't the type of confiding that led to marriage. She'd felt that. And it had proven to be true. She resolved that no matter what she did in the future, telling the truth to men was a bad proposition. She was so lost in thought that her grandfather's voice came as a surprise. She asked him to repeat himself.

"Lovely. Don't rightly know what'ta do 'bout him. A man has a right to go where he wants. If Ame and me hadn't took that right, we would've spent our lives among strangers."

Maud had never heard her grandfather speak of his past. And now she wasn't interested in it. Out of politeness, she said, "Your parents died?"

"Yep. Daddy were kilt by a fellow in a uniform. Funny thing, I comb my mind like I'm picking fleas and I ain't never been able to call up if it were gray or blue. Daddy warn't no soldier. He were a miller. The soldiers jist came through."

"Was your daddy a white man?"

He dropped some beans into the gourd. "I think he were. Mama were a Choctaw on her mama's side. Cherokee on her daddy's."

"A Choctaw?"

He snorted. "Odd, ain't it?"

"You came over here, why?"

"Looking fer Mama's family. Got confused. Thought they was the Singers. Took a while to figure out they wasn't. Meantime, Check Singer took me and Ame in. Gave us work. Paid the fee on us."

Maud wasn't interested in talking about the arrangements for non-Cherokees to work before statehood. Indian Territory had dissolved into Oklahoma before she was born. Others might jaw about the injustice of that, but she thought that was like whipping a dead mule. Being an Indian was a misfortune more than anything else. The only thing she felt glad to have confirmed was that her grandfather's father had been white. She turned the talk back to Lovely. No one had heard any reports on him.

Her grandfather said, "I was thinking maybe you could write yer pa. He's at his sister's, ain't he?"

"Sheriff Talley says not. But Daddy can hide out easy."

"Why don't ya think about writing yer aunt? Tell her Lovely's run off. To keep an eye out fer him."

"Lovely won't go to Daddy."

Her grandfather held the rattle up. "Do you think you could paint a face on this? Sompthing pretty?"

"Probably."

"Good. Put red on it somewheres. I'll glue the handle after it's painted." He put his hand on the stump and got up. Looking down at Maud, he said, "Mustard and Lovely was always crossways. But in my experience, blood goes to blood. It's worth a try. We don't want to lose the boy."

Shortly afterward, Maud started walking home. She was wearing one of her aunt Lucy's dresses and carrying a feed sack that held her dress and the gourd. She swung the sack like she was carefree, but her thoughts were about squaw root. She'd heard it whispered among girls at school that the plant could expel babies down outhouse holes. She was glad she'd picked up enough to roughly know what the plant looked like. And some had grown in Blue's woods in years past. She decided to find it and ask Viola about how to prepare it once she had it in hand.

She scanned the sides of the road for snakes as she thought

and walked, but when she finally looked up, she saw Billy and Early on Gourd's front porch. Billy smiled. She felt a little jump in the triangle between her legs. She shook her head, tossed her hair, and ran her free hand through it. Billy's smile got wider. By the time she got to the lane in front of the house, Early had gone inside. Billy said, "Baby okay?"

That startled Maud. Then she remembered Lucy's newborn. "Baby's fine. What have you been up to?"

"Jist chawing the cud with yer menfolk. Won a quarter offin Early pitching pennies."

"He'll make it up. Don't play cards with him."

Early appeared at the screen door. "Whose side are you on, Maud?" He grinned.

Early told Maud he'd secured Gourd's place to live in for as long as Gourd was piled up in his current woman's bed. He asked about the baby and paid Billy his quarter. After that, Billy said he probably should help Maud settle back in. Early arched an eyebrow and remarked, "Yer as helpful as a crutch, Walkingstick."

Maud and Billy hadn't been in her house longer than a minute when he grabbed her around the waist from behind. He turned her around, pressed her to him with his hands on the cheeks of her rear, and kissed her hard. The kiss went through her whole body. She felt like she was melting into a puddle, like her legs were giving way. She wasn't aware of how they made it all the way over to the bed. And they didn't bother with getting her aunt Lucy's dress all the way off; they just pushed it up and Billy went inside her. Once he was in, they began a rocking that moved the bed both up and down and against the wall so hard that the iron piece of furniture made noises like a hammer. Soon those noises were joined by Maud's and by a low hum of Billy's that sounded like the rush of a river. Maud came first with a high moan that could've been heard on the porch. Billy came with more thumping of the bed and more humming. Then they lay back, faces turned up toward the crack in the ceiling. They did the same thing twice again until they both finally fell into such a deep sleep that the cock crowed several times the next morning before Maud fully awoke and looked over at Billy. He was still asleep, his mouth open, his lips thick. She touched his thigh. He groaned. Then she touched his balls. His eyes opened. He pursed his lips. His eyelids dropped down again. He cupped Maud's hand with his own and moved it up to his penis. It hardened. Maud said, "I need to see to the chickens. Fox could have got them."

Billy said, "Too late now." Then he let go of Maud's hand, rolled over onto her, and started rocking again. They rocked with a smoother rhythm than the night before, and when Billy finished, he said he thought that would last him all day. Maud finished with the beginnings of feeling sore. She pushed Billy's shoulder and said, "We've ruined the bed."

"Okay. Tonight, we'll use the floor," he said.

Billy left after breakfast, and Maud started in on chores that the men folk who had been tending the animals hadn't noticed needing doing. That entailed a lot of washing and dusting, and it wasn't until midafternoon that she got to thinking again about the squaw root. She pictured the plant in her mind as a single stalk with bluish-green leaves and a flower that looked almost like a starfish. She thought a patch grew around some trees she'd been through when Blue had taken Lovely and her hunting for wild mushrooms. She wished she had a clock or a watch. She walked out to the pump to see what board its shadow was cast on as, in certain seasons, the shadow could be used to measure the time. She bit her under lip, tilted her head, and decided she didn't have enough space left in the afternoon to get to Blue's allotment and back before Billy was likely to return. She went into the house, got a pencil and pad, and walked over to the live oak tree. She brushed aside its branches and settled on a little stool that had, in her absence, found its way under there. She wrote the letter to her aunt that her grandfather had asked her to write. She thought about the dirt dobbers. She decided to mail the letter in Nan's box.

She closed the cover of the pad and set it and the pencil on the ground. She leaned against the trunk of the tree and looked out between its branches. She felt settled by her lovemaking with Billy. She'd felt settled all day. In fact, the day had been the best she'd had in a while, and the first time since Booker left that she hadn't felt bereft. She thought that if Billy and she kept it up she'd be able to forget Booker entirely. And that was what he deserved for leaving her alone without a word. She was tired of men moving around when they took a mind to, tired of them laying out. They didn't lay out in books, not routinely anyhow. And she thought in cities men didn't come and go as they pleased. City men settled down, went to work in the morning, came home in the evening, played with the children, and read the paper. She recalled the men in her family also did that sometimes. But other times, they just up and ran away. Booker was clearly in that mold. And if he was, well, it was good to be rid of him. She should've known he was a traveling man by the fact that he'd taken up peddling when his wife and child died. She'd been blinded by his looks and his books. Well, she could get over that. She had the remedy for it. Billy Walkingstick. Billy Walker. He would do. He would do just fine. She hoped Booker would come back and find them piled up in bed. She imagined that scene. He would walk in and there Billy would be on top of her, humming like rushing water. She'd be groaning, and she'd look over at Booker and say, "Why don't you have a seat on the porch? We're busy here." Maud giggled at that scene and then she thought of another.

In that one, she was sitting astride Billy, riding him like a horse. He was bucking and the bed was thumping so loud that she didn't hear Booker come in. He grabbed her arm and tried to get her off of Billy, but she jerked away from him, threw her head back, and shook her hair. In another, she and Billy were in the barn, up in the hayloft on a quilt. They hadn't heard Booker climbing the ladder until he was up there with them. She looked up. He was standing over them. His hand went into his pants. He started stroking himself.

That image shocked Maud. She jumped up from the stool, parted the branches of the live oak tree, and walked out into the yard. Chickens were pecking in the dirt. Clothes were flapping on the line. Off toward the river, a flock of birds looked like ants crawling across a blue cloth. Maud straightened her dress. She didn't need to be thinking such thoughts. She put her hand on her tummy. She needed to get rid of that thing before Billy noticed it. She resolved to walk to Blue's allotment the next day.

She and Billy spent that evening like the one before, only Maud got on top one time, just like she'd imagined under the tree. Billy let out a little laugh, but then he settled right into a rhythm, and she hung on to the iron rods of the bed over his head. They got up afterward and ate their supper, and then they went out on the porch to enjoy the breeze off the river. They took a quilt with them so they wouldn't get splinters.

The next morning, Maud gave Billy her aunt's letter to mail. She told him to put it in Nan's box, the second in the line, to avoid getting stung. As soon as he rode off, she grabbed her rifle and bullets, a flour sack, and three biscuits. She took an old cow path west toward Blue's allotment. The air was abuzz with insects and the sun was warming her back. Fairly soon, she was sweating, and she looked forward to the shade of the trees where she thought she remembered squaw root growing. She worked on keeping images of sex away by thinking about Sherlock Holmes. She was doing a fairly good job of that until the barrel of her rifle reminded her of a penis and she got to carrying it with a rhythm that recalled the one she and Billy used in bed. She got a funny feeling in her arm that made her want to thrust her gun in a jabbing sort of way. She shook her head. She was thinking unnatural thoughts. She cradled her gun in both arms and tucked her flour sack in her armpit, careful to keep the biscuits away from her sweat.

She walked on like that, trying to remember lines from *The Hound of the Baskervilles* until she got to the stand of trees she thought she recalled. She forgot about Sherlock Holmes and sex, and began searching the ground. She was looking for the specific plant and watching for snakes, which would, at that time of day, be likely to be curled in the shade. She was startled by a black racer that was longer than any she'd seen in a while. It escaped into the grass and was gone before she even thought about shooting it. She walked on and on, mostly crisscrossing, and was about to give up when she remembered the circle of trees Lovely had recently visited. She'd last been there when she was too young to know about squaw root, let alone identify it. But the circle was cool and had been a comfort to her as a child. She recalled Blue saying his grandfather had shown it to him, and he'd told her and Lovely stories about the old man living off the land on his long walks. Maud was thinking about her great-grandfather walking day after day all the way from Georgia when she caught a glimpse of bluish-green leaves. She forgot about her ancestor's walks. She used the barrel of her rifle to clear her way toward the plant.

It was a single stalk more than two feet tall sprouting clusters of flowers and pods. She was fairly certain it was squaw root. She didn't know what part of the plant she needed. She felt stupid for not bringing a knife. She needed to cut the whole thing down. But the stalk was fairly thick. She looked around for smaller ones but didn't see any. So she tore off branches with leaves, flowers, and pods. She stuffed those into her sack. She sighed hard. She was relieved. And suddenly hungry. Hungry so strong that it had to be the baby's fault. She said, "Quit gnawing at me. I'm gonna eat." She looked around. She thought the circle of trees wasn't far. She walked on, cogitating on what part of the squaw root she needed to take and in what dosage and how. She didn't want to poison herself. She just wanted to get sick enough to get rid of the baby.

She started figuring on how to ask Viola how much to take and how to fix it up. She didn't have any idea what her great-aunt thought about getting rid of a baby. She didn't mind delivering them, she knew that. And certainly birthing was bad. Maud shivered, recalling Lucy's screaming. Everybody had said it had been an easy birth. If that was easy, she didn't want to know what hard was. The only reassurance she felt from the whole mess was that Viola didn't shrink from anything.

At the same time she saw the circle of trees she'd been hunting, she heard a rustle in the woods. It was loud enough to be a large animal, and her mind went to wolves, panthers, and bears. Wolves ran mostly in packs at night. Bears and panthers left tracks on the sandbar. But they were shy animals and fairly rare. She recalled the wild hogs that had roamed the land in the past. They would charge a person, startle a horse into throwing a rider, run through a house. But were any of them left? People ate wild hog. They were probably all eaten to death. She wedged her sack under her arm and lifted her rifle to her waist. Humans were the most likely and most dangerous animals around. She listened. There was another sound farther away. She listened harder. She heard a racket in the limbs over her head. A squirrel. She heard a blue jay. She heard insects. They buzzed steady like always. She decided she'd scared away whatever had been prowling, and she walked on toward the circle, her gun back down and her sack in her hand. She was trying to recall if anybody she knew had ever tasted bear when she stepped into the circle of trees and saw a piece of blue cloth on the ground. Lovely's shirt.

She dropped her sack. She couldn't run. She couldn't bend. Scattered on the ground were pieces of clothes and chawed bones, Lovely's rifle and boots, Gilda's Bible. She dropped her gun. When she moved, she ran toward the river. Beyond the trees, she burst into the sun and sand. She ran to the water's edge. She kept on running until she saw a still pool cut off from the torrent by a low bank of sand. She ran into the pool and sunk to her knees until she was submerged to her shoulders. She wailed so loudly that she could hear herself screaming over the noise of the river.

She screamed and screamed. When she was so exhausted she could only gasp, she laid her shoulders against hard, wet sand. Her legs floated in the water. She looked up into the bright sky until the sun burnt her eyes. She panted. She looked down into the water. The sun glistened and sparkled there. She had to squint even looking down. Her dress was curved around her thighs. She saw her reflection. Its wavering took her out of time. She looked up again and again to the channel of the river. The water was furiously rushing, green, blue, and gray. The sound was like a train's.

She thought she could break through the wall of sand that protected the pool and join the river. It wouldn't take much; or even if she did nothing, the water would dissolve the bank, grab her, and take her away. She would float to Fort Smith, to New Orleans, to the sea. She would cease to exist or exist everywhere all the time in the air, in the sun. She slid farther down into the pool. It was lovely and cool. It protected her skin from the baking heat. She could lie there. The river would come.

A part of the sandbank broke away. New water came in. A school of minnows followed it. They moved in a silver sheet; the sun caught their backs. They swam up beside her leg, to her arm and her chest. One nibbled her. Two others joined in. Soon Maud felt her left arm being tickled. She shook it. The minnows darted away as quickly as a snake. But they left her feeling something. Feeling she was going to live. She slowly rolled over and started crawling. The sand was gritty and rough. It scratched her forearms. She stood up. She looked around for her shoes. She saw one stuck in sand. The other one she didn't see anywhere. She couldn't walk back through the woods barefooted. She would walk the sandbar. She could either go northwest around the bend of the river and find a cow path from there or she could take the ruts through the wild up next to Gourd's. The path to Gourd's was shorter. She looked around for a snake stick.

Her only walking thoughts were about where she was stepping. She stayed on the wet sand close to the river for as long as she could. Walking on dry sand felt like dancing on fire. When she finally got out of the worst of it to the ruts, she chose the left one and walked it until she got to patches of stones and pebbles. Then she switched to the right rut until she met the same thing. She kept her mind on her feet and pushed away thoughts as though they were wild animals. When she came close to the Mounts' path, she wanted to turn her face away from it, look up toward the western sky, and run. But the ground was rocky; her eyes had to go back to her feet. She got beyond the turn without conjuring up any vivid recollections and continued on, moving her eyes up and down on the ground and straight ahead, watching for rocks and looking for the roof of Gourd's house. When she finally saw a stovepipe, she started crying. She cried all the way up the rise.

Early wasn't home yet. She knew by the sun that he wouldn't show for a few more hours and neither would Billy. She walked her lane and washed her feet at the pump. They were bleeding from the sides and soles. She unbuttoned her dress and let it drop to the ground. She did the same with her slip; she stepped out of her drawers. She gathered her clothes up and walked to the porch. She left the garments in a pile, went inside, and dressed behind the sheet, putting socks on first. Spots of blood appeared in the cotton. She ignored those and lifted her overalls off a hook. She stepped into them and then into her boots. By the time she was dressed, she felt calmer than she'd felt in days. But she also felt disconnected. The sheet looked like millions and millions of little square boxes of thread, the crates of clothes like stacks of holes. Maud realized she was looking at each particular thing like it wasn't part of anything else, like it had no usefulness. She wondered if that was how Lovely had gotten to seeing the world. Things by themselves were frightening. She felt her heart thumping. She heard it. She brushed the sheet out of her way, picked out her mother's rifle from the corner and a few bullets from the tray in the top drawer of the chest. She walked out on the porch, looked toward the river, up at the sun, over to the live oak tree.

To avoid Nan's children, she walked to her grandfather's house by the back way. She cut across the bull's pasture, watching him out of the sides of her eyes. She slipped through that gate without undoing its latch. The house looked empty in the distance; the side yard the same. She figured the men were still in the fields; Viola and Lucy were probably in the kitchen. But then she noticed that her uncle Ame's car wasn't next to the barn. The thought crossed her mind that they'd all up and driven off, that she'd never see them again. The dog barked. The bark sounded sharp. Poker was treating her like a stranger. But when she called his name, he came, tail wagging. His friendliness pulled tears from her eyes. Her knees folded; she laid her gun on the ground, put her arms around the dog, and let him lick her face. She was wailing and Poker was whining when Viola came out the front door.

Viola took her to the kitchen, sat her in a chair, and handed her the dipper. She sat down next to Maud and looked out the window. She picked up a fan and fanned Maud's face.

They'd been sitting like that for some time when Maud said, "I found Lovely's body."

Viola stopped fanning. Her eyes didn't blink. "Where?"

"Circle of trees. Uncle Blue's allotment."

Viola laid the fan on the table facedown. "The men'll go get him when they come in."

Maud realized then that the house was quiet. "Where is everybody?"

"Lucy and Cole took the baby to town. She's sick."

The mention of the baby brought Maud's mind off of Lovely. She had Viola alone. She didn't know when that would happen again. "I went to the woods to find squaw root," she said.

Viola closed her eyes.

Maud waited for them to open. When they didn't, she went on. "I don't know how to use it."

Viola's hair was pulled back in a bun. She scratched her neck beneath it. "It's tricky."

"I figured you could teach me."

Viola sighed deeply. She licked the corner of her mouth. "You reckon Lovely took his own life?"

Maud felt guilt pierce her heart like an arrow. Lovely, her

brother and closest friend, was dead on the ground. Eaten, probably by wolves. She was at a table, thinking about her own life. She blushed all the way to her navel. "I'm sorry. I'm, I'm, I'm crazy with shock and out of heart. I don't know what I'm saying."

"You might wanta rest." Viola placed her palms on the table and pushed herself up. She carried the dipper to the pan and took a long drink. She offered the dipper to Maud. Maud shook her head. Viola looked out the window. "Nancy got the throw ups. Scared Lucy. Scared me after a while. I thought going to the doctor was best. When the men came in fer dinner, Cole took Ame's car. Don't know when they'll be back. Them doctors get backed up something awful. You can lie down if yer of a mind."

But Maud couldn't rest. They talked about Lucy's recovery, about a hen that had taken it into her head to roost in a tree during the day, about moles digging tunnels in the yard. Viola did most of the talking until they heard a horse. They looked out the window and saw Blue leading his into the lot. He came back to the pump. He was washing his forearms when Viola went out. Maud watched them from the door. Blue turned over a bucket and sat down on it. Viola put her hand on his shoulder. He put his face in his hands. Poker sat on his haunches. Viola seemed to be looking at the northeast sky. They stayed that way. Then Blue got up and walked to the barn. Viola came inside. She said, "Blue'll git Ame and Bert. He knows the place where Lovely's at. We'll start to cooking."

Early showed up after Blue left. Viola sent him to tell Nan and to put Maud's animals up and to bring her a dress. Lucy and Cole arrived shortly after that with their little boy and with a baby who was, mercifully, sleeping. When Blue finally pulled the wagon in, Viola went out to check the bed and talk to the men. She waved her arm, and Lucy led Maud out the door by the hand. Cole followed them. Lovely, or what was left of him, was wrapped head to toe in a couple of quilts. They all stared at the quilts until Bert said, "We'll take turns sitting up. But we're gonna haveta do it in the barn. It won't do to move him outta the wagon. You younguns" — he pointed to Blue, Early, and Cole — "take the early shift. Git some sleep and then go dig the grave when it's light. Maud, ya want him close to yer mama?" His voice cracked.

Maud put her hand on a wagon wheel. She nodded. Her mouth moved but no sound came out. Viola said, "No use you staying up. Come with me." She had her arm around Maud's waist and turned to go, but Maud resisted. Viola said, "Come on, now. You've had a shock, and it ain't over yet. It's just begun. You haveta preserve yerself."

She tugged Maud again, and Maud went with her, weeping.

The next morning, Nan, Ryde, and their children joined them. Maud sat with her grandfather and Viola in the seat of the wagon that carried Lovely's remains. Ame rode in the bed next to the body. The rest of the family except for Early, who rode his horse, piled into Ryde's wagon, on the seat and in the bed. They turned the wagons west at the section line cross, passed the snake lakes, and turned into the lane of the cemetery. When Maud saw the mound of dirt, she started crying again. When the wagon stopped, she wouldn't get off. Finally, Nan and Lucy convinced her she had to, and each one of them stood beside her at the edge of the empty hole. The men held the quilts by their edges. They lowered Lovely's body slowly.

Maud had picked some verses from Ecclesiastes that Lovely had liked, but she couldn't get the words out. Early took Gilda's Bible in his hands, and said, "Which ones?"

"Chapter three, down to thirteen."

"I'll give it a whirl." He stumbled only on the word *laboureth* and handed the book back to Maud.

Then Viola threw some crumpled-up leaves over the quilts. She said strong Creek-sounding words that Maud didn't understand. After that, everybody who wanted to speak said whatever was on his or her mind about Lovely. Everybody except Maud. When her turn came, she shook her head and buried it into her aunt Nan's shoulder.

Bert threw in the first shovel of dirt. They'd decided to bury Lovely fast and explain later what had happened to him. They had a bunch of good reasons for that, the top one being that another eaten body would remind Sheriff Talley of the earlier two. They wanted to collect their wits to tell the story the way they wanted it told. They talked about that at dinner and again at supper, and it fell to Maud to break the news to Gilda and Mr. Singer. But the next morning was Sunday, and Maud knew Sunday wasn't a day to spread bad news. So she went home after dinner. She found Billy had left her a note of a single word, *Where?* As she stared at the letters, she realized the day before had been August 18. She'd been standing at Lovely's grave when she should've been marrying Booker. Now, she was holding a note from Billy. He seemed like the only future she had, and that future seemed as heavy and black as a kettle.

She went to the front porch and sat in a rocker. She couldn't think in a straight line. She put her hand on her belly. She felt a little curve growing there. That made her heart sink deeper. She looked at a chicken scratching in the dirt by the steps. She looked at the live oak tree. At the pump. At Gourd's house. At the horizon beyond the wild and the river. She would never see a real city. Never Charleston with a man in a sweater. Never wear a dress that stopped at her knees. Never wear tassels or bob her hair.

Maud began to feel a growing hatred for who she was and where she lived. She was sick to death of dirt, sick of chickens, sick of guns and snakes, and, most of all, sick of dead bodies gnawed by animals. Her only chance for escape had been that bright blue canvas rocking her way. She cursed Booker out loud. She stormed at his character until she remembered he'd left her a letter. She just didn't know what it said. But that didn't really matter. He hadn't come back for their wedding. That told the words.

Maud stirred her misery until she whipped it so hard she couldn't bear to sit in a rocker or anywhere. She walked the yard. She picked up rocks and threw them. She went to the pump and washed her face. She walked to the barn and back. Looked at the house and thought she'd lose her mind like Lovely had done. She didn't blame him one bit. He was smarter than she was. He'd found a way out. She shouted loudly, "Good for you, Lovely. You go on. Land somewhere else. Have a real life. Goddamn this dirt."

She couldn't say why that outburst made her feel better. She sat down on a step, put her elbows on her knees, and looked at her hands. She'd never done her nails. They were strong and well shaped but without color. If she had a bottle of Cutex, she could paint them. But she didn't even have that. Didn't have anything she really needed or wanted. Except scissors. She did have scissors.

She jumped up from the step, let the screen door bang behind her, and opened the bottom drawer of the chest. She lifted out her mother's sewing basket. Between spools of thread and a pin cushion was a shiny pair of scissors. She went behind the sheet and lifted the mirror off the wall. She carried it and the basket out to the porch. She set the basket on the steps and put the mirror on the post nail where the men hung it to shave. She stood in the yard and peered in the glass. She held up her hair and turned her head to both sides. Then she picked up the scissors and started cutting.

She cut her hair into a bob with bangs. When she finished, she wasn't even sure she was looking at herself. But she decided she'd get used to it and like it, and that everybody else had better do the same. She left her cut hair on the ground to be blown by the wind and went to milk the cow. When she got back, she got water out of the rainwater barrel and washed her bob. She was standing at the edge of the porch marking a dress with chalk to cut it shorter when she heard the beat of hooves. She looked up. Billy. He waved his hat in the air.

He pulled up his horse at the trough. Walking toward her, he stopped midstep. His eyes grew round. He took his hat off and scratched his head. He turned and looked at his horse. He put his hat back on and then turned around again and looked at Maud. He said, "I'll shore miss Lovely."

"How'd you hear?"

"Early. Saw him on the way down." He took his hat off again, rubbed the brim with both hands. He looked off toward the barn.

Maud sighed. She didn't care if he liked her hair or not. It was hers to cut. But maybe he was just overcome about Lovely. She said, "I brought home some of Viola's cooking."

They ate on the porch. Billy talked about a horse he was breaking at work. Maud thought about her hair. She was thinking she'd made a mistake. She put her hand to the back of her head and felt her bare neck. She shook her head. Billy kept talking about the horse. She finally said, "Do you notice anything different?"

"Didja put a little color on yer cheeks?"

Maud threw her plate out toward the yard. The food went higher than the dish. The chickens squawked, fluttered away, and then rushed back, squabbling over the bits. She stood to speak. "You can just get out of here!" She pointed toward Billy's horse.

He grinned and leaned back in his rocker. "I sorta like a high-tempered woman."

Soon after that, they started making love against a porch post. They heard the beat of hooves in midthrust and moan, but they couldn't stop until they'd come all the way. Then they saw Early standing on Gourd's porch, staring toward them. Early waved. Maud said, "I don't give a rat's ass. Nothing he hasn't seen before." Billy waved back.

Inside, they lay on the bed and stared at the crack in the ceiling. Then Billy rolled over onto his side, propped his face in his palm, and said, "I wasn't shore I'd like making love to a boy." He caught some of Maud's hair between his fingers and pulled it a bit.

"You better get used to it. And I'm gonna cut my dresses down. Show my knees."

Billy ran a hand down her thigh and rested his palm on the scar on the back of her leg. "I like yer knees."

They made love once again and slept through the night like the dead. When Maud woke, Billy was standing over her, his elbow working. She said, "What're you doing?" He smiled. Then he reached for her arm, pulled her toward him, and said, "Open yer mouth. Put it in."

He came so fast he didn't get his penis much past the tip of her tongue. She pulled back, put the tips of her fingers to her lips. She swallowed. "It's salty."

"So I hear."

"You've done that before?"

Billy sat down, put his arm around her waist, drew her to him, and kissed her tenderly. When he pulled back, he said, "No, not really. I heared tell. Men talk, you know."

Maud didn't believe him. He'd had another girlfriend. She had big breasts. The thought of those breasts stabbed her with jealousy. "If I catch you talking about me, I'll do the same thing to you I did to my hair."

"Oh, Maud. Cross my heart. I won't talk about you." Billy paused. "I won't have to. Early'll do it fer me." He started giggling.

Maud pushed him down on the mattress and stood up. "I'll make a gelding out of Early, too. It's morning. Time to go to work."

Once Maud saw Billy out of the house, she went about her chores, focused on the conversations she needed to have with Mr. Singer and Gilda. Speaking with Gilda would be the hardest; Mr. Singer might make her feel better. When she headed out, talking to them in that order was her plan. She carried in a sack pulled to her chest Gilda's Bible and Mr. Singer's books. She stopped in to visit with Nan, took iced tea and pie there, explained her haircut as wanting to try something new, and found out that her grandfather had gone into town to register Lovely's death. When she got to the section lines, Mr. Beecher, headed out in his wagon, gave her a ride into Ft. Gibson. She dallied there, putting off calling on Gilda until after dinner so that the Starrs wouldn't try to feed her. She wanted to tell Gilda and get away fast.

Gilda's first reaction was to Maud's hair. But she quickly said, "You look all hollow in the cheeks. What's the matter?" She took Maud's sack and set it on a table. She put her hands on Maud's upper arms and looked her over.

Maud started to cry.

"It's Lovely, isn't it? Tell me. Take a seat." Gilda nodded toward a sofa.

But Maud didn't feel she could sit until she'd said what she'd come to say. "You better sit yourself."

Gilda did. She looked up at Maud and said, "Tell me."

"Lovely passed away. He'd been poorly since the rabies shots. Couldn't get over them."

Gilda's mouth fell open. "He died of his shots?"

Maud wanted to run out the door. But to get the rest out, she figured she needed to sit. She settled on the arm of a chair. "No. He was afraid he was going mad. We have a cousin that happened to. I guess he didn't want to be put away. I don't know, really." She shook her head. "If I'd known, I wouldn't have taken my eyes off him." Tears welled up. She wiped them away with a handkerchief.

Gilda turned her head. She shuddered. She looked back at Maud. "He killed himself?"

Maud stood again. Her voice caught as she spoke. "It's not your fault. Don't take any blame. If it's anybody's, it's mine. I should've tried to help him more. I didn't know what to do or how bad it was." She shook her head.

Gilda looked down. Maud thought she was praying. After what seemed forever, Gilda lifted her face. "He's with the Lord now," she said, but she was crying.

Maud wanted to escape. "Yes, yes, he is." She didn't believe that, but she didn't not believe it. And she would've said whatever it took to get out of the house. She handed Gilda her Bible and told her they'd read from it at the service. That the verses had been a real help and were what Lovely would've wanted. They tried to comfort each other with hugs and reassuring words. But as soon as she thought she could go with any grace, Maud got out the door.

She felt relief as soon as she got to the street. She threw the sack of books over her shoulder, and by the time she reached the center of town, she felt better than she had when she'd arrived. And she realized that, beyond her guilt, she, too, felt Lovely was better off where he was. He would've been haunted in his head for the rest of his life. Why was mysterious and beyond her reach. She didn't understand it. She didn't think anybody did.

She was given a ride out of town on the back of a horse ridden by a boy she knew. He took her all the way to the potato barn, dismounted when she slid off, and tried to talk to her about going off to the oil fields. Maud endured that as long as she could. Then she abruptly told him Mr. Singer was expecting her, turned, and marched toward the barn. But in there, the potato odor flew up her nostrils and down to her stomach. She suddenly became sick and retched in a corner. She didn't think that was related to the baby. She thought it was due to having to tell Gilda. She remembered her mother's death going to her gut. She sat down outside in the barn's shade until she was sure nothing else was coming up. Then she walked to a rainwater barrel and washed her mouth out. She scooped water with her palm onto her arms and neck to cool them down from the heat.

A few minutes later, she cupped her hand against the summer kitchen's screen door. The room was dark and a large table sat in the center, a fireplace at the far end. Lizzie wasn't in there, so Maud went to the back door of the main house and knocked. Nobody came. But the porch was shady, and she was exhausted. She sat down on a rocker with cushions on its seat and back, and fell asleep. Sometime later, she awoke to the sound of her name. Mr. Singer was standing inside his screen. "I didn't hear a knock. Then you looked so tuckered out, I let you sleep. Feel better now?" He opened the screen and stepped out.

"Yes. I'm sorry." She started to get up.

"Keep your seat. I'll lean against the post. An old man sits too much. Need to stir my blood."

"Thank you. I brought your books." Maud put her hand on the

sack on the table beside the chair. "They were good, especially the Sherlock Holmes."

Mr. Singer nodded. "I can read about Holmes late into the night. Often do." He patted his chest and reached into his shirt pocket. He drew out an envelope. "You might be interested in this." He handed it to her.

The handwriting struck Maud like a bolt of lightning. She stared at it, her eyes wide, her mouth open. Her breath was uneven. Mr. Singer continued. "Came enclosed with one to me. He may not be too sure how often you get to your mailbox."

Maud recalled the dirt dobbers and telling Billy to mail her the letter in Nan's box. She hadn't even checked their box since running into the wasps. They rarely got anything unless they'd ordered from Sears and Roebuck; they hadn't done that in a long time. Booker's first letter had come by way of Mr. Singer; she'd thought that he hadn't known her route number. She felt panicked over what she might've missed. She jumped up.

Mr. Singer jerked and stepped back. "Why don't I leave you to read by yourself? I'll shelve your books. I have a new one you might enjoy."

Maud wasn't sure she'd be able to talk after she opened her letter. And she still needed to tell Mr. Singer about Lovely. But her mind sped in another direction. She said, "I'd appreciate a new book." She sat back down. She studied Booker's handwriting while Mr. Singer was gone.

When he returned, he handed her a book and said something about it. But Maud didn't hear that. She felt like a field on fire. She blurted out, "Lovely's dead. He killed himself."

Mr. Singer's face grew as pale as his goatee. Maud stood to let him sit down. But he waved the seat away with his hand. He put a palm on a post. The other hand he wiped across his mouth.

"I didn't mean to be so forward. I'm upset." Her tears started again. She drew her handkerchief out of her pocket and wiped them.

Mr. Singer drew out his own handkerchief and blew his nose. "He was a fine young man. A credit to your family. To your grandpa and grandma. To your great-grandpa."

Maud forgot, just for a moment, how much she longed to be out of the place she lived, and she felt comforted by a memory that spanned generations. Mr. Singer's gaze went to the west horizon; his mind seemed to follow it.

She said, "We were all proud of him."

Maud left with the book clutched to her breast, the envelope tucked inside with the tip sticking out so she could keep a watch on it. She walked to the tree beside the highway. She sunk to the roots and wedged her back against the trunk. She opened the book and drew the letter from between its pages. Her thumb shook as she slipped her nail beneath the fold.

> Dear Maud,
>
> I have to confess I thought you'd at least answer my second letter. I know I'm at fault, but I'm not the only one. There's plenty of blame to go around. I hope you'll reconsider.
>
> I've moved from the boarding house. My new address is 355 So. Brier. Please write me and tell me what you're thinking. I didn't figure you would be so mad that we couldn't even be friends.
>
> Yours sincerely,
> Booker

She'd read the letter twice when she heard a motor coming over the bridge. The rumble of the planks came nearer and nearer.

She felt like her destiny was coming upon her and would appear momentarily. But by the time the truck had passed, Maud realized she didn't even know what city Booker was in. Muskogee? Tulsa? Oklahoma City? Some smaller town beyond that bridge? She needed to go back to Mr. Singer and ask him where the postmark on his letter was from. And she needed to look for the other letter. The second one.

Maud jumped up from the roots, dusted her dress and legs off, and stuck the letter and its envelope back in the book. She edged down the embankment sideways on an angled course from rock to rock to a clump of grass until she landed on level ground. But by the time she did, she heard a motor, looked up, and saw a black Chrysler coming along the road toward Mr. Singer's house. She stopped where she was. The car stopped at the end of the drive in front of the garage next to a hitching rail. A man, a woman, and three children tumbled out. Maud didn't recognize any of them, but she supposed they were Mr. Singer's family come to visit, maybe from a long way away. She turned back to the bank beside the highway and climbed it again. From there, she walked down the road to the section line and turned south.

She endured catcalls from the men at the school site. But nobody approached her, and she decided she'd walk that way again. If she didn't have the courage to walk down her own section line, she wouldn't have the courage to walk down the street in a city. She rushed on, thinking about what might be waiting in her mailbox. She thought about how many times she'd walked near it and about the letter Billy had mailed in the box next to it.

At the line of boxes, she stopped with her hand on the flap of hers, trying to remember one of the ancient Cherokee love formulas she'd copied from Mooney's book. But she couldn't bring one up that she felt sure was exact, and she didn't want to say one, even in her head, that might be incorrect and jinx the insides of the box. She focused her eyes on the beans in the field beyond. What if she opened the box and it was empty? She wouldn't be able to bear that. Still, she had one letter in hand. That was better than nothing. She stood to the side to avoid any angry dirt dobbers, tugged hard once, and then eased the flap open.

There was a dead dirt dobber lying on top of a flyer with a picture of a tractor on it. She tilted the flyer and dumped him off. She pulled out a handwritten offer from a well digger and a book of coupons. Below them was a letter addressed in Booker's writing and postmarked from Tulsa. Her hand shook as she held it. She dropped the book. It landed on her toe.

Bending over, Maud suddenly felt faint. She'd had too much excitement and heat and too little water. The back of her neck was burning where it'd never been exposed to the sun. She rose up slowly, afraid she might faint. Nan's house sat beyond the beans. She decided to walk toward it at a slow pace and read the letter there. She walked, both letters in the book, and took deep, regular breaths that she hoped would get her to within sight of her aunt's if her body gave out.

Renee was standing out in the road. She ran up steps to the pump, picked a tin cup off the top of the handle, and dipped it into a bucket. She came back out to the road and walked toward Maud, spilling some water as she came. Maud had never been so glad to see the child in her life. She drank noisily, drained the cup of every drop, and wiped her face with her forearm.

Renee said, "You're wobbly. And you look peaked."

"I feel peaked."

"Want me to carry your book?"

"No, I'll carry it myself. You carry these." She handed Renee the rest of the mail. "Thanks for the water. Can I lean on you a bit?"

Renee stepped to Maud's side and took the cup. Maud drew her arm over the girl's shoulders. They walked down the middle of the road. The house Nan was living in was built on a natural rise that had protected it from the flood. A wall of sandstone held back the rise where it was cut down for the road. Five steps led up to the yard. When they got to the steps, Renee said, "Can you do these?"

Maud shook her head. "Let me rest here. Go get your mama."

Maud was resting the side of her face on her book and the book on her knees when Nan shooed her kids away and sat down beside her. She rubbed Maud's back. "You can't be walking in this heat in yer condition. Not with the blow you've had."

Maud straightened up. "I've heard from Booker." She tapped the book's cover. "Two letters. In here."

"What'd they say?"

"I haven't read one of them."

Nan's hand stopped rubbing. "Let me see."

Maud opened the book and handed her the unopened enve-lope. "You read it. Tell me what it says. I can't face it alone."

Nan held the envelope up to the sun. She carefully broke open a side with little rips. She pulled the letter out and was silent. Then she said, "He's working in a store named Vandever's. His boss is Mr. Gary. He's selling men's ready-to-wear. He's living in a boarding house with three other men. The woman who runs it is a good cook but wears dirty aprons. One of the men is from Mis-souri. One is from Texas and the other one is from a place I can't make out the name. Evelyn and Arlene, that's his horses, right? Well, they're down the street in a stable. He don't say anything about his wagon or wares."

"Does he say anything about me?"

Nan bit her under lip. She read more. "He says he admires yer spirit and hopes you'll write and tell him what yer thinking."

"That's it?"

Nan nodded.

"Let me see." Maud pulled the letter from her aunt's hand. She read it silently. *I admire your spirit and hope you'll write and tell me what you're thinking* was the most personal thing in it. Maud growled.

"He don't know yer in a family way, do he?"

Maud looked up from the letter to the far side of the road. Over there, a few trees provided shade and the ground ample nesting for snakes. She said, "I have to get rid of this baby. Will you make Viola help me?"

Nan clasped her knees with her hands and tapped her thumbs together.

"Aunt Nan, I can't have this baby. I just can't. Booker doesn't know about it. We were trying not to get in a family way. And I can't show up on his doorstep and say it's his. He doesn't even sound that interested." She waved the letter in front of her face like a fan. "He's more interested in his job and people in Tulsa. And I've got another letter that says he wants to be friends."

"Have you written him?"

"No. I didn't know where he was. And now . . ." Maud looked down at her stomach.

"That's three letters in all. Sounds like he's still interested. He just needs some encouragement."

"Maybe he does. But showing up on his doorstep and announcing I'm carrying isn't likely to rekindle his interest."

"It might. He might want a baby."

"I want him to want me."

Nan seemed to study the trees. Eventually, she said, "That Billy's a worker."

"That might be, but the baby's not his."

Nan grunted. "He's too full-blooded to care."

Maud put her chin in her hands. Her elbows were balanced on the book on her knees. She knew Cherokee men weren't too bothered by who'd fathered the children in their own homes. Mostly, they parented their sisters' kids, their certain blood kin. That, Maud supposed, was the upside to their everlasting comings and goings. She said, "You don't understand. I've got to get out of here. Aunt Nan, the whole world's passing me by. Will you talk to Aunt Viola for me?" Her voice sounded high.

Nan sighed. "You haveta please yerself. But if ya do it, be sure it's in the right sign."

"What sign would that be?"

"I'd have to study on it. But not in the heart, belly, or reins. You'd bleed to death as quick as that." She snapped her fingers.

The snap startled Maud. And the thought of bleeding to death filled her with horror. She didn't think astrological signs were reliable, but most of her family was high on them, particularly for planting, hog killing, and tooth pulling. She didn't want to take any unnecessary chances. Bleeding to death in the bottoms would be worse than being snakebit and getting it over with fast.

Nan patted Maud's back. She asked her to stay for supper. And they were eating when they heard a wagon. Morgan hopped up to see who it was. He came back and slid into his seat with a grin on his face. Ryde said, "Well?"

"It's one of Maud's fellows."

Maud said, "In a wagon?"

"Yep."

"Does it have a blue cover?"

"Nope. Got a rocker and chest in the back. Saw a dog, too."

Maud burst out crying. She jumped up from the table and fled out the back door. She ran to the smokehouse, lifted the latch, stepped into salty dark, and pulled the door closed behind her. She turned her face to the wood, beat her forehead against it again and again, and sobbed. After she cried herself out, she wiped her nose and face on her handkerchief. She turned around and peered into the dark. Her uncle was renting this house and had been in it for only a couple of years. She was unfamiliar with its particular smokehouse, but she'd been in smokehouses all of her life. They didn't much vary. When her eyes adjusted, she saw three hams hanging from the ceiling and a curing chest against the back wall. She moved over to the chest, swiped her finger against the wood to test it for grease, and tasted the results. She sat down. She needed to think, if she could just get her head clear. She inhaled salt. It burnt.

7

When she got back home, she couldn't think any better. Billy was in the barn, his dog patrolling the front porch. Maud growled at the dog louder than he growled at her. She threw out a leg in his direction as she went inside. Billy's chair and chest were hunkered in the main room like a couple of contented hogs. The chest was particularly grating. It was sitting where Lovely's cot usually sat and it seemed solid and permanent. But Maud had already felt that living alone without the hope of Lovely returning was worse than living alone thinking he would show any day. So her feelings were running completely crossways.

Maud went to the cow lot, prodded Carrie into place with a little stick, and fussed at the cow, even though the animal was as cooperative as usual. She stood behind Carrie and smacked her on her rump more than once, trying to make the cow kick her in the stomach. But Carrie just turned a big brown eye and a wide, wet mouth Maud's way and flicked her tail like she was bored with the whole conversation. Maud gave up. She set her bucket and stool in place, rested her cheek on the cow's side, and closed her eyes. She tried to get some comfort from Carrie's hide as she milked.

When she came in from the cow lot, Billy was hungry, first for food and then for sex. Settled some by milking, she provided him both. But while she and Billy rocked back and forth, she got to thinking about Booker, seventy or eighty miles away in Tulsa, doing the same thing with a big-city girl. Probably a flapper with a long string of pearls. Maud started crying before Billy was through. She cried over Booker having a girlfriend in Tulsa, over Billy's furniture making her choice for her, over Lovely's death. Billy was so deeply occupied that his rhythm didn't change. But when he was through, he asked her what the matter was. She said, "I'm just crying for Gilda. I told her today."

As the days and nights wore on, Maud got used to the furniture. She also stopped worrying about Sheriff Talley showing up to ask questions about Lovely. Everybody knew Lovely had lost his mind; as gentle as he'd been, even Talley wouldn't think anybody in the family had killed him. She bought some stamps and wrote her sisters and her aunt, hoping one of them would get word to her father. She checked the mailbox every day, both for word back from them and for another letter from Tulsa. Twice, when Billy was off working, she sat under the live oak tree and tried to write Booker. But each time she tore up what she had written. She realized she didn't have enough information about his state of mind to know exactly how to cast her lines. And the thought of writing Booker the wrong thing and then waiting for an answer that might never come — or, even worse, might come and push the last hope she had away forever — was more than Maud could bear.

But more immediate, with her every day, was Lovely's being gone. She'd never been without him before and she hated the empty spaces he left in the house and on the porch. She had a hole in her chest that sometimes seemed so big she couldn't swallow. She felt like a hollowed-out tree. She got the most relief from her grief when she and Billy were having sex. But that always ended in tears, and the crying began to interfere with Billy's ability to keep his interest up. After a few wilting experiences, Maud told him that her tears were releasing her grief and that bed was the only place she felt safe enough to let it out. Billy perked back up after that and applied himself like a woodpecker to a tree. Maud enjoyed his hammering and the senselessness that came over her when she rocked back and forth with her legs locked over his rear.

She'd dropped the squaw root she'd gathered when she found Lovely's body. She couldn't go back there and pick it up. And she thought it was likely her grandfather and great-uncle had picked that sack up when they'd gathered Lovely's remains. She'd need to cut more squaw root, but she didn't want to walk to Blue's allotment and relive that awful day unless she knew for sure how to put the weed to use. She kept trying to get Nan to help her get rid of the baby. But Nan kept shaking her head, saying the signs were all wrong and recalling her uncle Tomahawk who'd died of a tooth pulled when the sign was in the heart. Nan said, "Bled plumb to death" more than once in such a somber tone that Maud began to wonder if Tomahawk had really died that way or if Nan had just made that story up.

On the day Maud brought the rattle back for the baby, she asked Viola to help her. Viola was watering flowers, dipping out of a bucket with a cup, and didn't respond. Maud hoped she'd get an answer when the bucket was empty, and she studied the petunias until her great-aunt turned the pail upside down over a cluster and finally spoke. "Sometimes I look at these flowers and see the faces of all the dead Indians in the ground. They killed us in ever' which way. Smallpox. Measles. Firewater. Starvation. Shot the ones who crossed them. Burnt our crops and houses to the ground. Ran us off our land. Stole ever' last thing we had. Preached hard religion that scared the spirits out of the world. Then told us we was going to Hell unless we took up their God." Viola handed Maud the bucket, spat, and marched around the side of the house.

So Maud went back to sex. She started grabbing Billy as soon as he cleaned up. She unbuckled his pants at the pump. She pushed him under the branches of the live oak tree and tickled him with twigs until once he came without even a hand. She sucked his dick right out on the porch. Inside, she rode him on top, pinning his shoulders to the mattress. She squeezed his butt like a vice while they were on their sides. And, under him, she lassoed his rear with her legs. She'd decided the only way to get rid of that baby was to fuck it out, and the more positions they tried, the better chance she had. She got to where she was sore between the legs all of the time. She greased herself with the salve her father used on sows when they were being nursed to nubs, and that worked not only to smooth her rough patches but helped Billy, too. His penis had gotten to looking like it'd been in a fight.

Lovemaking kept Maud's thoughts about Booker at bay. But sometimes during the day, he would appear to her as clear as a stalk of corn, as clear as a cow in the pasture, as clear as the live oak tree. She never caught a glimpse of him out of the sides of her eyes; he was always in front of her, full-blown, sometimes naked but more often with a book in his hand, wearing a white shirt and red suspenders, his bowler on the back of his head. At first, Maud thought those visions were real. Her breath left her body; she stood still. But then Booker melted away into the sun, into the air, into the branches of the tree. So when the apparition showed up, she made even more passionate love with Billy. And she sometimes thought about Booker watching them. That both excited her and provided a temporary balm to her feelings of abandonment and injustice.

But her crying got more frequent. She cried if the wind blew dust in her eye, cried if she saw an animal hurt, cried if she wanted her way. Billy started going to the barn or over to visit Early until the storm passed away. But that infuriated Maud. More than once, when he returned, she threw a cup at his head or pushed him down the steps off the porch. Billy, however, seemed to be able to handle a fighting woman better than a crying one, and when her temper was particularly elevated, he sometimes pulled his pecker out of his pants and stroked it up and down. That drove Maud into a frenzy and made her wet with desire. She and Billy started enjoying their fights because of the making up.

Maud didn't hear back from her aunt Matilda, who she wasn't certain could write. She did hear from her sister Peggy. She'd seen their father several days back and would tell him about Lovely when she saw him again. She didn't say exactly where Mustard was, but did say that he was following the oil and that he had come to her and stayed a few days after a fight that she thought would leave a scar over his left eye. Peggy was sorry she hadn't been able to travel with her children to get to Maud's wedding and wanted to know how she liked married life. Maud tore that letter up and put the pieces in a nest in the chicken house that was on the top row, rarely used and out of sight. She couldn't say at first why she didn't just burn the letter, but she knew she felt chagrined that she hadn't told Peggy the marriage was off, and eventually she figured out that she was lonesome for her daddy and didn't want to send any mention of him up in flames.

She didn't hear any more from Booker. And she didn't write him. She couldn't tell him about Billy or the baby, and she envisioned his head being turned by women in Tulsa. She calculated she couldn't compete with store-bought shifts, silk stockings, and shoes with fancy buckles. But even though she kept her hair bobbed and cut her three dresses up to the knees, she got to where she couldn't stand to look at the Sears and Roebuck Catalogue. When the new one arrived, she took it straight to the outhouse. Billy rescued it from there, and they had a fight over whether or not to leave it on the kitchen table. Billy won that fight by screwing her against the wall so long and hard that she slid to the floor and told him, "Do what you want. I don't care."

Still, seeing the catalogue on the table every morning, noon, and night reminded Maud of Booker. She didn't know enough about Tulsa to know what kind of store he was working in except that it sold ready-to-wear. But she imagined it looked like the Woolworth Building, whose picture she'd seen again and again. She also imagined Sears and Roebuck housed in that same structure. And after a while, Sears and Roebuck, the Woolworth Building, and Booker's store all merged into an image that loomed so large in her mind that it seemed like a force of nature as powerful as the river. She beat it back by going to the cellar and sitting on a bench until the smell of the earth brought Lovely to her. She carried on conversations with him about their parents, about books, about how the hens were laying.

And so September wore on with Maud tuned to her inside feelings and visions more than to the outside world until one Sunday evening late in the month, after a meal at Nan's and making love, Billy ran the palm of his hand over her belly and rested it below her navel. He said, "That ain't yer aunt Nan's cooking, is it?"

Maud looked past her breasts like she was checking on her situation for the first time. There was a definite mound there. She hated seeing it. "I reckon."

Billy's head was propped on his other hand. He pulled his chin in. "'You reckon?' Don't you know?"

She rested her forearm over her eyes to hide as much of her face as she could. "I've been suspecting. Just thought I'd wait and see."

"Do ya think we better stop?"

"Stop what?"

"You know."

"Stop doing it good?"

"Yeah. It might hurt the baby." Billy's brow wrinkled.

"Well, number one, we don't know there's a baby in there. I might just be over fed. A satisfied woman can put on weight."

Billy smiled, but asked, "What's number two?"

"There isn't a number two. I was just using an expression."

Billy frowned. He ran his hand over her stomach again.

Maud turned onto her side and cupped his balls with her fingers. "I've just eaten a big meal. When did you start wanting to talk in bed?" She squeezed just a little.

"I can feel that in the roof of my mouth." He started to say something else, but Maud kissed him on the lips; whispered, "Shut up"; and then kissed his neck and his nipples, and moved down in the bed. Billy didn't do anything but groan, and by the time she was through with him, he didn't make any sound at all. He slept without moving and went to work the next morning humming a tune.

But Maud was distressed. She'd been examining her body every day and had seen the changes in it. Her breasts were heavy, the brown around her nipples too dark, and the curve to her belly wasn't going away unless she did something about it. She was afraid she'd poison herself if she tried the squaw root without instructions, afraid she'd bleed to death if she stuck something up herself, and figured Dr. Ragsdale wouldn't help her out. The only thing she could think to try was jumping. She stood on the edge of the porch and jumped off of it until her shins hurt and dirt was ground into her palms. Then she sat on the steps and tried to feel if anything had changed inside. She decided it hadn't. But she resolved to jump every morning as soon as Billy went off to work. She went about her chores in a foul mood.

She was carrying a pail of milk back from the cow lot when she heard Billy's dog barking. He was on the ground in front of the porch, so she first looked past him for a snake. She couldn't see anything unusual in the dirt; she looked closer at the dog's head. It was up, not down; his ears were pointing forward. He'd heard something in the distance. Maud kept walking toward the house, and a car soon emerged from the trees on the section line. It was the sheriff's.

Maud was already so blue that the sight of the car stirred her interest more than her fears. She walked on into the kitchen and poured the milk into a pitcher while the sheriff negotiated the guards. When he called from the steps, she came to the screen and said, "Good morning, Sheriff Talley. Would you like a glass of milk?"

The sheriff licked his lips. But then he shook his head. "I'd like a word with ya. Could I come in?"

That request was unusual. The weather was still hot. Most anybody would prefer to talk on the porch. Maud recognized that Talley wanted to see if anybody else was inside. That probably meant he'd come about her father, not about Lovely. She said, "Have you located Daddy?"

Talley stepped up to the porch. "Do ya mind if I come in?" He took his hat off with his left hand.

Maud knew that meant he was saving his right hand for his gun. She didn't much like anybody seeing the inside of the house, but she really didn't have much choice. She opened the screen door.

The sheriff stepped into the kitchen, looked it over, and stepped into the other room. He pulled the sheet back and looked behind it. He let it go and paused in the threshold between the two rooms. "Laswell says yer daddy came by the feed store to pick up money owed him."

Maud's first reaction was to feel hurt that her father hadn't come to see her. She said, "When was that?"

"Jist let me ask the questions. Have ya seen him?"

"No. I wish I had. I don't even know if he knows Lovely's dead."

"I heard about that. Had a little talk with yer grandfather. I'm sorry. Do ya think the rabies sent him off in his head?"

"Could be." She didn't know what her grandfather had said and didn't want to contradict whatever it was. He'd never mentioned talking to the sheriff, and it could be that Talley was casting a line to hook her. On the other hand, it was just like her grandpa to say as little as possible about anything disturbing. Both to buy time and because she really felt it, she said, "Do you mind if we step outside? I'm overheating."

The sheriff held the screen door open. Maud stepped out on the porch. She didn't want to offer Talley a seat, so she leaned against a post, her hand cushioning her rear. The sheriff put his hat on, walked to the front edge of the porch, and picked a lighter and a pack of cigarettes out of his shirt pocket. He shook a cigarette out, crumpled the package, and stuck it back in his pocket. "I'd offer ya one, but I'm out."

"I just smoke at night." She waved her hand in front of her face. At that time of day, there wasn't a spot of shade on the front porch.

Talley lit his cigarette and pocketed his lighter in his pants. Something about that made Maud feel a little unsettled. She first wondered why he didn't put it back in his shirt pocket where it had come from. Then she recalled her father's Banjo. It was probably on top of the chest. Billy had smoked a cigarette with his coffee that morning; she didn't think he'd left it on the table, but he knew how much it meant to her and he never took it farther than the porch. What if Talley had seen it? He'd seen it a thousand times before; he'd recognize it. She flicked a bead of sweat off her brow.

"Laswell says Mustard's hand waz hurt."

"Hurt bad?"

"Evidently."

"Well, he fights a lot."

"Weren't his right hand, twer his left one." Talley took a drag.

"That's a good thing, I guess. Why are you telling me?"

"He's yer daddy. I thought you might like to know." He puffed on his cigarette again.

Maud thought it was unlikely the sheriff was being considerate. She took her hand out from behind her, leaned her shoulders against the post, and folded her arms below her breasts.

Talley took his cigarette from between his lips. "You know, men lose fingers, hands, even arms, in those oil fields ever' day." He flicked his ash. "I'm thinking yer daddy's days on a rig are over. Think about that. Where would a man go ifin he was out of work?" He looked directly at Maud. "He'd go home. Give me a shout when he shows. I jist wanta ask him a few questions." Talley stepped off the porch.

Maud went inside and watched the sheriff leave from the window. Then she sat down on the bed. She wondered where her father was. She hoped he'd show up, maybe come through the back way by the river. The thought of seeing him again brought tears to her eyes. She got up to get a handkerchief from the dresser and remembered the lighter. It wasn't on the dresser's top. She felt relieved. She drew a handkerchief out of the drawer, blew her nose in it, and looked over to Billy's dresser. The lighter wasn't there, either. She tried to recall for sure if Billy had used it that morning. She thought he had. She'd cleared the ashtray off the table. She stepped to the door and looked in the kitchen. The ashtray was on a shelf above the pan and the dipper. She stepped over there. The lighter wasn't on the shelf. Then she remembered Talley holding the door for her. Had he seen the lighter on the table and scooped it up behind her back? She pulled out a chair and sat down at the table. She thought taking the lighter was illegal. But maybe not if it was evidence. She didn't know. She felt her stomach knot into a fist. Then she remembered that Talley didn't know the lighter was evidence, didn't know it had been left at the Mounts'. He'd just think it meant her father had been around. But he knew that anyway. She felt some relief. But then she got to wondering where the lighter was. She searched both rooms again. She went out on the porch. She scanned it, and the west one, too. The Banjo was nowhere to be seen.

Maud knew she was working herself into a state over the lighter. And she decided the best thing to do was to get her mind off it by going see her uncle Ryde. He was more likely than anybody to know what her father was up to, and he may've even seen him. He'd also spent enough time in jail to know if the sheriff was a thief. She grabbed her gun from the corner and headed out. But between the cattle guards, she decided the sheriff could very well be at her aunt and uncle's house. She needed to wait to walk up there. Besides, her daddy might show up. She didn't want to miss him if he did. She turned back. She hung around the farm for the rest of the day, scanning her surroundings every few minutes, hoping her father would appear in the distance.

Mustard didn't show, but by the time Billy did, Maud had decided not to tell him about the sheriff's visit. She'd never gotten around to telling him about the Mounts. She was certain he knew they were dead, fairly certain, too, that he knew that her father and uncle had been suspects. But he was too Indian to have asked her about it. In that way, Billy was an improvement over Booker.

However, Maud wasn't too Indian to ask a question or two. The first thing she said when Billy came into the kitchen from washing up at the pump was, "Have you seen Daddy's lighter?"

Billy ducked his head. Then he looked up and smiled. He put his hand in his pocket and drew it out. The Banjo was in his palm. "I fergot what I was doing."

Maud had a cup of flour in her hand. She took a couple of steps toward Billy and threw the flour in his face.

The next morning, after she'd jumped off the porch seven or eight times, Maud put on the loosest dress she had and picked up her gun and *Show Boat*, the last book Mr. Singer had lent her, and headed out through the cattle guards. Her plan was to talk to her uncle Ryde first and then return the book to Mr. Singer and get another one on medical conditions and what to do about them. Her thoughts moved back and forth so many times between her father and how to ask for the book without raising suspicions that she was at the steps up to Ryde and Nan's yard before she realized the whole place seemed quiet. Their dog was in the yard, and the kids, except for Andy, would be in school, but there didn't seem to be any sign of her aunt or uncle, and the chickens weren't out. She said to the dog, "What'd you do with them?"; and she bounded up to the porch, calling, "Aunt Nan, Uncle Ryde," two or three times. The door was shut. She tried the knob. It turned. She went in the house, called again, and walked to the kitchen. Plates with half-eaten food were on the table. She went out the back door. She looked around. No sign of a human. The chickens were squawking. She walked over to the chicken house and opened the flap. The hens came running out.

After that, she didn't know what to do, so she washed the dishes. Her fear arose as she did. What if the sheriff had arrested them? They both knew that her daddy had killed Claude Mount. What if they confessed that? Maud scrubbed egg off a plate. No, that was as unlikely as a tornado at Christmas. Ryde had already held up under questioning and Nan would pretend she couldn't understand what the sheriff was saying. They had to be somewhere else. Maybe with somebody who came by asking for help. She thought they'd show soon; they had Andy with them. But by the time the dishes were dried and put up, Ryde and Nan still weren't back. Maud decided she'd walk on up to her grandfather's and see if anybody there knew what was going on. But then she saw *Show Boat* sitting on the table. She decided to go on to Mr. Singer's. Wherever her aunt and uncle were, they'd be back eventually. They hadn't locked the door.

When she got to Mr. Singer's, his front door was shut. Instead of knocking, she went around the side and saw that the garage was empty. She walked on toward the summer kitchen. As she got nearer, she heard whistling. She peered in the screen door, saw Lizzie, and said, "Hello, there."

The cook jumped and said, "You frightened me outta my drawers." But she invited her in.

Maud had seen the summer kitchen only from outside the door. Stepping inside it was like stepping into a book. A large rectangular table sat in the center of the room. Pots, skillets, and cleavers hung from the ceiling. Maud was staring up at them when Lizzie said, "You can sit."

She propped her gun by the door. "I came to bring Mr. Singer his book. I've kept it too long." She slid into a chair, glad to be off her feet.

"He ain't here. You look tuckered out. Want some tea?"

"Yes, please." Maud looked around. The windows were high up on the walls; the sink had both a spigot and a pump. The fireplace was huge. A pot hung on chains was inside it. The west wall was lined with shelves and cabinets. There was both a wood stove and an electric one. The electric one still had a tag on it. Mr. Singer's mother had sold some of their land to an electricity company before she'd died. Everybody knew Mr. Singer would be the first in the bottoms to get the goods when the plant was eventually built.

Lizzie went to a wooden icebox taller than she was and took out a bowl of ice with a pick in it. She chipped, jabbing quickly. When she set the glass in front of Maud, she said, "Hear anything from Mr. Wakefield?"

Maud didn't know any Negroes. There had been a bad killing of them over in Tulsa, and especially since then, most of them lived off by themselves. But she did recognize that Lizzie's asking a personal question was peculiar. She didn't know if that threw her or if she was thrown because the subject was Booker. However, she'd read *Show Boat* and didn't care for hatefulness toward anybody. And the cook had been a real friend to her. "He's written me; but I never answered his letters."

"Ahum." Lizzie poured herself some tea and leaned against the sink. She looked at Maud over the top of her glasses.

"He ran off and left me."

"Well, some of 'em do that." Lizzie took a drink. Then she looked over Maud's head. "But if ya can get ya a good'un, they's a blessing. I had me a husband fer twenty-two years. A good man. Appendix busted."

Upon hearing that, Maud's last uneasiness about talking to

Lizzie faded. She asked if she had any children. The cook had three, two sons alive and one daughter dead. Maud could tell the dead daughter was a painful subject, and she didn't want to dwell on the topic of children beyond politeness, so she was fishing around for another subject when Lizzie said, "Yer look whipped and hung up. Want some vittles?"

The mention of food made Maud's stomach growl. She took up Lizzie's offer, and as she ate, she fell into conversation with the cook so easily that she told her about Lovely's death, about the goings-on with the rest of her family, about everything except the sheriff's visit, Billy, and what was foremost in her mind, that she needed to get rid of a baby. However, at one point, the thought did come to her that Negroes probably had their own baby-ridding remedies and that they might work as well as any. Certainly anything would work better than what she'd been doing. But she couldn't approach the subject without giving herself away. She didn't know what Lizzie might, or might not, tell Mr. Singer, and she didn't want him to know she was carrying, particularly if she found a way to get rid of the baby.

After they ran out of conversation, Lizzie gave her a flour sack and let her search the library by herself. She left toting a medical dictionary, a book about the Spanish influenza, and *Elmer Gantry*. Rain clouds were filling the southwest sky. Maud had her gun with her and had endured the catcalls on her way over. She started out on that same route again but hoped to hitch a ride before she got to within shouting distance of the work crew. And she was on the section line, turning to look back toward the highway in hopes of seeing a car, horse, or wagon, when she felt a stir in her belly. Though it was new, she recognized the movement, and her heart jumped with the hope that the baby was fixing to leave her for good. But the movement came two or three more times, didn't interfere with her walking, and didn't have any pain attached to it. By the time she heard the whistles and yells, she realized that the baby was big enough to move around. She held off crying until she got past the building site and then burst out so loud that she startled a couple of quail out of the Johnson grass.

Maud was still crying when she heard a motor behind her. It was her uncle Ame's car. There was no place to escape. She wiped her face with the top of the flour sack, stood in the road, and waited for Ame to stop. Viola rolled down the window and said, "Hop in."

Maud knew her face looked like a gully after a rain, and she was afraid any sound she'd make would come out as a wail. She got into the backseat without a word. The car started rolling again without any remark from Ame. Viola talked. They'd been to Manard to work on their new house. The outside walls were up and the floor down. They were waiting on windows, plywood for the inside walls, and a sink.

Maud felt thankful for her great-aunt's interest in her own business, but she was miserable in every other way. Her great-uncle turned onto the ruts to her grandfather's house without asking if she wanted to go there. And because Maud was afraid of what her voice might sound like, she rode without asking to get out, wiped her nose on the flour sack, and hoped her eyes weren't puffy. When they stopped, she couldn't face more conversation with Viola and she didn't want to see Lucy's children. She said, "Thanks for the ride. Billy'll be getting in." She squared her shoulders and walked away, carrying her sack of books in one hand and her gun in the other.

In her misery, Maud had forgotten to ask her great-aunt and great-uncle if they knew where Nan and Ryde were. But by the time she got to their house, it was clear Nan and Ryde were back, and she slid past, hoping nobody would call to her. Nobody did, and as she was closing the last cattle guard at home, the rain moved in. She ran to keep the books dry, caught her breath on the porch, and watched the drops hit the dust and the chickens flee. She looked to the sky. Black clouds were racing at an unusual speed. But it was late in the season for a tornado; she took a deep breath and decided to watch and wait. She deposited *Elmer Gantry* and the book about the Spanish influenza inside on Billy's chest. She brought out the medical dictionary and took a chair on the only spot on the porch that wasn't getting wet. Billy's dog settled at her feet.

Maud had hoped she'd find useful information under the word *abortion*, but what she found was a definition, causes of, and complications from. The causes were explained in sentences sprinkled with words she didn't know and had to look up on other pages. She found the complications particularly stomach turning. She closed the book to put them out of her mind. She watched the storm. As she did, the baby moved again.

Maud was hardened by killing whatever animal they needed for food. She wrung chickens' necks without wincing, had helped butcher hogs since she was little, and routinely gutted fish. But with the exception of poisonous snakes and the occasional gar she shot in the head, she didn't kill anything she couldn't use. That was the way she'd been raised; she didn't know anybody who did any different unless they were mean. She thought about the Mounts. They'd killed just for the pleasure. Her mind returned to Betty, axed in the back. She saw her bawling in the dirt, struggling, wild in the eyes. She recalled the poke stalk standing up out of her wound, the terror on Lovely's face, how she'd looked down the barrel, waiting for her shot. To keep from thinking about the killing she wanted to do, she went inside, lay down, and looked at the crack in the ceiling.

She fell asleep and woke up when the bed shook with Billy taking off his boots. He said he'd waited out the storm at Nan and Ryde's. That he'd eaten there and that Sanders had been snakebit, but the doctor didn't think by a cottonmouth. That answered Maud's question about her aunt and uncle's disappearance, but not the one about their seeing her father. Billy said he was tuckered out, and she didn't want to ask him that anyway. He stripped, lay down beside her, and slid his arm under her neck. He was asleep before she could blink. She lay awake listening to his breathing, wondering where her father was and if she would see him.

The next day, she walked up the line and found Nan on her front porch. Her aunt told her the story of Sanders' snakebite, his screaming and crying, Ryde's cutting the bite with his knife and sucking it with his mouth. Maud listened to the story, thinking about both her young cousin and her mother. She was relieved when Nan got to the part about what the doctor had said and about the older kids not wanting to be left in town at school after the excitement. Sanders' ankle was swollen and bandaged, more because of the remedy than the bite, and he was, that morning, back in school with the others. The story went on with meanders off into Renee's reaction and Morgan's search for the snake under the house. After a while, Maud felt glad for the distraction, and she was thankful to have her aunt to herself. Andy was napping and Ryde was in the garden. Maud let Nan wear her story completely out before she said, "Talley paid me a visit looking for Daddy."

Nan was letting out hems in pairs of overalls. "Yeah. He stopped by here. Ryde told him we ain't seen Mustard. Spoke the truth. Mustard didn't come 'til after Talley left. I was aiming to tell ya, but we got distracted." She pulled on a thread and it unraveled in one long piece from a leg.

Maud felt hurt that her father hadn't come to see her. He'd been so near. She looked off into the trees on the far side of the road. "What's he have to say for himself?"

"Talked mostly to Ryde. They went to the side yard. But Mustard left something fer ya."

Maud's eyes turned to her aunt. "What?"

"Let me get it." Nan set the overalls on top of her sewing basket and went inside. She came out with an envelope, handed it to Maud, and sat down. The envelope had the feed store's address and symbol in the upper left-hand corner. It was sealed. Maud held it to the light and tore open a side. She shook the envelope and three ten-dollar bills fell out. "Daddy left this for me?"

"Yep. I reckoned it waz money. Held it to the light myself. Couldn't tell how much." Nan chuckled and took up the overalls again.

Maud fingered the bills. They were a token of love from her father that she sorely needed even more than she needed the money. Her tears came again. But they were coming so often that she had a handkerchief in her pocket. She set the bills and the envelope under a river rock beside her chair, wiped her face, and blew her nose. "Did Daddy know about Lovely?"

"One of yer sisters got him word. Peggy, I think he said."

"The sheriff said Daddy hurt his hand."

"Yeah. It were still bandaged. Said it got caught in machinery. Tore his little finger plumb off. Half tore the next one off, too."

"What's he gonna do?"

"That's what he and Ryde waz talking about in the yard." Nan picked a threaded needle out of a pincushion. "Maybe you oughta ask Ryde directly."

Maud figured her aunt knew as much as her uncle did. She wasn't a person who needed to be protected, and as hard as Ryde was on his kids, he and Nan got along well, after their fashion. So, in Maud's calculation, Nan was trying to wiggle out of delivering bad news. She asked, "He's in the garden?" Nan nodded, and said, "Stay fer dinner. I baked a pie this morning."

Maud found Ryde in the middle of what was left of his beans and squash. The vegetables had grown up tripods of sticks that looked like two rows of tepees, but the vines were brown and played out. Her uncle was tugging on them; the entire back of his shirt was wet; the hat on his head was ringed with a dark band of sweat. Maud knew he didn't take well to surprise, so she yelled to warn him. Ryde turned, took his hat off, and rubbed his forehead with his forearm. He said, "If this ain't hell, I don't know what is."

Maud asked how his squash and beans had done. And Ryde pointed out his cantaloupes and pumpkins, told her what kind they were, how long they'd been planted, and when he expected to harvest them. It was the calmest Maud had seen him in a long time, and she figured it was because he was away from his kids who got on his nerves. She was feeling empathy for him on that when he said, "Nan tell ya Mustard showed?"

"Talley told me first." Maud told her uncle about the sheriff's visit. Then she said, "What's Daddy gonna do?"

Ryde looked up at the sun. The day wasn't as hot as the last few had been, but the air was heavy and warm. "Let's go to the shade." He nodded toward a scrub elm tree. There was a little wooden bench under it, just big enough for two people. Ryde headed toward it, and Maud followed him. When they both were seated, Ryde took out a pack of cigarettes and held it toward Maud. She took one, and he lit it for her, cupping his hand around his lighter's flame. Then he lit one for himself. They smoked in silence for a couple of minutes, then Ryde said, "The last of Mustard's allotment bought that car of his. You know that."

Maud hadn't known it for sure. But her father hadn't talked about his allotment in years. Her uncle added, "He ain't gonna be able to labor with that hand. And he don't have any more education than I do. 'Bout the third grade."

Maud could tell her uncle had put some thought into her father's circumstances. And it seemed like he was laying out a defense. She felt anxious about that. She said, "So where's he off to?"

Ryde jerked his thumb toward the horizon. "The Cookson Hills."

Maud winced. But she didn't look up. She'd seen the foothills every day of her life. They loomed on the eastern horizon wherever there was a break in the trees. And even though sometimes at sunset when the summer had been particularly dry, they turned a beautiful, unnatural shade of pink, the hills were lawless. Over the years, they'd been the hideout for all of the Starr outlaws, Cherokee Bill, the Dalton Gang — the list went on and on. Maud shook her head. She took a drag off of her cigarette. She felt tears welling up again. She dropped her butt in the dirt and crushed it under her shoe. "Why's he doing that?"

Ryde took a long draw and dropped his cigarette, too. "Well, he said he were gonna look up Choc Floyd."

Maud looked at the dead butt between her shoes. She looked at the dirt on her left toe. "I thought Mr. Floyd was sent away."

"He waz. But he's due out any day."

"How would Daddy know that?"

"Mostly common knowledge. Remembered it from when he waz sent up."

"Does Daddy know Mr. Floyd personally or just from the papers?"

Ryde pulled the cigarette pack out of his pocket again. He lit up, not offering Maud another one. "Choc waz as big on the rooster fighting as we waz fer a while. 'Member Buster, that solid black'un yer daddy raised? Choc won a lotta money on him. That waz before he got into a more high-dollar business."

Maud remembered Buster quite well. He'd been as mean as the dickens, but she'd felt sorry for him. And she didn't think robbing grocery stores and filling stations was really a business. She said so. Her uncle stood up, turned, and faced her. He planted his feet wide, his toes pointing out. He waved his left hand toward the foothills. "Don't ferget, not five years back people waz starving up there. Choc and his buddies brought 'em food. They got it from grocery stores 'cause that's where it waz at." He shook his head. "No rain, no crops."

Maud could see she'd agitated her uncle. That wasn't hard to do. He raised his belt to whip his kids almost as often as he raised it to hold up his pants. But she didn't think he'd hit her. He never had. But she wanted him in a good disposition when her cousins got home from school. She said, "I remember all that. I'm not saying Mr. Floyd isn't good to his friends. But robbing eventually leads to killing. You know that, Uncle Ryde." She looked up at him straight in the eye.

Ryde took a long puff on his cigarette. Then he raised a leg and propped a foot on the bench where he'd been sitting next to Maud. He put an elbow on that thigh and leaned over toward her. In a quieter voice, he said, "Mustard's already crossed that line. And he's gotta make a living. Mustard and me, we understand each other. I don't cross him and he don't cross me. But if ya wanta try to talk some sense into his head, I 'spect he'll be slipping back." He nodded toward the eastern horizon. "Them hills ain't that fer away."

Maud stayed long enough to eat and see her uncle into a better mood. But she walked back home with her general blues replaced by worry. It was as clear to her as it was to her uncle that her father wasn't looking for Pretty Boy Floyd in order to drive a tractor for him. She hoped that Mr. Floyd was still in the pen and that her daddy wouldn't be able to find him. She thought that if he was out he was unlikely to be reformed. It was more likely that he would be worse. She hoped she could talk to her daddy before he got into some sort of robbing spree.

Within a couple of days, the whole thing put her in even a worse mood. Two evenings later, she started a fight over peeing off the side of the porch. She caught Billy midstream and she didn't like it one bit. It was a sign of laziness and showed a trashy attitude toward the yard. Not even chickens foul their own nests. Dogs find a tree or a stump; cats dig a hole and cover their messes up. Billy tucked in and retorted, "What about horses? They shit in their stalls." The two of them named every creature whose habits they knew until the argument petered out because neither one of them knew what foxes did in their holes.

Maud went inside and let the screen door bang. She undressed without going behind the sheet, and she assumed that Billy, who could see in the window, would get so aroused he'd storm in the door and they'd get down to some serious making up. But Billy stayed outside on the porch. Maud lay down on the bed and pulled a sheet over her. She waited. Billy lit a cigarette. She could smell the smoke inside. The smell felt sickening. She went to the screen door with nothing on. "When do you think you're gonna be through?"

"Is it late?"

"The sun's disappeared."

"It's not July."

"What's that supposed to mean."

"The days are getting shorter."

"Seems to me like something else is getting shorter."

"What's that supposed to mean?"

"If you don't use it, it shrivels up."

"I use it when I want to."

"If you're cheating on me, I'll take a gun to you."

"What the hell's gotten into you?" Billy crushed his cigarette on the sole of his boot and dropped the butt into a tin can.

"Are you not coming to bed?"

"Not yet." He sounded firm.

Maud began to feel ridiculous standing at the screen door naked. And she didn't want to appear to be begging or to have her stomach examined. She turned away, lit the coal-oil lamp, propped herself under a quilt, and tried to read. She figured Billy would soon give up and come to bed. But she fell asleep, and when she woke, the lamp was dark and Billy was on his side of the bed with his back to her.

The next night, Early came over and ate with them. Then he and Billy drank choc beer and the three of them played cards at the kitchen table until Billy ran out of pennies. The men switched to matchsticks and Maud went to bed. She tried to read, but she was too irritated to get very far. She laid *Elmer Gantry* on the table, dampened the flame, and watched and listened to Billy and Early in the next room. She pretended they were people she didn't know just to keep from getting up and hitting their heads with her book.

By Saturday, her irritation had turned to anger. The baby was wiggling. Jumping off the side of the porch hadn't done any good, and Billy, who was her only relief, was acting like he'd been neutered with a blunt knife. She decided that what he needed was a change of location. She waited until he was in the barn soaping his saddle, and then she walked out there carrying a hot piece of apple pie on a plate. She swung the plate in an arc just out of his reach and waved a fork in her other hand. She said, "I've got something delicious for you." She cut her eyes around and stuck out the tip of her tongue.

Billy's eyes widened. A grin spread across his face. "Oh, baby, my favorite," and he held out his hand.

Maud settled on a stool. She asked Billy about his saddle, about what he wanted to do in town that night, about whether there would be food at the fort to buy or if they needed to take a basket. When he was through eating, she said, "Delicious?"

"Best I ever had." Billy smiled in a lopsided way and kissed her. Then he took up his soaping rag.

Maud felt a jab of anger. But she shoved that away by reminding herself that she was on a mission. She unbuttoned the two top buttons of her dress. "How about some dessert for your dessert?"

"I'm a little busy here." Billy rubbed the horn of his saddle.

Maud didn't know what to do. Having to interest a man in sex was outside of her range of experience, and she didn't think it was quite natural. She said, "If you don't get your fire back, I may need that horn myself."

Billy ran his thumbnail down a crease in the saddle, scooped out some soap, and flicked it from under his nail.

Maud sat quietly. To wait him out, she looked at the scythe that Lovely had used. Her mind wandered back to that day until it reached Booker. She was trying to shake him out of her head when Billy said, "It ain't natural to keep poking a baby the way we've been doing."

"Natural? Of course it's natural. What're you jabbering about?"

Billy turned, the rag around his fingers. "So you admit yer in a family way?"

Maud instantly saw she'd been trapped. And she wasn't used to being on the short end of the smart stick. Her temper flared out. "What if I am? It's my own business."

"Is that the ground you want to stand on, Maud? I'd think that through if I were you." Billy cocked his head.

Maud didn't know what to say. And her emotions weren't under much control. She started crying big tears. She couldn't stop. Billy started twisting his rag in both hands. He said, "It can't be that bad," which didn't have any effect. Then he said, "Go on up to the house and take a rest on the bed." He turned back to his saddle.

Maud couldn't bear to go into town that night. She couldn't bear to be with Billy. She wanted news on Pretty Boy, but she couldn't stand to think about talking to anyone at all. She sat on the porch, and although the weather was perfect, she felt hot and then cold. Eventually, she went inside, lay down on the bed, and stared at the crack in the ceiling until she wasn't sure if she was seeing it in the dark or in her imagination. She was going to have to carry that baby to term. And then she would have to go through the birth. She recalled Lucy's screaming. She shuddered. But the birthing wasn't the worst of it. She'd be saddled with the thing for the rest of her life. She'd never get out of the bottoms, never get away from the dirt. If she got lucky, she might get electricity. But that would be a long time in the future; and even if she did, she would never see a city, never ride in an elevator, never shop in a store on the second floor. Those thoughts led her to Booker, who was doing all of those things; and she became even more infuriated at him for leaving and for being such a coward that he couldn't stand a little killing of people who were as mean as wild boars. In the midst of that anger, Maud remembered that she was unhappy with the thought of her father joining Pretty Boy Floyd.

She liked books, learning, and clean things. She liked folks being nice to one another. But most of all, she wanted to live in a place where people died of natural causes when they were old and were dressed up in suits and laid down in wooden boxes.

That night, Maud sank into a misery that not even reading relieved. She lost all interest in visiting. She spent most of her days on the porch looking out toward the river. The smells of cooking reminded her of horse piss. Billy began picking up food from Nan's for them to eat. When Maud wouldn't milk the cow or put the chickens up, he took over those chores. When she wouldn't wash herself, he led her by the hand to the rainwater barrel and washed her hair. But when he tried to undress her, she fought. She couldn't stand to have her stomach looked at. She started waiting until Billy rode off to work to dress in clothes that her father had left.

She stayed like that for weeks until, one morning in early November, she was sitting on the porch in Mustard's overalls and shirt with her stomach bigger than she wanted it to be but still small enough to be mostly hidden under the bib. She was worrying a river rock in her hand, turning it over and over, when she looked up and saw her aunt Viola leading a sorrel horse by a rope. Viola was wearing a long-sleeved checkered dress covered by an apron. Her hair was pulled back in a bun. Maud was interested enough to wonder why Viola had chosen to walk rather than ride that horse. But even that question soon left her, and the dull blankness she'd felt for weeks slid back into the space behind her eyes.

Viola tied the horse to the hitching rail and walked the stones to the porch. She stopped on the top step. When Maud didn't speak, Viola said, "I brung ya a horse."

Maud didn't feel like she could form words. She nodded. Viola took a seat on the planks, leaning against a post with her face to the sun. She started talking. Her voice sounded to Maud like it was coming from deep in a cave. Her words didn't make any sense.

Eventually, Viola said, "Ya got the blues bad," and Maud clearly heard that. She nodded.

"The thing is, this is a rough patch. Yer daddy's gone off. Lovely went and did hisself in. That man, what's his name, Booker, left. And now yer in an inconvenient way that ya don't seem to take to. My mama got inconvenienced when she waz fifteen. They waz living down in Texas. Her ma had broke with the first Early and had taken up with a mean man. She waz packing to leave him when he rode up on a horse and shot her dead in the doorway. Smack in front of Mama and her little brother and sister. But he didn't shoot them. He jist rode away. Mama buried her mother, gathered up her brother and sister, and started walking. She walked all the way from the Red River to 'round here carrying that baby in her belly. Gave birth to him at the end of that walk. That's my brother Frank. You've met him." Viola took a pouch out of her apron and pinched tobacco from it. She put the pinch in her bottom lip and tucked the pouch away. A rooster crowed. Billy's dog stood up from his dust hole, shook, and trotted off toward a fence post where he lifted his leg. Eventually, Viola said, "I hear tell if ya want rid of a baby, the best way is to ride it out."

Maud eyes widened a little. She looked at the horse.

Viola got up slowly. She walked to the hitching rail, untied the horse, and led it to the edge of the porch. "She don't take a bit. Tender in the mouth. You'll haveta use this hackamore. Let me see if ya can git on her from here."

Maud stood up, went to the edge of the porch, and threw her right leg over the horse's back. "What's her name?"

"Leaf."

"Whose is she?"

"Yer grandpa's now. Early won her offin a fellow and gave her to Bert as payment for something or other." Viola looked off toward the river. "We can't be losing Lovely and you both. Ya don't haveta ride her hard. Jist enough to keep arocking back and forth. I'm not saying it'll work fer total sure. How far along are ya?"

"Five months, as best I can tell."

"Then it's too late fer anything else. I'll open the guards fer ya." Viola started walking, talking over her shoulder. "You ride her up and down the line. Jist stay on her as much as ya can. But if ya get to cramping or bleeding, get to Nan or Lucy." She looked up at Maud. "Ame and me, we're gonna move in a couple of weeks. You can ride her up to our place and visit a spell. We'll be south of Manard on a hill. Yer cousin Minnie's allotment." Viola was referring to her husband's first wife. "The important thing is not try to deal with it alone if it starts to coming. It's too late fer that. There'll be a lot of blood and you'll be weak. Billy won't be much help."

Maud started crying. She cried until she sobbed. Viola drew a handkerchief out of her apron and handed it to her. Maud wiped her nose and tucked the handkerchief in her bib. "I'll give it back."

"Don't worry 'bout that. But ride over to see us tomorrow. I don't feel too good 'bout leaving ya down here with this remedy. Bert said to do it, so I am. But a delivery can be hard, 'specially if the baby ain't helping."

Maud understood that her grandfather was taking care of her and that she had to get help if the remedy started working. She promised to visit the next day, swore she wouldn't ride far off the section line, and agreed to get to family if she felt any cramping or saw any blood. At Gourd's corner, they parted ways. Viola walked east to see the spot on Nan's allotment where she and Ryde were planning to build a house, and Maud rode up the line.

She turned west at the cross of the section lines and rode on past the snake lakes to the cemetery beyond the water. She stopped at Lovely's grave and looked at the sandstone marker they'd put up until money was saved for a better one. The soil was still bare except for a few fallen leaves. She was cried out, too listless to get off the horse and figure out how to get back on, too foggy in her mind to form many words. But she did say to Lovely, "If I can't get rid of this baby, I'll name it for you." However, she regretted that as soon as she'd said it; the promise might keep the baby in her long enough for a live birth. She said, "Not if it's a girl. Only if it's a boy." She hoped that cut the chances of a live birth in two.

Maud didn't stop by her mother's grave because she knew her mama wouldn't be too happy with her. She stopped at her grandmother's marker only long enough to think that the tall slab of granite must've been bought in a year of good crops. She steered the horse around other graves so as not to step on any. She'd come to the cemetery to be with Lovely and to find a spot to bury whatever came out of her. She eventually found a place close to a little bush about fifteen feet south of Lovely's marker. She thought maybe the baby's remains would nourish the bush into something pretty. She wished it still had its leaves so she could determine what kind it was.

After that, she rode the section line west to the next one, turned south on it, and rode to Blue's allotment. His cattle were grazing there, and she watched them for a while. She didn't think about anything in particular, and the cows made her feel a little better. She decided she would ride over to watch them every day.

When Billy got home that night, he didn't seem surprised to see Leaf and didn't ask why she was there. And Maud didn't tell him. She figured that he didn't know horseback riding would bring a baby on and that he wouldn't approve of what she was doing if she told him. She did, however, feel well enough to boil some eggs for supper, and she opened a can of greens from the cellar and made some cornbread. Billy was so appreciative that when they settled to sleep he put his arm around her.

Maud rode the next day, the next, and the next. The following week, Gourd moved back into his house. He'd split the sheets with his woman, seemed glad to be home, and started visiting when Early did. When they came at night, she played cards with them some, but mostly she left them in the kitchen with Billy, went to bed with a lamp, and read Mr. Singer's medical book.

A few days later when Viola and Ame moved, Maud rode up in the car with them and helped them set up house. But she was anxious to return to riding Leaf, and her great-uncle and great-aunt drove her back the next day. They returned her to her grandfather's house, and they all stayed for dinner. Early was there, too, and he and Blue had been in town that day selling hay. Blue had heard at Taylor's General Store that Choc Floyd was still in the Missouri pen. But he said that Mustard had heard right. He'd been due out; he was serving extra time for having narcotics in his cell and socking a guard. If he could keep his behavior under control and didn't escape sooner, he'd be out in early spring.

Billy wasn't at that meal, and before it was over, Maud reminded Early, in particular, that family business was family business and that Billy wasn't yet kin. Early raised a fork full of sauerkraut and poked it toward Maud. "You might want to remedy that as soon as you can." He grinned and deposited the sauerkraut in his mouth. A string hung out on his chin. Maud said, "You can't even hit your mouth with your food. Don't be giving me advice." But the news that Mr. Floyd was still in prison made her feel better, at least for the evening, and she felt a small seed of hope that her father had found something to do for a living that didn't involve robbing grocery stores and filling stations, and that he'd come to see her soon.

The next day she took up her routine of riding the section lines and visiting the snake lakes, the graveyard, and the cows. The riding made her feel more hopeful. When she realized that, she supposed it was because she was doing something to rid herself of the baby. But as the days wore on, she grew less sure the riding would work. However, by then, that didn't seem to matter so much. And the riding helped with the aches in her hips and lower back.

By December, she'd completely given up hope that riding would expel the baby. She resigned herself to having it. She told herself that Billy would make a good father and that Nan and Lucy would teach her how to care for it. But she kept on riding because she understood that Leaf had restored her sanity. She began to suspect that her grandfather and great-aunt had had that result in mind from the beginning.

Shortly before Christmas, on a Sunday when the family was gathered at Nan's, her grandfather pulled a piece of paper from his overalls' bib. He laid it on the kitchen table in front of her and smoothed it out with his hand. He said, "Now, keep this safe. It's the paper moving yer mama's allotment into yer name." He continued in a low tone. "Blue'll go on and farm yer land, just like always. Unless ya got other plans?"

Maud couldn't think what her other plans might be. "I don't know that I have."

Bert nodded toward the porch where the younger men were congregated, waiting to be fed. "Walkingstick's not much of a farmer, is he?"

"His interest lies in horses, cattle, and airplanes."

"Don't know 'bout airplanes, but nothing wrong with horses and cattle. In fact, the way wheat prices seem to be turning that might be best. But, now listen to yer grandpa, Maud. Nearly ever' family we know has lost their allotments. You can't even imagine the stealing that went on before ya waz born. We've held on to our parcels, but there may be landgrabbing again. Anything in the world can happen. But ya need to understand, Maudy-Baby, nowadays most women lose their allotments to men. You hold on to yers." He laid his hand over hers, squeezed it quickly, and let it go. "Pin it to yer slip."

Maud was as surprised by her grandfather's hand as she was by the paper, and she only half heard him say something about having held the allotment for her and Lovely since their mother's death. But Lovely's name refocused her attention. She felt the loss of him all over again.

For Christmas, Billy gave Maud an oak cradle with a design carved into its head. She could tell the design was a bird, but Billy said it wasn't just any old bird, it was an eagle, and he'd carved it himself. He was so proud of the cradle that Maud wondered if he understood that the baby wasn't his, and she began mentally shuffling through all the hues in the family. Andy and Morgan were dark, so was Lucy's baby, Nancy. All of them had white daddies. But then so did Renee, Sanders, and Lee. They were pale. Her aunt Sarah's kids had a white daddy, too. Most of them tended to be light in the winter and dark in the summer.

She'd had Mr. Singer's books for more than two months. She'd avoided returning them for fear of his seeing her condition. She didn't particularly want to run into Lizzie, either. She didn't feel embarrassed about the baby in general, only irritated and depressed. But while most people had forgotten about Booker, Mr. Singer and Lizzie wouldn't have. They probably even knew how he was doing. She didn't want to know that herself. She didn't think she could bear hearing about his success. And she didn't want Mr. Singer or Lizzie feeling sorry for her.

But the books looked like snakes coiled on the chest every time she passed. And since it was cold outside, she was inside as much as out. She put the books in a drawer. But that felt like knowing a snake was hiding under a bush, and that was painful, considering the way her mother had died. So she brought the books back out, and on a day between Christmas and New Year's, she decided she'd take them back. Since it was the holiday season, she added three jars of plum jelly to the feed sack.

She put on her father's heavy coat. The only mirror was the little one behind the sheet, so she couldn't see her entire figure. But she held the looking glass down to her stomach to see if the coat hid her condition. She thought maybe, maybe not. Still, she figured she needed to return the books before she got any bigger. She set off on Leaf on a gray day into a wind that was cold.

If Mr. Singer was home, she planned to turn around and try again the next day. But when she got to within sight of his house, she was relieved to see that his garage was an empty hole. She rode to the hitching rail, tied Leaf there, and walked to the summer kitchen. Smoke was curling from its chimney and stovepipe, but the door was shut against the cold. She knocked.

Lizzie invited her in. The room was warm; fires were burning in both the stove and the fireplace. Maud set the sack on the table, brought out the jelly jars, and moved to the hearth. She held her hands over the flames while Lizzie heated up water for coffee. They talked as friends. Eventually, warmed by the coffee and fire, Maud started sweating. She moved away from the fireplace toward the door. But it was closed against the weather. She swiped beads of sweat off her upper lip with her forefinger.

Lizzie said, "You can take yer coat off."

Maud hesitated. But she was comfortable and had some company. Gossip was the only entertainment anybody had; Lizzie had probably already gotten word of her situation. So she unbuttoned the top of her coat and took the bull by the horns. "I'm in a family way."

Lizzie's eyebrows lifted. *"Ahum,"* she said. "Who's the lucky daddy?"

Maud had gotten accustomed to the Negro woman's directness. It was completely opposite from the way any Indian would react, and probably most Negroes, too, for all she knew. But she was used to directness in white people, and she figured Lizzie, having worked for Mr. Singer for so long, had acquired some white ways. Still, Maud stammered. "It's, uh, Billy Walkingstick's. I've been seeing him a good while." She suddenly felt even hotter and worried that she looked embarrassed.

"Coming soon?"

Maud ducked that question with "I wish it'd come today."

Lizzie turned to the sink. She pulled the plug. The water gurgled down the drain. When the noise went away, she turned around. She opened her mouth. Then she turned back to the sink. Maud wondered what she'd been going to say, but she was almost certain she didn't really want to hear it. She said, "You'll thank Mr. Singer for me, please?"

Lizzie let out a sigh. Her shoulders rose and fell. She turned around and said, "Yer'll be needing some more books. Can't do much with a big belly."

Maud left with three more books and was thankful to have them. She'd liked *Elmer Gantry* enough to read it twice, had read the Spanish influenza book twice, too, and parts of the medical dictionary again and again. But if it hadn't been for Leaf, the boredom and the loneliness of the farm, even with Billy there, would've been more than she could've taken. She sorely missed being able to talk about books and ideas with Lovely — and with Booker — if she let herself dwell on that. But she didn't. She rode past the school, and as construction had halted for the holidays, she walked Leaf around the new building. While she did, she day-dreamed about teaching. That could be something she could do. But she couldn't teach and tend a baby. And she would some-how have to get enough money to go the teachers' college in Tahlequah. She wished she'd asked Booker more about what all he'd done to teach. But when she thought about that, she found her blues coming back, and she'd learned to steer clear of them when she could. She turned Leaf away from the school, and be-fore she went home, she stopped in and visited Nan.

The family spent New Year's Day at her grandpa's. Ame and Viola came in with Ame's oldest two girls, cousins Maud particularly liked and rarely got to see. The women cooked; the men talked and smoked in the yard. The weather was warm and sunny. When the meal was over, everyone except Lucy and Viola went back to the yard and shot cigarette butts off of fence posts. Maud, for one day, forgot her condition, her grief, and her worry, and enjoyed the company, the shooting, and the hopefulness of the new year. 1927 and 1928 had been terrible years. She felt that no matter what happened, 1929 would be a better one.

At dusk, she and Billy rode home. They went at a clopping pace he set to protect her and the baby, and so slow that her mind and eyes wandered. When they were almost to Gourd's, she no-ticed car tracks in the dust. Two lines of them. She felt almost certain they hadn't been there when they'd gone up the line that morning. She looked toward her house. There wasn't a car in the yard. She peered east at the lane to Nan's allotment. The tracks hadn't veered in that direction. She looked down the road to the wild. No tracks there. The tracks were on her lane. Somebody had visited. Maybe her daddy. Billy kept talking about a bull he had his eye on, but Maud's mind was glued to who could've driven a car to her house. She peered into the lean-to in the distance. The light was almost gone; it was a black hole. Her father's car could be in there, and she wouldn't be able to see it. But there were two sets of tracks. The car had come and gone. Billy hopped off his horse to open the first guard. Maud studied the tracks. She couldn't remember the treads on her father's car, but he'd been gone so long he probably had different tires. She hoped that if he'd come he'd come alone.

Billy remounted after the guard was in place and dismounted again at the second one. He kept talking about building a herd of his own. Maud kept studying the tracks. She hoped nobody had come in and stolen everything they had. The house wasn't locked. The door didn't even lock from the outside. Maud looked to the chicken house. One chicken remained in the yard. She needed to scoot that hen in and close them all up.

Billy led the horses to the barn. Maud herded the stray chicken into the hen house, secured the door and flap, and went to the porch. She stopped at the front door, fearful about going in even though she knew whoever had come had already gone. She wished she'd taken her rifle with her and slowly turned the knob. The house was almost dark. The corners were in deep shadows. She went to the sheet and jerked it back. Crates and clothes. She felt relieved. Then she recalled the dead dog on the table. She turned to the kitchen, half expecting to see another one. But the table was clear except for salt, pepper, jelly, and the Calumet tin of pencils. All the guns they'd left behind were in the corner. She opened the top drawer of her chest. Her father's lighter was there.

When she picked the lighter up, she sensed her heart pounding. She felt faint and sat down on the side of the bed. The Banjo felt clammy in her hand. She was almost sure somebody had been in the house. She couldn't say why. Everything seemed in place. Her father would've probably taken his lighter had he come and gone away. And he would've known where she and Billy were. So it most likely wasn't him. Maud felt disappointed. She missed her daddy. She hoped he'd come home before he got into trouble he couldn't get out of. Grief overtook her again. She was familiar with it, knew that when she lay down it would crawl all over her like night descending and that she might not be able to shake it the next day. Still, she felt overwhelmed. She slipped out of her coat and her shoes. Without taking off her dress, she climbed under the quilts. She pretended to be asleep when Billy came to bed.

She got up three times in the night to pee. She took her dress off when she came back in the final time and rubbed her hands over her belly. She hated the baby in a way she hadn't in weeks, and she felt so heavy that the few steps to the bed seemed like walking in loose sand. When she got back under the covers, she lay awake staring at the place on the ceiling where she knew the crack ran, even though it was too dark to see it. She felt it cut across her from her collarbone; over her left, misshapen breast; down the crevice beneath it; up the hill of her belly; and down to her right hip bone. Maud wished the crack would open her up. She'd reach inside, snatch that baby out, and ... give it to some woman who wanted one.

She was still in bed when Billy rode off to work the next morning. She got up only when the sun from the east window was too bright to ignore. The weather had turned cold again. She put on her coat, went to the outhouse and the pump, let the chickens out, and came back in and took the pan of biscuits Billy had made out of the oven. They were still warm. She slathered a biscuit with butter at the stove, sat down at the table, and slathered it with jelly. She was trying to work up the energy for chores when she caught the sound of a motor. She focused her eyes on the pencil tin to listen harder. The motor belonged to a car. She put one hand on her back and the other on the table to push herself up. She went to the window. The car was stopped at the first cattle guard. It was bright blue.

A shock zigzagged through Maud's body. The baby kicked. A spasm grabbed her between her legs. Her knees buckled. She caught herself with a hand on a knob on Billy's chest of drawers. It slowed her fall, but she still crumpled to the floor. She looked for a place to hide. Behind the sheet was the only cover. She crawled over there. She pulled herself up by holding on to the crates. She looked in the mirror. The face staring back looked like a stranger's. It was puffed with fat and pale; the hair was chopped like a boy's. She was breathing so hard she heard herself wheezing. She couldn't let Booker see her looking so bad. She pulled the sheet completely closed and sat down on a crate. Billy's dog started barking. She waited.

Booker knocked on the main door. The dog kept barking. Maud heard Booker say, "Settle down." He knocked on the door to the kitchen. He said something else to the dog. It whined in a friendlier way. The porch steps creaked. Maud stayed put. She listened for the sound of the car. She heard the rooster. Its crow made her think that he'd check the outbuildings and barn. The dog was quiet. Maud wished she'd had time to get to the cellar. He might not check in there. She tried to smooth her breathing by thinking of the river. She closed her eyes and imagined the sand-bar. She thought about searching for rocks. Her mind's eye swept the ground. She felt her breath even out. She was thinking about holding a smooth red rock in her hand when she heard Booker open the door.

He pulled the sheet back. He was wearing a heavy coat and his bowler. His eyes were as green as ever, flecked with gold. He said, "I've come for you, Maud."

She looked down at her belly, in part to hide her face. "You're a little late."

"Mr. Singer called me last week. He told me the situation. He'd written before, suggesting I visit. But I was waiting to hear from you."

Maud looked up. "I didn't know where you were!"

"The post office forwards my mail. Why didn't you write? My Fayetteville address was in my first letter."

Maud looked down again. "That letter got destroyed."

"You tore it up?"

She shook her head. "No, I didn't tear it up. It . . . it's too hard to explain. It got destroyed in the rain."

Booker's voice raised a little. "Why didn't you let me know? You could've sent me a message by Mr. Singer."

Maud looked up. "I didn't know that, Booker. I didn't know where you'd gone. You up and left me without warning." Maud could feel herself getting more agitated, and she felt trapped by Booker and the sheet. She stood up. "Get out of my way. I need space to breathe."

Booker took his bowler off and held the sheet open with his other hand. He said more loudly, "You don't need to be so ill-tempered."

Maud turned to face him. "Ill-tempered! How dare you! I'm just getting my temper worked up! You leave me without a word and have the nerve to come back here and call me ill-tempered! You'll be lucky if I don't take a gun to you!"

Booker let go of the sheet. The muscles in his jaws tightened. "That's the problem, Maud. I'm not used to shooting people. It's not any way to live."

"I haven't shot anybody, Booker." Maud glared.

"No, but you're threatening to."

"It's just a figure of speech. Believe me, Booker, if I was gonna shoot you, I wouldn't give you any warning. I'm smarter than that."

Booker wiped his brow with his palm. He pointed to the bed. "Do you mind if I sit down."

"Do what you please." Maud thought about sitting herself. But she felt like she had the upper hand and she intended to keep it.

Booker sat on the edge of the bed, laid his hat beside him, and straightened his back. "Look, Maud. If you'd read my letter, you would've known I needed to do some soul-searching." He held up a hand. "I don't like being lied to. And I'm not used to lying to the law. I don't think I can adjust to that way of living."

"So you left me here to take care of everything?"

"I left you here to get my mind cleared out. I had to think. I knew I couldn't go back to teaching. I'd already outgrown all of that. And then I saw Tulsa. Maud, you can't believe what's over there. I can make us a real living in Tulsa. You can't live here." He held both hands up in the air and looked around.

"If this isn't good enough for you, maybe I'm not good enough for you." She put her hand on Billy's chest of drawers.

"I thought you wanted out of here?"

"I want to be with people who love me. That's more important than plaster on walls and rugs on floors."

Booker pursed his lips. Then he dropped his gaze. "I see." He slipped a hand into his coat pocket. He brought out a little box and set it on the bed between him and his hat. "Just let me ask you this first. Is that bump on your front mine?"

Maud thought she knew what was in the box. It looked like one Nan had. But she wasn't totally sure, and she couldn't be making any mistakes. She said, "Don't call my baby a bump."

Booker clasped his hands together between his legs. "Is that our baby, Maud? Miz Lizzie said it was."

"Lizzie?" Maud was startled.

"Yes, I talked to her when I got here. She told me about the baby, that it was mine."

Maud was beginning to feel uncomfortable standing, and talking about the baby made her feel even heavier. She slid into a rocker in front of the window directly across from Booker. "Well, I don't know how she figured that out. But, yes, it's yours."

Booker put his fingers on the box. He lifted it just a little and settled it back on the bed. Maud could tell his next question was going to be about Billy, and she wanted to put that off as long as she could. "Did Lizzie tell you about Lovely?"

Booker clasped his hands together between his legs again. He looked down. "Mr. Singer told me that." He looked up and touched his fingers to his brow. "I was sorry to hear it. Lovely . . . well, I liked Lovely a lot. What happened, exactly? If you don't mind me asking?"

Maud didn't mind. Talking about Lovely put off talking about Billy. "He shot himself. There's this place down closer to the river on Blue's allotment. He took us there when we were kids. When we were still pitiful over our mother's death. It's a quiet, peaceful place. Evidently, Lovely had visited it some over the years. I hope to think that he had some comfort there."

Booker sighed deeply and was quiet for a moment. Then he picked up the little box. "I should have gotten a bow on this. I've been paying for it on time. I picked it up in a rush when Mr. Singer called me to get over here. I still have one payment to go, but I work for the store. I cleared it with my boss." He looked directly at her. "Maud, you're the most exciting thing that's ever happened to me." He opened the lid. A diamond ring was nestled in soft blue cloth.

Maud was glad she was sitting down. She was sure her knees would've buckled had she been standing. As it was, she needed to hold back from reaching out. She gripped the arms of the rocker. "You've been paying all this time?"

"Well, I put a little money aside when I sold Evelyn and Arlene. Then I put a little more aside when Mr. Singer wrote me a while back. I made a big down payment, then paid a little every two weeks." Booker pointed toward the yard with his right forefinger. "I got a loan for the car. The brothers who own the store have put me in charge of men's ready-to-wear. If I do well at that, they're going to make me a buyer."

Maud was impressed. She hoped that didn't show. "Are you going to give me the box or are you planning on wearing that ring yourself?"

Booker reached across the space between them and handed her the box. Maud wished she hadn't asked for it. Up close, the diamond looked even prettier. In the light from the east window, it sparkled. That sparkle took Maud's breath away. But she was still afraid of what Booker was going to say about Billy. And she was worried about Billy. She snapped the lid of the box closed and covered it with the palm of her hand. She'd beat Booker to the draw. "This is all fine and dandy, but Billy's been tending to me while you were gallivanting around."

Booker stood up. He walked to the door of the kitchen and looked in there like he was making sure they were alone. Then he turned and stood in the doorway. "Yes, Billy. Miz Lizzie mentioned him. It's not reassuring to come back and find out you've been living with another man." Booker's voice was grim.

Maud felt at a disadvantage sitting down while Booker was in the doorway. But if she stood up, she'd be following his lead; he'd still be at the top of the pecking order and she'd be at the end. She stayed where she was, turned her face away from him, and looked out the east window. She didn't say anything.

Booker finally said, "Are you planning on commenting before the cows come home?"

Maud took a deep breath. She looked at the box in her hand. "Billy's been good to me, Booker. I can't just leave him."

Booker huffed. He stepped into the room. "Well, he can't come with us!" His face turned red.

"Don't get all riled up. And don't be standing over me. I'm not suggesting that. I'm just saying this is a big decision. Maybe I should stay with what I know. How can I be sure you won't up and leave me again?"

Booker stepped close to the sheet. "Don't be ridiculous, Maud. I'm not a man who gets his head turned by every girl in a dress. And don't act like you're totally innocent. You lied to me. You lied again and again." He raised an arm. His hand hit the sheet.

"Could you just sit back down and stop waving your arms all around? You look like you're swatting flies."

Booker pursed his lips into a hard line. He started toward the bed but instead sat in the rocker in front of the east window. He leaned way back in it. "Well?"

"Well, what?"

"Well, I guess you've been sleeping with him."

Maud started to laugh. But she caught herself in time to make the laugh sound like a cough. She put a fist to her mouth and cleared her throat. "I guess you've been Mr. Buttoned-up Pants."

"It's different for a man."

Maud jumped out of her chair like she'd been bitten. She went to the kitchen door. She had a mind to throw something, but the only throwable things in her line of vision were the Calumet pencil tin and a perfectly good jar of jelly with a knife sticking in it. The knife would frighten Booker. And she didn't want to throw the ring box. She whirled around. "So, you have been seeing other women!"

Booker stood up. "Not really. At least nothing serious. But for God's sake, Maud, don't turn this around on me!" He glared at her and pointed to the mattress. "This bed makes me sick. I know what's been going on here."

Maud was used to fights ending up in bed. But she was really too pregnant for that. She wasn't sure what to do. She slumped against the door frame. "Billy's been good to me, Booker. I don't know what I would've done without him. Daddy's still away. Probably for good. And Lovely's dead. And I didn't know where you were. Or if you'd ever come back." She put a hand on her stomach.

Booker sighed. He swiped a hand across his mouth. He glanced at the bed, winced, and then looked out a south window. "Maud, we both need to get out of here. Our baby deserves more." He turned, stepped closer to her, and looked her full in the face. "There's a whole world out there, Maud. It's sparkling clean. We're coming up on a new decade. Times are booming. You should see Tulsa. There's a hotel ten stories high. Oil companies are as thick as fleas on a dog's back. They're building a new train station. The store I work in has got everything you'd ever want to buy. Dresses and slips galore. Perfume. Creams to make your skin smooth. Baby clothes. I've rented a house. It's got radiators and indoor plumbing. An electric stove and refrigerator. We live in the greatest state in the country. It's overflowing with oil and wheat, and everybody is spending their money. These are the best times the world has ever seen. Come with me, Maud. We'll get married. We'll raise our child in the horn of plenty."

Maud felt like a tornado was on her. She needed to run without looking back. She squeezed the ring box. "We have to go before I change my mind."

"Let's go now. There's nothing preventing us. I'll call Mr. Singer when we get to Tulsa. He can tell your family."

Maud looked around the room. There wasn't much to take. There wasn't much to leave behind. Except Billy. She had to do something about him. But she couldn't say that to Booker. "I have some of Mr. Singer's books. We can drop them by and tell him then."

"Good idea. What else do you want to take?"

"Why don't you load that cradle." She nodded toward it. "Put the books in it. Let me change my dress and think about what else."

When Booker came back, Maud had thrown some clothes in a crate. She asked him to carry the crate and her mother's sewing basket to the car. When he came back again, she was dressed, and she handed him her gun and her mother's pistol and rifle. She stuffed her father's Banjo and her mother's cameo in her little handbag and handed Booker that, too. She told him to wait for her in the car; she needed to look around one more time to make sure she wasn't leaving anything she would want behind. When he cleared the porch, she turned to her chest, opened the top drawer, and pulled her allotment paper out. She studied the writing on it as she walked to the kitchen. She sat down in a chair and pulled a pencil from the Calumet tin. She scribbled "Yours" above the typed words and signed her name at the bottom. She pinned the paper to the table with the jelly jar.

Acknowledgments

I am grateful for the patience and support of many friends and loved ones who read for me, again and again, over years as I learned the craft of writing. Foremost in the group is Laura Derr, my college roommate, who thoughtfully and lovingly criticized no-telling-how-many drafts of books that might never see the outside of a drawer. I also want to thank the readers of this particular manuscript in its original draft: my partner, Jane Griffiths; my friend and business partner, Judy Worth; my friends Sue Weant, Lana Dearinger, Tunie Fairbanks, Martha Helen Smith, and Lisa Sharon. I want also to thank Adrienne Brodeur, a wonderful editor, for her insightful and diplomatic comments on a draft of this manuscript.

I would like to thank Roxana Robinson in particular, whose kindness, faith, and encouragement kept me going for years. I am also in Roxana's debt for her practical help in opening doors for me, especially the door to Lynn Nesbit, the consummate agent and professional who placed this book. Lynn's assistant, Hannah Davey, was also extremely helpful to me, as was my editor at Houghton Mifflin Harcourt, Lauren Wein, and her assistant, Nina Barnett.

I'd also like to thank Lillian Leeds, the matriarch of our family, without whose mothering and memories this book couldn't have been written. And finally, I'd like to thank the rest of my mother's family. They lived down and around Maud's section line and provided me firm and fertile ground to stand on. I am constantly humbled by the hardship of their early lives; by their humor, ingenuity, and determination; and by their courage.